Turn Towards the Sun

ALSO BY EMMA DAVIES

Letting in Light

Turn Towards the Sun

EMMA DAVIES

LAKE UNION
PUBLISHING

Published by Lake Union Publishing, Seattle

www.apub.com

Amazon, the Amazon logo, and Lake Union Publishing are trademarks of Amazon.com, Inc., or its affiliates.

ISBN-13: 9781503942301
ISBN-10: 1503942309

Cover design by Lisa Horton

Printed in the United States of America

To all my lovely readers, whose faith has got me this far

JANUARY

Chapter 1

Lizzie

Don't stuff it up, don't stuff it up.

I have no idea where I am. The bus turned off the main road about fifteen minutes ago, and now we're winding our way down a series of successively narrower roads. I'd been in such a panic this morning that I'd rushed out of the flat without checking the bus route. I only know what time we get to Wickford and, as we've been travelling for twenty-five minutes now, this is making my nerves worse. Sometime in the next ten minutes I've got to get off, but where?

I look around at the other passengers, wondering whether I've got the nerve to ask anyone where we are, but they're all old people, and most of them would sooner spit on me than talk to me. A lady across the aisle catches my eye, and she gives me that look, like I'm not supposed to be here, so I look away. I can tell what she's thinking; it's what they always think. A skinny girl with badly dyed frizzy hair, clothes that don't quite fit and nowhere else to be at nearly eleven o'clock on a Tuesday morning. I'm the sort of person her taxes are paying for. I'm bound to be trouble.

I pull my phone out again and check the time, and then I check my emails for about the twentieth time, but all it says is what I already know, that my interview is at eleven, and when I get there to ask for somebody called Finn.

A sudden lurch throws me forwards in my seat, and now the bus is stuck up against a massive lorry which is trying to get around the bend. I look down at my poor excuse of a smart skirt. It's two sizes too big, but it was all I could get at such short notice. I should have known better than to think anything would ever come of this. I was so amazed when I got the message about the interview – it's not the sort of thing that normally happens to me.

For a while I had begun to dream about what it might be like to work at Rowan Hill – not that I've ever been there, but just the thought of it felt nice. Somewhere no one would know me, somewhere I could finally try to be who I wanted to be, without being shouted at all the time. A place where people are nice to one another and where I'd be welcome, instead of just a hanger-on because I have nowhere else to go. But it doesn't matter what I think any more. I'm going to be late now, so I can kiss this job goodbye.

My mouth hangs open as the bus finally pulls up at the stop in Wickford. I know it's the right place. The village is bigger than some of the ones we've passed through; there's even a little school here, but I don't need to read the sign to know where I am. There's a huge wall that runs right along the street, way bigger than I am, with an old-fashioned brass thing on it that says ROWAN HILL. It looks exactly like I thought it would; after all, just the sound of the name tells you the kind of place it is – a bit posh, but very pretty, and welcoming in a friendly sort of way.

It's ten minutes past eleven, but maybe they won't mind me being late; there might have been someone in before me who talked too much and it's put them all behind, I think, as I practically run through the gates wondering where to find Finn. I hate being late. The road beyond the gate leads in two directions, but there's a wooden signpost that says one way is to the car park and the other to the courtyard shops and tea room. That's where I need to be. Blinking heck, the house is massive.

I don't stop until I hurtle into the courtyard, almost tripping over my feet as I skid to a halt outside a place that looks like it sells benches of all things. There's a bloke outside, whistling, pushing a wheelbarrow full of bark chippings, but no one else is around. I'll have to ask him, although I hope he doesn't think I want to buy anything.

'Are you Finn?' I ask.

The whistling stops immediately, replaced with a big smile.

'No, I'm Patrick,' he says, giving me the once-over. 'But I can get Finn for you if you like.'

I nod, trying to remember to be polite. This place is not like Phil's. 'Thank you,' I manage, although my teeth are chattering, I'm that nervous. *Don't stuff it up.*

'I've come for an interview, but me bus got stuck, and now I'm late.'

'I'll ring him now,' Patrick replies, smiling again. 'Don't worry. It'll be fine.'

I give him an anxious smile, scuffing at the floor with my feet to try and warm them up. There's a vile wind blowing around the courtyard.

'Do you want to come and wait inside? He won't be a minute, but there's a fire going. You could come and warm your hands at least.'

I try to peer through the doorway to his shop. 'You've got a fire in there – what, like a real one?'

Patrick nods. 'Come through. I'll show you.'

He has and all. 'Wow,' I say. 'I love fires like this. We had one once in a house where I stayed as a kid, and the lady that looked after us . . . well, it doesn't matter, never mind.' I shouldn't be telling him this. No one wants to know. No one should know, I correct myself.

'Lizzie?'

5

The voice is coming from behind me. A hand is being held out, but, *Oh My God*, he's gorgeous. What do I say? I can't give him my hand; it's shaking enough as it is.

'I'm so sorry I'm late,' I burst out. 'Only the soddin' bus got stuck up against a lorry.'

There's a momentary pause. 'Well, Lizzie, welcome to Rowan Hill. I'm Finn . . . I was just going to ask you if you'd had a good journey, but it sounds as if it might have been a little fraught.'

'Oh shit, I probably shouldn't swear at an interview, should I? Sorry . . .'

There are little crinkles at the corner of his mouth. The bastard's laughing at me! Well, I don't know what to say, do I? His hand is still sticking out in the air, so I take it. Might as well.

'Listen, don't worry about being late. It's bad enough when you come for an interview and you're really nervous, without public transport letting you down as well. You're here now, so let's go and meet Ellie. Do you want to come with me?'

He lets go of my hand with a big smile. Maybe he's just trying to be nice. Actually, he doesn't look like he's laughing at me after all, just being friendly.

We walk out across the courtyard, to a white door in one wall. I try not to look at his bum, but honestly the view is that good. He's wearing one of those chunky jumpers too, like you see on men in catalogues. I bet he's married.

He pushes open the door to the biggest kitchen I've ever seen. There's even a sofa in here. There's a lady sitting at a large table too, and she gets up when she sees me. I pull at my skirt, trying to get it to sit straight.

Don't stuff it up.

'Ellie, this is Lizzie, and Lizzie, may I introduce you to Ellie, who, among other things, runs the tea room for us.'

I remember to hold out my hand.

'Come and sit down, Lizzie.' She flicks a glance at Finn. 'Don't worry about being late. These things happen.'

I perch on the edge of my chair, while she looks at me expectantly. Finn comes and sits down too.

'You've got shops and everything,' I say. 'I read about this place, but I never knew all this stuff was here . . . It's cool.'

Ellie smiles and opens a notebook, looking at what she's written there. I'm too far away to see what it says, but then she puts the book down anyway.

'So, do you want to start by telling us a bit about yourself, Lizzie, what you've done in the past, that sort of thing?' she begins.

'What sort of stuff?' I ask, biting my lip. I'm beginning to feel really hot.

'Whatever you like,' she replies. 'Maybe a bit about your last job, or even something you've enjoyed doing?'

Ellie sits back in her chair; she doesn't look nervous at all. She's beautiful, I think, staring at her hair. She looks like one of those women out of the paintings, with bright red hair in big long ringlets. It's exactly how I wanted my hair when I had it done last year, but the hairdresser was just someone me mum knew and it went wrong. Now it's just all frizzy. Hers isn't. It's real, you can tell.

I get what she means then, and stop panicking a bit. I actually remember to smile. 'Ah, well, that's easy then.' I tuck my hair back behind my ears. 'I helped out on a farm for a while; that was really good. I had a boyfriend whose dad was a farmer and he took me to see the lambs being born. I mean, it was pretty disgusting and flipping freezing too – it was only March – but when they were all cleaned up the lambs were gorgeous. After that I just sort of stayed on, helping out. There was loads that needed doing.'

Ellie's been making notes, but her pencil stops scribbling and she looks up.

'I didn't see that on your application form, Lizzie.'

'No, well, it wasn't a proper job; I didn't get paid or anything. I just liked being there was all, and Darren's dad taught me loads of stuff. I even used to help with the milking by the end.'

'Oh, I see,' smiles Ellie. 'So how long did you do that for?'

I frown at her. 'Only a few months – till the end of the summer. Darren and me broke up, and after that it was a bit awkward. Shame, cos I really enjoyed it. I liked being outside, you know?'

Finn makes an encouraging noise in the back of his throat. 'I do know exactly what you mean, Lizzie. I don't think I could ever go back to being cooped up in an office all the time.'

I flash him a grateful smile, and feel myself begin to relax a bit, until I see Ellie turning my application form over and back again like she's looking for something. She leans forwards.

'Sorry, Lizzie, I think I'm a bit confused . . . according to your application form you've only had one job, the one in the restaurant, and you've been there under a year—'

I feel my heart begin to sink again. I know what she's getting at. 'You're right. I've only had the one proper job.' I lift my chin a little. 'It isn't easy to get jobs round where I live . . . except ones you don't get paid for.'

'Do you mean voluntary work?' The pencil is twitching in her fingers again. 'Have you done anything like that, apart from on the farm, that is?'

'Only at the charity shop, but I don't do that all the time, now I'm working for Phil, only when I can fit it in.'

Ellie sits back in her chair, a big smile on her face. 'Of course, you can put those things on your application form, Lizzie. You really should actually, because then people know a lot more about the sort of things you can do. Why don't you tell us some more about that now?'

'Well, I'm sort of in charge of the books there, cos no one else reads much. The first thing I always do when I get there is give the place a really good tidy, cos otherwise it looks a bit like a jumble sale . . . After that I do whatever I can see needs doing: serving people, or sorting out the stock, ironing the clothes even. I like looking after the books the best, though.'

'So you've actually done quite a few different things then?' says Finn, looking at Ellie.

I hadn't ever thought about it like that, but I suppose I have really. I sit up a little straighter. 'I like to be busy,' I add, nodding, 'and I'd get bored if I was doing the same thing over and over.'

Ellie gives Finn one of those smiles like they're sharing a secret. 'Well, that's one thing you'd never be here. I sometimes think I'd quite like to be bored once in a while – we're so busy that we never seem to get the time to stop. Having an extra person here who can turn their hand to pretty much anything would be a real godsend.'

'A bit like a gofer, you mean?'

Ellie sits back in her chair. 'Exactly,' she says, with a broad grin. 'Although I should mention that we don't always work nine to five here. That's one of the reasons why we're offering accommodation with the job. Would that be all right for you?'

I'm trying to stop myself from grinning like a lunatic. 'It would be perfect,' I say as calmly as I can. 'I, er, live with my sister at the minute . . . which is fine, but, you know, a bit awkward at times. Living here would be wonderful.' A teeny burble of nervous excitement escapes at my little white lie. I can't help it.

It seems a lot easier after that. I could kick myself for slipping up at the beginning but Ellie and Finn don't seem to notice, or maybe they're too polite to let it show. We go on to talk about all sorts of stuff, not just about the job and what it would involve, and I'm not sure whether what I say is right, but Finn and Ellie both smile a lot. Finn has such a beautiful smile. Ellie is so lucky, but then she's lovely too, so it's only fair that she should have a husband like him.

The journey back to Phil's flat seemed to fly by, although my feet were killing me by the time I got there. I was so hungry, I had to buy some chips from the place by the bus station, but then I didn't have enough money to get the bus across town and had to walk. I didn't mind; it gave me time to calm down a bit. Phil's diner was still in darkness as I passed it, which meant that the lazy bugger hadn't bothered to open for the lunchtime trade. He'd be back at the flat no doubt, swilling beer with his mates.

'Nice of you to put in an appearance,' he calls with a sneer, as I step through the door and pass down the dingy hallway.

I stop at the entrance to the living room. There are three of them in there, sprawled on the settee.

'Yeah, well, I told you I'd be out. Don't blame me if you can't remember.'

He considers this for a minute, raking through his tiny brain for any memory of this morning.

'Where you been anyway?' he asks eventually.

'Out,' I reply. 'Looking for somewhere to live, like you told me to.'

He takes another swig from the can resting in his lap. 'Good, cos that copper was sniffing round again this morning. Not the proper one, mind – one of those poncey community fellas. They're all the same, just waiting to dob me in. You know I'll lose me flat if they find out you're living here. You ain't supposed to.'

'Yes, Phil, I know,' I reply wearily. 'I'm working on it, okay? Which one was it anyway? What did you tell him?'

'The lanky bloke, the one with glasses. And I didn't tell him nothing. You think I'm stupid or something?'

I can barely disguise my snort. I know exactly who he means. Neil, his name is. He's not too bad actually. He has a kind face. He chatted to me once when I was hanging around, asked me where I lived, but I told him I lived with my folks and we were new to the area. He didn't believe me, of course, but he didn't push it either, just gave me a little card with his name on. I've still got it somewhere.

'Yeah, well, I'll be out of your hair soon.'

'You better had.'

'I will!'

It's quiet in my room at least. I've got the volume on my phone turned right up, and I check it again, but there's not been any calls in the last five minutes. I'm sure she'll ring. She said she would, *either way*, and she looked like the sort of person who does what they say they will. Either way . . . at least by tonight I'll know.

I sweep a pile of stuff off the bed and onto the floor. The bastard's been through my things again, but I don't care. That's why I leave it the way I do, because none of this stuff means anything to me – some of it was even here when I arrived, and I reckon that if he's feeling his way through these things he'll never think to look for my real stuff, the stuff that's mine.

I pull up the side of the mattress, and fish out my book, checking it's okay, and then I sit on the bed with my back against the wall and start to read. There's a nervous fluttery thing going on in my stomach, and I know that reading will calm me. It always does. It's only quarter past two; it might be ages yet before she rings. Ellie. I turn her name over in my head, liking the sound of it.

I've only read four chapters when my mobile rings, and I pick it up, looking at it, counting the rings. I've got to answer it in the next three or it will go to voicemail. My heart is pounding.

'Lizzie Macdonald,' I say, trying to sound like one of those business people I've seen in town.

'Hi, Lizzie. This is Ellie, from Rowan Hill.'

I swallow.

I can see my face in the mirror on the back of the door as I look up, and I stare at myself. Do I look any different, I wonder? Do I look like someone whose whole life might be about to change? A grin overtakes my face as I gaze; that can't be me surely, but then I'm rolling about on my bed kicking my legs in the air, burying my face in the pillow and squealing. I did it! I fucking did it!

And the best bit is that I can move in at the weekend. Two days, that's all. That's all I've got to wait. I can do that, no problem. I lie on my back, and stare up at the yellowing ceiling.

Don't stuff it up, don't stuff it up.

Chapter 2

LIZZIE

You know I actually felt a bit sorry for Phil in the end. Not for long, mind – he didn't deserve it that much. But you should have seen his face when he realised that me moving out of the flat meant I wouldn't be skivvying for him any more. What a muppet. Still, at least he signed my reference before I left. He didn't bother reading it either, but I didn't put anything in it that wasn't true, so the fact that he hadn't written it himself wasn't really cheating.

The bus is much quieter today. I'm still nervous, but it's nice to look out of the window this time and see where I'm going. I don't really remember much about the last journey, but today I see all the fields and the lovely houses as we go by. It's very pretty and I want to take in as much of it as I can. This is where I'm going to be living now – and not just living with someone else. I actually have my own flat, my very first place. I'm so excited about it and think that as soon as I get paid I'll buy some pretty flowers; the daffodils should be out soon.

After the interview, Finn showed me up to the flat; I was in such a tizzy that I can't really remember much about that either, but the absolutely very best thing, apart from it being mine, is that it's right in the courtyard, in the middle of everything, over one of the shops. Finn said it was a stable once. I'll be able to walk across the yard with the other customers, only I won't be a customer, of course; I'll be able to smile at them as if to say, *Yes, this is where I live*, and they'll think I'm so lucky.

I don't really know much about Rowan Hill, other than what Ellie told me at my interview, but I managed to get on the internet for a bit to find out more. I still can't believe I'm here and I'm determined to learn as much as I can. It's basically a really big posh house, which has been here forever, with a pretty garden and loads of woodland for people to walk in. The thing is, two years ago it was all just tumble-down. The courtyard was old stables and storerooms and none of the shops were here. Now all the buildings have been developed and the gardens made lovely again. The woods have had paths laid through them, and picnic benches and seats added too. It's only been open to the public since last summer. The shops sell the things that people make here at Rowan Hill, but there's also a tea room, which is where I'm going to be working some of the time. Other than that, I'll be helping anywhere I'm needed, and I wonder if that's why they offered me the job. I think they could see I got really excited about all the different things I might be doing here, and they seemed to like it when I said I like to be busy. I don't think I'll be working today, though. Ellie said she would show me around a bit and then I could get settled. I grin. That won't take long; I've only got one bag.

It's lunchtime when I arrive, and I go straight to the tea room, just like Ellie said I should. It's at the top of the courtyard, in an old barn, with a big wooden door and a little bell that tinkles as you walk through it. There's loads of people inside. A few are already sitting down, but some are still standing at the counter, waiting to be served. I can see Ellie now too, laughing. She doesn't look stressed out at all by how busy it is. She looks like she laughs a lot. I think I might just wait by the door until she's free, but then I spot Finn coming towards me from across the room. And that's when I see it. I don't think I've ever seen anything quite so beautiful before. Finn sees me looking and a big grin covers his face.

'It's quite something, isn't it?' he says.

'It's amazing,' I breathe. 'I didn't know this was a church.'

'It's not,' answers Finn. 'My brother made it . . . Not every day you see a stained-glass window in a tea room, is it?'

'No, it's not. But how did you get it in here?' I ask, confused. 'It's huge. But it's so beautiful – look, it makes the walls go coloured right up to the ceiling.'

'I know,' grins Finn, 'and you should see it on a day when the sun is shining. I'll introduce you to Will later on, and he can tell you all about it. That's what he does, you see, makes things from stained glass. He has his workshop here, so when we renovated this barn Will made the window especially for it, and for Ellie, of course.'

I look at him, puzzled.

'They're getting married.' He winks. 'This was sort of an engagement present.'

'Oh my God,' I say. 'I can't imagine having anyone love you so much that they'd make you that as a present. My last boyfriend didn't even buy me anything on my birthday, tight sod.'

Finn just smiles at me. 'Well, I hope that someone will one day,' he says, and I blush. Ridiculous – as if he would flirt with me.

'Listen, Ellie's still a bit busy. Why don't I take you over to the flat and we can get you sorted out? She can catch up with you in a bit.' He touches my arm. 'Wait here, and I'll let her know what we're doing.'

I do as I'm told and watch while Finn goes to talk to Ellie. I can't stop staring at the window; it's incredible. I thought Ellie must be with Finn, but obviously not. I doubt very much if he's single, though. I see her wave then, and mouth *hello*. I wave back.

There are steps up to the flat, and Finn carries my bag as I follow him up. We say hello to Patrick on the way too, as I'm right above his shop – well, half of it anyway. He's not got his wheelbarrow today but instead is carving something into wood. It looks like a signpost.

Finn unlocks the door, then hands me the key.

'Pop that somewhere safe,' he says. 'Only the door has a Yale lock; once it closes behind you, that's it. You'll probably get locked out at some point; we've all done it. Just in case you do, there are spares in the main house. I'll show you where later.'

I'm staring at him, trying to take in what he's just said. I'm nodding, but all I can think is that I actually have my own key. I slip it into my pocket with a grin.

'Shall I pop your bag through to the bedroom?' he asks. 'You travel light, don't you?'

I bite my lip. 'Well, I had to come on the bus and I wasn't sure how much I could carry. I've left my other stuff back at my sister's. I can pick it up any time.'

'Good thinking,' replies Finn. 'And in the meantime, there's pretty much everything you need here. Ellie's made up the bed already, and there's towels for you in the bathroom. Anything else you need at the minute, just ask. I think she's even popped a few things into the fridge for you as well. Nobody will ever starve while Ellie's around.'

I look around me in wonder. 'I can't believe you've done all this for me. It's very kind of you.'

Finn looks surprised but then his eyes do that twinkly thing again. 'Well, we like to look after folk here, Lizzie. That's all. And you're one of us now.'

I can't wait to meet Will. He must be totally off the scale if Ellie is marrying him and not Finn.

'Right, well, shall I leave you to it for a bit? I think you'll work out everything, but I'll just show you the wood burner before I go, if you like. They're not difficult to use but if you've not used one before, I can run through it.'

I nod vigorously. 'Please,' I say. 'I don't know about things like that.'

'No problem. I'll go and relieve Ellie afterwards. I know she's dying to show you around and introduce you to everyone. I think she also mentioned that you're having tea with us tonight, so I can introduce you to my partner, Ben, then as well. He's delivering a piece of furniture to a customer right now, so I'm afraid you'll have to wait until later to meet him.'

My partner, Ben – bollocks. Why is it always the good-looking ones?

I was going to put my things away but instead I just sit on my bed, staring around me. I can't believe I'm going to be living here, or that I have bathroom all to myself. And a living room, and a little tiny kitchen. There's a window in the ceiling, too, and I bet when I lie down at night I can see the stars through it.

There's a second knock on the door after about fifteen minutes and this time it's Ellie. I'm suddenly so excited that I pull her inside and give her a big hug.

'It's so gorgeous here, Ellie, it's so cute – I love it!' I exclaim, hugging her again.

She looks a little surprised. 'Oh good, well, that's a relief,' she starts, and I can see that she's a bit nervous too. 'It's a little bit quirky this place, but I like it too.'

'And look, a lovely lady has just bought me these,' I say, pointing to a big bowl of fruit on the table. 'I can't remember her name, though . . .'

'Ah, that will be Bonnie. She and her husband are market gardeners—'

She stops when she catches sight of my awkward look.

'—they grow fruit and veg? Their farm shop is just the other side of the courtyard; strawberries to die for in the summer.' She looks around the room. 'Did you get all your stuff in okay?'

I nod enthusiastically. 'Finn was great. He carried everything up here for me. I just need to put it all away now. He showed me how everything works too, including that thing.' I nod towards the wood burner standing in the hearth. 'I don't think I'll ever manage it; I've never used one before.' I bite my lip, wondering what else to say.

'You'll soon get the hang of it. It's pretty easy once you get used to the rhythm of feeding it.'

'That's what Finn said, but I dunno. He promised me he'd help me with it, but I'm a bit . . . well, stupid sometimes . . .'

'Aren't we all?' she smiles. 'You'll be fine, and Finn's a man of his word. Just let us know if you're having problems with anything.'

'That's what he said too. It's a shame, isn't it, really, him playing for the other team? Cos he's ever so good-looking. I bet you were gutted when you found out. I mean, I'm sure Will's nice but—' I stop suddenly, blushing furiously, my mouth making a small '*oh*' of surprise. 'Sorry . . . I didn't mean that. You're getting married, aren't you? So he must be lovely too. And you're all very kind, letting me stay here. It really wasn't my fault what happened in my old job . . . Some of the customers weren't very nice. I mean, you wouldn't like it if some fat, drunk bloke started leching on you, I had to say something—' I look up at her. 'I promise I'll do better here.'

Oh. Dear. Lord.

I smile faintly, trying not to let the panic show on my face. I can't believe I just said that.

'Oh, right . . . Well, look, don't worry. Let's take one step at a time, and see how things go, shall we? If you're ready I'll show you around properly and you can meet everyone, and then I'll leave you be for a bit to get used to things before tea tonight. How does that sound?'

'You know, Finn said you were lovely, and you are, but you mustn't worry about me. My mum used to say I was hopeless, but I'm not, not really.'

'So what do you think, Lizzie?'

We've just returned from a tour of the courtyard – even though it's quite a cold day there are still a few people about.

I smile a little nervously. 'I like Helen's the best,' I venture. 'The colours of all those things hanging on the walls were lovely in there . . . although the lady with the herbs, Patience I think her name was, smelled lovely too. Well, her shop did, not her . . . not that she didn't smell nice, I mean—'

Ellie lays her hand on my arm. 'Don't worry. I know exactly what you're trying to say. I often pop in there just to breathe in all those amazing smells.'

'I've got a bit of dry skin on my hands, look. I always get it in winter. Do you think one of her creams might work on that?'

'I'm sure it would. You can pop in and ask her sometime if you like. She won't mind.'

I give a hesitant smile.

'She doesn't bite, honestly,' Ellie adds. 'She's got a wicked sense of humour and can seem a bit intimidating until you get to know her, but I think that's because she's so tall and laughs very loudly.'

'I liked her,' I say. 'She made me laugh.'

'She makes me laugh too,' she agrees. 'Right, I think you've met just about everyone. I'll take you to meet Will now, and then we can go to the tea room, which is of course *the* most important place.' She winks.

'Is it true that Will made that huge window in there?'

'It is. Wait till you see it again properly. It still takes my breath away.'

She takes my arm. 'Come on, I'll introduce you to Will and then we can go and get a cup of tea and a piece of cake. I'm starving.'

Oh God, so am I.

19

Ellie leads me back up through the courtyard right to the top, where a big white door stands in the wall, right underneath the little tower with the bell in it. I had wondered before what was behind it because I saw some people go through there earlier with their dogs but as she pushes it open, I begin to understand.

'Pretty much everything that way is woodland,' she says. 'Rowan Hill, actually, which is where the estate gets its name from. Lots of people come here to walk now it's all open to the public. The trails start here too, out to the picnic spots, or just through the woods. You'll have to explore sometime.'

She cuts off towards the left. 'But along here are the formal gardens at the back of the main house. If you ever can't find Patience, she's usually through here. She looks after it for us but it's also where she gets all her herbs from. The room at the back there used to be the old conservatory but it's Will's workroom now. He needs the light, you see.'

Will is sitting at his workroom table when we finally get there, and the place is a tip; bits of paper scattered all over the surface in front of him, and photographs too. There are at least three mugs that I can see. It doesn't look like the sort of place that anybody could ever work in; it's far too messy. He pushes around the pile of papers as we go in, as though he's looking for something, and then pulls one towards him, glancing at it for a moment before putting it back down again. I'm not surprised he can't find anything. He stares up at me as I follow Ellie across the room, a quizzical look on his face.

'I know you're busy,' says Ellie. 'We'll leave you to it in a minute, but I wanted to introduce you to Lizzie.' She picks up one of the mugs of cold tea from the table, a horrible white scum on the surface. It looks like it's been there for hours, if not days.

Will pulls a face. 'I'm sorry, I would have come out to meet you before, but I needed to get this down on paper while it was fresh in my mind. It's really nice to meet you, Lizzie.' He stands up and breaks into a smile that totally transforms his face. He isn't anywhere near as good-looking as Finn, but there's something really nice about him, or maybe it's just the way he's looking at Ellie. No one has ever looked at me like that before.

'I saw your window,' I say. 'I think it's amazing, better than anything I've seen before, even in churches. It isn't so old-fashioned.'

He smiles again, his blue eyes all crinkly. 'Well, thank you. I think so too.' He drops his voice. 'Only don't tell anyone because the one I'm hoping to work on next is going in a church.'

I look down at the workbench. 'But there isn't any glass?'

'Not yet, no. I'm just working on the design at the moment. I have to show it to some people in London who will decide whether they want me to make it, or someone else. There are four of us that they'll be choosing from.'

'He's been stuck in here for days, Lizzie. I have to prise him out to eat and sleep, otherwise he'd be in here the whole time,' adds Ellie. 'And he's very modest, too. He hardly ever talks about his work. So if you've got a question, ask it now.'

'I can't imagine making something like this, a whole window, from lots of little bits. I mean, where do you start?'

Will clears his throat. 'Here, look. I'll show you.'

He gathers the papers on the table together, and pats the seat next to him. He passes them across for me to look at but it's hard to make out any detail as the pages are so dark.

'It's not very clear,' I say.

'No, and that's my problem, I guess. These photos are of a window from an old church that was bombed during the war. It was called St Luke's. It wasn't a particularly impressive church, which might be why these old photos are all anyone can find. After the church was bombed, a temporary structure was put up, a rather unlovely building, but sadly that building fell into disrepair too, and eventually the Church decommissioned it. For a long while, that was that.'

'So what's happening to it now?'

'Well, it's part of a restoration project; in fact, the church has been rebuilt, essentially, as part of the regeneration of the whole area. It's going to be a real part of the local community when it's finished. One of the final pieces of work is installing a new stained-glass window, which is where I come in, I hope.'

'And you will,' says Ellie. 'You said your first submission went really well and it's not long to go now before the final decision, is it?'

'No, it isn't.' Will leans in towards me. 'Trouble is, if I get the job, I'm going to have to work in London for a bit, which is really bad timing on my part.'

Ellie tuts. 'Will, the wedding isn't for ages yet. It will be fine.' She gives him a smile. 'Besides which, it's hardly going to be the celebrity wedding of the season. There's not really that much to do. In any case, now that we've got Lizzie to help us out, it will mean I won't need to be in the tea room quite so much. Not to mention that I'm practically falling over people here wanting to help.'

'Oh, I could help too . . . if you wanted. I'd love to.'

'There you are, then. As long as you don't mind me making a few decisions, it's nothing to worry about.'

'It's getting married that's important, not how it's done,' he replies, holding up a hand.

'Good, then let's not worry about it now. There are more important things to see to first.'

Will returns his gaze to the table, quiet for a moment, considering the papers in front of him. His blond hair is sticking up at the front. It looks like he's been running his hand through it without thinking.

'God, I want this job . . . It could really put me on the map.'

Ellie looks at him for a moment, a soft expression on her face. 'I'd like a map with you on it,' she says. 'I could highlight all the notable places to visit.'

The corners of Will's mouth twitch upwards. 'I could help you explore—'

She giggles, slapping at his hand. 'Come on, Lizzie. It's time we were out of here.'

I'm so tired by the time I get to bed. There are so many things chasing through my head as I lie looking up at my window, but it's been a totally brilliant day. I was right too; I can see the stars when I lie down.

Don't stuff it up, don't stuff it up.

Chapter 3

Lizzie

'Are you sure you don't mind, Lizzie? Only we might get a bit mucky,' says Ellie as we walk back out across the courtyard. 'No one's been in here for a while, and everything will be really dusty.'

I hurry to catch up with her. 'No, I don't mind at all. I'll help with anything.' We're heading for a little cottage that stands in a clearing just past the courtyard. 'Does this belong to you as well?'

'It does now,' she says. 'But when I first moved here it belonged to my best friend Jane and her husband. I rented the Lodge from them for a bit, before Will and I got together. When I moved out Jane wasn't sure what to do with it. She said it would feel weird having someone else living here, and I'm secretly rather pleased about that as I've got a bit of a soft spot for this place. In the end Will asked if he could buy it from them; not that we know what to do with it yet, but as we expand Rowan Hill it could come in very handy.'

'How long did you live here for?' I ask, squinting up at the building through the low winter sun.

'Not that long actually. Only about a year altogether, although it feels much longer than that looking back. A lot happened during that year; maybe that's why.'

Ellie pushes open the door, giving it a little kick when it sticks.

She laughs. 'It used to stick a lot then too. There isn't much furniture left. Some of it went into your little flat, but we don't need the rest, and Finn has the builders coming in tomorrow, so it's got to go. Ben won't be long and he'll give us a hand shifting some of the bigger stuff.'

I gaze around the room we've entered. It looks like the kitchen. There's one of those old-fashioned cookers like they've got in the big house, and a sink, but it doesn't look much like a kitchen otherwise – it's full of bookcases for one thing.

Ellie nods her head towards them. 'No cupboards,' she explains. 'I had to use them to store all my stuff . . . Actually, if you want anything, say so, won't you? Otherwise it will all go to the furniture recycling place Ben knows.'

I've never had a proper bookcase before.

'There's a smaller one in the other room, if you want to have a look,' says Ellie, catching my expression. 'Go and see.'

'Would it not be too much trouble?' I ask, coming back into the kitchen.

'Of course not,' Ellie smiles. 'I rather like the idea of you having some of my things. When I first came to Rowan Hill, it was a fresh start for me too. The Lodge might be small, and a bit basic, but it was my shelter for a while, my refuge when I first moved here, and everything in my life felt lost.' She looks up at me for a second, a wistful expression on her face. 'I don't mean that you're lost. Of course not. Just that I hope Rowan Hill can do for you what it did for me. It has that way about it somehow, a way of providing the very thing you need the most, exactly when you most need it, even if you don't know what you need yourself. I was at a bit of a crossroads in my life back then, but with a little bit of Rowan Hill magic I found the way forward. Maybe, if you have one of my bookcases, a little bit of that magic might rub off on you.'

It's a nice thought; I hope she's right.

There's the sound of a van door slamming shut outside.

'Right, that sounds as if the cavalry has arrived. Let's get our sleeves rolled up.'

We've been working for only an hour or so when Ellie's mobile bursts into life. She pulls it out of her pocket and checks the display.

'Oh God, this is embarrassing. I've got a prospective tenant coming this morning, and either I've got it wrong or she's turned up early. I haven't got time to go and get changed now, so dusty and dishevelled it is,' she says, slipping her phone back into her pocket. 'Would you like to come with me, Lizzie, and we could show her around together? If she does decide she'd like to come here, it will be good for you to have met her. Apart from that, she's got a very posh name . . . I feel a bit intimidated, to be honest, particularly as I look such a mess at the moment. I could do with some moral support.'

I nod enthusiastically. I wouldn't have thought that Ellie would be nervous about anything, but she's actually asking me to help. I can't believe it.

The woman's name is Fliss, I learn, as she shakes my hand a few minutes later, which is short for Felicity. Ellie's right; it's definitely a posh name, but Fliss seems lovely, not stuck up at all – when Ellie apologises for being late, and dirty too, she just laughs.

'You mustn't apologise for being busy,' she says. 'You've fitted me in at short notice, and I'm so grateful.' Her eyes flick momentarily to Ellie's hair, and she smiles. 'Here, let me,' she adds, pulling a cobweb out of Ellie's curls. 'I've been to loads of places, but I wish I'd saved my time and come here first. It looks perfect. My sister has been having a tough time lately, so I relocated to Shropshire a couple of months ago so that I could be closer to her, and while that's proved to be a really good move, to be honest I didn't think it would be so difficult to find somewhere for my business.'

Ellie moves forwards into the courtyard. 'Well, let's start with one of the finished units, shall we, and we'll see how we go? It might give you a better idea of how things could look for you. Lizzie just joined us yesterday, by the way.'

'That's lovely, Lizzie. We can be new girls together. What do you do? Not another jeweller, I hope,' she laughs.

I look to Ellie, not sure what I should say.

'No, Lizzie's here as my assistant. So if you need anything, you know who to ask.'

I nod, beaming at them both.

Ellie leads us both towards Helen's studio. 'You mentioned on the phone that you were looking for somewhere really light and airy: we have a textile artist here who also needs a lot of natural light for her work, so I thought I'd show you her studio, if that's okay.'

'Oh, lovely,' Fliss replies, looking around her at the array of buildings.

I can't see Helen at first as we enter the room, until I spot her legs sticking out from behind a desk, her top half bent double as she rummages in a large basket of fabric on the floor.

'Knock, knock,' says Ellie, waiting for Helen to extricate herself. She comes over and gives us both a welcome hug, as if she hasn't seen us for days, then thrusts out her hand in greeting.

'You must be Fliss,' she says, giving her a warm smile, just like the one she first gave me yesterday. 'Ellie mentioned that she'd be bringing you around this afternoon. You're a jeweller, aren't you?'

Fliss nods, looking around her, stunned. The whitewashed walls are filled with a riot of colours: wall hangings, tapestries and woven artwork. I know exactly how she feels. There's so much to look at, you don't know where to start. And then, when you've looked for the first time, you want to begin all over again.

'This is amazing,' Fliss says eventually, wandering over to peer at some of the weaving more closely. 'So clever.'

She stands back, looking at the walls this time, her neck stretching up to take in the room upstairs. 'I couldn't picture how the studios would look when you described them, Ellie, but now that I see it, well . . . wow. I've always gone for a really sophisticated look before. Flaming expensive, and to be honest extremely boring, but my designs will look amazing against these walls. I would never have thought it, but the contrast of the jewellery against the simplicity of the room will look incredible.'

'The light here is beautiful too,' says Helen. 'If you come here, your unit will be on the same side as mine, so you'll look out on the orchards. You'll have the same windows as I do, all along the back.'

Fliss turns to me. 'So what do you think, Lizzie? I bet you're as flabbergasted by all this as I am.'

I am about to reply, but then Fliss looks away. 'This is going to seem extremely rude, Ellie, but can we go and look at my unit now? Sorry, Helen, I'd love to stay and talk but I'm far too excited.'

Helen grins. 'No, you go. It is exciting, isn't it, when you begin to visualise your own business here? The minute I saw this place I knew it was the one for me.'

'Well, I'm sure I'm going to love it, so I hope to be able to come and see you again . . . if you wouldn't mind, of course.'

'Any time, Fliss. It's lovely to meet you.'

We walk back out into the courtyard. 'Of course, the unit we have on offer is much smaller than Helen's,' warns Ellie, 'but the principle is the same.'

'Heavens, I'd need to make an awful lot of jewellery to fill a place that size. Don't worry, Ellie, I'm sure it will be perfect.'

I haven't been inside this new shop yet, and I don't think it's quite finished as the walls still need painting. It is lovely and light, just like Ellie said, with big windows that face towards the sun.

'Just remember that this is only the basic shell,' says Ellie. 'The level of finish is up to you really. Each business has its own requirements in terms of space, fitments, and—'

'No, this is perfect,' says Fliss, crossing the room. 'Oh, and a little office space too,' she adds, pulling open the door. 'I could put my safe in here.'

She looks around again, nodding, and I can see that she's not really looking at the room any more but where she might put her things. I don't know what kind of jewellery she makes but I'm sure it would look beautiful in here, all laid out on shelves by the window, with the light making it glitter.

'How soon could I move in?' she asks. 'I'm serious, this is exactly what I need. If you'll have me, I'd love to be a part of things here . . . although that's something you'll have to explain to me, I'm afraid. I've never come across the co-operative way of working before, and I'm totally clueless. It does sound intriguing, though, a refreshing change from the modern dog-eat-dog world.'

'It works well for us,' replies Ellie. 'But don't worry – I'll get Finn, one of the owners, to explain all the legalities to you. It's quite straight-forward. The basic idea is that we're all part of a single community here, not so much concerned with just our own businesses but Rowan Hill as a whole, helping to make a profitable and, importantly, a sustainable future for us all. We share, we help each other out, and we take decisions jointly, that kind of thing.' She looks at Fliss's smiling face. 'I can see if Finn is free now, if you like.'

'Wonderful,' she says, offering her hand in reply. 'Thank you so much, Ellie . . . and Lizzie.'

By the time we show Fliss out, I can see Will hovering at the top of the courtyard by the tea room. Ellie gives me an anxious glance.

29

'Why don't you pop back to the Lodge, Lizzie, and see if Ben still needs a hand with anything? I'll just have a quick chat with Will, and whenever you're finished, come back to the tea room, and I'll meet you there.'

'Is everything all right?' I ask.

'I'm sure it will be, probably something to do with the project that Will is working on. That's all.'

'Okay then,' I smile, and start to retrace my steps.

I'm just about to go out through the gates when I hear someone calling my name, and turn around to see Ben waving at me. He's standing at the bottom of the steps up to my little flat.

'I'm all done in the Lodge, Lizzie, but I brought that bookcase back for you. Do you know where you want it? I can bring it up for you now if you like.'

I shake my head. 'I haven't had a chance to look yet. I hope it fits.'

'Well, shall we go and see? I'll pop through to my workshop and get my tape measure. Wait here a minute.'

He's wearing his dark hair tied up in a band today. He reminds me of a singer that my mum used to like, big brown eyes, a bit sad-looking, until he smiles his cheeky grin. He seems really nice, although I didn't get much of a chance to talk to him when we met last night. He seems much quieter than Finn.

In fact, when we look there's only one possible place that the bookshelf can go, but as I watch Ben roll out the tape measure to check the space, I can see it's going to be too small.

I shouldn't have got my hopes up. It's just that it seemed a really nice idea to have something that belonged to Ellie. I know she doesn't need the bookcase now, but I could have kept it safe for her in case she needed it again. I give Ben a rueful smile.

'Never mind,' I say. 'Thanks for checking anyway.' I thrust my hands into my jeans pockets.

'Not so fast,' says Ben. 'You're forgetting the golden rule.'

'Sorry . . . I don't know what you mean.'

'We never give up on anything at Rowan Hill . . . and that includes wayward bits of furniture that have the audacity not to fit what would be the most perfect space.'

I give him a blank look.

'You're forgetting I'm a carpenter. Come with me.'

I follow him back down the stairs and into his workshop, which is underneath us. I haven't been inside here yet, but the first thing that strikes me is not what I had expected at all.

'What's that smell?' I ask, looking around me. 'It's sort of . . . warm.'

'Do you like it?' replies Ben.

I smile at him shyly. 'Oh yes. I think it's lovely.' And then I catch sight of the things inside.

'Did you make all these?' I say, looking around me in wonder. My eyes flit from a table to a bookcase, chairs, cupboards and, right at the back, a huge dresser, like the ones you see in magazines.

'Yup,' grins Ben. 'Look, come through here.' And he takes me into the other room, very different from the first, not a showroom, but a place where things get made. The smell is stronger here.

'Is it the wood? Is that what I can smell?'

'Breathe it in,' he nods. 'It's lovely, isn't it? Something I never tire of. I come over here in the morning, open the door, and it's like an old friend greeting me.'

'Yeah, I get that. That is how it smells, sort of friendly and comforting.'

Just inside the entrance to this room is another bookcase, the one that belongs to Ellie, but it's not this that draws me in further. There's a huge round table in here, not finished yet, but the top of it has an amazing swirly pattern on it, almost right around the edge. It's towards the back of the room, right by the window in the back wall. On the floor beneath it are tiny curls of wood, like little bits of apple peel. I stretch out my hand to feel one of the edges.

'Does it make you want to touch it?' asks Ben.

I snatch my hand back.

He comes to stand by my side. 'No, it's good. It's good if you want to touch it. Go ahead. It should feel smooth.'

It does, it's like silk. I slide my fingers around the grooves, tracing each swirl into the next. There's no ending to them; they just carry on forever, all twisted together.

'It's a Celtic knot design,' says Ben. 'One of my very favourite things.'

I look at him. 'But how do you know how to do that? Where the pattern goes?'

Ben laughs. 'Well, you have to concentrate very hard, that's for sure. It would be easy to get it wrong. That's happened before, and then I have to change the design slightly and pretend it's what I meant to do. I don't recommend that, though.'

'It must take forever.'

'Well, this is a bit of a labour of love, certainly. I've had it on the go for quite some time, but the person I'm making it for doesn't know it's for her, so not a word, promise?'

I put my hand to my mouth. 'Who's it for?' I whisper.

'Ellie. It's her and Will's wedding present.'

I pull in my breath, suddenly feeling like I'm about to cry. 'That's so beautiful,' I manage.

'She saw it ages ago, in my old workshop before I moved to Rowan Hill, and she said then how much she loved it. It seems the perfect opportunity now she's getting married to finish it for her. I need to crack on with it actually, or they won't be getting it at all.'

'You're so clever,' I say. 'I wish I could do something like that.'

'Have you ever tried?'

My sudden snort sounds very loud. 'Sorry, I didn't mean that to come out—' Trouble is, I don't quite know what to say next. How could I possibly explain to Ben what it's like? How the kind of life I led before wasn't one where you could learn things like this, but one where people laughed at you for wanting to better yourself. I remember a couple of years ago, when I decided I'd like to learn Italian. Not that I knew much about the language, but whenever I heard it spoken, the words sounded so beautiful in my head. I'd have loved to understand what they meant, but the only place doing classes was right across town. The buses didn't run at that time of night, and when I asked my mum for a lift she just snarled at me. After all, why would I possibly need to learn the language when it was obvious I was never going to go to Italy? I stopped asking after a while. Ben wouldn't understand. None of them would.

He looks at me, like he's going to say something, but then changes his mind, which is fine by me. I don't want to have to talk about things before Rowan Hill.

'I tell you what. Let's have a look at this bookcase and see what we can do. You can help me with it.'

I stare at him.

'Come on.'

The first thing he does is to lay the bookcase on its back, tracing his hands along the edges.

'See? No disrespect to Ellie, but this is like a lot of pieces of furniture that you buy in the shops. It's not actually very well made. Can you see these little marks here? They're the holes from the pins that are holding this all together. And notice how the back is all just strips of wood. That's because it's much easier and cheaper to make this way – because you don't need as big a piece of wood. These were probably just offcuts.'

I nod, although I'm not altogether sure what he means.

'Look at this dresser here instead. Can you see how the edges are cut together, instead of pinned? Lace your fingers together and you'll see what I mean.'

And suddenly I do. I can see how the two edges of wood are both cut so that they slot together.

'That's so clever,' I exclaim.

'It's called a dovetailed joint . . . So there you go; now you do know a little bit about woodwork.' He smiles at me again.

'Ellie's bookcase would be really easy to take apart, and then all we need to do is shorten the length of all these pieces of wood and put it back together again.'

'Could we really do all that?' I breathe.

'Yes, of course. Would you like to?'

I nod rapidly. I can't believe anyone would do that for me.

Ben holds out his hand. 'Then it's a deal,' he says. 'We can work on it a bit in the evenings, if you like. And I'll have a word with Ellie too; perhaps if there's a day when it's quieter in the tea room, we could work on it then as well.'

I'm sure I must look like a complete lunatic, grinning from ear to ear.

Chapter 4

Lizzie

I practically run back to the tea room. I can't wait to tell Ellie, and I hope she thinks it's a good idea. I don't mind how long I have to work; I'll even go without my lunch break if I can help Ben for a bit.

Except Ellie isn't there when I rush through the door. Instead there's another woman standing behind the counter. Little dimples show in her cheeks as we stare at one another for a moment.

'Lizzie?' she asks.

I haven't a clue who she is.

When I don't answer, she comes around the side of the till. I can't help but stare; her stomach is enormous.

'I know. No human baby could possibly be this big, could it? I think I'm carrying an elephant.' She flaps at her face as if she's hot.

I'm not sure what to say. She might think I'm being rude if I agree with her.

'I'm Jane,' she says. 'Ellie's told me all about you.'

I know that name from somewhere, I think, trying to remember.

'Oh yes, you're the lady that used to own the little cottage?'

'That's right. I've popped over to give Ellie a hand this morning, until you're on your feet, but she won't be long; she's gone to see Will, I think.'

I nod. 'I know, I was there when he came looking for her.'

She's smiling, but then she suddenly narrows her eyes at me.

'Did they both seem all right? Not upset or anything?'

'I don't think so . . . I'm not really sure.'

'Hmm, we'll see,' is all she says in reply. She turns to go back behind the counter.

'Come round, Lizzie, you can give me a hand if you like.'

I hesitate for a moment. 'Is everything all right . . . ?'

She pulls a face. 'Oh, take no notice of me. Everything is absolutely fine; I'm just being an old mother hen. I worry about Ellie, that's all; we've been friends for a very long time.' She reaches underneath the counter and takes out three plates. 'I have a feeling that when she gets back, she might like a piece of cake or a scone even. What shall we have?'

I look to where she's pointing, at a display cabinet filled with cake stands full of delicious-looking treats.

'Erm . . .' I stammer. 'I don't know. Can you choose?'

She's just about to answer when the door tinkles open again, and it's Ellie. She must be very cold. Her cheeks are all pink.

'Jane, I'm so sorry,' she says. 'I got held up. Are you okay in here?'

Jane gives her a long look before calmly taking a plate of scones out of the cabinet. She straightens, arching her back slightly, and narrows her eyes, just like she did with me.

'Who held you up?' she asks, ignoring Ellie's question.

'Oh, I got caught up with the new jeweller – I think she's going to be joining us – and we got chatting to Finn.'

'That I know,' replies Jane drily. 'I'm just wondering who else held you up, because whoever it was made you do that thing you think you're good at. You know, the *oh, I'm absolutely fine, jolly hockey sticks, and if*

36

I breeze about no one will know that anything is wrong routine. I have known you too long, Elinor Hesketh, so don't try to pull the wool over my eyes.' She opens out her arms, as if offering Ellie a hug.

'I might have known I wouldn't fool you,' Ellie mutters mutinously. 'Don't hug me, though, Jane. I'm filthy. I probably shouldn't even be in here.'

Jane gives her another look, and shoos her to a table. 'I don't suppose you've had anything to eat either, have you?' She tuts. 'Sit there a minute. You too, Lizzie. I expect you could do with something.'

I do as I'm told.

'I'm sorry, Jane; you don't need to do this. Go on, I'll be fine. You need to get back to the girls.'

Jane waves a hand airily. 'I phoned Jack ten minutes ago. He's happy; no major disasters to report, so I can leave him for a bit.'

Ellie gives her a quizzical look.

'Well, Will came by about fifteen minutes ago, looking for you, and judging by the look on his face I thought perhaps you might need me to stay. So come on, Ellie, tell me what the matter is.'

'Oh, Jane, what would I do without you?' she sighs.

'Starve probably,' she says pointedly, putting down three plates on the table, and pushing one towards Ellie.

I feel a bit awkward, so I just sit quietly and eat my scone. It's very nice. Jane doesn't say anything either, just perches uncomfortably on her chair, with one eye on the counter in case anyone needs to be served, and it's not until I'm chasing the last of the crumbs around the plate with my finger that Ellie starts to speak again.

'Will had a call from his old boss about an hour ago. The final meeting to decide who gets the commission was brought forwards to Friday apparently, and this chap has just had an email saying that they're going to be inviting Will up to London early next week to offer it to him. It's not all been formalised yet, or all the details worked out, but even so—' She's talking really fast, but stops suddenly.

Jane takes hold of her hand.

'But this is a good thing, isn't it?' she says gently, her brown eyes on Ellie's.

'It is, yes, of course it is,' she nods. 'But I think it's only hit me now what this actually means. It's an amazing opportunity for Will. It's the kind of thing he dreamed would happen after we opened here and people got to see his work again. I'm so happy for him really, but it's just . . .' She shrugs helplessly. 'Just that he could be away for months, and I'm not sure how I'll cope. Not when I've only just found him.'

Jane's eyes widen. 'You, not cope? What utter rot. Have you forgotten what's happened over the last year? You were the only one who *was* coping, Ellie, may I remind you? And, like I said, this is a good thing – but I also know that you love this man passionately and can't bear to be away from him for longer than about three hours.'

'More like two,' she smiles ruefully. 'How pathetic is that?'

'You're in love, Ellie, and God help us, but where would everyone here be now were it not for that? None of this would exist. Not this tea room, not this beautiful window, none of these happy customers, and none of the other amazing people at Rowan Hill who owe so much to you and Will.' She stops then, catching sight of the look on my face.

'Sorry, Lizzie, I should explain, because Ellie is far too modest to tell you. Everything you see at Rowan Hill is down to Ellie. All of this was her idea. When she came here about eighteen months ago, nothing was here then. In fact, the estate was feeling very sorry for itself, as was Ellie, to be honest, although that was entirely justified.' She cups one hand to the side of her mouth. 'Horrible break-up from an absolute bastard,' she adds in a stage whisper. 'But she fell in love with Will, and had all these wonderful dreams about how Rowan Hill could be, and together they made them come true.'

'Aw, just like a fairy tale!' I sigh.

'Exactly like a fairy tale. Only Ellie has to be reminded occasionally that she's got the castle and the prince. Well, she soon will have, and she can stop worrying!'

'Actually,' comes a small voice, 'I may not get the prince after all.'

I look at Ellie, but she's staring at her plate.

'Right,' says Jane, briskly. 'Come on, spit it out, what else haven't you told me?'

'That once Will goes, he might not get back until the middle of June.'

'Ah,' says Jane, in understanding.

'But isn't that when your wedding is?' I ask.

'Exactly,' says Ellie. 'On the twenty-first.'

'So what does Will say?' asks Jane, frowning.

'That it won't make any difference, that we can still go ahead with the wedding as planned, and that he'll make sure nothing changes.'

'So . . .'

'I know, but what if things don't go to plan? What if things do change? Will is as excited as I am about our wedding, but this kind of work is all he's ever dreamed about, and I'm worried that something is going to have to give. It might put him in a really difficult position. I don't want to have to make him choose.'

'Oh, Ellie, I'm sure it won't come to that. And you can't go through the next few months worrying about what might happen. Just wait and see what does happen. You of all people know how to keep faith. Just trust in Will and believe that whatever happens will happen for the right reason. *And* remind yourself that we'll all be here to help you, and that everything will be fine.' She squeezes Ellie's hand.

'You're a very wise woman, Jane, has anyone ever told you that?'

Jane rolls her eyes. 'Yes, frequently, but that's because I'm so old.'

'You're younger than me!'

She grins. 'It must just be because I feel so old then.'

'Jane, you're blooming! Look at you, you're beautiful.'

'Fat and old.'

'Pregnant!'

Ellie giggles and we both look at Jane's tummy, which looks like it's going to escape from the top she is wearing. She looks really pretty, actually. Her hair is bouncy and shiny, and her face glows like she's been outside a lot.

'You need to be taking it easy,' Ellie adds. 'You'll be seriously out of action soon. It should be me running around after you, not the other way around.'

'I offered to mind the tea room for this afternoon, not the whole of next month,' she says.

'Yes, and I'm here now,' I say. 'I can help with anything you want.'

Ellie blushes. 'You're both right, I've got plenty to keep me busy, and lots of lovely people to help me. That's what I need to focus on. What's six months in the grand scheme of things? It's nothing.'

She stares up at the stained-glass window at the far end of the tea room, even in the dull January light looking so beautiful.

'Actually, Will wants to let everyone know, so we're going to get folks together in here at the end of the day for his announcement. Would you mind hanging on a minute while I go and tell people?'

Jane wafts her hand. 'Of course. Off you go. Lizzie and I can look after things here, can't we?' She grins.

She waits until Ellie has left the room before turning to me. 'It's a very special place this, Lizzie, and that's one very special person. I'm glad you've come to help, and I'm sure you're really going to enjoy being here, but would you do me a favour?'

I nod.

'I can't be here all the time and, like I said, Ellie is a very good friend. Would you keep an eye on her for me? I obviously didn't want to say too much before, but she has been let down very badly in the past, and although she and Will have a beautiful relationship, I'd hate for anything to damage that. They haven't been together that long, and given that Robbie betrayed her in the worst possible way, it would only be natural for her to worry from time to time. She might need a bit of cheering up while Will is away.'

I think of all the kindness that Ellie has shown me, in fact all the kindness that everyone here has shown me since I arrived. I might not feel like I deserve it, but I'm not going to ruin this chance I've been given. Not ever.

'I will,' I say, determined. 'I promise.'

The tea room suddenly seems full of people. We've shut for the day and everyone has gathered to hear Will's news. There's lots of laughter and everyone seems to be talking at once, but although I can see them all through the kitchen door, I'm quite happy to stay on the other side of everything and finish off the washing-up. I made a right mess of things this afternoon, and I feel awful. It was only a few hours ago that I promised Jane I'd help, but now I've only made things worse. Ellie was very nice about it, but she must think I'm a real idiot. She's trying to look cheerful, but I don't think she is, not really.

I wasn't thinking, that's the problem. I got so carried away with how nice everything was here that I forgot I can't act like I did at home. That was my old life, and I'm not going back there again. Ellie didn't tell me off, but I think she thought I should have known better. I've been in enough shops to know that you don't use your fingers for things – the customer I was serving gave me a filthy look when I put the cake on her plate. When Ellie apologised, she was very nice about it, but then I panicked and dropped the plate. I look down at the soapy water. At least I can wash up; I don't think I can get that wrong.

A champagne cork pops, making me jump, and I see Finn handing glasses round to everyone.

'Speech!' someone yells, but Will shakes his head, laughing. He raises his hands, and at his signal the noise in the room trails off.

'God, the jungle drums work fast around here,' he remarks. 'I must remember that for the future. Listen, I don't want to make a huge speech, but it means a lot that you've all come to share in my news. I don't think it's quite sunk in yet, but I also want to say thank you in advance because I know that you'll all be covering for me in different ways while I'm away, and I'm happy knowing that. Thank you.'

A cheer rises up and glasses are chinked together, then the chat starts up again as Will goes around to talk to everyone, as does Ellie. After that they all sort of drift off, until just Ellie, Will, Finn and Ben are left, looking at each other a little nervously, as though they're not sure what to say first, or who should be the one to say it.

Ellie throws her arms around Will, kissing him firmly on the cheek. 'I knew you'd get it,' she says, kissing him again. 'God, it's so brilliant – you're so brilliant.'

I can see his blue eyes on hers as he lets out a breath. It's like he doesn't ever want to look away. 'Thanks to you, Ellie,' he says quietly. 'Where would I be—'

'Oi, enough of that. It was only a matter of time. Make no mistake, this is down to you, your vision, your ideas, and above all your brilliant, brilliant skill,' Ellie replies.

'Hear, hear,' says Finn. 'Come on, man, tell us all about it.'

Will gives a small smile and takes a breath. 'So . . . I'm really pleased; it's a great opportunity. The project is fantastic; I'm really looking forward to working on it. I've negotiated a good fee, and I'm chuffed to bits that they've picked my work over three others, but . . .' And he lets his breath run out, halting his flow. 'I will have to leave pretty soon, maybe even next Sunday.'

I hear Ellie make a small noise. I don't think she can help it.

'The project is part funded by a grant from the Churches Conservation Trust, with the stipulation that it's delivered to their deadline. Without that assurance, there is no grant, which gives us about five months to pull it off. Hence the need for an urgent start.'

Ellie runs her hand down the length of his arm, sliding her fingers around his and giving them a little squeeze.

'But it's still fantastic news, Will,' she says, although it's weird because she's doing that thing with her face that Liam used to, where his face looked all smiley, and the things he said were nice things, but his eyes weren't saying the same thing at all. That was usually just before he hit Mum, and I know Ellie isn't going to hit anyone, but I wonder if Will has noticed.

'I might get to come home at weekends,' he adds, laying his hand over hers. 'And I'll try and send at least one slushy or suggestive email a day, I promise.'

Even in the dim light, I can see her blushing. 'That's okay then,' she smiles, looking up at him.

Ben leans forwards, raising his glass. 'Congratulations, mate, well done,' he says, catching my eye and waving the glass at me as if I should join in, but I shake my head and look down. They don't need me.

Chapter 5

ELLIE

After yesterday's emotional goodbye to Will, I'm determined to make this day a good one. I'm hurrying across the courtyard to welcome Fliss to the family, already worried that she's been here more than two hours, and I've only just managed to leave the tea room. I had to draft in Ben to help Lizzie before I came across, as I daren't leave her on her own yet, but I can't worry about that at the minute. Right now it's time to help Fliss feel at home.

'Special delivery!' I call out, as I stick my head around the door.

'Ellie, hi, come in,' she greets me. 'It's so lovely to see you again. Close your eyes, though. I'm still in such an awful mess.'

It doesn't look a mess, I think, as I eye up the glass cabinets and their twinkling contents. It's a whole lot of gorgeousness and already beginning to look pretty much ready for business.

'I probably don't have your eye for detail,' I say. 'I think it looks amazing.' I cross over to take a better look at one of the cabinets, which has already been filled with an array of silver and glass pendants. 'You're going to have me bankrupt in no time, I can tell, these are so pretty.'

Fliss straightens up from one of the displays. 'Aw, thank you,' she gushes. 'Anyway, in here is fine; it's in there that's the problem.' She grimaces, nodding her head in the direction of the little office space to the side. 'I've closed the door on it, and now I think I'm scared to go in. Look.'

She walks over to the door and flings it open at arm's length, jumping back as two cardboard boxes tumble into the room, landing at my feet. She immediately picks them up and throws them back, whereupon another falls out.

'See,' she laughs. 'It's chaos.'

I peer in as best I can. An explosion in a packing factory would be one way to describe it. There are boxes and paper and bubble wrap piled high.

'I'm like a swan. Outwardly all seems graceful and serene,' she says, wafting her arm around the studio, 'but underneath I'm paddling furiously in the weeds. Your hair is beautiful, you know,' she adds, out of the blue, smiling generously. 'It's one of the first things I noticed about you.'

It's fair to say that most people don't miss my hair; it's very long, very curly and bright red, but I'm also equally certain that the last time we met it was looking far from lovely. Now it's my turn to thank her for her compliment.

'I brought this over for you as well,' I add. 'Look, your first letter – Miss F. Warrender, Silver and Gold, how fab is that? You'll get to know our postman, Brian. He must be about ninety-odd, but still going strong. He generally brings all the post to the tea room and we farm it out from there. Hope that's all right?'

'Oh, that will be fine. It sounds like a great excuse to pop over for a cuppa.' She smiles again. 'You know, I'm so pleased I managed to grab this place before someone else snapped it up.'

'Well, it's looking really good. Will it suit you, do you think?'

'It's perfect,' she raves. 'You were so right about the light here, and having the walls with just the bare stone painted white really shows off my pieces; it's such a marvellous contrast. I can see I shall need to take your advice going forwards.'

I blush at her generosity, feeling a little ashamed that throughout her preparations for moving in, I've had to leave all the detail to others.

'I think you have Finn and Ben to thank more than me, but that's kind of you to say. I can help you to get sorted now, if you like. Make a start on cardboard city through there.'

Fliss crosses to a small table by the side of one of her units, picking up a brochure. 'I would take you up on that, but that darling girl Lizzie said she'd give me a hand later once the tea room closes. She's been so helpful, I said I'd take her out for a pizza – the poor thing looks half starved.'

'Fliss! You don't need to do that,' I exclaim, but smile inwardly at hearing that Lizzie has proved herself to be useful.

'No, I know I don't, but fair's fair: she's giving up her time for me. It's the least I can do.'

'It's still lovely of you. She's found it quite hard settling in, I think, and now I feel a bit like I'm nagging her the whole time. A trip out will be a nice change.'

Fliss winces. 'Yes, she mentioned that she's broken one or two things.'

And dropped cake in someone's lap, flooded the kitchen and burnt two trays of scones, I think to myself.

'We'll get there,' I say. 'It's early days yet.'

Fliss's smile is warm. 'I'm sure you will. She didn't say much, but you only have to look at her to know that things here are a little different from what she's used to. With our help she'll soon feel more at home, but you must let me know if I can help with anything else.

Anyway, come and sit over here for a minute. I want to show you something.'

I cross to where Fliss motions, a round table laid with a deep blue cloth, and take a seat on one of the three chairs covered in matching coloured velvet.

'This is where I'll meet with clients to discuss their requirements – and I'd like you to be the first, Ellie.'

I look at her in puzzlement. 'I'm sorry, I don't follow . . . ?'

She takes my left hand in hers. 'A little bird tells me that you're getting married soon. Please tell me that you haven't sorted anything out yet? You will let me make the rings for you, won't you?'

FEBRUARY

Chapter 6

Lizzie

'We should have done this weeks ago, Lizzie. I really don't know where the time has gone.'

I look around the dim room with its stiff white tablecloths, and return Fliss's wide, easy grin with a nervous smile. When she said she'd take me out for a pizza, I thought she meant to Pizza Hut, not to a proper Italian restaurant, with candles on the table and a wine list. I'm grateful that the menu has been translated into English, but I've never eaten an artichoke in my life, and I'm not sure I want to start tonight. I feel out of place enough as it is, without having to cope with alien vegetables.

Fliss's head is bent to her menu. 'I wish these places didn't feel like they had to invent increasingly adventurous toppings all the time. I mean, what's wrong with pepperoni anyway?' She turns a page back and forth. 'I don't know about you, but I think I might just have the Margherita.'

I feel my shoulders drop a little, and flash her a grateful smile. 'Yes, me too, and a Coke, if that's okay . . . I'm not sure I should have anything else, what with work in the morning.' The wine list goes on for two pages, and it sounds like a good excuse.

'Sensible girl. I'm getting far too old to be able to drink during the week, and in my line of work it pays to have a steady hand. I might have a lemonade, I think.'

I lay the menu back down on the table. 'I think the things you make are lovely,' I begin shyly. 'It must take ages to learn how to do it. And to come up with all those different designs as well.'

Fliss runs a finger around the edge of her sleeve to free her bangle. 'I've always made things, even used to thread buttons from my mum's old tin on to elastic when I was a child. But, yes, then I went to university to learn how to make jewellery properly. I'm still learning – what colours work well together, how different types of materials handle. Sometimes I have a really great idea for a design, but in practice it's just not possible. Then I have to go back to the drawing board.'

'So you've done it for a long time then?'

Fliss nods, both at me and to the waiter to catch his eye. 'Although I've only had my own business for about six years. A lot of my orders come through my website, but now that I've got my own shop at Rowan Hill, I'm over the moon. I still can't believe I'm here. I never thought I'd find anywhere so perfect.'

She breaks off to speak to the waiter, rattling off our order without any hesitation. I wish I could speak the way she does, although I am getting better, I think.

'And you've done a brilliant job in helping me to get sorted out, Lizzie. I can't thank you enough. I've had so much to think about, moving here and getting things settled for my sister, that I haven't been half as organised as I usually am. Still, improvements on that front too, so it's all looking good.' She beams.

I fiddle with the edge of the tablecloth, lining it up in a straight line across my knees. 'Is she all right?' I ask, politely.

Fliss takes a huge gulp of her drink the minute it's put down on the table. 'She will be,' she says. 'Her husband died earlier this year, and although it's early days yet, I think she's beginning to find her feet a little. He'd been ill for some time, but there was always hope, you know? It's Isla, my niece, who's finding it so hard. She's only five, and old enough to sort of understand. There've been a few issues at school, and what with worry over finances too, it was the least I could do to try and help. She only lives a couple of miles from here as well, so it's no hardship moving in with her for a while.' She takes another sip of her drink, before sitting back in her chair and raising her glass to me. 'Anyway, I didn't come here to talk about me, or my sister's tale of woe. I'd much rather hear how you're settling in. I think you're so brave, you know.'

I nearly splutter my Coke across the table. I've been called many things in my life before, but never brave.

'See, there you go again,' says Fliss, leaning forwards. 'Why don't you believe it when someone pays you a compliment? You always think the worst. And besides, I do think you're brave. I know you feel you've made a few mistakes, and I might have got this wrong but I sense that Rowan Hill is a little different from what you're used to? Coupled with the stress of moving away from everything that's familiar, I think you're settling in really well. It *is* brave to do what you've done and strive for something better. Not many people would do that.'

'Well, they would if they had my shitty life,' I mutter, forgetting my manners for a minute.

'But they don't. You see it all the time, on these TV programmes, for example. People on benefits, smoking and drinking, never a care for the children they're supposedly bringing up. It might sound harsh, but to me a lot of them look like they're quite happy in the gutter; they have no aspirations whatsoever. You're different, Lizzie. You want something from your life, and it takes a lot of guts to go after that.'

'Or stupidity,' I reply. 'I don't seem to be doing a very good job of it at the moment.'

'Teething troubles, that's all,' smiles Fliss. 'We all get them. It does takes time to settle in somewhere new, and I know I can't speak for everyone, but you really have been a huge help to me.'

I look down at my lap, uncertain of how to ask my next question. 'Would you tell me, Fliss? If I was making a mess of things? Only I'm not sure Ellie is all that pleased I'm here. I don't mean to make mistakes, it's just that I get so flustered when I think everyone is looking at me, or talking about me—'

'But why would they be doing that?' she interrupts.

'Because they usually do. You don't see it, Fliss, but I've spent most of my life having people talk about me, or sneer at me just because I come from the wrong end of town and don't have any money. People are very quick to judge.'

Fliss stares at me for a moment, a soft frown on her face. 'Yes, I suppose they are,' she says. 'But only a few people are like that; the rest are decent human beings. And I've honestly never heard Ellie say that she was in any way unhappy with what you've been doing. You really must try not to think like that. Just keep on doing what you're doing, and it will all turn out brilliantly.'

'I hope so.' I shiver involuntarily. 'I really love it at Rowan Hill, and there's no way I'd want to go back to where I was before.'

'Then you won't,' she reassures. 'No reason why you should.' She leans back as our plates are placed in front of us, inhaling deeply. 'Now that smells really good,' she adds, and raises her glass to me as if in a toast. 'To Rowan Hill,' she says.

I smile properly for the first time since arriving at the restaurant. 'To Rowan Hill,' I echo, touching my glass to hers.

Chapter 7

Lizzie

I'm being taken out today, to some big stately home near here. Ellie says she thought it would be nice for us to get to know each other a bit better, but I thought we were doing fine before.

It's not that I'm ungrateful, but for Ellie wandering around some big posh house and having tea after is a nice day out; all it does for me is make me nervous. I've never been anywhere like that before, and I know I'll feel out of place.

'So what do you think of Attingham Park, Lizzie?' Ellie asks a few hours later.

I gaze around me at the smartly painted tea room, with its high ceilings and huge bay windows.

'It's nice, but not as nice as ours. They don't have a pretty window for a start.'

'I didn't really mean the tea room. I meant the place in general, the house and the grounds, the deer park even. What did you like best?'

'Oh, the house,' I say straight away, becoming more animated. 'That was amazing. That big room laid out for dinner, all posh plates and bowls and all those knives and forks. I wouldn't know where to start—'

'Yes, me too,' Ellie replies. 'I love to imagine what it must have been like to live here; when it was a family house, I mean, before the National Trust owned it. Imagine journeying along that huge drive in a carriage, and the parties they would have had. Or strolling in the grounds with your guests on a Sunday afternoon, before taking tea on the terrace.'

'I wouldn't have liked to work here, though. All those fireplaces to clean, traipsing up and down stairs all day, and all that silver to polish.'

'No, I don't suppose that would have been so much fun. It would have taken a lot of work to keep the household running, and even now there's an army of people employed here to keep things ticking over, or repaired and preserved, so that we can all enjoy them.'

I'm quiet for a moment, looking at the menu in front of me. I knew the minute she asked me to come here with her why we were going; I've been let down 'gently' before.

'Why did you bring me here really, Ellie?' I ask softly. 'I'm not stupid.'

'No one is calling you stupid. Whatever made you say that?'

'I've seen the way you all look at me. I know I've dropped stuff and got things wrong, but I'm not thick. I want to get things right so much . . . but however hard I try, it all seems to go wrong.'

To my horror a slow tear makes its way down my cheek and falls to my hand, which is shaking as I clutch the menu.

'And we'll help you,' says Ellie, reaching forwards to me. 'We'll all help you.'

I sniff, looking up at her, meeting her eyes for the first time. 'Aren't you going to sack me?' I whisper.

'Sack you?' she replies, puzzled. 'No, Lizzie, I'm not going to sack you – is that why you thought I'd brought you here?'

I nod glumly. 'I thought you were just trying to be nice about it. Bringing me out here and then buying me tea so I wouldn't feel too bad and cry all over your customers.'

She watches me for a moment. 'Well, you know, if I were going to sack you, that might not have been such a bad idea, but as I'm not, let me tell you the real reason I brought you here.'

She pauses for a moment as the waitress appears with our cakes. The scones are nowhere near as big as Ellie's, but she's brought cream as well as jam.

'When I asked what you thought about this place, I was very interested to know what you liked about it. Why do you think I wanted to know?'

I lay my knife down for a moment, mid-mouthful. I'm not sure whether to speak with my mouth full or keep her waiting while I swallow my scone. In the end I gulp down half and manage to mumble through the rest.

'Dunno really. Did you want to see if I agreed with what you think?'

'No – the opposite, in fact. I wanted to know what you liked best because, actually, your favourite thing isn't the same as mine at all. I like the house, the inside of it, but what I *love* is the setting of it all, the way the house and the courtyards are arranged, the grounds, the woodland and the gardens. I love the way they make me feel.'

'I felt a bit like I was in one of those TV drama thingies when I was in the house. You know, like the lady of the manor.'

'Rustling skirts and tight corsets?' she smiles.

'Yeah, a bit,' I say, shyly.

'So why else do you think people come here?'

I look down at my plate. 'The tea?'

'Yes, that's certainly one. What else?'

'Erm . . . walking? Lots of people were walking their dogs.' I look around me, suddenly seeing the people in the tea room for the first time. 'There's quite a lot of children here too. I always thought these places were for old fuddy-duddies.'

'So why do you think they come?'

The seconds tick by, stretching.

'How about if you had been at work all week, rushing about and madly busy?' she prompts.

'Then you might come for a day out,' I reply.

She smiles. 'Do you remember coming to places like this with your parents as a child? I never wanted to go when mine suggested it, and I always moaned a lot, saying how boring they were. The funny thing was that whenever we got to where we were going, I always had a brilliant time. Now that I'm older, of course, I understand why they wanted to visit these sort of places.'

I bow my head. 'I've never been anywhere like this before,' I murmur, embarrassed. 'Not ever. I never knew my dad, and Mum could never be bothered to take me out.'

Ellie looks shocked at this, and instantly apologises, but I can't say I blame her. Most people's childhoods weren't like mine.

'Lizzie?' she says gently. She reaches forwards to touch my hand again, waiting until I look at her before she starts speaking again. 'Can I ask you another question?'

I give a slight nod, swallowing hard.

'Why did you apply for the job at Rowan Hill? Were you really living with your sister before?'

I shake my head slightly. 'I don't even have a sister.'

'I'm not angry with you, Lizzie, but I do expect you to be honest with me.'

I take a huge bite of my scone, chewing it slowly; she has no idea what it was like.

'I didn't lie to you,' I protest. 'Well, not about me job. I did work as a waitress, but I only got the job cos Phil – the bloke whose flat we lived in – felt sorry for me after Mum died.'

'Oh God, Lizzie, I'm so sorry.' There are even tears in her eyes, and that makes me mad.

'Don't be. Not about her, any road,' I say, knowing how bitter I sound. 'She wasn't worth it. She never cared about me, not all the time she was alive. Dragged me from this place to that in search of new boyfriends and parties. I thought when we came to Shrewsbury that things might be different. She seemed to like it, and for a little while things were a bit better. She even got a job, but then she met Liam and the drinking and drugs started up again, but worse this time. She got into a fight one night when she was drunk and some bloke broke her arm really badly. She lost her job then and all.'

'So what happened?'

I shrug, looking around me at the people deep in conversation. How on earth can I possibly explain what happened next?

'She died,' I say, knowing my words don't cover the half of it. 'She died,' I repeat, 'and I had to find somewhere to live. I don't know why Phil let me stay really, or why he gave me a job, but I knew it wouldn't be long before he chucked me out . . .'

'And that's when you saw our advert?'

I nod. 'It was because you said the job came with a place to live that I applied for it.'

'Oh God, Lizzie. And we were worried that no one would want the job because we couldn't afford to pay very much.'

'Yeah, well, when you've got nothing, little things can mean the world.'

She sighs. 'I take it your reference wasn't real?'

'Sorry. Phil told me that he'd give me a good reference, but only cos he knew it would get rid of me and he couldn't be bothered to write it himself. He wasn't supposed to have anyone living in the flat, see; the council would have thrown him out if they knew.'

We sit in silence for a few moments.

'I bet you're going to sack me now, aren't you?' I mumble, licking my lips.

She thinks for a bit. 'No. I want to show you something,' she says, to my astonishment. 'I brought you here to talk to you about how you can help us out, and that's what I'm going to do. Finish your scone.'

Back outside again, Ellie makes purposefully for the path that leads off to one side of the house. I trail after her, totally confused. How can she not want to sack me?

We're following the signs to the walled garden, and once inside Ellie leads us straight to one of the benches.

'I know it's a bit chilly, but I want you to sit here for a minute. Don't say anything. Simply sit for a moment, and just be. I'm going to do the same.'

I close my eyes, not knowing what she means, and when I open them a few moments later hers are still shut. I close mine again, and try to sit still. At first I don't feel anything. The wind is cold; it's making my face ache, and I can hear the cawing of the crows in the big trees behind the wall, but I'm not sure what I'm supposed to be waiting for. And then just when I feel my nose start to itch, it suddenly seeps into me, that feeling you get when you're just about to drift off to sleep. When everything about the day has been forgotten and you're calm for a minute. Except I don't fall asleep, and the feeling doesn't go away. It fills me up, warm and comforting, and I feel more peaceful than ever in my life before. I slowly open my eyes and watch Ellie for a minute, her face soft, her bright red hair blowing this way and that in the wind. Almost as if she knows that she's being observed, she suddenly looks at me.

'Is that what you feel?' I ask.

She laughs. 'I don't know! What do *you* feel?'

'It's weird. I've never done this before, but it's really peaceful . . . and then, it's not. It's sort of buzzing, like it's alive . . .'

'You should come here in the summer, when the bees are mad with pollen and the flowers light up every part of the garden with a different colour. Then it's fairly humming with energy; you can almost see the air vibrating.'

'What is it?' I ask.

'I don't know what you call it, but I know how it makes me feel. There are places like this everywhere, if you look to find them, and Rowan Hill is one of them. It has this sort of special feel about it. I noticed it when I first moved there, and I'm sure other people think the same.'

'Is that why people come here then, to Attingham Park?' I ask, looking around me.

'Partly. Some will, but I don't think everybody feels things the same way. People come here for all sorts of reasons, like we said earlier. Some come for a walk, or to see the house, or perhaps because they're interested in history or architecture. I think others come simply for a nice afternoon out and a piece of cake, and in the winter it's beautiful here with the deer. Other people might come because it's a good place to be when you've had a busy week and are tired of rushing around. You can't rush here; it just won't let you.'

'Yeah, I get that.' I tuck my hands under my legs to get them out of the wind. 'Rowan Hill is like that too.'

'It is, if you can stop to listen to what it has to say. The trouble is that now we're all so busy it's hard to remember to do that. We made Rowan Hill for people to feel what we've felt today, whatever they're doing, and I need your help, Lizzie, to remind us all of that fact.'

'And not throw their tea all over them in the tea room?'

She smiles. 'Something like that. Rowan Hill is a special place for me. It's a special place for all of us. Last year, when we were only just beginning to get our ideas for it together, we were all a bit lost, but little by little we found the things again that made us happy, that made us feel a part of something. We're like a family now, and I want our visitors to feel special when they come to Rowan Hill, whatever their reason – and I want them to keep coming back. None of us can afford to lose the things we've found over this last year or so. I think the same is true for you, Lizzie. I think you have a lot to offer Rowan Hill, and I think it can help you too.'

'But how can I help?'

'By working hard. By listening carefully. By noticing things.'

'What do you mean, noticing things?'

'Seeing what needs doing, and then doing it, even if you think it might be someone else's job, or observing things that have gone wrong and looking for a way to fix them. That's how we work at Rowan Hill. We're a team.'

'But I'm no good at that stuff. What if I don't notice?'

'You will. Just look with your eyes and your mind open. Think about everything that's going on around you, and then ask yourself if there's something that's not quite right, or that needs attention.'

'Like the waitress back in the tea room, do you mean?'

'Which one?'

'The one that served us, the one that was doing everything. The other girl was stood about, like some dozy arse.'

She grins. 'You might want to call her a lazy so-and-so, rather than a dozy arse, when you're in public, but you see, you do notice things. I know you've been helping Ben out in his workroom. He said you've been brilliant.'

A smile creeps up my face. 'Can we go now?'

'We can,' she replies. 'I think we've got what we came here for, don't you? I took a chance on you, Lizzie, because I could see that you needed a little help. If you let it, Rowan Hill can give you that help, but you have to give it back in return, is that a deal?'

'And if I get things wrong?'

'Well, as long as you ask if you need help, that's the main thing.' She rises from the bench, and I get up too, feeling the coldness seeping into my toes. 'Speaking of which, let's get going, I want to introduce you to someone very special.'

I thought we were just going back to Rowan Hill, but instead of turning in through the high wall of the estate, Ellie swings the car into a driveway just short of it. I follow her down the path to the house a little nervously, not quite sure what to expect. Ellie has told me nothing about who we're going to see.

It's a surprise when the front door is pulled open and an elderly lady stands there, and an even bigger surprise when she throws the door open wide and beams at Ellie, pulling her into a hug. She looks tiny and quite frail, but judging by the *oof* that Ellie makes, she's stronger than her appearance suggests. She looks a bit like I should know her, and exactly how I always dreamed my granny would look, if I'd ever met her.

'And you must be Lizzie,' she says. 'I've certainly heard a lot about you, so it's lovely to finally meet you.'

I look at Ellie, and she nods at me slightly to move forwards. I look down at the carpet suddenly and blush, struggling to get my shoes off in case I get mud all over the creamy hallway.

The lady takes my arm and leads me away into the living room as if I'm the only person here. I'm sure she's staring at me, but I keep my eyes down.

'Now you must sit there, dear,' she says to me, 'so that I can see your face. If we're to get to know one another properly I must at least know what you look like. I love this room, but that corner there is always gloomy, no matter what I try to do to it.'

I flick Ellie another nervous glance.

'Lizzie, this is Alice,' she begins, joining me on the settee. 'Alice is a very good friend of ours, and whatever you do, don't make the mistake of thinking she's a helpless little old lady. She's lived next door to Rowan Hill since before Will and Finn were born, and thinks of us all as her own. She's as protective as a lioness towards her cubs, aren't you, Alice?' she smiles. 'Cross her at your peril.'

Alice gives a very audible *tut*.

'She is, however,' she continues, leaning into her words, 'a bit of a softie, and despite the fact that when I first met her I thought her a hideous old witch, she keeps an eye on us all, and makes sure that none of us upsets the apple cart.'

Another *tut*.

'You're putting the fear of God into the poor girl, Ellie, stop it at once.' She twinkles at me. 'Whatever will she think?'

She turns to me again, smoothing down her skirt. 'I'm not half as bad as she makes out, dear. You and I will get on famously, I'm sure of it.'

'I think I've heard of you,' I stammer. 'Didn't you write something in the paper a while ago? I saw it when I was . . . well, before I came here.'

'I did,' she replies, and looks pleased. 'I did an article on Rowan Hill not long after it opened, about why us old people should learn to accept change, embrace new ideas and move on. It's a valuable lesson to learn, for all of us.'

'We've been up to Attingham this morning, Alice,' says Ellie. 'And we had a chat about how Lizzie can help at Rowan Hill.'

'I see.' She gives me a big smile.

'Lizzie has found settling in here a bit difficult . . . like a lot of us do at first. Exactly like I did, in fact, when I arrived.'

'Well, then, let's fix that straight away. There's no better place to put things right after all, and I think that you and I might help one another too.'

I look up, not sure what she means.

'I'm getting on a bit now, and much as I love Will or Finn coming in each day to see to my fires, they're always in so much of a rush. They never let me see that, of course, but I was thinking . . . if I show you how, do you think that's something you could come and do each day – clear the grate out and re-lay the fire for me? My old bones do feel the cold, and you'd be doing us all a big favour.'

I look at the pile of logs in her fireplace, all burning brightly.

'Oh, could I? I love fires like this. It's just like the one Patrick has in his workshop.'

'Of course, then we can have a little chat . . . about all sorts of things. Maybe I can help you out with some of the things you find difficult too. How does that sound?'

'Would that be all right?' I ask. 'Wouldn't I be in the way?'

I look over at Ellie, but she's smiling too.

Alice waves a hand in the air, and laughs. 'Dear, how can you possibly be in the way? That would be fine with you, Ellie, wouldn't it? You wouldn't miss her for a little bit each morning. I love a good natter and, believe me, I've got some stories to tell.'

MARCH

Chapter 8

Lizzie

My stomach's making loud rumbling noises, so much so that Ben laughs at me.

'Now I can tell you're feeling more at home, Lizzie – your clock is definitely set to Rowan Hill time.' He checks his watch. 'See, I was right: eleven o'clock. Time for cake. Come on, let's finish up here for a bit.'

I run my hand over the piece of wood we've been working on. 'It's looking good, don't you think?' I ask.

'I think it's coming along brilliantly. In fact, I'm surprised at how quickly you've got the hang of it. The trick is in working it until it's as smooth as silk, and then we can put a bit of colour back into it.'

'I like the dark woods the best, the ones that look really glossy . . . and I think it might go with the colour of the beams in my lounge better.'

Ben crosses to the cupboard along the far wall of his workshop.

'Come and see,' he says. 'There are all sorts of polishes in here. We can try a few if you like on one of the pieces we've cut off so we don't spoil this, and you can pick your favourite.'

I look at the rows and rows of tins and bottles. 'Could I really? Wouldn't you mind?' I say, wondering how much I can get away with.

'Of course I don't mind.' Ben tips his head to one side, and narrows his eyes. 'On one condition.'

He has very kind brown eyes.

'That if you ever use anything from this cupboard, you promise to put it back when you're finished? There's stuff in here that can do some serious damage if it's messed around with. Just like Ellie has her rules for the tea room, these are my rules for in here . . . If you ever catch me leaving stuff out, you can tell me off, okay?'

He winks at me, and I know he's trying to be kind. I just wish he didn't have to remind me about the tea room. I haven't been in there yet this morning, not since I broke a teapot yesterday. It was heavier than it looked and it slipped off the tray before I could stop it. Ellie said she didn't mind but she still found me jobs to do elsewhere this morning.

Ben takes hold of my arm. 'Let's go and have that break. You know, you're doing really well, Lizzie. You just need to have a bit more confidence.'

I smile back, but I'm not really feeling it, to be honest.

By the time we get to the tea room, Finn and Patrick are already there, loaded up with a plateful of gingerbread and coffee and walnut cake. They always have the same thing every day. So does Ben, only he prefers the lemon drizzle. I can never make up my mind.

Ellie gives me a big smile as I go up to the counter, which makes me flush a bit.

'The usual today, is it, Ben?' she asks, as he comes around the counter too. She pushes at his arm. 'No, go on, shoo. Go and sit down. Lizzie and I will bring the tea over, won't we?' She flashes me another smile.

I catch Ben's eye and, remembering his words, give a little nod. I've got to do this.

'What are you going to have today, Lizzie?' she adds.

They all look so good. 'Can I have the blackberry and apple?' I ask.

'Coming right up . . . No, I tell you what – why don't you plate up, Lizzie? I need to check on my scones for a minute.'

I look back down at the counter, at the rows of cake stands to one side. I've got a horrible feeling I'm going to drop one of them. A vision of an entire lemon drizzle cake crashing to the ground fills my head. I take a deep breath, trying to remember what to do first. The tray, that's it.

I set the tray down and take out two plates from under the counter. *Take the plate to the cake*, I mutter, *not the other way around*. That's where it went wrong last time. I take the dome off the first cake stand and put it down carefully. *Plate to the cake* . . . I pick up the tongs and go for the nearest piece of lemon drizzle, holding the plate as close to the stand as I can. I hold my breath and slide it across.

'Actually, Lizzie,' calls Ellie from the kitchen, 'could I have a piece of gingerbread too? I think I might join you today.'

I pick up another plate and try again.

I've just got my own cake on my plate when Ellie comes back through.

'Look at that,' she grins. 'You're a total pro now.'

I beam at her, and put down three napkins and three forks on the tray. I even manage to get the tray to the table without losing any of the contents.

Finn looks up as we join him. His T-shirt and jeans are covered in paint, and there's a splodge in his hair too.

'Good day?' he asks.

'Mmm, not bad,' says Ellie. 'Those ladies from the walking group came in again,' she says with meaning. 'I'm sure we seem to be seeing them rather more frequently now. Not that I'm complaining, of course. I just wondered if that might have anything to do with you at all.'

'Me? Whatever do you mean?' he replies innocently.

'Oh, nothing really. But since you carried a certain lady with a turned ankle back the other week, they seem to be an almost permanent feature.'

Finn winks at me, leaning past Ellie to scoop up a crumb of her gingerbread. 'Can I help it if they enjoy walking?' he says, and then frowns. 'Although . . . I'm not altogether sure that her ankle was as bad as she was making out.'

'You don't say,' she replies, slapping his hand as he reaches across again. 'Will you leave my cake alone, Finn? You've had yours, and I'm starving.'

'Haven't you eaten?' asks Finn, picking up the teapot and pouring out more tea. 'Ellie, you'll fade away to nothing. There should be no excuse now that Lizzie's here. Make sure you stop and get something. Ben, tell her.'

'Huh? Tell her what?'

'That she should eat properly. She can't be trying on wedding dresses if one minute she's, oh I don't know, this big,' he says, holding up his hands about two feet apart, 'and then the next minute she's, like, this big,' he concludes, narrowing the gap to about twelve inches.

Ben laughs. 'I should watch it, Finn. You'll be wearing that cake in a minute. Ellie will look beautiful whatever.'

'I never said she wouldn't,' argues Finn indignantly.

'And we all know that she's going to wear the dress I picked out for her anyhow.'

'Ben, that was ages ago,' remarks Ellie. 'I doubt they even have it any more.' She looks at me. 'He's talking about the wedding-dress shop in the village, Lizzie. It used to be a tea room, and it's where I started the whole cake-making thing when I first came to Rowan Hill. When the shop was sold, Ben made the display cabinets for the new owner and he spotted this dress, which he thinks I should have, and which will have long since been sold.' She rolls her eyes at him.

'Wouldn't hurt to look, though, would it?' adds Finn, a little twitch turning up the corners of his mouth.

Ellie looks at Patrick, but he just shrugs.

'Hey, don't look at me,' he grins. 'I'm just here for the cake. Although you might want to mention that chat you had with me the other day – you know, the one about the double wedding, and Finn and Ben . . . I was wondering if I could be best man to all three of you . . .'

Finn picks up his cake as if to throw it.

Ellie sighs. 'Gentlemen. Can we *please* talk about something else? You know I don't go in for big wow dresses.'

'Yes, but presumably you will be wearing a dress of some kind. I'm not sure that the good folk of Wickford are ready for their first naturist wedding ceremony.'

'Oh, very funny,' says Ellie. 'And yes, Patrick, I will be wearing a dress. I just haven't got around to thinking about it yet, that's all.'

Finn pushes Ellie's plate a little further towards her. 'Eat,' he says, holding his hands up again, only this time a mere six inches apart.

I watch as Ellie finishes her cake. A thought has just popped into my head, but I don't want to mention it, not yet, although I'm sure it would help. Ellie's always so busy, and this would be so much fun. Plus, I'd love to know what kind of dress she's going to wear. She's going to look so beautiful.

'Has Helen been in this morning?' I ask, as we're clearing the plates away. 'Or any of the others?' Finn, Patrick and Ben have long since gone back to work.

'Not today, no.' She gives me a little look. 'Why?'

I put the plates carefully into the dishwasher. 'I just wondered if they might like some cake as well. I could take them some – if you like.'

Ellie stops what she's doing and turns around to face me. At first I think she might be a bit cross, but then she gives me a pleased look. 'That's a brilliant idea, Lizzie, how lovely.'

'I won't be long,' I say quickly. 'I'll start with Helen, as she's nearest.'

Ellie grins. 'What would she like, do you think?'

'Chocolate brownie!' we both chorus.

Helen's work still makes me grin every time I enter her studio: it's so cheerful, a rainbow of colours shining out from the whitewashed walls. Her studio is on two floors, with an office upstairs and a huge canvas that hangs from the top of the stairs over the banister down into the main room below. It faces you when you walk through the door, and I've heard people gasp when they see it for the first time.

There are no customers in here at the moment, which is unusual, but good for me; at least I'll get the chance to talk to her properly. I can see her, sitting at the table, bent over a canvas, a heap of cloths beside her, and her mouth full of pins.

She looks up, smiling a greeting her mouth won't allow her to say, and waves for me to sit down. She takes a pin out of her mouth and pushes it through the material she is holding on to the canvas, making a small tuck as she does so. Then she does it again, and again, until the material stays put. She holds it a little distance away, judging the effect before grinning up at me.

'Hello,' I smile, looking at the piece she's holding. 'Is that something new?'

'I'm fiddling really, trying out something a bit different. I must be mad. I've got two commissions to finish and then I go and get this daft idea in my head, and I can't get it out until I have a play. I'll get over it in a bit.'

'Or it will turn out to be another fantastic idea, like all your others,' I remark. Helen just smiles.

'That's what I keep telling her,' says Fliss, appearing from the little kitchen area at the back of the studio, and carrying two mugs of tea. 'She's far too modest for her own good.'

Now what do I do? I wanted to speak to Helen on her own, but I didn't know Fliss was here and I've only got one piece of cake.

I fidget with my feet. 'I'm sorry, Fliss. I was going to ask Helen something, but I didn't know you were here; I've only brought one brownie.'

'That's okay, Lizzie,' says Fliss, taking the plate. 'Helen won't want this anyway.'

Helen looks up sharply. 'Oi,' she says. 'Back away from the plate, madam.' She laughs. 'Go and get your own.'

Fliss puts the plate back down on the table. She shrugs at me. 'Ah well, it was worth a shot . . . Don't worry, Lizzie. I'll pop over and get something in a bit.'

I really like Fliss. She's so funny.

Helen already has her mouth full. 'What can I help you with, Lizzie?' she mumbles.

'I popped over to ask a bit of a favour really.'

'Oh?'

'We were talking in the tea room a few minutes ago about wedding dresses and things, and I saw an advert in the paper last night for a wedding fair in Ludlow this weekend. Do you think we should see if we can get Ellie to go? Her wedding isn't very far off now.' I fiddle with my fringe. 'I didn't say anything, because I know how busy she is, but I don't think she would go on her own, and I wondered if maybe you could go with her?'

Helen's face falls. 'Oh, Lizzie, I can't, I'm sorry. Tom's working this weekend. It's not his turn to be on call, but he's covering for a colleague whose wife is very ill. I've no one I can leave the boys with, and I certainly couldn't bring them along too.' She shudders, perhaps at the thought of the combination of sticky-fingered little boys and pristine white wedding dresses. 'It's a brilliant idea, though. Maybe there's another fair we could go to sometime.'

'I could ask Jane, but with her bump being so big, I don't think she'd fancy it.'

'No, they're busy places, these events,' agrees Fliss. 'But Helen's right; it is a great idea. I could go with Ellie, if you like? I've done a few wedding fairs in my time, believe me, and it pays to know your way around these places.'

'Oh, would you?' I say, realising that although it wasn't what I had in mind originally, this could work just as well. 'That would be perfect. I don't know a thing about wedding stuff, and I could stay here and look after the tea room.' I pretend I don't see the looks on both their faces. 'I'd get someone to help me.'

Helen takes another bite of her cake. 'Ellie's going to need some persuading,' she says. 'You know what she's like. She doesn't want a big wedding, or any "fuss".'

Fliss grins. 'Leave her to me. I'll talk her round. Make sure you can get someone to help in the tea room, Lizzie, or she'll never agree to it.'

'I will,' I nod excitedly.

Fliss looks at us both. 'Right, well, strike while the iron's hot and all that. Damn good excuse to go and get a piece of cake, I reckon. What do you think?' And with that she rushes off.

Helen turns to me, smiling. 'Well done, Lizzie. That was a really thoughtful thing to suggest. Ellie will love it, and it will give her and Fliss a chance to get to know one another better as well.' She licks her finger. 'Listen, if it's quiet this afternoon, and Ellie can spare you for an hour, would you like to come back and help me cut some more material? It was such a big help last time.'

'I'd love to,' I reply, a huge grin on my face. This is turning into such a brilliant day.

Chapter 9

Ellie

The sky is the palest blue this morning, and the spring sunshine is doing its best to make a mockery of my mood. I am looking forward to the wedding fair; it's just that I'm rather anxious about the whole thing too, and Fliss's kind explanations of what to expect have only made this worse. I feel out of my depth before I've even got there.

I didn't want to go to start with, when Fliss first mentioned it, but then she told me that it was actually Lizzie's idea, and I couldn't refuse; she's been trying so hard lately. I probably do need to go, in all honesty, and I know I'm only putting the planning off because Will isn't here. As Fliss said, I'm simply nervous about making a start and I'll feel better once I've got some things organised. I'm sure she's right.

Fliss is due in half an hour. I'm not sure why we need to go so early, but apparently that's inexperience on my part. I'm just finishing my toast when I hear a knock on the kitchen door, and am mentally girding my loins when a cheery 'yoo-hoo' echoes across the kitchen. She's early. And cheerful.

Fliss walks in, looking very elegant in a bright floral dress and heels. Her long blond hair is straightened to a mirror-like sheen.

'Morning. Hope you're up for this, Ellie, it's going to be a fantastic day!'

I look down at my jeans and fleece, and sigh.

Fliss has actually made a list in a pretty flowery notebook. She bought it for me to keep, so that I can record all the arrangements I make as I go along. It's to help me plan, she says. I think I'm supposed to feel reassured by this suggestion, but instead I'm not sure I can live up to the expectation.

'I've made you an appointment for eleven,' she says, pulling out of the driveway and into the village. 'That way we can get our bearings for an hour or so first and then be ready to get down to the serious stuff.'

'I'm sorry, what? What appointment? I thought you could come and go as you wanted at these things.'

'Oh you can,' smiles Fliss, 'but the makeovers and dress fittings have to be booked in advance, otherwise you'd never get a slot, would you?'

I fumble with my mobile, wondering how early I can call for help. 'Erm, makeover? Do I need one of those?' I reply, panicked.

Fliss glances askew at me as if I'm mad and then returns her concentration to the road ahead. The seconds tick by.

'Ellie? Do you mind if I say something to you, something quite personal – but don't get offended or anything, will you?'

What on earth do you say to a question like that?

'It's just that I'm not sure you realise quite how beautiful you could be. I mean, you're very pretty now, but with your hair done properly and the right make-up you would look truly stunning.'

Somehow that wasn't what I was expecting, and I turn and stare at her.

'It's true. Why don't you believe me?'

'Well, I've never really thought about it before, I suppose. I'm quite happy with the way I look, and to be honest most of the time I'm too busy to be that bothered.'

'Exactly! So on your wedding day, the one time when you can make the effort, don't you think you should show Will what he means to you, by giving him a day he'll never forget, and a bride he'll never forget?'

I chew at my lip. 'But I'm not sure that Will is really all that fussed either. We're both happy with a simple wedding.'

'Are you sure about that, Ellie? I might be speaking out of turn here, but your tea room has a huge stained-glass window in it – a stained-glass window, for God's sake! Not only is it stunningly beautiful, but it was made by a man who loves you so much that nothing else would declare his love for you in quite the same way. *And* he dedicated it to you publicly in front of a huge crowd of strangers. There's nothing simple, or subtle, about that.'

Oh. I've never really thought of it like that, and suddenly my cheeks begin to burn.

'Most women would give their eye teeth for such a romantic declaration. You don't need to have a big wedding, Ellie, but like I said, the devil's in the detail, and if I were you I'd make it the very best it can be, to show *your* love for Will.'

My face is on fire, I'm so ashamed. How did I not see this before? How could I be so unconcerned about the most important day of our lives? I'd taken Will's low-key stance on the wedding to mean that he agreed with my way of thinking, but what if he's just going along with it because he doesn't want to upset me, especially now that he's away? What if he's actually really disappointed I'm not making more of an effort?

I feel Fliss's hand on my arm, giving it a sympathetic squeeze. 'I'm not questioning your judgement, Ellie – please don't think that – but I thought it might help to see things from a different point of view, especially as—' She trails off here, her eyes suddenly fixed on the road ahead. 'Look, perhaps I shouldn't have mentioned anything, but, well . . . Helen told me that Will has been married before. I'm sorry, I know it's not really any of my business, but if it were me, I'd want to make damn sure that everything was streets ahead of his last wedding. It can be a tricky thing being a second wife.'

I blink at her, surprised, and sudden realisation falls with a dull thud. I hadn't thought of that either.

'I don't suppose you know what kind of a wedding they had, do you?'

I look down at my lap. 'I don't, no . . . It's not something we've ever discussed. Things were very strained with Caroline, and it was rather a difficult time for Will personally, not just because of his marriage. It's not a period he likes to dwell on, that I do know.'

'And you've not seen any photos or anything?'

'No, there are none around. But I do know she was very beautiful, very elegant . . . I don't know much about her, but I can only begin to imagine the kind of wedding it would have been: straight from the pages of a glossy magazine.'

I begin to twiddle with the strap on my bag, until Fliss reaches across and takes my arm, giving it a squeeze.

'I'll help, Ellie – whatever it takes. We'll make it as perfect as we can, and we'll make you the most beautiful woman he's ever seen, don't you worry.'

'Thank you,' I manage, gratefully, blinking rapidly.

The setting for the fair is like something out of a fairy tale. It's a hotel I've never visited, and now that I've seen it, I understand why. At the end of a long and tree-lined drive, three round turrets can just be seen poking through the trees ahead. As the driveway opens up into a sweep of immaculate gravel, a huge cream building comes into view. The whole place screams money, a sentiment echoed by the complimentary glass of buck's fizz that is gently pressed into our hands as we pass through the door.

Fliss takes my arm and leads me swiftly through the rooms, 'doing a recce', as she puts it, so that we know where to focus our energy. Her little notebook accompanies us, and at intervals she adds a note, of what I've no idea, but I'm happy to let her take the lead.

After half an hour or so we're back in the main foyer with its welcoming fireplace and carefully placed armchairs. Fliss commandeers a small sofa for us amid the general throng of people.

'So what do you think?' she asks me, a broad smile on her face.

'I never imagined there would be quite so many people here,' I confide. 'It's a bit of a bun fight, isn't it?'

Fliss laughs. 'Well, it can be, but that's where I can help. You have to plan these things with military precision.'

'Oh' is all I can manage. 'You sound like you've had a bit of practice?' I glance down at her hand again, but I haven't missed anything; she doesn't wear any rings.

'Yes, quite a bit, at one time,' she replies, a slight tightness crossing her face for an instant. 'Actually, it's how I started as a jeweller, touting myself around fairs every weekend, trying to get commissions, but that was many moons ago now,' she finishes. 'I've never been married myself, but I've come into contact with a lot of wedding planners in my time, and I know these kinds of affairs like the back of my hand. Essentially they're all the same.' She takes out her notebook. 'The trick is to spot the people worth doing business with. A lot of people here are two-bit outfits and you can waste an awful lot of time in talking to them. Once we've picked the right ones, we start a meaningful conversation and they'll happily supply all the information we need to know.'

'Oh, right . . . but that sounds a bit serious. I'm not sure I want to sign up to anything today. I mean, I would probably want a bit of time to think about things,' I say, feeling nervous.

'Ellie,' says Fliss quietly, 'we won't be signing up to anything today. All the people here worth anything will be booked up for the next eighteen months or so. They would never be able to accommodate a wedding in three months' time.'

I'm confused now, and more than a little disappointed. The whole thing is beginning to sound like a monumental waste of time, just a silly day out. 'Then why are we here?' I ask, whispering for some reason.

'To get information. To find out what you like and what you don't like and then see how we might be able to replicate it ourselves. We won't be using these suppliers, but they don't know that. We need to be a little bit creative in our conversations with them, that's all.'

My eyes widen. 'You mean lie to them?'

'Not exactly, no, simply pretend a little. You have to trust me on this one, Ellie. Just follow my lead.' She looks at her watch and pops her notebook away again. 'First, we need to make Cinderella worthy of going to the ball.' She takes my hand with a grin. 'Come on.'

I've never been so intimidated in all my life. I am taken into a tent thing in the middle of a large room, which is absolutely crammed with people. Inside the brightly lit tent is what looks suspiciously like a dentist's chair, together with a rail of gowns and three people, two of whom are men. I am swooped on with undisguised glee and led to the chair, where I sit nervously, hoping that the man who appears to have modelled himself on Gok Wan does not have the same hands-on tendencies as most flamboyant TV makeover gurus seem to.

Fliss is off to one side talking in a low voice to the woman, who nods every now and then, waving a fistful of brushes around as she does so. Eventually she comes over to me with a bright but rather toothy smile and starts to direct traffic. I must say they're all very complimentary, and as they start to comb my hair and massage oil into my hands I begin to relax a little. It's actually rather nice just to sit for a bit and not have to think about anything.

I'm not sure what length of time passes before I'm pronounced ready by the toothy woman, but on her cue a very large full-length mirror is wheeled into the tent. Marc 'with a c' helps me out of my chair, his anxious eyes on my hair lest his creation topple. The rack of gowns is brought across and one is selected for me by Fliss. It's very fitted and heavily beaded, nothing like I would choose myself, but apparently that's the whole point.

Eventually I'm buttoned in and stood to one side to wait for my *ta-dah* moment. The mirror is wheeled across and slowly turned around to face me.

It's mid-afternoon by the time we eventually leave and I am in sore need of a sit down and a gallon of tea. I feel strangely buoyant, though; Fliss's tales of our wedding to be became ever more elaborate as the day wore on and I am a little bit giddy from too much giggling. I didn't feel entirely comfortable to start with, but as I began to understand what Fliss was trying to achieve I realised how clever she was being, and decided to go with the flow. Now the little notebook is crammed full of names of suppliers and ideas that we can put into practice ourselves.

Instead of having to find a florist who isn't booked up, we now have the name of our favourite florist's supplier in the Birmingham market, together with a photo of the most beautiful bouquet and a list of all the names of the flowers it contains. Apparently my prospective mother-in-law is very superstitious about flowers and needs to approve each variety before they can possibly be used. Fliss used a similar technique for wheedling all sorts of information out of other suppliers: once they got the whiff of a potential big-budget wedding coming their way it was astonishing what they were prepared to share with us.

Fliss was such good company and, as I climb back into her car ready for the drive home, I realise how much I've enjoyed myself. In my bag are several photographs, souvenirs of my makeover, and I hug the thought of them to me with a secret delight.

Now, as we're heading back, my thoughts return to Rowan Hill, and I wonder what kind of day everyone has had. The fair suddenly seems like another world, and I'm not sure that I'm ready for the return to normality yet.

'So that wasn't so bad then, was it?' asks Fliss. 'What did you think?'

I think carefully before committing to an answer. 'I've been surprised, mainly,' I say. 'I thought it would all be pretentious rubbish. But there were some really beautiful ideas there, things I hadn't even considered, which could be lovely. Do you really think that we can make it work, with the things you've suggested? There isn't that much time.'

'Well, I've been thinking about that actually. What would you say if I were to offer to organise everything for you? I know how busy you are and I'd love to do it. To be honest, it's something I've been considering for a while now, extending my business to include wedding planning. It would make sense, and I think I'm quite good at it.' She touches my arm. 'I would need to build up a portfolio, and some testimonials, so how about you be my first official client? We'd be helping each other out, and I wouldn't charge you anything, of course. You have some wonderful friends here who are only too willing to help, but you need someone to co-ordinate things, and now that I've seen the things you like, I can start to put your plans into action. I think our list is pretty much complete now, so why don't I hang on to the notebook and then I can make a start pretty much straight away?'

'Fliss, I can't ask you to do that!' I protest. 'What about your own work?'

'I can easily do the two. A lot of this will involve phone calls and emails initially and I can do that from my studio, but you can't from the tea room.'

She has a point. 'But it's still too much. You did all this for me today as well.'

'It was fun, though, wasn't it?'

'Oh yes, brilliant!'

'Well, then. I promise I'll keep you updated every step of the way and I won't do a thing without your say-so. Deal?'

'Deal,' I grin. 'And thank you, Fliss – thank you so much.'

'My pleasure.'

Chapter 10

LIZZIE

I open my front door to find Ellie standing on the top step, swinging a takeaway bag. Even from here it smells good.

'Please tell me you haven't eaten yet?' she says.

I shake my head, more surprised than anything. I'm not used to having visitors, but then I'm not used to having my own place either, I remind myself.

'I thought we could have tea together,' she continues. 'Ben and Finn have gone out and I wanted to say thank you for suggesting the wedding fair. I thought you might like to hear how we got on.'

I smile, feeling a little shy. My first proper visitor. I lead Ellie through to the living area and move the book I was reading off the sofa so that she can sit down.

'It smells good,' I say. 'What is it?'

'Well, I didn't know what you liked, so I got beef in black bean sauce and chicken chow mein.'

'I'm not really sure what either of those taste like . . .' I say tentatively, 'but I'm sure I'll like them. Shall I put them on some plates?' I add, hoping she doesn't think I'm a complete loser. I've never been able to afford a Chinese takeaway before.

Ellie hands me the bag. 'I like both, so I don't mind which you want, or we can split them, if you like. There's rice too.'

I pop through into the kitchen area, my mouth watering like crazy. Ellie's voice floats through the doorway a minute later.

'That's never my bookcase,' she calls. 'It looks amazing.'

I stick my head back through the doorway. 'Doesn't it? Ben has been so lovely helping me. I thought he might get sick of all my stupid questions, but he hasn't. Well, at least I don't think he has—' I look back at the cartons of food on the side. 'Hang on a minute, or these will all get cold.'

I finish dishing up the food and then go and sit back down with Ellie, balancing the plate of food on my lap. 'I thought we were just going to chop the ends off the shelves and then put it back together again, but Ben thought we should do it properly, so we stripped it all down, and then sanded it. After that we waxed and polished it. That blinking well nearly killed my arm, but it was so cool learning how to do it all. Ben's got me making a stool now. He says I'm a brilliant student . . . but I think it's only because he's a great teacher.'

I'm aware that Ellie's eyes stay looking at me even when I've finished talking.

'What?' I say, wondering if I've done something wrong, and then I realise. 'Oh God, I'm sorry, you wanted to talk about the fair, didn't you, and I'm rabbiting on—'

'Lizzie,' says Ellie, gently. 'You're not rabbiting on at all. It's lovely to see you so excited. I'm really pleased that you've settled in, and I hear that you and Alice did a fab job in the tea room today.'

'Really?' I ask eagerly.

'You did,' she says firmly. 'Alice rang me a little earlier on and, believe me, she would have mentioned if there were any problems. You're doing so well.'

I'm sure I must be blushing from ear to ear. No one's ever said anything like that to me before.

She touches my arm. 'Come on, dig in, and then I can tell you about today.'

There's nothing else said for a bit after that, as we both eat without stopping. I hadn't realised how hungry I was, and my food soon disappears. I finish way before Ellie does; she'll think I'm a total pig.

She's grinning at me. 'Am I right in thinking you enjoyed that?'

I'd lick the plate if I could.

'I brought something over to show you,' she says, still chewing. 'It's in my handbag. But I'll only show it to you if you promise not to laugh.'

'What is it?'

'I had a photo taken today, at the fair. Fliss made me go into one of those makeover tents, and I had my face and hair done. Then when I came outside there was a massive crowd waiting.'

'Blimey, I bet that was embarrassing.'

'It was, a little . . .' Ellie stops for a minute. 'Anyway, would you have a look at the photo and see what you think?'

She rolls to one side and fishes around in her bag on the floor. The photo is a bigger size than normal and she looks at it for a moment before passing it to me.

I stare at the image in front of me.

Ellie looks beautiful, transformed. Her hair is loosely pinned up, with what look like pearls dotted here and there. Soft coils have escaped and some hang to her shoulders; one grazes the side of her cheek. Two huge green eyes smile out from skin that looks like cream, and her lips and cheeks are the softest pink, like smooth rose petals.

I stare up at her in wonder. She doesn't look a bit like this now. You can see her freckles for one thing, and her hair is loose, but there's something else in the photo that I can't see now, something that I've never seen in Ellie before. It's hard to put into words exactly, but as I look at her expression, I wonder whether this is why she's here.

'Don't you like it?' I ask.

Ellie looks down at the photo again, and spears a piece of chicken on her plate, pushing it around in the sauce.

'I do like it,' she says slowly, 'which is a bit weird, because it doesn't really look like me at all . . . It's an odd feeling.'

'Well, I think you look beautiful. You only look different in the photo because you don't normally wear that much make-up.'

'Hmm, maybe,' Ellie replies, but she's staring into space. She puts her fork back down on the plate and just looks at it. She doesn't say anything for a very long time.

I start to fidget, wondering what on earth I can say to break the silence, but my mind has gone completely blank. I look at my bookcase, but there are only three books on it so far, including one that Fliss let me borrow. I'm just about to suggest a cup of tea when Ellie suddenly speaks.

'Can I ask you a question?' she says. 'Only I didn't think I was going to enjoy the wedding fair today, but I did, and now I've got home I can't decide which is right and which is wrong.'

I look at the photo again. 'What with? The dress? I can't really see it that clearly but it looks stunning.'

'No, not the dress . . . well, yes, I suppose so . . . All of it really.' She stares at me. 'I'm not making much sense, am I?'

I shake my head slightly. 'But I'm a bit thick sometimes,' I reply.

'Do you ever get that thing when you're absolutely dead set against something, but then something makes you change your mind and you feel a bit guilty about it, or wonder if you're right at all?'

I think for a minute. 'Like tattoos, do you mean?'

Ellie narrows her eyes at me.

'I had a friend at school who loved tattoos,' I say, 'but her parents would have gone mental if she'd got one. We spent hours looking at designs and she swore that she'd get one as soon as she left school. She wanted me to get one too, but I hated them . . . I still do. I think they look really ugly . . . but I kind of wanted to stay friends with her too, so I got one . . . Just a little one; you can't really see it.'

'And you like it now?'

'No, I hate it . . . but for a bit I didn't, for a bit I felt really cool, cos everyone kept asking to see it, and I felt really great when that happened.'

'So what made you change your mind about it?'

'Well, for one thing, my friend turned into a class A bitch, so I stopped talking to her . . . but mainly it was because I realised that it wasn't me. I liked the feeling it gave me for a while, but that wore off after a bit and I was just me again – the me that doesn't like tattoos.'

A bit more of Ellie's dinner finally makes it into her mouth. She nods rapidly.

'That's very perceptive of you, Lizzie.'

I look at her blankly.

'It's very smart that you understood all that about yourself.'

'Well, I spent quite a lot of time on my own before I came here, a lot of it trying to figure out why people do the things they do; I like watching people too. Sometimes I get it wrong, but mostly I'm right.'

'So do you know why I asked you that question a minute ago?'

I smile at her; Ellie's not stupid either.

'Well, I think you look pretty all the time, but you don't seem to think that. Sometimes you do, when Will looks at you, maybe, but mostly you just apologise for looking a mess. I think today the people at the fair made you look like someone else, like a beautiful princess, and now you want the fairy tale, even though you think you shouldn't.'

Beside me, Ellie heaves a sigh. 'Is it wrong?' she whispers.

'God, no,' I laugh. 'Who wouldn't want to look like that on their wedding day? I bloody would, I know that. In any case, it's only for a day, isn't it? It's not like my tattoo.'

'No, that's true,' agrees Ellie, thoughtfully. 'Fliss said something too, which got me thinking. I've never thought about it before.'

I make an encouraging nod.

'About Will. I'm not sure if you know, but he's been married before. Caroline, her name was.'

When I shake my head, Ellie continues.

'I don't know a great deal about her, only that she was very beautiful, although not a very nice person, by all accounts. Fliss thought it would be as well for there not to be any, well, comparison between us—'

'I don't think Will would think like that, Ellie. Have you seen the way he looks at you?'

'I know . . . It's not that . . .'

'You just don't want the evil cow to get one over on you?'

Ellie splutters 'Something like that,' before collapsing into a giggle. 'Oh, Lizzie, trust you to hit the nail exactly on the head!' She looks down at her plate, and then back up at me.

'Can I?' I giggle too, hating the thought of the food going to waste.

'Be my guest,' replies Ellie, passing me the plate. She tucks her legs up underneath her. 'I'm so glad I came around here tonight.'

'So am I,' I mumble through a mouthful of cold but still delicious rice. 'I haven't had food so good in ages.'

The laughter fills my little sitting room for quite a while.

'You're not worried about Caroline, are you?' I say eventually.

'No, not really. Our wedding will be nothing like theirs, and Will despises Caroline now, if anything. I know I'm not competing against her, but it's hard, especially with him being away. I can't talk to him about any of the wedding plans, or how I'm feeling.'

'You haven't known him that long, have you?'

'No, not at all, only about eighteen months.' She screws up her face. 'But I've got it bad. I feel like a lovesick teenager.'

'I think it's lovely. I haven't had many boyfriends and never one that I felt that way about, or one who was worth sticking with. It must be a nice feeling.'

'I sometimes wonder if it's a bad thing, being so happy?' she says. 'I'm worried that it's all too good to be true, and I'll wake up one day and find I've been dreaming.'

'Nah, I don't think so. Will's not really the stuff of nightmares, is he?'

She smiles dreamily. 'I don't think so, but then I got it all very wrong before, not that long ago actually, only a year before I moved here.'

'Yeah, but we've all had dodgy boyfriends.'

Ellie snorts. 'Mine was more than dodgy, he was married-with-a-wife-and-child dodgy.'

'No!' I exclaim. 'What a bastard! How did you find out?'

'He used to travel a lot with his job, backwards and forwards between Edinburgh and Cambridge, which is where I was living at the time. His wife lived in Edinburgh. Simple, really. I only found out when I had an accident, just up the road from here actually. I was on the way back from visiting Jane and her family and swerved to avoid a pheasant, and my car ended up in a ditch. I smashed up my arm and broke my collarbone.'

'Oh God, that's awful,' I say, covering my hand with my mouth.

'It wasn't the best day I've ever had, no, but in a bizarre way it was the start of my life here at Rowan Hill, and with Will too.'

I lean towards her. 'Why, what happened?'

'A passer-by came to my rescue . . . a lovely man with bright blue eyes. I had no idea who he was, of course, and when they carted me off to hospital all I knew was that his first name was Will.'

I nearly choke on the last of my dinner. 'No! Not your Will?'

'One and the same.'

'I can't believe it, that's so sweet. And you kept in touch all that time, and then moved here too.'

A gentle smile crosses Ellie's face. 'Not exactly, no. I never saw or heard from him again. That is, until a year later, when I moved to the Lodge and realised he was my next-door neighbour. I was on my own then, of course, nursing my wounds after the whole sorry episode with Robbie, and the rest, as they say, is history.'

'That's amazing. It's like it was always meant to be; the perfect ending.'

Ellie grimaces. 'Well, yes, eventually, but I did have to go through a really crap year beforehand after I found out about Robbie. I was a bit of a mess when I came here.' She looks at me before continuing. 'When I was in the hospital I tried to call Robbie, of course, to let him know what had happened but I couldn't get hold of him on his mobile. I called his office, who told me he was working from home that day, and when I rang, his wife answered the phone. That was a pretty short conversation, I can tell you. After that the spineless bastard even tried to make out it was my fault, and after six years together I decided that my judgement as far as men were concerned was seriously lacking.'

'But, Ellie, Will's nothing like that.'

'I know, but he's had a bad few years too. It hasn't always been easy for him, and sometimes, not very often admittedly, but sometimes I can't help but wonder if I could get it wrong again.'

'We all have problems,' I reply, thinking back to my own past. 'But Will is mad about you, Ellie. Anyone can see that. Don't give this Robbie loser another thought. Sounds like you're lucky to be rid of him.'

Ellie is staring at me, an amused expression on her face. 'How did you get to be such an agony aunt?' she grins.

'Listen, my mum had more boyfriends than you've had hot dinners, and every single one of them gave her the runaround. I know a bastard when I see one. All you're suffering from is a few wedding nerves, that's all, and that's easily fixed.'

Ellie raises an eyebrow. 'Oh, and how do I do that then?'

I cup my hand around my mouth, leaning into her slightly. 'Lots of sex,' I whisper. 'How long before Will's home next?'

'Two weeks,' she groans.

APRIL

Chapter 11

Lizzie

I look down with pride at the rows and rows of green plants, their leaves glistening in the morning sun. I rest the watering can on the ground for a moment, and straighten my back, lifting my face to the warmth and feeling a gentle air blow about me. Spring has arrived at Rowan Hill, and as I watch the soil around the plants deepen in colour after being watered, I realise that, for the first time in a long time, I'm looking forward to the coming weeks.

I helped Patience to plant these, and I can even remember the names of most of them. They were tiny little things when we first put them in, but now – only a few weeks later – they're three times as big and will soon be able to come out from under their glass covers and be planted up into the painted pots that Patience has ready and waiting. She's going to fill the courtyard with them, and I can't wait to see the colours bursting out. Some of them smell good too, she said. Ellie told me that last year she stood great troughs of lavender outside her studio which blew the most amazing smell across the courtyard all summer.

It's been my job to check on these plants and water them each morning, and today it's lovely and warm inside the red-brick walls of the garden. The forecast is good too, warm sunshine for the whole week. It doesn't seem possible, but I love the way being out here feels, whatever the weather. I check my watch, but it's only eight o'clock, and still a bit early for my morning visit to Alice. She certainly won't need her fires lit today, that's for sure, but I can make her a cup of tea anyway.

I place the glass covers carefully back over the plants and pick up the watering can, making my way around the outside of the garden to the shed at the far end. I walk beneath the tea-room window, dark-looking from this side, though I know that from inside the room every colour will be shining out. I might go and see if Ellie needs anything before I visit Alice; Will is coming home this weekend and, as Alice puts it, she's in a bit of a tizz.

Ellie's laughter reaches me even before I'm through the door. Jane is standing in the tea room, and she's trying to give Ellie a hug around her very large belly.

'Oh my God, Jane, look at you!' I exclaim without thinking.

Jane flaps the envelope she's carrying at her face like a fan. 'I know, I know. Just when you thought it couldn't possibly get any bigger.'

I blush, but Jane is not the type to take offence, fortunately.

'But I only saw you last week,' grins Ellie. 'What's happened? Are you sure you've got your dates right?'

'Unfortunately, yes. I saw the midwife yesterday. I've still got three weeks to go, although if this one is the same as the other two, you can add a fortnight on to that.' She pulls a face. 'I just hope I don't have to be induced this time. I'd like a nice, quick, simple labour, if you please, no drama with number three.'

Ellie frowns at her. 'Well, I hope you're remembering our deal – no going into labour at two in the morning and dragging me out of bed. I'm looking after the girls,' she adds for my benefit.

'I'll see what I can do,' Jane laughs. 'Anyway, I've popped over to see how you're doing and to harass you and Finn about the new brochures. Apparently Jack has a window before his copy-edits arrive later in the week, which I think is code for "please can I have any alterations back", and I'm trying to get my jobs done early, so that I can slink off this afternoon for a crafty feet-up before the kids get home from school. Well, that's the plan anyway, but the state of the house may mean that I spend all day cleaning instead.'

Ellie grins at her, shielding her eyes from the sun. 'We all had a chat about them again last night, as it happens. The marked-up copy is in the kitchen, back at the house.'

'I'll go and get it,' I volunteer. 'I know where it is.'

I slip out and run back across the courtyard. I pull my keys out of my jeans pocket, but when I get to it, the back door is open. One of the boys must still be there. I shout a hello, and cross the kitchen to where I know we left the leaflet. Typical; somebody's obviously moved it.

I can hear Finn in the study. He's talking to someone, probably Ben, and I push open the door expecting to find them poring over the plans for the Lodge, but instead he is deep in conversation with Fliss, who is perched on the edge of his desk.

'Oops,' she grins, as she spies me. 'Pretend I wasn't here . . . time I wasn't anyway.' And with that she hops off the table and squeezes past me.

'Ah,' says Finn slowly, his eyes narrowing, 'secret wedding stuff.'

'Oh, I *see*. Come on then, tell me.'

Finn grins, his blue eyes twinkling. 'Well, I'm not allowed to tell you, am I? It's *secret* wedding stuff.'

'Oh, that's not fair! You know I won't tell Ellie.' I punch his arm lightly. 'Come on, tell me.'

'God, you're all as bad as one another,' he says, raising his eyebrows. 'Right, well, swear you won't say anything, because if you do, I'm toast, but Will wants to take Ellie on a surprise honeymoon, so she's not to know anything about it, okay? Fliss wanted to check that Ellie has a valid passport; Will has no idea apparently. I said I'd try and find out . . . Actually, you might be able to help me with that.'

'Oh yes, let me! I can be Fliss's secret agent,' I say.

Finn groans.

'That's not very nice. I can do it so that Ellie doesn't twig,' I say indignantly.

'You better had or there will be hell to pay,' grins Finn.

'I will . . . Anyway, I need to get back. I only came over to get the new brochure, but I can't find it now.'

'By the side of the bread bin. I thought I had better put it in a safe place.'

I arch an eyebrow.

'Yes, well . . . it seemed like a good place this morning after I nearly threw my coffee over it twice.'

I fetch the brochure and rush back to the tea room, where Jane and Ellie are now sitting with a cup of tea. I lay it on the table between them so that Jane can see it.

'There's very little to change actually,' starts Ellie. 'Only one or two alterations and additions,' she adds, showing Jane the changes. 'And Lizzie had a brilliant idea, but perhaps I need to talk to Jack about that in a bit more detail. Initially it would mean a bit more work, but once it's set up it will mean less changes overall.'

'Oh?' says Jane. 'Go on.'

'Well, we're really happy with this brochure now, and the original one was brilliant, but we have rather outgrown it. This includes everything we have to offer here but, as Lizzie pointed out, if anything changes we have to have the whole thing redesigned. If we left the main brochure as it is but had a series of inserts for each of the businesses instead, not only would it provide a great advertisement for them, but also, if anything changed, we'd just scrap that insert and not have to amend the whole thing. I'd like to think we're all going to be here for a while, but you never know.'

Jane purses her lips. 'Yes, I see what you mean. That sounds like a fine idea; I'll ask Jack about it later.'

'Well, there's no rush, but if he thinks it's doable, perhaps you could work with him on it, Lizzie,' says Ellie.

I look up from the paperclip I'm twiddling on the table. 'Me?'

'Yes, why not? It was your idea.'

I grin at her. 'If that would be all right . . . I'd love to.'

Jane scribbles the last few notes. 'Right, well, I'll take these straight back. I'll ask him about the other thing too, although after the end of this week, he'll be on an editing deadline again for a few weeks, so I can't promise.'

'Jane, it's no problem. I wouldn't dream of intruding on his writing. That's far more important than this favour he's doing for us,' Ellie replies.

Jane winks at me. 'Don't you dare tell him his writing's important; he'll be unbearable.' She levers herself out of the chair. 'You know, I can't believe this weather. If it stays this warm, we should try to grab a get-together on Friday, once Will is home. Why don't we have a picnic, our first one of the year? What do you think, Lizzie?'

'Me?' I ask. 'Why, would I be coming too?'

'Of course,' grins Jane. 'Everyone goes. You'll love it. They've become quite a tradition here.'

I look at Ellie, slightly alarmed. I don't know what to say.

Ellie sighs. 'It is a lovely idea, Jane, but I'm not quite sure how we'd manage it with all of us now. Some folks would have to stay here and mind the shop. In any case, are you really sure you're up to that?'

'Well, we could all chip in, like we've done before, but I take your point that not everybody will be able to get away. Shame, though. I mean, let's face it, once this baby elephant arrives, it will put paid to my social life for a while, and you'll all be so busy in the summer, not to mention a certain wedding—'

Chapter 12

Lizzie

'I'm sorry I couldn't come across first thing,' I say, handing Alice her cup of tea, the cup clattering against the saucer. 'We're off on our picnic later and Ellie needed me for a few jobs.'

'I can imagine,' replies Alice, 'but it's nice to see you whatever the time of day, and of course there is a huge benefit to coming a little later.'

When I don't reply she reaches behind her and picks up the triangular tin that I've come to know and love. Even the sight of the jaunty little Scottie dogs don't help this morning, but I dredge up a smile.

'Alice, you and your biscuits; you're worse than I am.'

She gives the tin her best enticing rattle. 'I don't have many vices, but Ellie's chocolate-chip shortbread I can make an exception for. Besides, it's gone eleven and we have now entered into legitimate biscuit-eating time.'

Normally I'd have the lid off before you could say 'pass me a biscuit', but today my tongue is pretty much stuck to the roof of my mouth. It has been all morning.

'You have one, Alice,' I say. 'I'm trying to save myself for later; you should see the mountain of food that's coming with us.'

'And I thought you had hollow legs, Lizzie,' she replies, watching me.

I pick up the dishcloth by the sink and begin to wipe imaginary spills from the work surface.

'Is there anything else you need for this afternoon?' I ask. 'Any jobs you need doing?'

Alice leans forwards and takes the cloth out of my hand. 'No, I don't think so, and even if there were, I wouldn't dream of asking you, not when you've got such a fun afternoon ahead of you. Don't you be thinking about me; just have a lovely time and enjoy yourself.'

She stands in the centre of her kitchen, hands on her hips, beaming a smile at me, which I know I'm meant to return. I manage it, but it's a bit of a grimace, to be honest. I should say something really, it's just that . . .

'At least the weather looks like it's going to stay fine,' I say instead.

Alice's hands remain on her hips. 'Are you going to drink that cup of tea, Lizzie? Or are you going to tell me what it is that's making you refuse a biscuit, start cleaning my kitchen and look like the proverbial rabbit caught in the middle of the road facing the oncoming car?'

My shoulders sag as I pick up my cup. 'You'll think I'm really silly . . .' I begin.

Alice's reply is to frown, tut and pick up the biscuit tin all at the same time. 'Since when have I ever thought you silly?' she admonishes, but her voice is soft as she slides a gentle arm around my shoulders. 'Come on, come and sit down, and mountain of food or not, you're having a biscuit.'

I follow her to the table, smiling to myself. Alice is the grandma I always wished I had and I feel like I've known her my whole life already.

'I'm a bit nervous about going on the picnic,' I start, knowing from past experience that I might as well just come out with it. 'Which is really pathetic, but I can't help it. It's different when I'm helping people, because then there's usually just the two of us, and I know what to say. But there will be seven of us at the picnic today, all the girls together, and I don't know how to be.' I look up to see an answering nod. 'Before, when it was just my mates and that hanging out, it was easy to say stupid stuff and drink and laugh along with them, but everyone here is a proper adult, married or with children or their own businesses. They own houses and cook dinners and know things that I never will. I'm scared I'll make a complete idiot of myself.'

Alice smiles at me in that way she has. Not agreeing that I'm stupid, but showing that she understands how I feel. 'And you're not a proper adult? Or one that has a wicked sense of humour, has read countless books, is practically a carpenter now and picks up new skills more quickly than anyone I know? In what way does that make you an idiot?'

I look down at the table. 'But it's different for them.'

'Only in your head,' she replies. 'Because you think they're better than you are.'

I trace the roses around my saucer with a finger. I know she's right. I know I shouldn't think like that, but it's so hard not to. I reach out tentatively for a biscuit.

'You know, sometimes confidence doesn't come from how you feel,' continues Alice, 'but how you act.' She takes another biscuit for herself. 'The one can often lead to the other, I've found . . . and the biggest thing I've learned over the years is that young people often feel so self-conscious, but despite what you think, people are not watching you, or thinking about you every minute of the day. In fact, they rarely are.'

I look up in surprise.

'So whereas you think everyone will be looking at what you're wearing this afternoon, or how your hair looks, or what silly things you might be saying, I can guarantee that they won't be. Ellie will be thinking about what to give everyone for tea, Patience will be thinking about the very attractive new client she has and Jane will be desperate to get her bra off and her pyjamas on.'

I giggle. 'You're right about Jane. She even said that to me the other day.'

'Well, there you are then. You really mustn't worry, you know. I can understand how you feel, but you must remind yourself that you have just as much to say as anyone else, are just as important and just as entitled to enjoy the picnic. Be yourself, Lizzie. That's all anyone needs.'

I sit back in my chair and grin. 'Thanks, Alice. You always know how to make me feel better.'

'So do you actually, if you think about it,' she smiles. 'But you're very welcome, always.'

I still might have chickened out if Ellie wasn't going, and even though I'm determined not to let my worries get the better of me, I'm not sure she really wants to go either. Will came home for the weekend late last night, and this morning he decided that he couldn't face the picnic. He's tired, but there's something else too, like he's not really with us yet. He insisted that Ellie go anyway, and I know he didn't mean to look relieved when she agreed, but I hope Ellie didn't see his expression.

As soon as we set off, Helen and Patience forge on ahead of us on the path with Bonnie and are nattering away, leaving Ellie and Fliss just behind them. They're rabbiting on about the wedding, so I think Ellie's happy enough. Fliss is so excited, anyone would think it was her getting married, but it's nice for Ellie – having Will away most of the time means she can't always share these things with him. Every now and then Patience shrieks with laughter, and it's very peaceful apart from that. It's a nice sound; it makes you want to grin.

Jane and I are bringing up the rear, going slightly slower so that Jane can keep up. She's puffing a little bit.

'I know I shouldn't complain, seeing how early it is in the year, but I hope this weather breaks sometime soon-ish,' she says. 'I was so hot in bed last night, I couldn't get comfortable, and my back aches like hell today.'

Perhaps we're not used to the warmer weather yet, but although it's been lovely and sunny all week, it's cloudier this morning, a bit like it's going to rain. Maybe Jane will feel better once it's cooler.

'Are you sure this is a good idea then?' I reply. 'I know we're not going far, but will the walking make your back worse?'

'No, it'll do it good, stretch it out a bit and get rid of this heavy feeling. So no fussing,' she admonishes. 'You're beginning to sound like Ellie.'

I stand back a little to let Jane pass on ahead through a narrower section of path. 'So how are your girls, then? Are they getting really excited now?' I call on ahead.

Jane stops to wait for me to catch up before replying. 'You know, Tilly is driving me mad. Every day for weeks now it's been *Mummy, are you getting the baby today? Mummy, are you getting the baby today?* like it's something I'll pop on the bottom of my shopping list next time I go to Tesco. I swear, when it finally does arrive, she'll take one look in the cot and go *oh*, like she's checking out what type of biscuits I've bought. The anticipation is always much more exciting than finding out it's bourbons again.'

I laugh at Jane's pained expression. 'Aw, that's so sweet.'

'I know,' she smiles in return. 'And Grace is so very grown up about the whole thing. They'll make brilliant sisters.'

Up ahead Fliss slows down too as the path widens.

'Have you always wanted a big family, Jane?' she asks, squinting in the sunlight.

Jane laughs. 'To be honest, I don't think I ever consciously thought about it. That sounds dreadful, doesn't it? But once we were married, Grace just came along, and after a couple of years it felt like the right thing to do to have another.' She thinks for a minute. 'My problem is I love being pregnant, but I think once this one's born we'll have to call a halt. I'm not sure my pelvic floor can stand the strain.'

Fliss winces. 'How about you, Ellie? You must be thinking about children now that you're going to be married soon?'

'Blimey, Fliss, one thing at a time,' she exclaims. 'Maybe one day, I don't know. It's not something that Will and I have on our to-do list right now, and I'm probably a bit old anyway. I'm quite happy being Auntie Ellie to Jane's gorgeous girls.'

'But I thought Will was really keen?' Fliss adds, looking at me for confirmation. 'Or did I mishear? I thought you were talking about it the other week?'

I struggle to remember our conversation, and shrug in confusion. 'Erm—'

'Yes, I'm sure that's right,' interrupts Fliss.

Ellie looks between us both, a little surprised and annoyed. 'Well, that's news to me,' she remarks. 'Will's got rather a lot on his plate at the moment; babies are the last thing on his mind.'

'I can't see it either,' says Jane in agreement. 'I mean, Ellie has to remind him to eat and drink. I don't think he's up for the demands of parenthood right now.' She passes a hand over her enormous belly. 'How about you, Fliss? Is it something you have planned for your future?'

Fliss laughs, but it's not the same sort of laugh as when you find something funny. 'Ha!' she replies. 'I need a man first, but that's a very long story. Besides, I hate being fat.'

It's a good thing Jane doesn't take offence easily. She rolls her eyes at Ellie, but Fliss doesn't even notice.

We come to a little clearing. Helen, having got there first, is already beginning to throw down the rugs to sit on. It's lovely and warm here, out from under the trees. Patience puts down her rucksack and the camping chair that she's brought for Jane.

'Where would madam like to sit?' she quips, turning the chair this way and that.

'Oh, thank you, my lady, just here would be absolutely wonderful.'

I unroll my own rug, which I've been carrying, making to sit near to Ellie.

'Will you be all right here, Lizzie?'

We all turn around to see Fliss standing at the edge of the clearing.

'Me?' I ask. 'Yes, why?'

'I just thought, you know that thing you said the other day about how much you hated spiders. I thought we were going on to the picnic benches. That way you wouldn't have to sit on the ground.'

'Fliss, it doesn't matter. Here will be fine.'

Ellie is looking at me, and then at Jane.

'We could go on, but it's that bit further, Lizzie, and we thought here would be okay?'

'It will be, honestly. I do hate spiders but I'm not phobic or anything.'

There's a silence that begins to lengthen, and I feel really awkward. I'm about to say it's fine again and sit down, when I hear a creak beside me as Jane begins to lever herself out of the chair.

She puts her hand out to me so that I can help to pull her up. She's laughing at her efforts. 'Well, if I can ever get out of this chair, it's no problem; we can go on.'

I look at her quizzically.

'It's fine, honestly. It's only another few minutes.'

'It's nearer ten to be fair, Jane,' says Ellie, tugging at her hand.

'No, come on. Look, I'm up now. Don't stop me now; I'm in full flow.'

'Sorry,' adds Fliss. 'I didn't mean to embarrass you, Lizzie. I just thought you might feel a bit awkward, and knowing you, you wouldn't say anything.' She gives a broad grin. 'At least now our picnic won't be punctuated with blood-curdling screams when a spider crawls up your leg.'

I smile nervously, but Jane doesn't seem to mind at all.

It's a lovely afternoon. I don't know why sandwiches taste so much better outdoors, but they do, and there's so much to eat that I make a complete pig of myself. Still, I'm not the only one who's in a food coma. Everyone else has stopped talking too, and Patience looks like she's actually conked out.

'I don't want to break up the party, but I think I need to get back now.'

There's an unusually sharp note to Jane's voice that makes me look up suddenly. She's still sitting on the picnic bench, a hand curled around one of the wooden slats that make up the table. Her body looks taut. I pull myself up into a sitting position.

'Are you okay, Jane?'

'I'm fine,' she says, biting her lower lip, a glint of alarm in her eyes. 'It's just that I think I might be in labour.'

Chapter 13

LIZZIE

Ellie stares at Jane incredulously, as our surroundings suddenly rush in on me.

'Are you sure?' I ask.

'No . . . I thought they were Braxton Hicks. I've been getting them for days, but I think they're a bit stronger than that somehow . . . and a bit closer together.'

'How close?' asks Ellie.

'About every five or six minutes.'

Fuck.

'I'm sorry, guys. I honestly thought they'd go away in a minute.'

Ellie crouches beside her. 'Jane, whatever you do, don't you dare apologise,' she says sternly, finding her friend's hand. 'Can you stand up?'

Jane nods, manoeuvring herself to get better leverage, and slowly gets to her feet. Her hand, I notice, stays clutching the table. She takes a step, which is immediately followed by a strange and surprised intake of breath. The dark leather of her shoes has turned a shade darker as liquid flows onto them.

'Please tell me you've peed yourself?' whispers Ellie.

'Sorry, no . . . it's my waters,' comes a small voice.

That can't be good. I pull my phone out of my pocket in a flash, as everybody else starts rushing around, gathering up food and rugs.

'Shit!' I say loudly. No signal. Great. What the bloody hell do we do now?

'Jane, if we take it really slowly, do you think you could walk back to the house?' asks Ellie. 'We'll help you.' Everyone rushes forwards as she nods, still smiling.

We inch around the edge of the table, making for open space, and for a moment it looks as if it will be okay, until a sudden flapping of Jane's hand catches my eye. I hold out my hand and she grabs hold of it, curling it into her own fist as a grunt of air escapes her and her head drops down in concentration.

'Sorry,' she breathes. 'That was most definitely a real one.' Slowly she lets go of my hand.

'Can you carry on, do you think?'

'I think so,' she replies, although I see the beginnings of real alarm in her eyes.

'Is that a good idea? Only won't the walking bring it on quicker?' asks Helen softly. 'I'm beginning to think that walking here in the first place wasn't a good idea,' she adds, shooting a look at me.

Ellie is looking at me too. We need to go and get help.

'I'll go,' I say immediately.

'Get Will,' she nods, thinking the same. 'Phone for an ambulance as well . . . and don't forget to ring Jack,' she yells at my back.

The path is quite flat, but it's hard to run at speed; little dips and dents keep jarring my feet, and I crash about from side to side. I've no idea how long it will take me. I lurch into the side of a sharp bush that scratches my face but I keep on running, my breath coming faster and faster.

I think I can see the end of the path now. There's a five-bar gate at the end of it, which leads back through to the gardens and the main driveway to the house. I crash into it, making it rattle against its hinges, and fumble for the catch that will allow me to fling it wide. Jesus, my side feels like it's splitting open. I wish I hadn't eaten those last two fairy cakes.

It isn't a great idea to lurch into Will's workroom when he's holding a huge piece of glass in his hand, but I don't think about that as I hurl myself through the door shouting. The glass is down on the bench in an instant, but not before I hear the sharp crack it makes as it connects with the edge of a metal ruler, and Will instinctively looks down at his hands. He rips off his gloves and drags me out into the kitchen, where I stand and explain as I gasp for breath.

'Where's my bloody phone?' he yells, his eyes racing around the room as I try to fumble mine out of my pocket. I practically throw it at him.

There's a strange moment then while I'm waiting for him to dial; I suddenly become aware not only of the sound of my breathing but of everything else as well. The faint tick from the clock on the wall, the water dripping from the tap into the sink, the sound of birdsong through the open door. It's as if everything has slowed down so that instead of a jumbled blur, every thought passes through my head like it's on a screen in front of me, like I'm reading it, showing me what to do. Then there's a dial tone, and a voice, and I hear Will speaking. Everything flies away from me again, rushing out to the corners of my mind, until all I can hear is my breathing once more, and the sound of Will's voice. But it's enough. I race upstairs.

Behind one of these doors must be what I'm looking for. I reach the first and yank it open, then the second. I know even before I open it that the third one is the airing cupboard; it's slightly narrower than the rest. I heave at the pile of stuff in front of me, sending it all crashing to the carpet. Amber needed blankets and towels that time, and Jane will need them too. I snatch up four or five and run back down the landing, hearing Will's voice yelling for me as I reach the bottom steps. He's holding my phone and a first-aid kit. His hand reaches out to mine.

Jane has been led back to the table, where she's standing, gently swaying and rocking her hips. Nobody knows what to do, but as we burst into their silence another contraction hits, which forces the air from Jane's body in hissing rushes. Ellie rubs the small of her back for something to do.

'What the hell kind of a picnic is this anyway?' mutters Jane, beginning to get her breath back. 'No one told me I'd have to get my knickers off.'

Jane's contractions are really kicking in now; it's like someone's turned on a tap. She's not speaking any more as she fights to stay focused ahead of the pain that's gripping her. Her hips rock from side to side. It's instinctive, I think; there's nothing she can do but go with it.

Someone has poured her a cup of water, which she gulps gratefully, and as I take her other hand I feel the pressure from it begin to rise again.

'It's okay, it's okay,' I murmur, as I find myself starting to rock in time with her. 'It won't be long.'

I'm not sure what 'it' is – a rescue, the birth, someone who knows what they're doing – but it sounds good. It sounds like the sort of thing you should say to a woman in the middle of a wood who is about to have a baby.

I need to think, but there's too many people here scattering my thoughts. I need some quiet and some calm, and I'm sure Jane does too.

'We probably ought to have someone back at the house to direct traffic,' I say. 'We've called an ambulance but there needs to be someone around to let them know where to find us. Helen and Patience, do you think you could do that?'

Helen nods, looking anxious. 'Will you be all right?' she asks.

I look back at Jane and then across to Will. 'Yes, we'll be fine. Help will be here before you know it, and Will and I can look after Jane until then. I helped a friend who was in labour once before, and besides, I think it's best if we're not all crowding round.'

They don't need to be asked twice, gathering up bags and rushing off, glad to have something to do.

'Maybe you should both go back too?' I say, looking at Bonnie and Fliss. 'I couldn't get hold of Jack. Take Jane's mobile and keep trying him, can you? There's no answer at home.'

'He'll be doing the school run,' pants Jane.

'So keep trying his mobile.' I look at Jane then. 'I think Will should stay here, Jane. Is that all right with you?'

She sounds her agreement.

Will turns back to the table and opens the first-aid kit he snatched from the kitchen cupboard. Somehow I don't think a plaster is going to fix this.

'You know, I'm very honoured that you've chosen my wood to give birth in.'

Jane looks up, eyes widening in alarm as the enormity of what Will has said sinks in. He hands her the cup of water, supporting her while she sips, until she gives another sharp gasp and clutches hold of the end of the bench, and starts rocking again, the noise rapidly rising as her fingers turn white against the edge of the wood. I spread my fingers wide over her belly, my other hand resting gently against her lower back.

'Keep breathing, keep breathing,' I say, trying to remember the words I heard used before. 'Jane, you're doing brilliantly.'

Jane straightens slightly. 'I need to sit down,' she pants. 'Like on all fours.' She steps out of her knickers, and I look away, grabbing at one of the thick fleeces I brought from the house. I pass it to Will, who spreads it open on the ground.

'I'm so sorry, Jane,' soothes Ellie. 'I know this is horrible, but let's get you as comfortable as we can until the ambulance gets here.' She helps her friend to the ground, sitting on the end of the bench so that Jane can lean into her.

'You should put your head down,' I say. 'Like, stick your bum in the air.' Three heads swivel around to look at me. 'I saw it before . . . It's supposed to stop the baby from coming so quickly.'

Jane drops her shoulders, giving a low moan.

'I didn't know they covered childbirth on first-aid courses, Will,' she pants, eyeing up the gloves he's taking from the first-aid box and giving a faint smile.

'They don't,' answers Will truthfully. 'Everything I know is out of a textbook. But you know what to do, Jane. You're two up on me already. Your body's done this before and it will know how to do it again. Listen to what it's telling you and you can do this.'

She nods, more enthusiastically this time, managing a small smile. Almost immediately her face contorts.

'Oh God, it's coming again,' she hisses.

Her head lifts suddenly, her back arching upward, straightening her spine. 'I need to push, Will . . . I can't help it.' A low guttural sound escapes her as her eyes close in concentration.

This isn't good; this is just like it was with Amber. A sudden rush of tears stings my eyes.

'I need to lean up against something.'

I shake open another fleece and spread it out in front of the other end of the bench, which faces out into a more open space.

'Ellie, can you come and sit here?' I ask, tapping the bench. 'Jane can use your legs as a brace and you can help support her.'

Will looks at me and nods. He can see what I'm thinking. 'Right, let's get you moved across now,' soothes Will, holding her shoulders. 'Jane, come on, that's it. Let's get you over here now . . . Jane?'

'I can't do this,' she blurts out, frightened now. 'I don't want to move. Let me stay here.' She's shaking her head as if trying to clear it.

'We can't, Jane. We need you to move so we have more space if we need it.'

She shakes her head again more violently. Will looks at Ellie, real concern on his face, before he turns back to Jane again, sinking to his knees so that he's right at her level. He rips his gloves off and very gently cups Jane's face in his hands and softly rubs a thumb across one cheek.

'Jane, listen to me. I would love for you not to have your baby here, but I swear to you we will do everything in our power to make it all right. I know you want Jack here, and doctors and nurses, somewhere comfortable, and something to take away your pain, but I don't think your baby is going to wait for any of those things. Your baby is going to be born right here, with just us three, and the only one who's going to know the difference is you.'

Jane's lips move almost silently, but it's enough for Will to hear. 'Good girl.' He nods and lets her go, taking her hand in support. Slowly she gets to her feet and moves the small distance over to where Ellie is waiting for her, arms outstretched. She bends to her knees again, almost immediately snatching Ellie's hand as she leans into her, wrapped in the contraction that takes hold of her.

I look at Will. I don't want to say it, but as I feel him looking at me, I know I don't have to. He's already guessed how close Jane is.

Will starts rummaging in the first-aid box and my stomach gives a weird lurch as he takes out another pair of gloves and hands them to me. There's a questioning look in his eyes.

I take a deep steadying breath and Will swallows hard. He looks terrified, and I know that I'm the only one here who has seen a baby being born. I have to do this.

'Will, can I have two blankets here, opened up halfway . . . that's it. Right underneath. We can leave the towels there for now.' I wait until he joins me. 'You okay?' I ask, hearing his rapid breathing.

He takes a deep breath and looks straight into my eyes. We're in this together.

'Come on, Jane. You're doing so well,' I whisper, stroking her back and dipping my head to see better. 'That's it, keep going, keep going,' I cry. 'Oh my God, I can see the head!'

Jane sucks in air, panting, trying to fill her lungs with as much air as she can before the next contraction hits her. 'Jesus!' she hisses through clenched teeth, straining hard.

'Will, I think you should come here, this side.'

He does as I ask, as my heart pounds in my chest. I feel a gentle breeze ruffle the hair around my neck, and for a moment experience that same feeling I had at Attingham Park; like everything is just as it should be. I open my eyes, not even realising that they were closed, and my fear leaves me.

'Okay, that's it! Gently now . . . pant for me,' I urge Jane. 'Gently . . . gently. Don't push; let your body do it.' I duck my head again. 'Will, put your hands here, and hold. Like this, don't pull, just hold.'

He does as I ask, nodding at me in encouragement, as amazed as I am that this is happening at all. It's not gross; in fact, I don't think I've ever seen anything so beautiful.

I catch a glimpse of something blue then, right where my fingertips are. I duck my head under Will's arm to get a better look. No, that's not right, that's not right at all. I've seen it before.

'Wait,' I whisper to Will, nudging him. I don't want to panic Jane, but she needs to stop for a minute.

'Jane, don't push,' I say urgently. 'Hang on. I need to move the cord, Will.' I hold his hands, placing them where my own were just seconds earlier, and run my finger down the side of the baby's neck, slipping my fingers underneath the cord, just enough to free it a little. I need to be quick, I can feel Jane struggling to hold on, the urge inside her to push reaching a climax. She lets out a strangled sound as I wiggle my fingers further still.

'It's okay. Go for it now, Jane. Come on, last one!' I choke.

She does as she's told, and with one last push, the baby is born, cradled in Will's hands as I swiftly move the cord up and away from its neck. There's a moment of absolute silence as all of us look at one another. A moment that if I live to be a hundred I swear I will never forget. Will reaches forwards and gently takes up a towel, wrapping it around Jane's child, whose kitten-like cries rise up to join the birdsong that has welcomed it into the world.

I sink down beside Jane, who reaches out with shaking arms to hold the baby to her.

'Oh my God, Jane, look at her, she's perfect,' splutters Ellie, choking back sobs.

'She is, she's beautiful. You have a beautiful daughter, Jane. We did it, we did it!' Will pushes back the hair from her face a little and rubs the side of her cheek.

'Thank you, thank you so much,' she whispers. 'I can't believe it, just look at her. Look at all that hair.' And she traces a finger around the baby's face and the shock of hair, which even though it's bloody and wet, looks suspiciously red.

Will takes another towel and passes it over the baby's head. 'Typical redhead. Couldn't wait to get into the world, could you? Far too impatient.' He clutches Ellie's hand, grinning. 'It's the red-haired ones you've got to watch, I'm told.'

'Thank you,' Ellie mouths at us, her green eyes shining with emotion.

'I held her head,' I say in wonder.

Ellie moves behind Jane to a clean patch of blanket so that she can change position and Jane can lean up against her, and the two of them sit like that, Ellie's arms around them both in the deep quiet, where for a few minutes nothing needs to be said.

I can't stop looking at the baby, and at Jane, who looks so peaceful. I hope that if I ever have a baby, it's just like this, full of love and wonder, not the fear and hopelessness that I'm used to. The spring air hums around me, just like it did that day back at Attingham Park, and I wonder how in only a few short months the pictures I hold in my head of my life before can fade until I almost can't see them. Today I chased a few more of those memories away.

A few minutes later the ambulance men arrive and for a bit it's all go again, but even this is calm and without panic. They let Will cut the baby's cord. I think they assume he's the dad, which Jane finds very funny and Will doesn't.

Nobody's really sure how to get Jane back to the house, but in the end a small wheelchair is produced and they set off slowly, with Ellie holding the baby like she's made of glass. I start to pick up some of the rugs, hanging back a little bit. It's not that I don't want to go with them, but just that I want to have one last look at this place before I leave. Whatever else happens in my life, I don't think I will ever find anywhere as special as this.

I look around one last time, before hitching the blankets under my arm and setting off, only to find Will waiting for me, just on the edge of the clearing. He looks as if he's going to say something, but instead he holds out his arms and pulls me into his chest. He's shaking like a leaf, but he's warm and safe all at the same time. I've never been held by anyone like this before, and I wonder if this is how it is for Ellie. I hope so.

By the time we get back, there's an eager crowd of bodies waiting on the periphery of the courtyard, each of them straining to catch a glimpse of us and find out what's been going on. If I were Jane, I'd want to yell at them all to piss off and leave me alone, but instead she's smiling and chatting with everyone. Even the baby is already being passed around.

A car swings into the bottom of the courtyard and Jack climbs out of it, looking about him in confusion. He spots the ambulance and comes hurtling towards us, probably thinking that he's come to hold his wife's hand on the way to hospital. I'm not sure what he's been told, but he surely won't know yet that she's actually had the baby.

When the penny finally drops his face is full of emotion. He bends to one knee beside Jane so that he's at her level. 'Is everything all right?' he manages, not knowing what to say first.

'We're both fine,' says Jane. 'You have another daughter, darling – it's a little girl.'

'Oh good, I know what to do with those,' he murmurs, looking between her and the baby, and then dropping the softest of kisses on the baby's nose. He hands his daughter to Jane, where she lies sleepily, totally untroubled, and not minding in the slightest that she was born in the middle of a wood.

'I'm sorry, sir,' a voice interrupts. It's one of the ambulance crew. 'But we really ought to get your wife off to hospital now. Not that anything's wrong, but because of the circumstances of the birth, they both need to be checked over by a doctor.'

Jack gets to his feet. 'Yes, of course, sorry,' he apologises, and then suddenly thinks about what the man has just said, and looks back at Jane. 'Oh God, where was she born?'

'Very elegant,' says Jane drily. 'Holding on to a bench in the middle of the picnic area.' She turns, smiling. 'And on to Ellie, of course, whose hand I nearly crushed to a pulp.'

Jack's mouth hangs open. 'Seriously?' he asks.

'A pretty much textbook delivery, I believe. Your wife did amazingly well,' answers the paramedic, which makes Jack hold out his hand to shake.

'I can't thank you enough, really, thank you,' he gushes.

'It's not me you need to thank actually,' comes the paramedic's reply, just as Jane cranes her head around to ask where Will and I are. Her favourite midwives, she calls us. I'm standing behind as many people as I can, and Will is hiding behind me, but Jack still spots us and comes crashing through the crowd.

His hug nearly knocks Will off his feet altogether, and he plants a very wet kiss right on my mouth.

'Mate, I could bloody kiss you too!' he cries to Will, and then does just that, planting a smacker right in the centre of Will's forehead, which Finn finds hysterically funny.

Chapter 14

Lizzie

It's seven o'clock, and I think I could probably sleep in the middle of the road, I'm so tired. I'm sitting in the kitchen with Will and Ellie, and it's some time now since Jack, Jane and the baby were whisked away. After that everyone else gradually drifted off home, until there were just the three of us left. I managed to make us a drink and, at first, still gripped by excitement, we chatted away, telling each other what had happened over and over again. A bit daft really, seeing as we were all there. No one's spoken for ages now, though, and we're all slumped at the table, thinking our own thoughts in the gloomy kitchen.

Ellie feels really guilty, saying that we shouldn't have gone on the picnic at all, and that Jane and her baby could both have died. Will and I tried to talk her out of it, but now that she's said it, I know we're both thinking about all the bad things that could have happened as well. It didn't really feel like that at the time; back in the woods it felt like things were always going to turn out right. With Amber I was scared shitless. It all seemed so loud and confused and chaotic, but with Jane it was different. It was like it was always meant to be. I think Ellie's just trying to be a good friend, but she really shouldn't blame herself. I don't think she's let Jane down at all.

The trouble is now she's got me thinking too, about the comment that Fliss made before the picnic. I know she was only looking out for me, but I don't hate spiders that much; I wouldn't have minded sitting on the ground. I hope Ellie doesn't think it was my fault that Jane walked on further than she should have.

The back door bangs open as Finn and Ben return, carrying an armful of takeaway bags.

Finn flicks on the lights, throwing the room into sudden brightness. It makes me jump, and I wish he hadn't. It's too bright and it was quite nice sitting here in the dim room.

'Come on, you lot, grub's up,' he announces, dumping the bags on the table. Ben is already opening cupboards and fetching plates. 'I don't know about you three, but I'm bloody starving.' I look up to see Finn watching us all intently. 'We've brought all sorts; didn't know what you'd fancy.'

I nod in reply, trying a small smile. 'I'm not really fussed, Finn, thanks. I'll just have a bit of whatever's left.'

'Will? What about you?'

Will just shrugs. Ellie doesn't reply.

Wordlessly, Ben places the plates on the table as Finn unloads cartons from the bags. He spoons their contents out, dividing them between the five of us. I hear a drawer opening and closing and the clatter of cutlery on the table. A plate is placed in front of me.

'No arguments . . . Eat,' says Finn, handing me a fork and passing one to Will and Ellie also.

Ben and Finn are giving each other that *what are we going to do with them?* look, but I look away and gaze back down at my plate of food. Not that I want to eat any of it. Eventually, though, I manage a mouthful, surprised suddenly at how good the salty-sweet chicken tastes.

'This is really good,' I say, which makes Finn grin.

I eat steadily then, noticing that Will and Ellie are both doing the same, taking occasional swigs at the cans of drink that Ben has handed around. I'm surprised by the speed with which I clear my plate. I look up eventually to see Finn give me a wink.

'Better?' he asks.

I nod again, more enthusiastically this time. 'Yes, better, thanks. Sorry, I hadn't realised how hungry I was.'

'It's the shock,' says Ben. 'You need to replace your sugar levels. It's why you're feeling like you are.'

Will looks up then. 'Really?' he says. 'Because I thought it was the realisation that what happened this afternoon could have been one almighty fuck-up.' He passes a hand over his face and up through his hair, leaving it sticking up in places. 'Sorry,' he adds unnecessarily.

'You don't need to apologise, Will,' says Ben gently. 'I know how you're feeling, but you shouldn't be giving yourself such a hard time over this; none of you should. What you guys did earlier was amazing. For Christ's sake, you delivered a baby!'

Will looks at him then, the rather fierce expression on his face fading. 'Thank you,' he says. 'It's utter bloody madness, isn't it? It doesn't seem real somehow.'

Ellie lays her fork back down on her plate.

'I'm very proud of you, you know,' she smiles at Will. 'Listen, I've done the whole guilt-trip thing this afternoon too. I shouldn't have let Jane go on the picnic, and I certainly shouldn't have let her walk as far out as she did. We can go on forever thinking about what might have happened but no one can change what was going to happen: that baby was going to arrive regardless of anything we did. The miracle is that we were all around when she did decide to come. Can you imagine what would have happened if you'd hadn't been here this afternoon? Or Lizzie, with her supersonic legs and expert knowledge, for that matter.' She grins at me, tucking a piece of hair behind her ears. 'The truth of it is you were both amazing. Will – you were so beautiful with Jane, you know, you made her feel so calm and at ease—' She breaks off, to wind her fingers around his. 'And, Lizzie, I never knew you could run so fast, but how on earth did you know what to do?'

I don't have to tell them, I know that, but sitting here feels nice. I don't feel any different from anybody else, and I like that – it's not something that's happened much to me before. Maybe this is what having a family feels like.

'I had a friend once,' I begin. 'When I was at school. Amber, her name was.' I look up at the faces watching me. 'She got herself pregnant, but there was only me that knew – her dad would have killed her if he found out. Neither of us knew what to do, and then it got too late to do anything. So she had the baby.'

'And you were there?' asks Ellie gently.

I nod slightly, relieved to see that no one looks particularly shocked. 'She didn't have anyone else. I knew something was up cos she got sent home from school with stomach ache but by the time I got to her house the baby was already coming.' I can still see it now in my head, Amber lying on the floor screaming. She shouted at me too, horrible words.

'I had to call an ambulance, and they got there only a few minutes before the baby was born. That's how I knew about the cord thing. I saw the ambulance woman do it.'

'How old were you?' asks Finn.

'Fifteen . . . so was Amber. I really liked her, but she could be a silly cow. I told her that, but she didn't listen. She was fat you see, really fat. It never bothered me, but the other girls were right bitches. I think that's why she went with the boys all the time, so she'd feel like she had some friends. I dunno.'

Ben makes a small noise in the back of his throat. He actually looks like he might be about to cry. 'What happened? Were they both okay?'

'Kind of. The baby got sent away and then after a while Amber did too. Her dad threw her out. I think if it was just her mum she would have let her stay, but her dad was a bit handy with his fists, if you know what I mean, so Amber had to go . . . I think she's all right now. I had a postcard from her a year or so after, from some place by the seaside. I think her auntie lived there. But I haven't heard from her again.'

'That's so sad,' says Ellie, releasing Will's hand to take mine. 'I can't believe in this day and age that things like that still happen.'

'Well, it was a while ago now, but of course it still happens. It always will while folks are happy to look the other way.'

I regret it as soon as I say it. Ellie's head drops, and Will stares out of the window even though it's dark outside. All four look embarrassed, but I didn't mean for them to. I really didn't. They're not that kind of people.

'That's why this afternoon was so amazing,' I say quietly. 'It wasn't so much what happened, but how it felt. I didn't know people could be like that with one another until I came here, and I never thought I'd ever be somewhere like this . . . I wanted to say thank you.'

Will lays his hand over Ellie's, which is still resting on mine. 'Well, I for one am mighty glad that you are here, Lizzie. We couldn't have done it without your help today.'

'And Jane will love you forever, don't forget that,' grins Ellie.

A sharp noise sounds as Finn pushes his chair back from the table. 'Do you like champagne, Lizzie?' he asks me. 'Because it's about bloody time we cracked open a bottle. Come on, people, is this a party or what! Let's get the weekend started.'

Chapter 15

ELLIE

'I've got a surprise for you,' I announce after breakfast the next morning. Will looks up from the list he's making, not altogether sure that he likes surprises.

'Go on,' he answers slowly.

'Jane has invited us over this afternoon. Can you believe that woman? Gives birth yesterday, right as rain today; I don't know how she does it. Anyway, I know you're busy, but I think they want to thank you properly, and we still need to get Jack's car back to him. I thought maybe I could drive that and you could go in your car.'

Will glances back at his list, not quite as pleased as I thought he'd be.

'Don't you want to go?' I ask.

'It's not that; it's just that I thought we might go out today. I didn't think Jane would be up for visitors yet.'

'Well, she is,' I challenge.

Will is getting quite good at reading my facial expressions. The apology comes quickly.

'I'm just tired, Ellie, sorry,' he says, with a rueful glance.

'And?'

'. . . and I'm being a complete pig.' He catches my smile. 'So, yes, thank you for the perfectly timed and well-deserved nudge. I am also, as I know you are only too aware, a bit nervous about going because I know they'll make a huge fuss over me, which I'll hate . . . but I know you're dying to see the baby, so of course we'll go.'

'Are you sure?'

'Stop toying with me,' he answers. 'Yes, of course I'm sure. We should get some flowers or something.'

I nod. 'I'll pop into town this morning while you're doing whatever it is you need to be doing.'

'Speaking of which, I need to go and see a man about a window. I'll see you later.'

Jack is out of the door before the car even comes to a standstill. He must have been lying in wait for us. I pull forwards into the space his car normally occupies and wait for Will to pull up behind me. Jack comes to open the car door.

I hold up a hand in greeting. 'I know, I know, I'm only the side show. The main attraction will be here in a minute. I lost him on the way over,' I laugh, clambering out.

'None of that, you gorgeous girl. Come here,' he retorts, pulling me into a ferocious hug. 'Although . . .' he teases, looking over my shoulder. 'Will he be long, do you think?'

I stand back, giving him an appraising once-over. 'You look sickeningly well for someone who's probably had very little sleep,' I remark.

'Ah well, just . . . high on life,' he smirks.

I motion sticking two fingers down my throat as Will pulls into the drive.

'Humour me,' says Jack. 'I have to do all the schmaltz outside, because I can't get away with it inside. Jane tells me off.'

'Sounds like she's back to her usual self,' I point out with a grin. 'Is everything all right?'

'Fan-bloody-tastic in every sense of the word. It's at times like this that I'm reminded exactly why I married her.'

Jack takes a couple of steps forwards then, breaking into a huge grin.

'And here he is, the man of the hour,' he greets Will, who looks, as expected, rather embarrassed.

'You're not going to kiss me again, are you?' he asks Jack, jokingly.

'Not unless you want me to, mate.'

'Come on, Jack, that's enough fawning. Can we go in now? I'm dying to see the little one.'

'I'll get us something to wet the baby's head,' he agrees, leading the way straight into the kitchen, where Grace and Tilly are finishing some sandwiches.

'Late lunch today,' says Jack, by way of an explanation. 'Pretty much late everything,' he says darkly, 'seeing as I'm on kitchen duties.'

Tilly jumps up, running around the table, and grabs hold of my hand.

'Auntie Ellie,' she shouts. 'I've got a baby sister, look, come with me!' And she drags me off down the hall. I throw a helpless glance back towards Will, but he's in good hands.

Jane is sitting down, I'm pleased to see; I'd half expected to see her polishing the silver. She looks beautiful, her dark hair vivid against her creamy skin, holding the baby to her in a relaxed pose while she feeds. There's something vibrant about her, and so alive.

I let go of Tilly's hand, who immediately scampers off, and squash myself up beside Jane on the sofa. I lean up against her, dropping a kiss on her cheek.

'Hey you,' I say, reaching across to stroke the baby's head. 'Oh, Jane, she's beautiful,' I breathe, feasting my eyes. 'How are you?'

'Bit sore,' she admits. 'These are a bonus, though,' she adds, lifting up her top to reveal two enormous breasts. 'I think it's safe to say that my milk has well and truly come in.'

'Bloody hell!'

'I know. I think I'd like to keep these.'

'You and me both,' I laugh, looking down at my own chest. 'I think Tilly has probably gone to fetch Will,' I add, rather unnecessarily, as we can both hear her excited chatter. A moment later, Will is propelled into the room, looking distinctly uncomfortable.

Jane expertly slips her boob back into her bra in one swift movement and gets up to greet Will, who motions that she shouldn't move, just at the same time. There's a slightly awkward moment as Will remembers that he's seen parts of this woman he really shouldn't have, and he doesn't quite know where to put himself. Jane, if she feels it too, doesn't show it, but kisses Will warmly and takes him by the arm, leading him over towards me.

'Come on, sit down. I know you want a cuddle.' She looks between the two of us. 'Who wants her first?' she asks.

Immediately I waggle my fingers towards her, but then think better of it. 'Actually, I've just remembered I've got something in the car. Will, you take her.'

'I'm not very good with babies,' he admits sheepishly, but holds up his arms anyway. He flicks a quick glance towards me. He looks terrified.

'About time you learned then,' I tease. He swallows hard.

'Don't worry. You don't need to do anything. She's so stuffed full of milk she'll just sleep.'

I look to Tilly, who I can see is eyeing me carefully. 'Want to come with me?' I ask her, knowing that she has correctly guessed the opportunity for a present. She doesn't need a second invitation.

By the time I return from the car with a rather large carrier bag, everyone has gathered in the living room, where Jack is dishing out drinks.

'You'll have one, won't you, Ellie?' he asks, as I enter. 'Will says he's driving.'

'Just a small one, Jack, please.'

I return to my seat, where Grace materialises beside me.

'Have you bought the baby a present?' she asks, eyeing the bag I've brought in.

I open the top a tiny bit and peek in.

'Erm, no. Oh dear, I don't think I have.' I have a fish about in the bag. 'I have got this,' I say, bringing out a long cylinder. 'Perhaps you should have this, Grace. I think it's a bit big for the baby.'

She takes the package from me. I didn't have time to wrap it, but she knows what it is anyway, as she pops the top off the cylinder. She draws out a long tube of paper as a pack of felt-tip pens falls into her lap. It's one of those huge colour-in posters that I know she loves.

'Oh, look, it's the castle one,' she tells me. 'Thank you, Auntie Ellie,' she says, studying the picture intently.

I take another peep inside the bag. 'I think this must be for you then, Tilly.'

She shrieks in delight at the paper dressing-up set, complete with six different cardboard dolls.

'Can I go and do it now, Mummy?'

Jane smiles at me. 'Yes, but on the kitchen table, mind,' she says. Both girls rush off.

'Thank you both,' she says. 'That was really thoughtful.'

'I thought it might keep them occupied for a bit,' I explain. 'We did actually buy something for the baby too . . . Boring clothes, I'm afraid, but a certain gentleman not too far from here has commissioned himself to make something a little more memorable for you. Oh, and there's a bottle of something gorgeous in there for Mummy too,' I add, handing Jane the bag.

She holds up the package with her favourite L'Occitane cream inside.

'Yummy. Thank you so much. You really shouldn't have. Have you two not done enough for us already?'

'Hear, hear,' says Jack. 'Which brings me to our toast. I want to thank you, Will, for being so absolutely bloody marvellous. I know you don't want to hear it, but Jane and I want to say how much what you did means to us . . . and of course we also want to thank you for agreeing to take Ellie off our hands come June.' He winks.

Dear Jack.

He raises his glass. 'To Will,' he toasts.

'And to Jane,' I add, as glasses are clinked together. 'Congratulations.'

'Of course, you know what this means, don't you?' asks Jack. Blank looks are exchanged. 'That Jane will want Will as her personal physician at all subsequent births.'

Will's head jerks up.

'Only kidding! In fact, I suspect I shall be wheeled off to the vasectomy clinic first thing Monday morning.'

Jane nods enthusiastically, beaming at her husband. I risk a look at Will, who has not said one single word. He's smiling, but it doesn't go anywhere beyond his mouth. Poor sod, he really doesn't take compliments well. I'm not sure he has an affinity with babies either. He's brilliant with the girls, but I suppose he's had no real experience with newborns; he's holding the baby like she's about to spontaneously combust. I reach across to take her from him.

'So, come on then. Don't keep us in suspense any longer,' I say. 'What are you going to call her?'

Jack flashes me a huge grin. 'Well, actually, that's what we hope will be a nice surprise,' he says.

'Oh, how come?' I ask, not sure where this last statement was headed.

'It's my fault really,' explains Jane. 'I was so sure that this one was going to be a boy that we'd sort of discounted girls' names. It sounds stupid, but I think yesterday I was so overcome by events that I didn't even think about it. Then when we got up this morning, there it was, the perfect solution.'

Jack chips in. 'Fortunately I happen to agree, otherwise I don't know what we'd do.'

'I'd have my own way,' argues Jane amiably. 'You don't give birth in a wood and then not get to choose her name.'

I interrupt before Jack can make any further comment. 'And? Out with it then. What have you called her?'

'Rowan,' says Jane warmly. 'We've called her Rowan Elizabeth Manning.'

I look down at the still-sleeping child in my arms, a weighted silence settling around the room. I hear the breath catch in Will's throat beside me.

'That's perfect, isn't it, Will?'

He nods, blinking rapidly. 'It's beautiful,' he mumbles.

And then the mood turns as we all start talking at once, an excited chatter, recognising the need to move away from the poignancy of the moment before.

'Well, we could hardly call her Will, could we?' exclaims Jane. 'This seemed to be the next best thing, especially with that hair.'

'I'm jealous already, and she's only a day old. I always wanted hair that colour,' I admit.

'But your hair's beautiful,' insists Will.

'It's ginger. This is auburn. Rich, dark, like a rowan.'

'Still beautiful.'

I notice the look exchanged between Jack and Jane.

'So where did the red come from then?' I ask.

It's Jack who answers. 'My grandma. Christ, she was a feisty one. If this one's anything like her, we'll be in real trouble.'

'My mother was a redhead,' says Will quietly. 'Her name was Rowena. My father used to joke about it – said he should change the name of the farm to Rowena Hill.'

'I never knew that.' I look at him in surprise from where I'm inhaling the top of Rowan's fragrant head.

'Oh God, watch out!' quips Jack. 'Your offspring will be scarlet.'

I find myself blushing furiously, glancing at Will, expecting him to be doing the same thing. Instead he's looking at me like the world's about to end.

There's very little said in the car on the way home. Of course, Will recovered quickly, and dragged a smile back on his face in an instant. In fact, I don't think Jane and Jack noticed anything wrong, but I saw the look on his face. Although the rest of our time with them passed very pleasantly, his expression sat there in the periphery of my vision, mocking me. I thought Will understood that I don't want children, and although I've never outright asked him whether he does, whenever the subject has been touched upon he's always given me the impression that it wasn't something he wanted either. Although I stopped short of telling Lizzie that Will had had a breakdown before I came to Rowan Hill, the people close to us know what happened and they also know that his ex-wife's solution to his problems was to try to start a family. It's one of the reasons why they split up. Will's never given me any indication since that he's changed his mind about wanting a family, but judging by Fliss's comment back in the woods yesterday, he has. I thought at the time she must have got it wrong, but now I'm not so sure. The look Will gave me at Jane's was pure sorrow – how could I have got it so wrong?

Will's replies to anything I say are verging on the monosyllabic, but the clock is ticking; he has to go back to London soon and these last hours will be the ones that sustain us through the next few weeks until he comes home again. Every minute is precious and needs to be savoured, and I can't let what happened this afternoon colour them grey. What can I do? These next couple of months are also the last before we get married and this is not a discussion we should leave; it's too important for our future together – but I can't broach it today. I can't have Will leave so soon after what might very well turn into an argument and, although I resolve to talk to him about it as soon as I can, for now I just want us to enjoy the last evening we'll have together for a while. I spend the rest of the way home thinking about how I can turn the situation around.

I guess Will must have had the same thoughts. I head for the kettle as soon as we get in, but it's not long before I feel his arms around me, the warmth of his body comforting against my back. He doesn't speak, but lays his head against the back of my shoulder. There's nowhere I'd rather be than right here. I don't want to have to think about anyone else, or talk to anyone else, and I certainly don't want to have to share Will with anyone else. I turn to face him, and my expression mirrors his.

The evening is quiet, with a sweet poignancy to everything we say and do, and it is exactly how I want this time to be. Finn and Ben are nowhere to be seen, and even this makes me feel loved. I know that they will be there for me in the weeks to come, but right now they have given us time alone, and it's all I could ask for.

Despite the warmth of the day, it's cool as we finally climb the stairs, turning out the lights one by one. The light in our room stays lit, though, for a long while, as if we never want to lose sight of one another again, and although my eyes flutter closed as I feel Will's hands on my skin, whenever I open them his eyes are on mine, deep and dark with longing.

Chapter 16

LIZZIE

'Why is it that as soon as you have flour all over your hands, you need to scratch your nose?' laughs Ellie, screwing up her face to try and get rid of the offending itch.

I look down at my own hands, which are equally white. 'Oh, don't,' I reply. 'Now I'll need to scratch mine too.'

Ellie jostles her shoulder into mine as we both giggle. It started off as a perfectly serious attempt to get me to learn how to bake, but somehow we've spent most of the time laughing. The problem came when I tried to weigh out the flour into a big bowl, and although I began cautiously enough, I upended the bag a little too quickly. A huge clump of flour fell out of the bag and landed in the bowl with such force that a cloud of white dust coated most of my face. Ellie couldn't look at me then without laughing, and as the golden rule when baking is not to touch your face, hair, or anything else dirty until you've finished, she wouldn't let me wipe it off either.

We're rubbing in. Taking the flour and butter and sort of pressing them together through our fingers to make a breadcrumb-like mix. Except that Ellie's is perfect, and mine is full of big clumps. But I'm learning, and if I can do this, then I can make loads of things apparently: it's one of the basic skills of baking. Today we're trying out scones.

Ellie's been a bit quiet today, so I'm glad that now the tea room is shut she's suggested our cookery session. I think she only did it because Will left to go back to London very early this morning and she doesn't want to be on her own tonight, but she seems happier now, and even if I'm a crap baker, at least it's cheered her up.

'Don't press quite so hard, Lizzie. I think that's your problem. Pretend your handling something really fragile that you don't want to hurt, and do everything gently. That's the secret with most cakes really. You need what my mum used to call "light hands".'

I lift up another clump of flour and butter and try again. 'Is that where you learned how to do all this?' I ask. 'With your mum?'

'I guess so, yes,' Ellie replies. 'It's not something you really think about at the time, but I often used to stand on a stool when I was little and just watch what my mum was doing. When I got a bit bigger she'd let me help, and when I was bigger still I had my own little baking set. A bowl, rolling pin, and some fancy cutters, that kind of thing. Not surprisingly, shortbread was one of the first things she taught me how to bake.'

I swallow, thinking how different her childhood had been to mine.

'Did you have your own tiny apron too?' I grin.

'Crikey, I did actually . . . That takes me back. It had bright green parrots on it for some reason.'

I look down at my own blue and white striped cover-up. 'Nice . . .' I comment, which has Ellie laughing again. 'It must have been lovely doing things like that with your mum,' I add. 'When I was little, a cake was just something that came out of a packet, if I was very lucky. I don't think it even occurred to me that people made them.'

Ellie peers into my bowl. 'That's looking better,' she says. 'It's what you're used to, I suppose. My mum was a good cook; she always baked, and so I thought everyone else did too. They didn't, of course, but as I got older the love of it stayed with me, and I carried on making more things, different things.'

I let the mixture trickle through my fingers. 'And now, here you are, baking cakes for a living.' I smile back up at her. 'She must have been a good mum to teach you all that.'

'She was . . . She still is,' she smiles wistfully. She looks down at her own bowl in front of her, her lips pursed together. 'Didn't you ever do things like this with your mum then?'

The snort comes out of my mouth before I can stop it. 'Sorry,' I say automatically. 'My mum would spend as little time as possible with me, and then even when she was around it wouldn't have ever occurred to her to try and teach me anything, or do anything for fun. She was too busy off boozing, or with her boyfriends, to bother being a mum.' I'm wondering how much more to say.

'Oh, Lizzie, I'm so sorry. I can't imagine a childhood like that. You always think everyone's are like your own.'

'Well, everyone I knew had one like mine too,' I reply, but then catch sight of the look on Ellie's face. 'Just different, that's all. It wasn't all bad . . . In fact, I went to stay with another family for a while, fostered like, and Yvonne was lovely. She was a big, warm woman, with a big, warm house, and she did try and do stuff with me. Trouble was, there were five of us, so there was never very much of her to go around.'

'But you couldn't stay there?' asks Ellie, sadly.

'Nah, me mum convinced the social she was off the booze and drugs, and I had to go back.'

There's silence for a moment or two, before Ellie picks up the jug of milk we've already measured out.

'That's looking brilliant,' she says, peering into my bowl. 'Pop the sugar in, give it a stir and then we can add the milk.'

She watches while I follow her instructions. 'You know, full credit to you, Lizzie, that you're so determined to make something of your life.

I can't begin to think how it must have been for you growing up with no parents around to speak of, something I took utterly for granted.'

I shrug. 'I had no choice when I was little, but I do now. I know I get a lot of it wrong, but I am trying. It might just take me a little while.'

Ellie's smile is warm. 'And you're doing brilliantly . . .'

'Let's just see how my scones turn out, shall we?' I laugh, trying to sound a bit less serious. 'And it's knowing that there's something else out there, something different, that's half the battle. If I ever have kids, I'll make sure that they do as many things as possible. Learn as many things as they can. I might never have much money, but giving your kids time costs nothing.'

For a minute I think Ellie might be about to cry. 'And you'll be an amazing mum, I know it,' she says.

I smile at her. 'Well, I didn't have a good teacher like you did when I was a kid, but I've got one now. I can just see you with your own little ones some day, and as long as you don't make them wear aprons with green parrots on them, I'm sure they'll turn out to be amazing bakers too.'

I start to stir as Ellie pours in the milk. 'Gently now,' she says. 'I'm not sure I'm cut out to be a parent actually. It's weird given that my best friend is probably the most maternal person in the world, but I've never really felt the urge to have children myself. I love them, don't get me wrong, just other people's.' She smiles. 'That way I can give them back when they start being horrible. Will's the same. At least I think he is—' She breaks off to bite her lip. 'He's far too caught up in his work right now anyway, and that's far more important. He's only just got going, so to have children now would be . . . difficult,' she finishes.

I feel my face fall. 'Aw, I always thought you'd make a great mum and dad, but I get what you're saying. It's a big job, isn't it? And you're both so busy. Has Will never wanted kids either then? I thought Fliss said the other day that he does?'

This time Ellie's eyes do begin to fill with tears. She wipes the back of her hand across her nose.

'Oh God, look at me.' She grimaces. 'And don't you dare ever do that when you're baking. I don't think I realised how emotional Jane's baby made us feel, but seeing them yesterday was quite hard in a way. I've never felt under pressure to have children before, but as soon as you decide to get married it becomes something everyone expects. I don't think Will has changed his mind, not really, but he was a bit quiet when we visited Jane yesterday and I think he's feeling it too – like he should want to have children even if he doesn't . . .' She stares at me for a moment. 'Am I making any sense?'

'A bit broody, do you mean . . . ? But not like you really want children, you only think you do because you've just had a lovely cuddle with one and it seems quite appealing. Then you remember all the nights with no sleep and the dirty nappies . . .'

'Yes, that's it,' says Ellie, her face brightening. 'That's exactly it. Can you imagine what either of us would be like with no sleep at the moment?'

I look back down to the bowl, waiting for my next instruction. Ellie's voice sounds a bit jumpy, like she's trying too hard. I hope I haven't upset her. I was trying to make her feel better, not worse. Maybe I should get on with making the scones and change the subject.

I poke a finger into the soft mound of dough in the bowl. 'Are you sure this looks right? It's a bit mushy.'

Ellie peers into the bowl again. 'Is that a technical term?' she grins. 'The mushy stage . . . I quite like the sound of that, although, bizarrely, that's exactly what we were aiming for. Now we just tip it out onto the floured work surface and give it a gentle knead – that's the technical term for poking it a bit . . . And just remember—'

'I know,' I interrupt. 'Soft hands!'

MAY

Chapter 17

LIZZIE

I love being in Patience's workshop. It smells like the middle of summer, even when it isn't. Patience has put bunches of herbs and flowers on a sort of rack that hangs from the ceiling, and when you open the door you can smell them straight away. The scent in here is even stronger if the door to her kitchen is open because then you can smell all her oils as well. And when she's melting cocoa butter, it smells exactly like chocolate.

She isn't making anything today; she's been seeing patients – or clients, as she calls them. They come for all sorts of things, and whatever is wrong, she makes something that puts it right again. A bit like the potions master from Harry Potter, but in a good way.

It's been quite quiet this morning, so Patience has popped out to get some honey from the chap in the next village. His honey is the best apparently, and she won't use anything else. It feels nice sitting at her desk, in this peaceful room, and I take a big bite of my cheese and pickle sandwich hoping that the telephone doesn't ring. I've only got to take messages, but I don't want to sound a complete idiot.

I've only had one visitor so far, but that wasn't a proper customer, just Patrick bringing Patience some grapes to go with her lunch. He must think I was born yesterday – like I'd believe he was only here to make sure Patience doesn't go hungry. You'd have to be blind not to notice how many times he pops over to see her. Patrick's nice, though. I like him, and although he's quite shy, I think they'd make a lovely couple.

Once I've finished my sandwich I wander over to the display stand in the corner of the room. This is where Patience keeps her Little Pots of Goodness for people to buy, and I straighten up the beautiful green glass pots so that all the pretty labels face the right way. She's put some out that you can try as well, and I take the lid off one now, sticking my nose close to the contents. I poke my finger in and take out some of the cream, rubbing it on the back of my hand. I think this one might be my favourite.

My hands are still a bit greasy when the phone rings, so I have to swipe them down my jeans. I think it's one of those sales calls at first when I answer, because I can hear the person talking to someone else, but then, after a bit of a pause, a loud voice almost shouts, "Patience Connelly?"

That's a bit rude.

There's another silence after I explain that she isn't here. I'm not even sure that the caller is listening to me at all.

'Right, well, I haven't got all day. If she wants this order you'll have to take a message. Can you do that?'

'Well, I can, but she's only just popped out, she won't be long and I can ask her to call you back.'

'No, that won't work. I'll be in a meeting then. Look, just write this lot down, it's not difficult.'

I pick up the pen by the phone, my ears beginning to burn.

'Okay, I've got a pen.'

What follows is a long stream of words spoken so quickly that I can't even begin to get half of them down. She's got a strong Irish accent too, which doesn't help. I've got to get this right, though; it's important. I think I've got the first two things okay, but when I ask her to repeat everything, she gives a loud *tut*.

'Look, do you want the order or not?'

I'm beginning to get cross now; this is not fair at all.

'Patience *will* want the order, but you're talking too fast. Can't you just slow down a bit, so I can make sure I've got it right?'

'Oh, for heaven's sake . . . Right, I-want-eight-of-the-sleep-balm . . . six-of-the-hand-healing . . . Have you got that? Eight-of-the-sleep-balm . . .'

Bloody cow. I'm getting crosser by the minute. She doesn't have to speak to me like that. I don't know who she is, but I wouldn't want to sell anything to her. I continue scribbling everything down, until my thoughts come back at me suddenly.

'Wait – I don't know who you are. Where are you ringing from?' I gabble, before the phone is thrown down.

Another loud *tut*.

'Neeuv O'Connor.' And she's gone.

Neeuv, is that what she said? It doesn't sound quite right to me, but she's gone now so I can't ask her again even if I wanted to. I look down at the gobbledegook on the piece of paper in front of me, and feel a hot flush creep over my cheeks. Patience will never be able to read this.

I nearly jump out of my skin when the phone rings again, but this time it's just a lady who needs to rearrange her appointment, and she doesn't mind one bit when I say that Patience can ring her back. I finish writing her number down and look back at my scribbled list. My heart beats suddenly in my throat as I look down the items. There's one I can't read at all, and I can't remember what it was either.

I pick up the paper and take it over to the doorway; perhaps a bit more light will help. I pull the door open just as Fliss touches the handle to come in. She almost lands in my arms.

'Oh, thank God you're here,' I exclaim, pulling her further into the room.

'Well, I wasn't expecting that good a welcome,' she laughs. 'Are you all right?'

'Yes . . . no . . . sort of.' I look at her, frowning. 'I was holding this in the light to see if I could read it better. It's an order for Patience from some snotty woman on the phone. Talk about rude – she wouldn't give me any time to copy down what she wanted, and I'm not even sure where she's from. She's got some stupid name as well.'

Fliss takes the piece of paper from me, peering at my swirly writing. 'Christ, I might need my glasses. It's a bit small, Lizzie.'

'I know. I always write tiny when I'm in a hurry. I used to write much bigger when I was at school, but I got into trouble so many times for being slow I thought writing smaller might help. It doesn't, though, does it? Now I just can't read it. I can make out most of what it says, but it's this one here – I can't remember what it was for.'

The paper is turned this way and that, but it's obvious Fliss can't make head nor tail of it either.

'Perhaps you should write it all out again, neatly. It might come back to you then.'

I hurry back to the desk. 'That's a really good idea.' I take a new page from the notebook and start again, trying to make my writing as neat as possible.

'Will Patience be long, do you think?' asks Fliss. 'Only I've got a massive crick in my neck today. I wondered whether she might be able to unkink it if she wasn't too busy.'

'She won't be long, no. She's only popped out to get some of Mr Green's honey. He's a bit of a chatterbox, but she should only be another ten minutes or so. I can look in the diary if you like.'

Fliss picks up the leatherbound book on the desk. 'Is this it? Don't worry. You carry on with that. I can have a look myself.' She flicks through the pages. 'Have you remembered what it was yet?'

'No,' I reply, peering hard at the page.

'Would it be something from here?' she asks, putting the diary down and crossing to the display I looked at earlier. 'I can read out their names if that would help.'

'Oh, would you? It's got to be really, hasn't it?'

She reads out three or four before we hit on it.

'That's it, ex . . . eczema cream! It's because I couldn't spell it, I've just sort of scribbled anything down. How do you spell it anyway?'

I copy it down just as Fliss says, looking at my list, pleased that it now appears neat and ordered.

'Can you help me with this as well, Fliss? Only I'm not sure how you spell her name. I think I heard it right, but it sounds weird to me.'

Fliss comes back over to the desk and perches her bum on the edge of it. 'What did it sound like?'

'Neeuv,' I say, trying my best to sound like she did. 'She had a strong accent as well.'

'What's her last name? Is she Irish?'

'It's O'Connor.'

She smiles at me. 'Well, then, I think it's Niamh. You did pronounce it right, but it's spelled N-i-a-m-h.'

'How do you know stuff like that? I've never heard of it.'

Fliss shrugs. 'It's not all that common over here, and no, you are not stupid, before you say it. I doubt that many people would know how it's spelled.'

It's kind of her to say, but I still feel a bit of an idiot. I mean, I even need help to write down an order, for God's sake. How difficult can that be? I check the list again, making sure that I haven't made any mistakes. My mobile dances across the desk in front of me as a text message comes in. That's probably Patience telling me she's on her way back, I think. It isn't; it's Finn.

Ellie's delivery has just arrived. Are you free to help unpack? Fx

I'm not sure what to do now. Some of the things in the delivery are for the fridge and the freezer and need to be put away pretty quickly. I look at my watch and bite my lip, wondering what I should say to Finn. I'm not altogether sure how long Patience will be.

'I can hang on here if you want to go,' says Fliss.

'Oh . . . would that be all right? Only . . . well, I promised Patience that I'd stay until she got back.'

'I know, but I'm sure she won't mind just so long as someone stays. I don't mind, really. I could do with a chat to her as well, actually, wedding flowers and all that. Things are getting a bit close.'

'Oh, now I want to stay too! That's far more exciting than unpacking boxes. What sort of flowers is Ellie going to have?'

Fliss looks down at her feet, stretching them out in front of her as if to admire her shoes. Then she slowly puts them back down again.

'Well, I'm hoping it's not going to be too awkward, only Will loves lilies apparently. Very, very elegant, but—'

She looks back at me with her eyebrows raised. I'm not sure what she means. She stares at me for a moment longer, until finally her mouth makes a tight little twitch.

'We don't grow lilies here . . .'

I still don't get it – why is that a problem?

'And if we don't grow lilies here, then it doesn't make sense for Patience to do the flowers. The florist we want to order from will probably do them. I just hope that Patience won't be too upset.'

'Oh, I see,' I say, finally understanding what she means, even though I don't think it would be a problem. 'I don't think she'd mind, not really. She'd just want Ellie and Will to have what they want, surely?'

Fliss looks down at her feet again, before she smiles back up at me.

'Yes, I'm sure you're right.' She checks her watch. 'Listen, you should get going . . .'

I grab my mobile off the desk and stand up.

'Why don't you put the order under the phone, to keep it safe? Then you can be sure that Patience will find it. I'll tell her if you like.'

Oh Christ, what am I like? I'd bloody forgotten about that. I flash Fliss a huge smile so that she'd think that's what I was about to do anyway.

'Okay, thank you! See you later,' I call, then I'm off out the door.

Chapter 18

Lizzie

'Stop looking at me like that, Alice. I'm fine,' mutters Ellie mutinously, banging her bags of shopping about. 'So, where do you want your carrots?'

I take them from her without a word and put them in the fridge. I smile to myself. We've only been here ten minutes and already Alice has guessed that Ellie's in a bad mood.

'Saying you're fine and actually being fine are two very different things, Ellie, as you well know, but that's all I'm going to say on the matter for now.'

Alice turns to me. 'I wonder how long it will be before the strawberries are ready for picking?'

'Goodness, Alice, where did that come from?' asks Ellie, shaking her head softly. 'I shouldn't think it will be for a while yet. I can ask Bonnie if you like?'

'No, it doesn't matter. I had a sudden yearning for them at breakfast. That's all.' She gives me a slight wink, more of a twinkle really. She's so funny.

'With all this great weather we've been having, they'll probably be ripening up nicely. I would think they'll be at least another month.'

'I suppose so. They'll be worth waiting for, though, don't you think? As all good things are.'

Ellie stares at her, amused. 'Are we still talking about strawberries?' she smiles.

Alice narrows her eyes. 'Possibly not, dear, no.'

This is just like Alice, and one of the reasons I love coming over here. She always knows how I'm feeling the minute I walk through the door, particularly if I'm worried about something. She won't let me go until she's found out what it is either, which makes me laugh now. To start with, I didn't realise she was doing it, and I found myself telling her all sorts of things and then wondering why as soon as I left, but now I've cottoned on to Alice's ways and I'm used to her gentle interrogation.

'I am fine, you know,' repeats Ellie. 'And, yes, I've made it through another whole week without Will, and our wedding will be very special and worth waiting for, as will he.'

'I'm fussing, aren't I?' replies Alice.

'Yes, and so is everybody else,' Ellie replies, through slightly gritted teeth this time. 'I lose count of the number of times every day that I get asked how I am, or if everything is okay. I can't remember anyone doing that before Will went away, and it's getting to be a little annoying the longer it goes on. Actually, Ben is the only one who isn't fussing. He's very sweet. He just rushes up to me from time to time, gives me a big hug, and then rushes off again, looking embarrassed.'

'We just want to look after you, Ellie, that's all. You can't blame us for wanting to do that – it's something you do for all of us, after all.'

'Hmm, well, I don't know about that,' Ellie replies, thinking about Alice's words for a moment. 'I've been so busy this week looking at wedding stuff every spare minute of the day, I don't think I've actually talked to anyone properly. I know everyone means well, but you know how it is when you're trying to forget about something and everyone keeps asking you about it, all it does is remind you of that very thing.' She looks a bit sheepish. 'Ungrateful, I know.'

Alice nods in sympathy. 'Not ungrateful, Ellie, understandable. You probably feel like you want to keep out of everyone's way, but folks just want to help. You have a busy time ahead of you and you don't have to do everything yourself, just remember that.'

'I know.' She smiles at Alice's gentle telling off. 'But at least things are going well in that direction. Fliss has been amazing. She's so organised.'

'Well, that's good, dear. I expect the others are all getting excited too. I remember my own wedding like it was yesterday,' she adds wistfully. 'I had such fun. We couldn't afford very much, and my dress was quite plain, but it's the flowers I remember best, great armfuls of them from the neighbour's gardens. I bet Patience has loads of wonderful ideas for you.'

'Yes, except that she knows the names of every flower that ever was, and I don't. Before we settled on the lilies, she had to keep stopping to show me pictures of what things looked like. I'm completely clueless.'

Alice's eyebrows are raised.

'Lilies?'

'Yes . . . arum lilies. Why, what's wrong? Don't you like them?'

'Well, I don't dislike them,' Alice replies, but it's clear she's struggling for what to say. 'I've always thought them a bit funereal, to tell you the truth. And that's what Will wants too, is it?'

Ellie seems a bit surprised by her comment. 'Yes, that's what Patience said,' she replies. 'Admittedly, I was a bit surprised; they wouldn't have been my first choice, but Patience showed me some different arrangements, and I can see how they would look – they're very elegant.'

Now it's my turn to be surprised.

'So Patience knows about the lilies?'

Ellie glances at me, a bit irritated. 'Yes, of course she does, I spoke to her about them at the beginning of the week.'

'And she doesn't mind?'

'Why would she mind? In fact, it was her who gave me the name of the florist to use. Someone she's worked with before apparently.'

I must have misunderstood the other day. I thought Fliss was worried that Patience would be upset when she found out that Ellie and Will aren't going to have flowers from the gardens here, but that can't be right if Patience already knew about the lilies.

I'm about to speak when Alice steps in. She's smiling, but her brows are still drawn together. 'No one's being critical, dear, you must have what you want, of course, and I'm sure they will be beautiful.'

'Yes, they will, and it's not as if Patience isn't helping with the other flowers. She's going to do the table decorations here.'

Alice looks at my face for a moment, and gives me one of *those* looks, in other words, *shut up.*

'I'm sorry, Ellie dear, just ignore me. I didn't mean to interfere over the flowers, and now I've upset you. The most important thing is that it's your and Will's special day, and you must have whatever you want. I'm very old-fashioned in my views. You young things know much more than me.' She folds up her shopping bags, stowing them in a drawer. 'Now, have you got time for tea, or are you both rushing off?'

'We ought to be getting back to the tea room,' Ellie replies. 'People will be wanting their elevenses soon, and Ben can't cover for too long today. He's got a pile of stuff still to do in the Lodge. I might pop in on Patience first, though; make sure she really is happy with things.' She kisses Alice on the cheek. 'You're a wily old bird, Alice,' she sighs. 'What would I do without you?'

'What a nice idea, Ellie. She's probably up to her eyeballs, though it is very exciting.'

'Sorry, Alice, what is?' asks Ellie.

'The big order that came in.'

'Well, I know I've been a little preoccupied this week, but not *that* preoccupied,' Ellie frowns. 'I still have no clue what you're talking about.'

'The big order for her Little Pots of Goodness. From that lady with the funny name,' I fill in. 'Wouldn't it be great for Patience if they wanted more and more and more?'

Ellie is beginning to look worried.

'When did this come in, Lizzie? I didn't know anything about it.'

I think for a moment. 'A couple of days ago. Tuesday, I think, so she'll have sent it off by now.'

Ellie stares at me, a horrified look on her face, and I start to feel that familiar churning in my stomach.

'How can she possibly have sent it all off by now, Lizzie, when she has to make everything from scratch? A big order would take her days to make, a week even. I can't understand why she hasn't mentioned it, or asked for help for that matter.'

I stare first at Ellie, and then back at Alice. 'But I didn't know that! I thought she just took stuff off of shelves, put it in a box and sent it off. No one told me she had to make everything when an order came in.'

Ellie clapped her hand over her mouth. 'Oh, Lizzie, I'm so sorry. I think we all assumed you just knew – but how could you have?'

I can feel my eyes begin to fill up with tears. I have no answer for her. It's not her fault. I should have thought about it. But Ellie isn't finished yet.

'But that's not what's concerning me right now.' She looks at Alice. 'There's still something not quite right about this,' she mutters. 'Patience would have said something about a big order like this, particularly if she was struggling to fill it. It's almost as if she doesn't even know about it.' I can feel her eyes on my face then. 'I think you'd better come with me,' she says.

'I'm sorry, Patience, I came as soon as I heard,' Ellie says as she crashes through the door with me in tow.

'Jesus, Ellie, that's a pretty scary entrance,' Patience drawls. 'You could give someone a heart attack.'

I look around the room, where all is neat and ordered. The small desk to the rear of the room where Patience sits is empty except for an opened book, her hand still marking the place she is reading. Her notebook beside her also lies open, a pen aligned along its centre. To her left the door to her treatment room is ajar, and the couch stacked with white towels is just visible, while the edge of the curtain blows gently around the open window. The door to the kitchen is closed.

'You don't know about it, do you?' Ellie pants. 'Surely you can't have done it all!'

Patience gets to her feet, her long dark hair tossed back over her shoulder.

'Well, it's nice to see you too, Ellie, but what are you talking about?' She looks totally confused.

'The big order that came in; Alice mentioned it just now. Lizzie said it came in a couple of days ago.'

'You poor, love-starved puppy. You've actually gone quite mad, haven't you? Shall I speak slowly and clearly in words of one syllable and then we can see where we go from here, because I have absolutely no idea what you're talking about.'

Ellie is looking about the room, trying to make sense of what she's seeing, or rather, what she's not seeing.

Patience shakes her head. 'No, still nothing.' She smiles in amusement, but then her eyes narrow, as she finally takes in what Ellie's been saying.

Oh God, please don't say it, this can't be right.

'Hang on a minute . . . what big order? I haven't had a big order.'

My breath catches in my throat. I feel sick. How can she not know? I left the order right by the phone, I know I did.

I push past her to the desk, pushing the phone aside and picking up her notebook. There's nothing there. I give it a shake. Still nothing.

'Lizzie . . . ?' There's a warning note in her voice as Patience comes back to stand beside me.

I stare up at her in panic. 'I left it here, under the phone. You must have seen it.' I shake the notebook again, until she takes it from me, putting it back down on the desk.

'No, there's nothing here. I would have noticed.'

I'm searching my head for anything that might help. 'Your diary was on the desk,' I stammer. 'Maybe that's where it is.'

Patience yanks open the desk drawer sharply and pulls out the blue book, upending it over the desk and jiggling it. She doesn't say a word, and her mouth is a thin hard line.

'Nope, no order,' she says eventually, glaring at me.

'Lizzie,' begins Ellie, more gently. 'Can you explain to us what happened when you found out about the order, what was said, and what the note said? It's really important that you remember.'

I nod, my eyes wide. 'I think it was on Tuesday,' I start nervously. 'Yes, it must have been because you had popped out to pick up the jars of honey from Mr Green.'

Tuesday was two days ago. I can feel Patience stiffen beside me. Ellie nods encouragingly.

'The phone rang and it was the lady with the funny name – Niamh? I told her you weren't in and asked if she wanted to ring back, but she was in such a hurry, she said she hadn't got time and I should just take a message if you wanted the order.' I chew on my lip. 'She was a bit rude, actually. She practically shouted the order at me, and I had to write really fast to keep up with her. I knew it was important, so I made her wait while I repeated it back to her to make sure I had it right. She didn't like that.'

'So what happened then?' asks Ellie.

'Well, my writing was a bit messy so I started to write it out again, all proper, so you could read it. Ask Fliss, if you don't believe me.'

'Hang on a minute. What's Fliss got to do with this?' asks Patience.

And then I remember. Fliss can help me out.

'Fliss can tell you I'm not lying. She came in to talk to you about something just as I was writing everything down. She saw me.' I try to think clearly about what else happened. 'She helped me spell Niamh, and then when I'd finished she suggested I put the piece of paper under the phone, where you would see it.'

'But you didn't think to tell me that when I came back?' says Patience, exasperated, her voice rising.

I look indignant for a moment. 'I would have, but I wasn't there when you got back, don't you remember? Finn called me over to help unpack a delivery and I wasn't sure whether to go and help or not, but Fliss told me not to worry. She said she would hang on and wait for you to come back instead of me, and that she would make sure to tell you.'

Patience snorts. 'Well, it bloody well doesn't matter much now anyway, does it? Not unless you can remember exactly what the order was . . .' She glares at me, and I flinch as I see the look in her eyes. 'No, I thought not,' she finishes.

There's not much point in me saying anything else. I'll only make it worse. I have no idea where the list went, but I should have checked that Patience had seen it. I shouldn't have been so stupid.

I hang my head. 'I'm so sorry, Patience,' I say. It doesn't mean anything, of course. It's just words to her. 'I didn't know that you had to make up the order either. I thought you just put the jars in boxes and sent it off.'

'It had to be her too, didn't it?' she adds bitterly. 'That "woman with the funny name", as you put it, is from the garden centre. She's been the bane of my life recently, looking like she was interested and then not, wanting all sorts of information and then not returning my calls for weeks. Then when she goes and actually places an order, I'm completely clueless about it. Jesus, how good is that going to look?'

Ellie touches her arm gently. 'Look, I know you're upset, Patience, but let's see what we can do about this. Lizzie, can you remember any of what was on the order, or do you think Fliss could? Why don't you go and have a word with her and see what the two of you can come up with?'

Patience sighs. She doesn't want to be comforted, or reasoned with. I can see in the way she's standing – arms folded across her body, jaw clenched – that she just wants to be angry with me, and I can't say I blame her. Perhaps it's a good idea for me to go and see Fliss, then she and Ellie can have a good bitch about me. It might make her feel better.

'I really don't see that you have any other choice,' Ellie says half an hour later, placing a mug of tea on the table.

Patience gives a groan from where her head is buried in her arms. Her dark hair is spilling over her desk. She retreated there about five minutes ago, when I got back from visiting Fliss, and hasn't moved since.

I look at Ellie, who gives me a little smile. I know she's disappointed in me, but at least she isn't cross like Fliss was. I wasn't accusing Fliss of anything, at least I don't think I was, but now she thinks I'm blaming her for having lost the list. I'm not going to say anything else. Whatever I say just makes everything worse.

'The only thing you can do is be honest,' Ellie continues. 'Anything less will sound contrived and very fishy. If you want my opinion, come clean.'

Patience raises her head from her arms.

'And look a total dingbat?' she winces. 'That really bodes well for the future.'

'Well, maybe this Niamh has a softer side you could appeal to.'

Patience's look is not far off a glare.

'Okay, well, maybe not. But you have no order at the moment. What difference does it make?'

I wish I could turn the clock back. There's no way Patience will get this order, not from that grumpy cow. She didn't seem like the kind of person who would give anyone a second chance. Even if she really likes Patience's stuff, she'll think she's really bad at her job. And she isn't. I am.

Patience gets up from the table. She looks tired now. 'It doesn't make any difference at all, does it? So I might as well ring her and get it over with.' She picks up the phone from the desk. 'Excuse me.' And she goes into her treatment room, closing the door behind her.

It's quiet for a very long time.

Ellie clears her throat after a while and I can feel her watching me, but my head stays firmly looking at the floor, my hands shoved into the pockets of my jeans. I don't know why I'm still here. I should go back to the tea room so that Ben can get on with his work. Ellie said he didn't mind staying for a bit, but he's only saying that because he's so nice. I bet he's cross with me too now.

'You know, if by some miracle Patience does get this order,' whispers Ellie, 'then she's going to need a lot of help . . . Perhaps you could start thinking about how we can support her.'

I look up in surprise. The possibility that I might be able to help hadn't even occurred to me. I raise my eyes to Ellie and give a tiny nod, and then I turn my head and fix my gaze on the treatment-room door. Please don't let this be over.

〰️

There is a sudden loud explosion of noise as the door flies open, then Patience is standing there, chest heaving. She stares at Ellie for a moment and, without warning, gives an almighty snort and bursts out laughing.

'I bloody did it. Flaming sanctimonious cow, but I did it! One mahoosive big bloody order, and it's all mine.'

She stops as she sees me, and I wait to see the expression on her face, but then she grins, and I feel a huge swoosh of relief wash over me.

I rush to hug her, as does Ellie, and the three of us jump up and down for a minute like six-year-olds, our collective hair, one side red, one dark, one blond, swirling around us.

'Come on then, spill,' says Ellie, breathlessly. 'Tell us all about it.'

'Look at the pad. I wrote it down this time, that's for sure.' Patience grins. 'I've got a week to turn it around. I got a bloody lecture too, mind, about my failings as a businesswoman, my general incompetency and rank unprofessionalism, but . . . one of my creams did sort out her nasty bit of eczema' – she laughs like a drain – 'and so I'm in. I've been given a second chance, and not many people get those, apparently.'

'You don't say.'

'She wanted the order by today originally. Can you believe it? I told her I wasn't prepared to compromise on the quality of my product and neither should she. I've got to deliver that lot next Friday so they can have it ready for the weekend.' She grins. 'Jesus, I'm going to have to work all bloody night.'

'No,' I correct her. 'I'll help, as much as it takes.' I look at her list. Knowing what I do now, the quantities seem impossible. 'What are you going to do first?'

Patience grimaces. 'Work out what I need. I've nowhere near enough stock, and not just oils, herbs too.' She eyes the fragrant bunches tied to the rack over our heads. 'Niamh wants a load of herbal pillows too, and I can't use these, they're not fresh enough. Oh God, I need fabric too, and my green pots . . .' Her eyes widen at the enormity of what lies ahead.

Ellie puts a hand over hers. 'What we need is a battle plan, and I know someone who is really good at making lists.'

Chapter 19

Lizzie

It makes perfect sense when I think about it, but I still feel disappointed. Patience beamed at me when I offered to help, and I thought that would mean actually helping. Instead I had to go and get Fliss so that they could start making plans, and I'm stuck here polishing her shelves while she's over with Ellie and Patience.

Still, I suppose I don't mind that much. It does mean I get to look at all her pretty things. She was in the middle of making a necklace when I arrived and I'm not to touch that or anything on that table – not that I'd dare.

Instead I move to the row of glass display cabinets that are on two sides of the room. They're a bit taller than me, and each one is locked, obviously, but once you've opened the door at the front there are three shelves in each, with see-through cubes on them, all of different sizes. This is where Fliss puts the jewellery she's already made for people to look at.

I think it's the big lights that show up every speck of dust. And all the fingerprints, and it takes ages to take each bit of jewellery out and then polish the shelf and the cube and put it back as it was before. You have to wear little cotton gloves too, otherwise you just make everything mucky again, and the grease from your fingers makes the silver dull, Fliss says. I like to imagine that I'm a famous actress and that these are all in my dressing room. Now which one shall I wear today?

It's quiet today. Normally I stop if anyone comes in because if they see you fiddling with things, they won't come over and have a look, but today no one's been in at all, and I finished the last cabinet about ten minutes ago. I wish I knew how long Fliss was going to be because it's nearly half past two now and I'm starving hungry. I wander through to the back office. Fliss usually has some fruit in a bowl on her desk, and I'm sure she won't mind if I have an apple.

Her computer is making pinging noises, which must be emails or something, but the screen is blank so I ignore it. She lets me use it sometimes, just so I can look at stuff on the internet, but I don't want to touch it if she's not here. It could do with a dust, though. I glance around the rest of the room, at the shelves and the filing cabinet. Perhaps I'll just give them all a quick flick with the duster, and then if she's still not back I can have something to eat when I'm done.

There's a couple of books on the desk, and I pick one up while I crunch into my apple. I can't think what else I can do. I didn't want to disturb Fliss's papers and things too much, so I've sort of tidied them and dusted around everything as best I can. I sit back in her chair and turn the book over in my hand. It's a crime novel, with a cover I recognise – it's a bestseller, I think.

I open a page at random and start to read, my eyes skipping the words a bit. I turn the page and read a bit more. Some woman is looking through a photograph album, *fear flickering through her body*. It's dark and the wind is rattling at the windows. Well, of course, it always is. I turn another page, waiting for the blood-curdling scream that I'm sure is coming, automatically moving Fliss's bookmark out of the way to continue. *There's a creak in the hallway outside* . . . I close the book with a sigh. I bet it's the husband. Still, I'd love to find out. I rifle through the pages again to find the place where Fliss was up to, and replace her bookmark, turning back to the beginning of the book. I wander back out to the main shop and settle myself at the small table before opening it at chapter one.

The buzzer on the door nearly makes me jump out of my skin. I'm not sure how long I've been reading for, but seven chapters have whizzed past. My heart is already pounding. It doesn't need any more exercise.

'God, you made me jump!' I exclaim as Fliss bustles back through the door.

She holds her notebook across her chest, and tucks a stray piece of hair back behind her ear.

'Well, that was a bit of a tall order, but I think we've got there now. Patience has calmed down a bit anyway.' She grins. 'Thanks so much for covering for me here, Lizzie. It was a big help.'

'I haven't done very much,' I say. 'I didn't know how long you'd be and I didn't want to interfere with anything, but I've polished all the glass and dusted around a bit in your office.'

Fliss looks around her. 'Yes, I'm sorry. It took longer than I thought, but thank you, that's brilliant.' She eyes the book – I still have one finger pushed inside, marking my place. 'What do you think? I can't really get into it myself.'

I blush furiously. 'I was a bit bored – sorry. It's just that it was on your desk when I was dusting.'

'Borrow it if you like,' she replies, waving a hand and going through to the office. 'I don't mind. I'm not sure I'll bother finishing it.'

I follow behind her. 'Wouldn't you mind, honestly? I think it's fantastic. I'd love to know how it ends.'

'No problem,' she replies. 'Anyway, do you want to get going now? Just to let you know that we're all going to meet up in the big kitchen once we've shut up for the day. There's quite a list of things that Patience will need help with, so we thought it best to divide the jobs up a bit. There are some things I'm sure you can help with too. Would that be all right?' she asks.

'Of course,' I say, wondering what to add.

Fliss's smile is warm in reply. 'Lizzie, no one blames you for this – it was a mistake, that's all. You and I both know you wrote that order down. Where it's got to now is beyond me, but these things happen, and I'm sorry I snapped at you earlier. Please don't worry about it.'

There's quite a crowd in the kitchen, once we've all gathered together: Patience, Fliss, Ellie, Helen, Patrick, Ben, Finn and myself. The teapot has been emptied and a good chunk of a delicious orange and almond cake devoured. Lunch, apart from the apple, never happened after all, and any tea will be a good while away yet.

Fliss took charge almost as soon as we sat down, bringing her big notebook out again. Not the one that she keeps for Ellie's wedding stuff, but another one with butterflies all over it. She seems to have a never-ending supply of them.

During the afternoon she and Patience had written down everything that would be required to make each item on the order. Then they looked at what Patience already had in stock, and made a list of what they would now need. It was a very long list apparently, and buying everything on it would be the first job. After that they made what Fliss called a production schedule, which would tell them when they needed to make each product and in what order. It was to stop them all getting confused.

'So this shows us what we need to make first, second, and so on, depending on the amount of time each item takes. That way we can decide which tasks can be got on with while we're waiting on something else, and we can all see where help will be needed along the way. As well as the help with sourcing ingredients, as I've just explained.' All heads turn to look at Fliss and nod in unison.

'I'm your man for supplies,' volunteers Patrick, waving his car keys. 'Where do you get all this stuff from, Patience?'

'Birmingham mostly,' she moans, pulling a face. 'Some of the oils, the solvents. My containers too.'

'Make me an idiot's buying guide and a list of addresses. Then tomorrow me and my satnav will do the rest.'

'But some of these places are on industrial estates. They're not open to the general public and I don't think you can just go along and buy stuff. I have to phone my orders through.'

'So we'll ring them first and explain how urgent this is.' He grins. 'I can be very persuasive when I want to be.'

'The only problem is, I don't get them all from Birmingham,' Patience adds in a quiet voice.

'Oh well, no problem. I'll go wherever.'

'Cambridge?'

'Oh, bloody hell, Patience,' exclaims Ellie.

'I know, I know. It's a particular oil that I can't get from anywhere else. It comes from a small specialist, but it's the key ingredient in the eczema cream, which is also the thing that takes the longest to make. It's not a problem when I have time to order it advance, but now . . .'

Ellie looks straight at Finn and Ben. 'You two didn't have anything planned for tomorrow, did you?' she says.

'Ellie, it's a six-hour round trip!' protests Finn.

'I'll make you some sandwiches.' She grins. 'It's a lovely day for a drive in the country. Besides which, you pair can charm anything out of anybody.'

Patience heaves a heartfelt sigh. 'So true. Sex on legs, I think I called you once. Such a shame—'

Helen giggles, glancing at Finn, who stares at Patience open-mouthed. I'm looking at Patrick, who is actually blushing at Patience's words, and I wonder whether anyone else has noticed.

Fliss looks at her list once more. 'Right, so Patrick, Ben and Finn on supplies. Helen, are you okay to get going on the fabric front? And then us ladies are at Patience's beck and call picking herbs.' She looks up, smiling. Somehow I know her last statement doesn't include me.

'Is there something I can help with?' I ask, if only so that Patience will know that I've offered.

I'm not imagining the pause in conversation that goes on longer than it should, nor the look that Ellie gives Fliss before she replies.

'What I would love for you to do is to help out with the cakes, Lizzie, if you could,' she says. 'We've been saying for a while that you should have a go at making some on your own, and it's going to be really difficult for me to be in two places at once. So how about we make you tea-room manageress for a few days, cake-making and all.'

I don't know why I'm surprised really, but I guess I'm not quite forgiven for my 'mistake' after all. Ellie can dress up her last statement any way she wants, but whatever they had already decided between themselves, it's clear that my help isn't really wanted. I'm holding the fort, and she and I both know it.

'I thought I might find you here,' comes a voice from across the room. I look up in surprise, not just because the voice was suddenly loud in the quiet space, but also because I wasn't aware that anyone knew I had taken to coming in here apart from Patrick.

'I don't blame you. It's a nice little corner, isn't it?' Ben comes forwards to sit in the seat opposite me.

I'm curled in the corner of Patrick's workshop, sitting back with my feet up on an enormous rocking chair to one side of his fireplace. A cushion and blanket are keeping me company, along with my book, which is propped on my legs. Patrick's only just left and, although it's not cold, the fire he lights every day is still glowing faintly. The smell of the wood around me is warm and comforting.

'By my reckoning, you haven't had any lunch or tea, so I thought these might help.' Ben places a mug of hot chocolate and a pizza box on the table between us. 'Although Finn has pinched all the pepperoni, of course – sorry.'

I lay the book back down in my lap. 'Patrick knows I'm here,' I say. 'I lock everything up when I go.'

'Mm, I know,' Ben replies, staring at the embers of the fire. He doesn't seem to want to say anything else.

'I come here quite a bit,' I continue. 'Patrick doesn't always go home straight away at the end of the day, and he's nice to talk to. I help him tidy up sometimes too.'

Still Ben says nothing.

'Maybe it's because he was the first person I met when I came here – I dunno – but I like this place.'

Ben leans forwards and picks up the mug, holding it out to me. 'Here, don't let this get cold,' he says, smiling as I take it. 'There's no hope for the pizza, I'm afraid.'

''S okay . . . I like cold pizza,' I reply. 'Thank you.'

He looks at me properly then, for the first time since he came in here. His eyes are very dark in the dim light, but soft.

'Do you know the expression "a little cog in a big wheel", Lizzie?' he asks, finally.

'I've heard it,' I say, staring at the froth on top of the chocolate. I take a swallow. It's deliciously sweet. 'And although I probably don't understand exactly what it means, I know you're only trying to make me feel better,' I add.

He pushes the pizza box towards me. 'And how do you know that then?'

I fix him with a stare. 'Because Patrick left just five minutes ago, and I got a pep talk from him too. About how I shouldn't always think the worst, and that I should be pleased I'm being left in charge of the tea room instead of thinking it's because no one wants my help. About how I should have more confidence and faith in myself; that my cakes will be amazing and I should see it as an opportunity to prove myself to everyone here, not that any proof were needed . . . Do I need to go on?'

Ben shuffles his feet on the floor. 'Ouch,' he says. 'And there's me just thinking you might like some pizza—'

'Liar,' I pout, although I can never be mad at Ben.

He gives me an answering wink. 'Patrick might just have a point, you know,' he says, softly.

I take a huge bite of pizza, chewing it slowly and rather enjoying keeping Ben waiting for my response. 'I do know that,' I say eventually.

His smile is gentle as he looks up at me. 'Then let me say something else instead. I'm not trying to be cute here, or judgemental, but why are you always so down on yourself, Lizzie? You've no reason to be, you know.'

My anger flares in an instant. 'No? You don't think so? Well, how about if your whole life everybody told you how shit you were, or that whenever anything went wrong it was always your fault? I got blamed for living and breathing. I was the reason me mum never had a job, never had any money, drank like a fish and poisoned herself with drugs, cos if she hadn't had me, her life would have been so much better . . .' The words pour from me like lava. 'And then she went and fucking died and that was my fault as well . . . cos I just couldn't keep her safe . . . She just wouldn't listen . . .'

Ben's arms go around me in an instant, and I sob into the chest of the only person I have ever shared my pain with. 'All I ever tried to do was to get us out of the gutter,' I hiccup, 'but it's so hard when all everybody else tries to do is put you back there.'

'Oh, Lizzie,' murmurs Ben as he strokes my hair. 'I'm so sorry . . . I didn't know, but you're safe now, away from all that, and no one here will ever make you go back. That I can promise.'

I cling to him even tighter. If only that were true.

We stay that way for some while, until a sudden sneeze takes me by surprise and I pull away, searching for a tissue up my sleeve. Ben hands me his in an instant.

'Please don't tell anyone,' I whisper.

'Tell anyone what?' Ben replies, wiping a stray tear from the end of my chin. He gives me a soft smile. 'I only came in here to make sure you got something to eat. We had a nice chat, and then I left you reading, simple as.'

He picks up the book from my lap, where it's become a little crushed. 'I hope you know that no one is judging you, Lizzie. We all want you to be happy here; you're as much a part of Rowan Hill now as the rest of us, and your past can only hurt you if you cling on to it rather than let it go. Take the opportunity you've been given, even if today it's hard to see what that might be.'

I manage a small smile and offer him my tissue. 'I don't suppose you want this back, do you?'

He wrinkles his nose. 'I think I can live without it. So think about what Patrick and I have said this evening – we're on your side, you know. And on that note I really will leave you to your book. Don't stay here too long.'

'I won't.' I smile. 'Thanks, Ben, really – thank you.'

He nods. 'No problem. Sweet dreams, Lizzie,' he calls, and is gone.

I stare down at the book in my hands, and the bookmark that has fallen out of it once again. You can tell a lot about a person from the books they read, I think to myself, unfurling my legs from the chair. It's time I wasn't here; I have a lot of thinking to do.

Chapter 20

Lizzie

I start with the cakes, early in the morning while it's quiet. I've made some with Ellie a few times now, so I should be able to do it. I won't be able to chat to people and do six other things at the same time, of course, but if I concentrate and take my time I should be okay. The book of recipes is propped on the side and I read each one through carefully, until I have a list of five that aren't as difficult as some of the others. I tie my apron on, take a sip of my coffee, and reach for the bag of flour.

I don't notice it at first, perhaps because I'm so busy, or more likely because I'm so nervous of messing up the cakes, but as the morning ticks by I begin to relax again and get into the rhythm of weighing and mixing. I find myself stopping every now and then, like I'm listening out for something, but there's nothing there. It's a strange feeling. And one that doesn't go away.

At eleven I stop and plate up five cakes, sending Helen a quick text to let her know they're here. A row of kisses comes back, and minutes later she rushes in, her face flushed, busy but grateful, then rushes out again to make sure everyone has their mid-morning pick-up. I turn out a lemon sponge and clean the kitchen.

By one o'clock the sandwiches are on plates, along with some salad on the side and a few crisps. I text Ellie, who races in, asks if I'm all right, gives me a hug and rushes off with everyone's lunch. I finish the rest of the crisps, turn out a carrot cake and some brownies, and clean the kitchen again.

At three thirty, Bonnie comes over and we cut a little melon into chunks, slice up a few apples, and add these to bowls with a few grapes. She very kindly offers to deliver them to everyone for me. I take the last tray of scones out of the oven and have a cup of tea.

Five o'clock comes and I say a cheery goodbye to the last of the customers, put the chairs up on the tables and cut up the last of the shortbread. I sit at one of the tables for just a minute, and then when I've convinced myself this weird feeling is not my imagination, I get up to check that all the cakes are wrapped, collect the vases from the tables, ready for fresh flowers in the morning, and go and fill the mop bucket with hot soapy water.

I thought I'd feel on top of the world, like I'd had a Christmas and birthday present all at the same time. I've had a brilliant day; I've done everything that Ellie does, I haven't spilled or broken anything, and I'm pretty sure all our customers were happy. I've cleaned and made cakes, and remembered everything else I'm supposed to. But still something is missing. I don't feel happy, or elated by my successes today. I just feel flat; Rowan Hill feels flat.

I lock up the tea room, slipping my bunch of keys back into my pocket and, although I had originally intended to make my way back to the main house, I find myself reaching for the latch on Ben's workshop instead. I know why. There's too much buzzing around my head, and Ben and his calm ordered workspace are just what I need to untangle the knot of thoughts in there. There's no sign of Ben, but my stool is right where I had left it the day before, and without even thinking I take up my seat beside it and reach for a fresh piece of sandpaper. The rhythmic movement of the paper against the grain of the wood is soothing, and I let my mind wander back over the events of the day, lost in the quiet space around me. I continue for a few moments more before pausing and blowing gently at the small drifts of wood dust I've made, watching as they billow gently away from me, the only movement in the room.

I look back up at the familiar workshop, a space that has remained undisturbed today until now, and I suddenly long to be elsewhere. I stand, my mind now clear, and let my eyes roam around the room, giving it one final check before moving purposefully for the door.

Today felt weird because the people were not where they're supposed to be. I hardly spoke to a soul, apart from customers, and that's not right. I'm on my way back to the kitchen in the main house but I stop and look back at the courtyard, lifting my chin towards the sky, my eyes suddenly filling with tears at the thought of how easily this could all end. I understand now that it's the combination of people here who make the difference, the people who give Rowan Hill its voice. It needs the right people to keep it turning, and it needs someone with the right kind of eyes and ears to look out for it when those people are too busy to do so. I think about that day at Attingham Park and how Ellie told me that they were all so busy she was scared that they would forget to feel how special Rowan Hill is, and how to listen to what it has to say. The trouble is, I'm even more scared of what might happen if Rowan Hill changes, if it stops saying those things we need to hear.

Suddenly, holding the fort seems like the most important job in the world.

It's the most amazing smell, like walking into everything that makes up a summer's day all stuffed into a jar. Ellie is sitting at the kitchen table surrounded by herbs of every variety, which cover the huge table in a blanket of green. She has a stem of something in her hand, picking off the leaves one by one. It reminds me of when I was at school, and we sat out on the playing field at lunchtime with our skirts rolled up to get our legs in the sun. Picking the petals off a daisy; *he loves me, he loves me not.*

There's a cup of cold tea on the table beside Ellie, and a banana skin with half the banana left in it. She looks like she hasn't moved for a while, but her smile is bright as she looks up.

'Is everything okay?' she asks, and then, panicked, 'Oh my God, is that the time? The boys will be home in a bit, and I haven't even begun to think about tea yet.'

I smile reassuringly. 'That's fine, I'll sort something out.' I take a deep breath. 'How are you doing? It smells gorgeous in here.'

Ellie looks a bit surprised. 'You know, it's sad, I can't even smell it any more. Definite nose overload, but we're pretty much there, I think. Well, the picking and sorting . . . Tomorrow we've got to try and dry this lot.'

She pulls off another couple of leaves, checking them first before laying them down to join the others.

'Has everything gone all right today? I'm so sorry I haven't been able to spend any time with you at all.' She pulls a face. 'I didn't realise this would take quite so long.'

'Well, I didn't poison anyone, stab anyone with a fork or throw their cake at them, so I think it's been a good day.'

She nods absentmindedly.

I wait for a few seconds, until her head shoots up, and I laugh. 'No, seriously, it's been a great day. No drama, lots of folks eating and drinking.'

She puts the stem down in her lap and smiles properly then. 'That'll teach me.' She grins. 'Maybe it's time to stop now.'

'I think it's definitely time to stop now. Listen, why don't you go and have a shower or something, and I can start to make tea?'

'I can't do that—'

'Why not?'

'Well, because—' she glances around the room as if that might help her decide what to say. She looks back at me, and gives a helpless shrug.

'Do you know, if you really don't mind, that would be absolutely wonderful.' She gives a small smile and rises stiffly from the chair. 'I don't suppose you know someone who'd like nothing more than to give me a full body massage, do you? Ah well, never mind, it was worth a try.'

I wave her away, a bubble of happiness growing inside me. Now I just need to not stuff up the tea.

Finn and Ben appear first, the back door banging open as they saunter through the door. Finn stares around, trying to adjust his vision from the brightness of the day outside, while Ben dashes through the kitchen. 'Sorry, back in a minute. I'm desperate for a pee!'

He returns a few minutes later with Ellie, who looks much more awake now, I'm pleased to see.

'I've been praying that there's beer in the fridge for the last twenty miles,' says Finn, crossing the kitchen to look.

'Thank God,' Ben adds, taking a bottle from him.

'How did you get on?' asks Ellie.

Finn fishes in his jacket pocket and produces a small brown parcel.

'Mission accomplished. This is on the list just below gold dust apparently, but job done, as they say.'

'Thank you. I'm sorry for hustling you off to get this, but it means a lot to Patience.'

Finn waves his hand. 'It's no problem. We wanted nothing more than to sit on the motorway for six hours. We've had a lovely afternoon.'

Ben tuts. 'He's just teasing, Ellie. It was fine. The traffic was very light and we were treated to tea and toasted teacakes while we were there. I think the lady took pity on us.'

I raise an eyebrow. 'Nice lady, was she?'

'Very nice,' confirms Ben, nudging Finn. 'Took a bit of a shine to you, didn't she . . . as did her dog.'

Finn grimaces.

'A beautiful English setter by the name of Daisy,' adds Ben.

'Who sat on my lap the entire time we were there, tea, toasted teacakes and all.'

'Well, Patience will be very appreciative of your sufferance on her behalf,' grins Ellie.

Ben stares at the kitchen table. 'What's this? Some kind of weird health-food kick for tea, is it?'

'Not exactly,' laughs Ellie. 'I'll explain later. Actually, I don't know what we're having for tea. Lizzie is treating us.'

I move away from the worktop so that they can see behind me. 'I didn't have much time, I'm afraid, but I think you all like this. I made some tomato salad to go with it, and there's bread as well.'

Ben comes over, breaking into a low chuckle. 'What a bloody star! She's only gone and made chicken Caesar salad.' He swipes a chunk of chicken out of the bowl with a wink. 'Do you know this just about makes up for playing second fiddle to a big hairy dog and its "old enough to be my mother" owner all afternoon.'

Finn blows a kiss from across the room as Ellie snorts into her beer. I turn back to the food so that Ben doesn't see the grin on my face and start to dish up.

I don't know why I'm awake. I thought I'd need a bomb to wake me up after yesterday's sleepless night and the busy day today, but I'm gradually aware that not only am I awake, but I'm listening for something. A quick glance at my clock confirms that it's nearly one in the morning. Everything seems quiet, and yet something has woken me. It's not normal wakefulness either; it's not that sleepy turning over sort of wakefulness that lets you go straight back to sleep, nor is it of the too hot/too cold variety. I lie still, not wanting even a rustle of my duvet to cause me to miss a further clue, and then I hear it again. A bump from below me, somewhere down in the courtyard. I fling back the covers and reach for my trainers.

I look out of the window first, but the little pools of light in the courtyard are steady. Nothing crosses them, no unexpected shadows. I flick on the light on my phone, pressing my hand against it for now, and move slowly to the front door. There's a tiny click as I open the door, but then nothing. I hold my breath, but the seconds stretch out, and I let them go, knowing that as soon as I step out, a loud creak from the wooden stairs will sound out across the courtyard. Still nothing.

I've reached the bottom of the courtyard now and am looking out down the lane towards the car park, but it's empty too, just like the rest of the yard. I've walked the whole way round, and everything looks just as it should. I even stand under the shelter by Patrick's workshop for a few minutes, hidden in the darkness there, but apart from the chime of the church clock and the odd car passing, the night is silent. A sudden loud buzzing makes me almost jump out of my skin. I look down at my phone, still in my hand. A message flashes up.

Lizzie, what are you doing?

I look up at the window on my right, where I know Ellie must be standing.

Can I come to the kitchen?

I reply, and as I look, I catch her face turned towards me in the moonlight.

Yes x.

177

She lets me into the dim room, lit only by the under-cupboard lights. Her face looks tired and agitated.

'What were you doing out there?' she asks, pulling me further into the kitchen.

'I heard a noise outside, like a door banging shut.'

'You shouldn't go out to investigate things like that by yourself, Lizzie. Ring one of us, okay?'

'I didn't want to wake anyone,' I say, looking at her bare feet. 'Couldn't you sleep either?'

'No, not really . . .' She trails off.

'Did you hear it too then?'

'No . . . I was looking out of the window, that's all. I saw you.' She looks a bit distracted. 'Just missing Will, you know; feeling sorry for myself.' She gives a weak smile.

'Shall I put the kettle on and make us a cup of tea?'

Ellie looks at the back door and nods. 'I might go and wake Finn or Ben, just to be on the safe side. They can do a quick check.'

I perch on the edge of a kitchen chair as she disappears, before returning shortly with Finn behind her. He's still pulling the belt around his dressing gown.

'Where was the noise coming from, Lizzie?' he asks, dragging a hand over his face.

'I don't know. The other side of the courtyard maybe, but there's nothing there. I checked.'

Finn and Ellie exchange looks.

'I've already told her it wasn't a great idea,' she says.

I frown. 'Honestly, I'm not a pushover, you know. I've fought off enough of me mum's drunken boyfriends before now. Anyone messes with me and I give as good as I get.'

'I'll go and give the place the once-over anyway; it wouldn't hurt,' says Finn.

He reappears about ten minutes later as Ellie and I sip our tea in silence.

'All as it should be,' he announces. 'Rattled all the doors, and everything's secure. There's no one around.'

'I wasn't making it up.'

'No one thinks you were, Lizzie, but I expect it was just a cat or something. If it ever happens again, ring across for one of us. It would be awful if something happened to you.'

'Or to one of you,' I reply. 'You're the ones in the big posh house, not me,' I add, thinking he's rather missing the point. 'That's why it's good me being over there. I can keep an eye on things.'

Finn doesn't reply straight away, but I don't miss the surprised look he gives Ellie. 'I think we must all look after one another,' he says eventually, 'and you're on your own, so no playing the hero. I think we would all rather you were safe.'

Ellie touches my arm. 'Come on, drink up,' she says, 'and Finn can walk you back home. We've all got an early start in the morning.'

Whatever else I'm thinking, this is most certainly true.

Chapter 21

Lizzie

'But I really hadn't made any assumptions about the flowers, Fliss. Why would I? What's important is that Ellie and Will have beautiful arrangements, and they obviously know what they want . . . which is exactly what I said to Ellie when we talked about it.'

Fliss fiddles with a button on her cardigan as she steps aside to let me pass. 'Oh, well, just ignore me then. I must have got it wrong. Don't worry.'

Patience is standing in the middle of her studio, her hands on her hips. I look from one to the other, knowing that now might not be the right time to open my mouth, but I can see that Patience is not about to let it go.

'Wait a minute,' she says, as Fliss turns to leave. 'What did she say?'

'Well, nothing really. She seemed a bit stressed this morning, that's all. She was a bit off with me actually. I know she didn't mean to, but she mentioned something about the flowers and I wondered if there was a problem. No worries; it can't have been you that upset her.'

'No, it wasn't,' pouts Patience.

'She seemed fine when I saw her this morning,' I interrupt, keen to smooth the prickles. 'Maybe she's tired.'

'She did mention she hadn't slept very well,' agrees Fliss. 'Between you and me, I don't think she's coping with Will being away, poor thing. It must be awful for her.'

I think back to her words last night. I hadn't really noticed any change in her before, but perhaps Ellie is finding things much harder without Will than she's letting on.

'We'll all keep an eye on her, Fliss, don't worry.'

She smooths down the front of her skirt. 'I know you will,' she says. 'Now please promise you'll let me know if there's anything I can do to help today, Patience. Sorry I've got to run, but my client can only do early mornings.' She beams a smile into the room, and disappears through the door. Patience looks horrified.

'Are you sure you're all right?' I ask. 'I'm sure Fliss didn't mean—'

She flaps her hand at me, rings sparkling in the early sunshine.

'No, it's not that . . . I can't believe I've forgotten about them,' she moans. 'I've got clients in myself all day today and tomorrow as well . . . I'll have to cancel them . . . I can't possibly do—' She looks through to her still room, the surfaces of which are covered with all manner of boxes, bottles and tubs of ingredients, ready to be transformed into her magical potions.

'Give me your appointment book,' I say. 'I can cancel them for you. It's only early, and people will understand. I can say you're poorly or something.'

Patience's eyes grow round. 'Would you?' she says, blinking at me. 'Oh, that would be brilliant, if you could. One less thing for me to worry about.' She fishes in the desk drawer behind her. 'Listen, don't worry about rebooking anything. Just apologise and say I'll be in touch in a day or two.' She holds out the book for me, her hand wavering for a moment. I'm still not sure she totally trusts me; despite me constantly saying sorry, she probably thinks I'm going to make a mess of things. I can see she's running through all the things she has to do in her head and, just as importantly, what everyone else is doing too.

'Ellie and I have got the herb drying sorted between us. We're going to take it in turns, so you don't need to worry about that either.'

She flashes me a grateful, if slightly nervous smile. 'You're such a star, Lizzie. Thank you so much. I meant to say yesterday how lovely it was with all that food you made for us. It made such a difference.'

I can feel my cheeks beginning to colour a little. Perhaps she has forgiven me after all. 'I'll see if I can bring lunch again today. Now sit down with a cup of tea before you start, and have a few minutes to yourself. You'll feel clearer about things if you do.'

For a minute I think Patience is going to well up, but then she gives a shake of her head. 'God, what am I like?' she says. 'That's a very wise head you've got on your shoulders there, Lizzie. I'll do just that. And let me know if there are any problems today. I don't want Ellie to feel even more stressed than she already is.'

'I will,' I say, nodding.

✲

It looks like Ellie is in sore need of her cup of tea too. She seemed all right first thing, but perhaps a lack of sleep is catching up with her now. Either way, she looks a bit sorry for herself as she sits confronted by what looks like a million green leaves, all of which need to be dried today. She's staring at her hair slide, which also sits on the edge of the table, but the beautiful nuggets of red, gold and yellow amber must be a blur; she's not really looking at it at all. I know it reminds her of Will, and judging by the expression on her face, she's missing him dreadfully. He gave it to her the first year she came to Rowan Hill, a magical Christmas before they even got together, and it was only then that she realised the strength of his feelings for her. She caught me staring at it once and let me look at it properly; it's very pretty, but to her I think it's the most precious thing she's ever owned.

Ellie's gaze switches back to the table as I come and sit down beside her, and I can see her mentally shoving her thoughts back into the box she's been keeping them in. I do wish she would talk to me.

'Now, are we sure we know what we're doing with all this?' she asks.

'I think so,' I reply, looking down at the trays in front of us. We've spent the first hour this morning rechecking for any damaged and discoloured leaves and then laying out each batch of herbs in a single layer on wire racks, ready to be dried. I read through Patience's instructions one last time.

'Are you sure this is going to work?' I ask.

'Well, it's not how she normally does it, but she knows lots of people who oven-dry their herbs, and it seems to work for them. I don't think we really have any other choice. They're probably better if they're dried more slowly, but we simply don't have the time. It's this or nothing.'

I pull a face. 'Yeah, thanks for reminding me.' No pressure at all, I think. Ellie and I are in charge of checking the racks every half-hour and rotating them. The temperature has to be really low, so we're using the Aga's bottom oven on a very low heat, but it's not a tried and tested method unfortunately. Patience will have to check them carefully.

'Right, well, I'll load this lot and then pop over to the Lodge to make sure Finn has lit the Aga over there.'

It's going to take several hours to dry each batch of herbs, so we need all the help we can get. The Lodge might be looking like a building site at the moment but the Aga is still in place, and that's all that matters. I head over as soon as I can, popping the kitchen timer in my jacket pocket.

Despite the warm sunshine of early morning, the day is already beginning to cloud over, with a forecast of rain later – not the kind of day we need at all. Sure enough, by the time I've crossed the courtyard, I can smell the coming rain.

The weather never completely stops work at Rowan Hill. There's always plenty to do inside and out, and even now Finn and Ben have headed out to replace a gate. I hope that by the time the rain comes they'll be finished. The tea room will be quieter too, and that's no bad thing. Our herb-drying duties are going to seriously limit the time we can spend on anything else today, and I'm glad I made up enough cakes yesterday to see us through. We'll be opening soon, but I've just got enough time to start ringing around Patience's customers.

I get to the tea room only moments ahead of Ellie, a little worried to find the door already open, but by the time she arrives my slight anxiety has turned to shock as I stare at the counter. When I left late yesterday afternoon, everything was in its rightful place. I most certainly did not leave the leftover cakes on the side, uncovered and now – my touch confirms – hard and rather crispy on the surface. I flick my eyes around the room, but there are no more surprises that I can see on first glance.

'Oh, for goodness' sake, Lizzie, this is basic stuff!'

If she wasn't standing by my side, I would never have guessed it was Ellie; I've never heard her speak like this before.

'These are all completely ruined. How could you leave it like this?'

'Er, I didn't.' I might have masked the sarcasm in my voice a little more if I wasn't so pissed off. 'These were all put away, as they should have been. I didn't bloody slave my guts out yesterday only to make more sodding work for myself this morning.'

Ellie ignores me. 'Well, what the hell are we going to serve first thing, until I can get some more made?'

I push past her, moving to the other side of the counter, where I pick up one of the offending cake stands and carry it through to the kitchen. What a waste. I intend to make a lot more noise opening and closing the bin than is entirely necessary, and the first half of a Victoria sponge, thrown from a height, makes a satisfying thud as it hits the bottom of the fresh bin bag.

To my left a cupboard door is yanked open and a bag of flour removed and dumped onto the work surface. I can feel Ellie's glare on the side of my face. She reaches in again to remove something else, at which point I pick up the flour, and pull open the other side of the cupboard and put it straight back again.

'Being childish isn't going to help, Lizzie. I haven't got time for this.'

'No, but perhaps if you stopped jumping to conclusions and bothered to look in the cool room you'd find the five, yes, count them, five batches of cakes I made yesterday.'

It's as if time rewinds for a moment, as Ellie replays the last few minutes in her head, looking between me and the door to the cool room. She doesn't want to be right, but then she doesn't want to be wrong either. It's the lesser of two evils. Her hand goes to her mouth, and for a horrible moment I think she might be about to cry, but then she fixes me with her green eyes and a soft smile.

'You didn't leave all that mess out there, did you? And I've just made a complete prat of myself. No, worse, I've been rude and insulting, and if I were you, I'd either slap me or never speak to me again.'

She makes me laugh. Ellie couldn't be rude or obnoxious if she tried, not really, but for some reason she's not her usual sunny self. A cup of tea might help, or a hot chocolate, I think; that's an even better idea.

My hand is on the door to the cool room, before it occurs to me that all might not be well inside. I mean, if I made sure the cakes were all put away last night before I left, and then when I get here this morning they're not . . . My heart is in my mouth as I pull open the door, and for a minute I imagine scenes reminiscent of a cake fight – lemon icing dripping from the walls and sultanas slowly falling to the ground from their sticking place on the ceiling. But the room is cool and ordered. Just as it should be.

Ellie almost crashes into my back as she rushes to the door in haste. 'Is everything okay?' she asks, panicked.

I step aside to let her pass beside me. 'It's fine, don't worry. I just thought for a minute that—'

She lays a hand on my arm. 'I know,' she says, moving into the room and looking around her. When she turns back to me, her eyes are bright with tears this time.

'I can't believe you've done all this, Lizzie. It's amazing, just look at it all . . . They look beautiful!'

'Did I do okay?' I ask shyly.

'Oh yes,' nods Ellie, grinning. 'You did very okay.' She comes across to give me a hug. 'I am so, so sorry,' she says. 'I've been an absolute bitch to everyone this morning. I don't know what's the matter with me.'

I look at her anxious face. 'I do – but I'm not sure a hug from me is going to make much difference. We could have a drink, and you could tell me about it?'

She nods, with a rueful smile. 'I'll get the milk, and then apart from moaning like a lovesick teenager, we can try to work out what on earth happened here this morning.'

I must have left the door open – that's the only explanation I can come up with. As far as I know I was the first one over here this morning, and yet the door was already open when I arrived. It feels wrong, though; it feels like the sort of thing I used to do, and while I can accept it's possible I *did* leave the door open, I know I didn't leave all the leftover cakes uncovered. But if I didn't do it, then who did? If I hadn't made up those cakes yesterday we'd have been in real trouble this morning . . .

I'm still trying to gather together my rag-tag thoughts when Ellie hands me a mug.

'I'm probably over-reacting, I know that,' she begins, 'but I had an email from Will this morning, and it seemed . . . "Harsh" is the only way I can think to describe it. He certainly wasn't his usual self anyway. Let's put it like that. It's really upset me.'

'Maybe when he sent it he was in a rush or wasn't thinking. Things come over wrong in an email sometimes, don't they? Not like when you talk face to face or on the phone.'

'I thought that. It was sent very early this morning, and he is really busy . . . It just all seemed so confused: things I'm supposed to have said about the wedding, which I don't remember, and things he's supposed to have said for that matter. I don't know, maybe I'm just overtired.'

'What did he say?' I ask, looking at her pale face. 'Although don't tell me if you don't want to.'

Ellie starts to take a sip from her drink and then changes her mind, putting down her mug once more. 'Has he ever said anything to you about a honeymoon, about going to the Seychelles?' she asks.

Her question catches me by surprise and I look away quickly, pretending to study something on the counter. 'I don't think so,' I reply carefully. 'Why? Is that where you're going?'

'But that's just it, Lizzie. We're not going anywhere on our honeymoon, least of all to some fancy islands, and yet this morning Will wanted to know why I'd got this ridiculous idea into my head.'

I frown at her, puzzled. 'I'm not sure I'm with you,' I reply.

'He was cross with me because we'd agreed we weren't having a honeymoon, and now apparently I've changed my mind. According to Will I can change it back again because he's not going anywhere . . . but he's the one being ridiculous – I couldn't go to the Seychelles even if I wanted to. I don't have a passport, and he knows that.'

My ears prick up at the mention of Ellie's passport, but what she said doesn't sound quite right. I give an encouraging nod.

'It needs renewing, but there's no point doing it now before we get married, or I'll only have to change it again. I told him that when we first talked about going away, but then as we both agreed not to, it didn't matter anyway.'

'Oh, I see . . .' I say. 'Maybe Will just forgot?' I suggest.

Ellie frowns, and I can see it makes no sense to her. It makes no sense to me either, but why else would Will need Fliss to find out if Ellie had a passport? He must have forgotten. I study Ellie's face. There are tears in her eyes again, and I give her a hug. 'Look, why don't you have a chat with Fliss? She can put you straight about it, I'm sure, and anything else to do with the wedding that's bothering you. It's probably a misunderstanding, that's all.'

Ellie finally picks up her own mug and takes a reflective sip, before very deliberately placing it down again. She inhales deeply and gives me a reassuring smile, as if to say that normal service is being resumed.

'So what do you think happened here this morning, Lizzie?' she asks, changing the subject. 'It seems such a bizarre thing to just leave all the cakes uncovered. Had any of them been eaten?'

I stare at her. The thought had never even occurred to me.

'I honestly don't know,' I reply, trying to remember exactly how everything looked this morning. 'I was so cross, I just picked them all up and dumped them in the bin, but I don't think so . . . Although the door was unlocked when I got here.'

'And you locked it before you left last night.'

I pause just long enough for Ellie to tut. 'It wasn't a question, Lizzie. I'm sure you did. After the fab job you did in here yesterday, you wouldn't have forgotten that.'

I smile at her. 'I might have.'

She rolls her eyes. 'You might, but I don't think so . . . and anyway, that doesn't explain what happened with the cakes, does it?'

'No, I guess not.'

'And we'll probably never know either. It's not like we can finger-print everyone, is it?' She grins. 'So let's just forget about it for now; we've got more important things to think about today. I will check with everyone to see if they were over here first thing, but I doubt it; everyone else is madly busy too.' She pauses to take a deep breath, and looks at her watch. 'Right, let's make a start on these herbs for Patience, shall we?'

The rest of the morning passes quickly in a series of seemingly never-ending triangular trips between the tea room, the Lodge and the main house to check the herbs, and so far things seem to be progressing well. By lunchtime, though, the rain is falling in a steady curtain, and with each successive visit, although the herbs become drier, we become wetter.

I'm finishing a quick sandwich when my buzzer goes off again. 'Back in ten.' I smile at Ellie before grabbing my still-wet coat and heading out of the door.

The first of the herbs are all dried now, and their smell is pun-gent as I start to remove them from their trays. The lemon balm is a particular favourite of mine; it's a smell that I never tire of. Even on a wet day such as today, it reminds me of how a summer morn-ing should smell, fresh and bright. I can smell it on my fingers, and I crush a couple of leaves, crumbling the pieces into my palm to lift them to my nose, and for a moment their scent takes me to a place I can only ever dream of. Patience told me once that the herb grows wild on the hillsides in Italy – how amazing must it be waking to a new day there with the sun warming your skin in the gentle lemon-scented air. I lift my palm once more. Maybe one day I'll get to go and find out for myself.

I'm loading up the trays with a fresh batch of herbs ready for their stint in the oven, when a bedraggled-looking Ben appears.

'I've had enough of it out there today,' he says with a frown. 'I'm really not in the mood. I need to finish my dresser anyway, and this is as good an excuse as I'm likely to get. Even our hardy woodsman has sloped off to help Patience.'

I smile at his words, thinking of the number of times that I've popped in on her today and found Patrick somewhere in tow.

'And, yes, it hasn't gone unnoticed,' continues Ben, reading my mind.

'Aw, I think it's sweet,' I reply. 'Don't you?'

Ben just laughs. 'She'll eat him alive, poor man.'

'Probably,' I agree. 'But then maybe they're quite well suited. Patrick is like the calm after her storm.'

Ben ducks his head back out of the pantry.

'Have you seen my keys?'

'On the hook probably?'

'Yeah, I thought so too, but they're not there.'

'Well, they were there yesterday. When did you last have them?'

'Yesterday morning, I think,' says Ben, coming back into the kitchen. 'But I know I put them back then.'

'Well, you must have put them down somewhere. Why don't you take Ellie's for now? I expect they're in her handbag,' I nod, motioning towards the chair in the corner.

I slide the trays back into the oven, wedging the wooden spoon in the door to prevent it from closing. Right, next batch over at the Lodge.

'See you later, Ben,' I call.

Patience is melting another batch of cocoa butter as I walk through to her kitchen, and the scent of chocolate in the air is heavenly. It's enough to make your mouth water. I collected another batch of dried herbs from the Lodge as well, so now I think we might even have enough for Helen to start making up the little bean bags that will contain them. She's found the most beautiful fabric, covered with soft green, yellow and white flowers, and has spent the morning cutting out the cloth templates ready for sewing.

I lay the herbs out on the table so that Patience can pass judgement. I wait while she washes her hands again.

'How's it going?' I ask.

Her face brightens. 'Good, I think. We're gradually ticking things off the list, and so far it's all going according to plan – if anything, we're a bit ahead.'

'Well, I think these are good to go,' I say. 'Stick your nose in there; they smell amazing.'

'So what have we got?'

'Marjoram, lemon balm, camomile and rosemary so far,' I reel off, proud of myself. Two days ago I didn't even know what any of these were called. 'And the lavender isn't far off either. Can Helen make a start, do you think?'

'These are perfect, Lizzie, they're just perfect.' Patience's eyes are shining all of a sudden. 'I can't thank you enough, you know, and Ellie too. I can't believe you're all doing this for me.' She flaps a hand at her face. 'God, what a baby. Sorry.'

It doesn't seem right accepting praise when I feel responsible for all this manic activity. All I'm doing is trying to make amends. I've still so much to learn about everyone's businesses here; if it hadn't been for Alice's chance remark about Patience's order, she still might not even know about it. I can't believe I thought she would fill the order from the oodles of stock she had here, when it was bloody obvious that there was no oodles of stock anywhere. I should learn to open my eyes and stop making assumptions.

I give her a weak smile. 'No apology necessary. Just glad we can be here to help.'

'And there's no need for that look,' she replies, looking up at me through her lashes as if she's forgotten she's not wearing her reading glasses. 'The order going missing was a silly mix-up. Things get mislaid every day, so you need to stop berating yourself for it. I judge people by their actions, or their reactions, I should say, and you've more than made up for any mistake you might have made.' She holds up a handful of the herbs for me to smell. 'And here's the proof, if any were needed. Don't they smell wonderful?'

I breathe in the scent, feeling myself relax slightly. I smile again, but this time it turns the corners of my eyes up as well as my mouth.

'So that's settled then,' grins Patience, her words having a definite ring of finality about them. 'No more apologising and no more feeling bad about things. Is that a deal?'

I nod, several times over.

Patience hands me a large metal spoon. 'Come and give this a stir for me for a minute, can you? Gently, mind, and then you can help me with something else too. I just need to add a little almond oil.'

I wait while Patience measures out the oil into a small funnel-shaped jug and adds it to the mix. The smell intensifies. She motions for me to keep stirring.

'Now then. Ellie didn't seem her usual sunny self when she came over earlier, and Fliss clearly thought something had upset her too. When I asked her she muttered something about a mix-up with the honeymoon. I wondered if she'd said anything about it to you?'

'Only that she got an email from Will about it this morning which really upset her. She's been a bit snappy with people ever since, but I think it was just a misunderstanding.'

Patience nods, her face full of sympathy. 'I can understand why Will might not want to go away again, not after being away from here for so long. But a honeymoon's a bit different, isn't it? No wonder Ellie is upset.'

I stare up at her – she's obviously misunderstood too . . . But no sooner has the thought flitted through my head than I understand. Of course Will would have to pretend that he didn't want to go away. How else was he going to be able to keep his secret from Ellie? The trouble is that now she's got the wrong end of the stick. Oh crap. I can't say anything or it will ruin the surprise. I look up at Patience's waiting face. I should tell her really; I know she'll keep the secret, and maybe between the two of us we could make something up that would throw Ellie off the scent. But a promise is a promise, and I told Finn that I wouldn't say a word. Maybe it's him I need to speak to.

I'm just about to make some general reply to Patience when the door bangs open, and right on cue, Finn appears. But he does not look happy. Not at all.

Chapter 22

Lizzie

Finn gives Patience a quick half-smile, before grabbing my hand and fairly dragging me out.

'Hang on a minute, Finn. I've got stuff to sort out for Patience.'

'It can wait,' he says grimly. The look on his face convinces me it can. 'Where's Ellie?'

'In the tea room. Why? What's the matter?' I ask, pausing our march across the courtyard.

'Have you lent Ben's keys to anyone?'

'No. Why? Hasn't he found them yet?'

He shakes his head. 'Someone has, though.'

'What do you mean?'

Finn says no more as we reach the door to Ben's workshop. I look to him questioningly, but he stays silent, his mouth a thin hard line.

I'm not sure what I expect to see when I enter the room – carnage of one sort or another, I suppose – but all appears as it should. A few pieces of furniture stand, just as they always have, as a showcase for Ben's work, testament to his skill as a carpenter. Everything is neat and tidy, the usual warm woody smell filling the air. It's not until my eyes settle that I realise Finn and I are not the only ones in the room. Through the doorway, into the workshop proper, I can see what appear to be the soles of Ben's shoes, and as I take a couple of steps forwards I realise he's kneeling on the floor, almost as if he's praying.

I look to Finn for explanation, his jaw still clenched tight, his eyes dark with anger and something else: compassion, and unbelievable hurt carried for someone else.

I move forwards until I can see what Ben sees, and understand what has caused the colour to drain from his face so completely.

He's kneeling on the floor in front of the dresser he was working on. It's a stunning piece of furniture, a beautiful light oak, three cupboards underneath a top part with glass doors, and decorated here and there with the amazing Celtic carving for which Ben is rapidly becoming known. My eyes and fingers want to follow it forever.

And then I see it. The dark spreading stain from an overturned bottle. Like a poison it has spread, sinking into the soft welcoming wood that surrounds it. It's crept across the top surface, from one side to the other, where a great pool has gathered against the turned support for the cupboard above. The liquid has overflowed, seeping down the front of the cupboard in an almost perfect straight line. By the look of things, the bottle has been upturned for quite some time, and Ben has made no effort to remove it. It doesn't matter. The piece is utterly ruined. A violent heat rises up from my toes. How on earth could I have been so stupid and forgetful?

I move to kneel beside Ben, at a loss to know what to say. It feels like my heart is breaking too.

'Can you fix it?' I whisper. He doesn't look like he's noticed I'm even there, but there's a slight shake of the head. 'It's wood stain,' he says bitterly. 'It does what it says on the tin.'

'But can't you polish it out or something?'

'Look at it, Lizzie. It's been there for hours. It's deep into the grain. There's no way it can be removed.'

He looks at me then, looking for answers where he can find none. 'I don't understand why. That's all I want to know. Why someone would do this?'

I feel a small shiver ripple through me.

I look at Finn for a moment, panicked by Ben's words. He gives a slight shake of his head in warning, misunderstanding me. He's trying to stop me from asking the obvious. If you look around this workshop its plain to see what kind of a craftsman Ben is. His tools hang on their hooks, where they are returned each evening. His oils and solvents are kept in a cupboard that stands against one wall. The door is closed. Even the floor is swept clean from dust and shavings. There's no way he would have left the wood stain out where it is now.

'What do you think happened, Ben?' I ask.

'Well, it's bloody obvious, isn't it, Lizzie? Come on, think about it,' interrupts Finn, his voice strident. 'Think back to last night. Bit of a coincidence, don't you think?'

It takes me a moment to fully understand what he's saying. I struggle to form a reply.

'What other explanation is there?' demands Finn. 'Someone must have come in here during the night.'

'I didn't leave it like that,' says Ben.

'No, I know,' I say softly, knowing that to accuse Ben of such slap-dash behaviour would be almost as bad as having the dresser ruined. It's not his fault.

'And I can't find my keys either,' Ben adds, as I feel my eyes fill with tears.

I realise we're both still on our knees, and I reach out to offer him my hand, rocking back on my heels to make ready to stand and hoping he'll come with me.

'There has to be some other explanation, Ben. It must have been some sort of an accident, surely?' I say.

Ben lurches to his feet all of a sudden.

'I didn't realise I was so disliked,' he says coldly.

I exchange horrified looks with Finn.

'Ben, how you can you think that!' I say, shocked. 'We all love you. This hasn't got anything to do with you. It was just an accident. It wasn't personal.'

'Well, it may as well have been. I'm not some two-bit chippy, churning out mass-produced mediocrity. Everything I have is in that piece, same as it is in all of them. It's as simple as that, and everyone here knows it.'

Finn takes a step closer.

'Ben,' he starts, but gets no further before Ben pushes past both of us and stalks from the room. I look at Finn, hating to see the anguish in his eyes and knowing that he feels even more helpless than I do.

'I'm so sorry, Finn. I don't know what to say. Shall I go and get Ellie?'

He nods absentmindedly. 'Although I don't suppose there's anything she can do either. Perhaps later on, when Ben's had a chance to calm down, he might take another look and see if there's a chance of salvaging something.'

I nod sadly.

'I should go,' adds Finn, looking at the door.

'Yes,' I whisper, knowing that wherever Ben has gone, Finn will find him. Finn is the only one who can comfort him now.

I stand alone for a few moments, looking at the still room, and then I walk quietly back out into the rain.

Ellie says she will wait until after closing time to tell everyone, so the afternoon wears on just like any other. Laughter still rings out around the place as people move about their business: Patience and Fliss are hard at work in Patience's kitchen; Helen distributes cake for me before going back to her sewing; and Bonnie picks strawberries for everyone as a late-afternoon treat. Ellie and I move between them all, drying racks of herbs, turning them, rotating the trays and checking them over and again. But none of it feels real. I see and hear it all as if I'm under water, swimming through crashing waves that are trying to suck me under, the roaring in my ears almost unbearable at times. I want to turn the clock back to when none of this had happened, but I can't; it's already done. And what's done can't be undone.

At the end of the day, Ellie tells them all what has happened quickly and quietly, with the minimum of detail, and I hate myself even more for watching their faces closely as she does so. But all I see reflected there is confusion and sadness, not the guilt I was looking for.

'Wait till I catch the little fucker,' snarls Patience, voicing what everyone seems to feel. 'They'll wish they'd never been born. How could someone do this to Ben of all people?'

'I don't know. It must have been an accident; anything else is unthinkable,' Ellie says.

She shoots me a warning glance and I know why. She doesn't want to tell anyone about the noises we heard last night. That would be a step too far. The last thing any of them need to worry about are intruders. Much better to believe that a member of the public got into Ben's workshop during the day. Everyone's livelihoods are here, after all.

They all want to help and they all want to know where Ben is, but we have nothing to offer them, and after a little while their shared sense of helplessness becomes uncomfortable.

'Listen, I promise to tell you if I hear any more, but I don't think there's anything any of us can do,' adds Ellie. 'You may as well go home; there's still an awful lot to do tomorrow.'

'I feel really guilty now,' says Patience. 'Perhaps if we hadn't all been so busy sorting out my mess, we would have noticed something.'

Heads are shaken, including my own.

'You mustn't think like that,' comforts Ellie. 'It makes no difference, and it will be good for all of us to keep busy over the next few days – and that includes Ben. He's taken this very personally; it's important to show him how much we all depend on him.'

In a moment or two there's just me and Ellie left. I eye the room wearily; I just want to escape.

'I'll stay and help,' I say. 'I can do the floor if you like?'

She smiles at me gratefully, not welcoming the thought of these last few jobs of the day either.

'Only if you're sure, Lizzie. You've had a long day too, running backwards and forwards.'

'It's all right,' I say, biting my lip.

We're almost finished when the door opens again and Finn appears.

'He's back at the house,' he announces to Ellie's unspoken question.

'Is he okay?'

'Well, I found him beating the crap out of a tree, so I think he feels a little better now he's vented some of his anger, but I don't suppose it makes any real difference.'

'No, I guess not,' she says. 'I can't believe that anyone could do this to Ben. None of us can. I don't know if there's anything we can do to help, but I hope Ben knows that he only has to ask if he needs anything.'

'I'm not really sure he's even thought that far ahead, to be honest. For now he's reeling from the shock, and I think all we can do is carry on as normal and let things subside a little.'

She nods at him in agreement before turning back to me. 'Come on. You get away home now. I'll finish the rest.'

I don't argue, and shrug on my raincoat. Ellie looks dead on her feet, and I don't suppose she's looking forward to this evening either, but she still smiles at me reassuringly.

A sudden sharp noise fills the quiet room, like the cry of an injured child, and as I pull my hand slowly from my jacket pocket, I realise that it's me. I gasp for the breath that seems to have left my body. In my palm lies not one but two sets of keys: one belonging to me, and the other dangling from a worn oval bezel of rosewood. It's a set of keys all of us would know at a glance – and unmistakably those belonging to Ben.

Ellie's eyes fix on mine, widening in a horror that mirrors my own, as the enormity of my discovery hits her too. She shakes her head and holds out her trembling hand for the keys, but they're suddenly so heavy that I can barely find the strength to hold them. As she stretches further to take them, I burst into noisy choking sobs and drop the keys, wanting only to flee the tea room. They clatter to the floor, skimming past my fingers as if teasing me with the truth, so close to being caught, and yet so far.

The last thing I hear as I run through the rain is the bellow of Finn's voice behind me.

'What the hell is going on?'

Chapter 23

LIZZIE

It's killing me standing inside the door listening to them outside, and I know I should move away. It's stupid even standing here, like I could stop them from coming in even if I wanted to. Finn is furious, and I don't blame him. I can hear him tell Ellie that he wants some answers, but I can't let them in. I'm in such trouble.

I rest my head against the door, sensing that Ellie is probably doing the same, if only to ignore the rain that must be dripping down the back of her neck.

'Lizzie, come on, let me in so that we can talk,' she pleads. 'You're not in any trouble,' she adds, knocking on the door softly.

I feel another tear fall from the end of my chin and plop to my T-shirt, where the dark patch of material is getting bigger by the minute. I look down to see another tear right on the edge of my vision, dangling from the end of my nose, and wipe it away in disgust. I made a promise to myself that I wouldn't make any more mistakes, and that, if I did, I wouldn't run from them. I promised myself I'd be responsible for the things that happened in my life. I'd spent far too long around people who made out that everything was always someone else's fault and never their own. It was about time I became that person I so desperately wanted to be.

I open the door, and step aside to let Ellie and Finn inside. She gets no further than two steps before her arms go around me. Whatever I was expecting, it wasn't this. I'd expected noise and anger, not something that feels like sympathy, and I cling to her like a limpet, a fresh bout of crying gripping me.

I've left my bag on the floor and Finn picks it up, moving it to one side. I can hear him crossing the room and then clattering about in the kitchen, and I slowly try to disentangle myself from Ellie. Finn must want to yell at me, to pass on all the hurt he feels for Ben, hurl it at me in accusation – yet he doesn't. Despite his anger he's making a cup of tea. I know I'll never forgive myself for hurting these people.

Ellie leads me over to the sofa, sitting beside me and holding my hand, rubbing the top of it with her thumb, round and round in a soothing gesture. She finds a tissue up her sleeve which she passes to me, almost in apology that it can't be any bigger to cope with the flow of snot and tears that I seem to be producing.

To my amazement, Finn comes to sit on the other side of me, placing an arm around my shoulders and pulling me gently to him.

'Come on now, Lizzie, what's this all about, eh?'

I take a long shuddering breath, sniffing hard.

'I never meant to hurt Ben. I'm so sorry, Finn. I've let you all down so badly,' I whisper. 'When all you've ever done is be nice to me.'

I can feel Ellie looking at Finn over the top of my head. She's waiting for the moment when he blows, but she doesn't need to protect me; I deserve everything I get.

Another breath shudders from me.

'I'm not a bad person, really I'm not. I've been trying so hard to help everyone, but all these bad things keep happening and I don't know why, but I know it's all my fault.'

'What do you mean, you don't know why, Lizzie? Sometimes accidents happen despite our best intentions and the best thing to do is just be honest and admit to them. I don't suppose anyone will think what happened to Ben's dresser was done on purpose, but by hiding the keys all it did was make you seem like you were guilty.' Ellie's eyes are warm on mine.

I stare at her, shocked. 'But I didn't take them!' My denial is instant, but then my face crumples again. 'But then I must have, mustn't I? If the keys were in my pocket I must have taken them.' I drag a hand across my nose. 'I don't remember doing it, Ellie.' I look at her beseechingly.

Finn gives my shoulders a squeeze. 'When did you last see the keys?' he asks. 'Did you find them somewhere perhaps and pick them up for safe keeping?'

I think for a moment. 'I don't think so. I mean, I know where they're kept, on the hook in the house, but I haven't seen them anywhere else.'

'So the first time you saw them today was just now when you found them in your pocket?' he continues.

I nod, turning a little to look at him. 'And I'm sure they weren't there this morning neither, because I couldn't find my own keys when I went to leave. I looked in my jacket pocket to check if they were there and they weren't. They were under the bed in the end.'

He looks at me sadly. 'Well, I don't suppose it matters much, given what happened afterwards, but why didn't you come and find one of us as soon as you'd spilled the stain? If you had done that, maybe Ben could have done something about it.'

My stomach heaves in shock. Is that what they think? I think I might be sick, and my hand flies to my mouth.

'Lizzie?'

I swallow, trying to breathe, searching Finn's face for any clue that he might be joking, but he isn't. He really thinks it was me that did it. I feel Ellie's hand grip mine a little tighter.

'Lizzie, did you spill the stain?' she asks softly.

I shake my head violently, my hand still over my mouth.

'Then why did you say it was your fault?'

'Because it is,' I gasp, fresh tears spilling down my face. 'I promised Ben I would make sure that his workshop was tidy, that everything was put away as it should be. A promise is a promise and I check every day, but I knew I heard something in the night. I should have checked then. I should have gone inside and made sure properly. If I had, then none of this would have happened. It's all my fault.'

I hear a small catch in her voice. 'Oh, Lizzie . . . that doesn't make it your fault,' she says. 'We all could have checked the workshop last night, and none of us did. In fact, none of us heard the noise apart from you, so we're all to blame.'

I feel Finn pull away from me slightly.

'I think we're all missing the point rather,' he says stiffly. 'And I'm beginning to get a little confused. Lizzie, if you didn't tip the stain over Ben's dresser, and you didn't take his keys, then who did? This doesn't make any sense at all.'

I hang my head, sniffing again. 'But it must have been me, because of all the other things that have gone wrong too, the other things that have been my fault. I think I must be going mad.'

'What other things, Lizzie? What are you talking about?'

'The mix-up with the flowers, and then losing Patience's order.' I falter for a moment. 'No, not the flowers, don't worry about that, but the other thing; that must have been my fault.'

'Lizzie,' Ellie admonishes gently, 'we don't really know what happened there. You mustn't blame yourself. I think it was a case of crossed wires really.'

'No, no, it wasn't,' I argue, my voice rising again. 'You don't understand. I thought I put the piece of paper with Patience's order on it under the phone like Fliss told me to, but I must have got it wrong because the paper was never there.'

More looks are exchanged over my head.

'Lizzie, I don't think we're really following what you're trying to tell us,' says Finn. 'You were sure before that you wrote all of Patience's order down, and that you left the note for her to see. Why have you changed your mind?'

I push his arm away, starting to cry again. I stand up instead and walk towards the table, which is littered with mugs, clothes, bits of make-up and magazines. I move a sock, picking up the thing that lies beneath and bring it back to sit once more, my shoulders hunched and shaking.

Wordlessly I hold out my hand, offering a balled-up piece of paper. I don't think I need to tell them what it is.

'It was here all the time,' I whisper, not daring to look up. I actually flinch when I feel Ellie's warm fingers against my chin, a gentle pressure pulling my face upwards until I have to look at her.

'Lizzie?' she says, waiting until she has my full attention. 'How did the list get here?'

It almost feels like a giggle, this wave of shock that passes up over me, a thing that wants to burst out of me in surprise. 'I don't know,' I reply.

There's a huge space before what comes next. It's silent and loud both at the same time, and I wait through this living, breathing thing, fearing what will come. Knowing it has teeth enough to hurt me.

Instead what comes is a soft sigh and a gentle kiss to the top of my head as Finn's arms go around me and he pulls me from the sofa.

'Right, come on,' he says. 'I've had enough of this. Get some things together, Lizzie. I'm not having you stay here by yourself. You can come back to us tonight. I don't know what's going on, but whatever it is we'll get to the bottom of it.' He draws my head away slightly, holding both sides of it, forcing me to look at him. 'I don't think you've done anything wrong, Lizzie. None of this is your fault. Do you understand?'

I nod very slightly. 'Are you sure?' I say.

Finn tuts, pulling me towards him again.

'I'll get some things together, shall I?' says Ellie. 'A toothbrush and your pyjamas maybe. Is there anything else you want to bring?'

'I'll get them,' I mumble, trooping off to the bathroom and leaving Finn and Ellie staring at one another in the quiet room.

I look around for something to put my things in, spying a carrier bag on the floor, and as I do so Ellie joins me in the bedroom.

'What was going in the bag, Lizzie?' she asks. 'The big holdall by the door?'

I look at her sheepishly. 'I didn't think you'd want me here any more. I was going to leave.'

'Oh, Lizzie, where would you go?' she sighs, her own eyes shiny with tears. 'No one ever solved their problems by running away. You're part of our family here now and we'll get through this, okay?'

I nod forlornly, which at the moment is about the best I can do.

They think I'm asleep, and I probably should be. I'm more tired than I ever remember feeling before, and after I wolfed down the cheese and bacon toasted sandwich that Finn brought me, I sank back against the squishy cushions on the sofa and closed my eyes. Someone came to the door. I think it must have been Ellie because the feet crept away again, but after a few moments I heard them once more and felt the soft warmth of a throw settle over me. But I can't speak. My head is so full of words that there is no room for any more, inside or out, and so I keep my eyes closed and let the chaos swirl around my mind.

Now, I can hear them talking in the kitchen. The smell of bacon is still enticingly in the air, and the chink of glasses and crockery signals the sounds of normality returning.

'How is she?' asks Ben.

'Asleep.' It's Ellie's voice this time. 'I can't imagine how she must have been feeling, thinking that somehow she was responsible for everything that's happened.'

'You believe her then?'

'She's hardly a criminal mastermind, is she? But that aside, it doesn't fit with the Lizzie we know, does it? Something just doesn't add up.'

It's hard to hear Ben's reply, but he must have stuck up for me too because I hear Ellie tell him that she agrees with him.

'So what's going on then?'

'Honestly, Ben? I have no idea. I'm not sure I can even think about anything at all at the moment. Are you all right, though?'

'Yeah, I'm fine,' he replies. 'Hurt my hand beating a tree, but we'll both live.'

'I didn't really mean that, Ben.'

'No, I know, but I don't know what to say.'

Finn chimes in then, his voice louder, but still anxious.

'No, none of us do. I don't want to blame Lizzie for any of this, any more than you do. It seems ridiculous that she could be even capable of it, but you have to agree that it certainly looks like she's the guilty party. If she is, then she's a very accomplished liar and an Oscar-winning actress to boot. I also have no idea what would motivate her to do such things, but be honest, how much do we really know about her? I think we need to do a little gentle digging, just to be on the safe side. Hopefully we won't find anything untoward, but if we do . . . well, forewarned is forearmed. Of course, the other big question is, if it's not Lizzie, then who is it? Someone seems able to wander around Rowan Hill at will, and that worries me more than anything. If Lizzie didn't bring that piece of paper with Patience's order on it back to her flat, then someone else did.'

A small shiver runs down my spine as I take in the full implication of his words. That someone else could have been in my flat, going through my things. My thoughts begin to whirl again, and I almost miss what he says next.

'So, for the time being, Lizzie stays here. That way we can keep an eye on her, guilty or not.'

I almost fling back the covers then, but I don't. Instead I push aside all the other thoughts, all the other conversations crowding my head except for one. A memory of that thing Ellie said about noticing what was going on around me and deciding when things weren't quite right. Seeing when things have gone wrong and looking for a way to fix them. And then I let all the other conversations come back to me, one by one, sifting them, thinking through them, not like I usually do, but carefully this time, with a smart head on. Rowan Hill needs my help, and I'm not sure how I'm going to help it yet, but I'll find a way. And if I can't, then I think I know someone who can.

Chapter 24

LIZZIE

Ellie left me to lie in the next morning, and although I understand her reasons for doing so, I'm in such a panic when I wake up; all I can think about is getting to the tea room. It's only when I get there to find Finn behind the counter looking relatively chilled and smiling with customers that I remember it's my day off. That suits me fine; I've got a lot to do today.

I let myself back into my flat, eyeing my things as if I'm seeing them for the first time, although my gaze lingers longest on the bookcase I made with Ben. It only has four books on it, although now some other things have crept on there as well. I scoop them up angrily and dump them on the coffee table. It should be used for what it was made for.

I run my fingers over the smooth wood, picking up one of the books that I had brought with me. I flip to the rear of the book and pull out the card that I had placed there a couple of months before. Not hidden, but tucked away somewhere I'd be sure to remember, just like I always had done. Creatures of habit, I heard someone say once, and I let the phrase roll around in my head, thinking of someone else I know who likes to keep their important things stashed inside a book for safe keeping.

The call to Neil connects almost straight away, which makes me smile, and I imagine him standing on a street corner, waiting to pounce on his ringing phone and launch into action. He doesn't remember me at first, which doesn't surprise me. In fact, maybe he never even knew my name, but he knows my dad's name right enough: that gets his attention, and then he knows who I am. He is very helpful; I knew he would be. He has a kind face, you see, the sort that still believes that people do good things.

I promise to call him again as soon as I can. 'Thanks, Neil,' I say, and hang up, still smiling. And now to number two on my list of things to do today.

The noise has never bothered me; in fact, even though Ben and I are rarely here at the same time, I like the sounds that come from his workshop. They're busy sounds, making sounds, and I can almost feel the transformation of the wood that will result from them.

There's no point knocking, and in any case it's quite nice standing here, watching Ben without his knowing, because I can see that, underneath it all, he's unchanged. I can't imagine how he must be feeling after yesterday – like a piece of him is broken, I should think – but after all that he's still here, running his hands along the grain of the wood as if he's talking to it, or like it's talking to him. And he's working on Ellie and Will's table, which makes me more pleased than anything.

'I needed something nice to work on today,' he says, turning to smile at me and waving me forwards into the room.

I don't say anything for a moment, not really sure how to begin, or even if Ben wants me there at all. I run a finger around a whorl on the edge of the table.

'It's still beautiful,' I say tentatively.

'It is,' he agrees, running a hand back across his dark hair in thought. He stands back to survey his work.

'You know, I thought you might not come back here for a while,' he says. 'But I'm rather pleased that you have.'

I still my hand, catching the smile in his brown eyes. It gives me the courage to continue. 'I wanted to know that you're okay . . .' I begin, pausing for a moment to watch the expression on his face.

'And . . . ?'

I'm not sure how to say this, without him thinking I'm being soppy.

'I can smell this place in my flat, the wood and stuff.' I prod at a tiny, curled shaving on the floor with my foot, turning it this way and that. 'I like it; it makes me feel like I'm home. I mean, I know I am home, but you know . . .'

Ben stares at the carving tool in his hand. It's called a gouge; I know that now. I can feel him testing the weight of it in his palm, feeling how it sits perfectly, the wooden handle worn even smoother from hours of use.

'That's how I feel too,' he confides, his voice hushed. 'And it's also how I know that whoever was responsible for what happened yesterday, it wasn't you.' He registers the surprised look on my face. 'Anybody who feels wood the way you do could never bring themselves to destroy it in such a way.'

I mustn't cry; I don't want to cry. But Ben's gentle words mean more to me than he will probably ever know.

'If you had really wanted to hurt me you'd have gone for Ellie and Will's table. What happened yesterday was bad enough. I've lost a lot of money for one thing, but I can start again with the dresser. The table is something else entirely; there's too much love gone into that, and I'd never be able to replicate it. Therefore, whoever did this doesn't know me all that well. I thought yesterday that this was a personal attack on me – a natural reaction, I suppose, given the shock I'd just had – but now that I've thought about things a little more rationally, I don't think it was. Meant to cause damage and upset, but opportunist rather than aimed at me in particular.'

'So somebody still did this on purpose?'

'Absolutely,' he says. 'Think about it for a minute. We hear noises in the night, but when we check there's no one to be found. The place is locked up as it should be, just how it was this morning, in fact. Let's pretend for a moment that I *had* left the stain out and someone had been careless and knocked it over. Would they really have broken in here in the middle of the night, been careless, and then carefully locked up again? No, I don't think so either. It was a deliberate act, I'm sure of it. I just don't know why.'

'But I should have come in when I heard the noise. Something might have been left out – the stain – and if I'd have checked—'

Ben traces his finger around the carved edge he's been working on. He flicks away a tiny curl of wood.

'Lizzie, you and I both know that you've been coming in here every evening to check on things. Just as you and I know that you've never found a single thing out of place—' He holds up a hand to stop me from interrupting. 'I don't mind you coming in here; in fact, I rather like the idea that you've been keeping an eye on the place for me. But, like I said, I know you'll never have found anything anywhere other than where it should be, because that's not how I work. This wasn't an accident, Lizzie, and the more I think about it the more I think that Finn is right. This place wasn't broken into, but someone came to Rowan Hill in the dead of night, intent on doing harm, and whoever that someone was, they had keys.'

I look up into the sadness I see on his face. Perhaps if I told him, perhaps if I shared my suspicions with him, like I have with Neil, I could rid myself of the guilt that's churning my stomach every minute of the day, but I can't – not yet. Neil was really helpful, but I have no proof of anything yet, just my own fears, and that's not enough, particularly from someone with a reputation like mine. I'm not strong enough; I'd be blown away like a piece of yesterday's newspaper, and so, for the time being at least, I must bide my time.

I stretch up onto my tiptoes and lightly kiss Ben's cheek, leaving him staring at his table, his thoughts somewhere way off in the distance. His cheek twitches into a slight smile as he registers my touch, but he says nothing more and I leave the room as silently as I entered it.

I did wonder whether Jane would find my request to see her a bit strange, seeing as I don't really know her that well, but if she does, she makes no mention of it. Her greeting is as sunny as ever, just like the day outside.

The bus dropped me at the end of their lane, and as I walked the quiet distance to their house, the only sound was that of the bees, buzzing madly in the bright yellow gorse bushes by my side. Life must be so much simpler if you're a bee, I think.

I was a little bit nervous about coming here, not sure what I was going to say. But I made a promise to Jane, and a promise is a promise. I've scarcely seen her or baby Rowan since the day she was born, but I guess when you've helped to deliver a baby in the woods you share a bond that is not so easily broken.

As I touch my hand to their gate, I spy Jane going through to the back garden, a tray of plants in her hand, and by the time I get to her she is scooping up armfuls of compost. Little Rowan is strapped to her in a front carrier, gurgling gently, her bare toes curling and unfurling in the soft air.

'Morning!' waves Jane cheerfully.

She looks amazing. She's probably been up half the night, and every night before that, but she still looks beautiful.

She comes forwards to kiss me hello. 'You look like you've had a heavy night,' she observes, with her usual accurate assessment of anyone's condition.

'Thanks, Jane,' I say. 'You don't. You look great. Aren't you supposed to look knackered and like you could sleep on a washing line?' I bend to kiss the top of Rowan's head.

Jane laughs. 'Probably, but she's a little dream, this one. I just stick her in her cot, she waves her arms and legs around for a bit, gurgles and then sleeps the whole night through. She's pretty amazing.'

Rowan makes a soft cooing noise, as if in agreement.

'Come on. Let's go and put the kettle on,' says Jane, touching a hand to my arm.

'Are you sure it's okay for me to be here? I can see you're busy.'

She waves a dismissive hand. 'I can do this any time. I'm only out here because Jack has taken the girls out for the day. I'd much rather be chatting with you. Come on.'

Without waiting for a reply, she abandons her plants and leads the way along the path to the back door, where she kicks off her shoes. They land in a heap, beside a jumble of others.

'We can sit outside, if you like; it's quite warm out by the summerhouse where there's no wind.' She smiles down at the baby still strapped to her. 'And this little one loves being in the fresh air.'

'Not surprisingly,' I remark.

'I know. I'd have had all my babies in the woods if I'd have known. Admittedly, she seemed in rather a hurry to arrive, but now that she has, she seems pleased to be here.'

She lifts Rowan from the carrier and passes her to me. 'Time for Auntie Lizzie cuddles,' she smiles.

I take the little bundle from her; she's beautifully warm and smells just like the baby aisle in the supermarket. I hold her against me, swaying gently, as I've seen Jane do.

'I wonder if Will and Ellie's biological clocks will ever start ticking?' says Jane, her back to me as she fills the kettle. 'It would be so lovely, wouldn't it? A summer wedding followed by a spring baby.'

'It would, but Ellie's right really.' I smile, playing with Rowan's toes. 'She and Will are only just starting out, not like you and Jack, and they're both so busy I don't know how they'd manage to look after a baby as well.'

'I know. I just can't help getting all maternal on their behalf. Still, I know them well enough by now to know that they both feel the same, which is the main thing. It might cause awful problems for them if they didn't. In any case, they've got plenty of time to change their minds if they want to.'

I try to hide the flicker of concern that crosses my face, but Jane sees it anyway. She narrows her eyes at me.

'What's that look for?' she says. 'Do you know something I don't?'

I shift uncomfortably. 'Not exactly,' I mumble.

Jane gives me that look. You can tell she's a mum. 'Come on. Out with it. What's the matter?'

I rearrange the hemline of my top. 'It's nothing really, but you obviously think neither of them want children right now, and that's what I thought too. Ellie and I even talked about it once, but I've heard differently a couple of times now, and I'm wondering if that's why Ellie has been a bit upset lately. I mean, it's a bit of a biggy, isn't it, right before you get married?'

Jane takes down two mugs from a cupboard, lining them up on the work surface, and then pushing one so that it lies exactly in line with the other. Her fingers linger on it for a moment.

'Is that why you've come to see me today?' she asks, still looking down. 'The real reason? Not that it isn't lovely to see you,' she adds quickly, 'but you mentioned Ellie on the phone too.'

I stare at the kettle, willing it to boil. 'Well, you asked me to keep an eye on her for you, and so, well . . . I've been trying to, but there are one or two things I think you should know, and not things I'd be happy to say to Ellie.'

Jane eyes me steadily. 'So what exactly is it that you've heard twice now?' she says. 'I think you'd better start at the beginning.'

Now that I'm actually faced with talking about Ellie, I feel rather nervous. Jane is her oldest friend and it makes me feel awkward discussing things behind her back; at least, that's what it feels like. What if I've got it wrong? Maybe I'm worrying for nothing, looking for things that aren't really there.

I wait until we're seated in the garden before I start to explain my anxiety. Jane pushes a packet of chocolate biscuits across the tray towards me.

'Come on. You can stuff your face with some of those and tell me all about it.'

I jiggle baby Rowan on my knee, wondering where I should begin.

'It was Fliss that first brought up the subject of Will wanting children, that day back in the woods when Rowan was born. It obviously surprised you at the time, and now that I've had the chance to speak to Ellie about it, it makes sense for them not to want a family right now. I wouldn't have thought any more about Fliss's comment if Patience hadn't said the same thing to me about Will as well, just yesterday . . . and I wondered if that's what had upset Ellie too.'

Jane is about to take a sip of her tea, but the mug stops halfway to her mouth. '"Too"? What do you mean, "too"?'

'She had an email from Will – she didn't say much about it, only that there seemed to be some confusion over what's been said about various wedding arrangements. The email was a bit stroppy, I think. Anyway, it really upset her, and she was biting the heads off everyone.'

'Okay, let's back up a bit, Lizzie . . . I'm not really following what you're trying to say here. It's possible my brain is still addled by pregnancy hormones but you're talking about things I know nothing about.

Let's go back to the first thing, shall we? What was it that Patience said yesterday?'

I pause to watch a ladybird make its way along the edge of the garden table. 'Well, I can't remember it all, but she basically said that Will was really keen to have kids and wasn't it a shame that Ellie didn't want any. She wasn't gossiping; I think she was just worried for them both. She even said for me not to tell Ellie in case it upset her.'

'And how come Patience knows that's what Will wants? Has she spoken to him?'

I look at her, puzzled. 'Oh, I don't know . . . She didn't say.'

'Then maybe it was just something she overheard too. Think about it, Lizzie. Will has been away for weeks. I doubt very much that Patience would have spoken to him about anything much, let alone whether he wants to have children.'

'No, I suppose not.'

Jane pulls apart the top of the packet of biscuits and takes one, looking at it thoughtfully before dunking it into her tea. She lifts it to her lips, licking the melted chocolate from the top. Birdsong fills the silence between us.

'Do you know what I think?' she says eventually. 'I think Ellie is tired, stressed out with stuff for the wedding and missing Will like crazy. He's the one person she really wants to talk to, and the only one she can't, but even if she could talk to him properly she won't because she doesn't want to make him feel guilty about being away, and she doesn't want to upset him because she knows how important this project is to him.'

'Blimey . . . so—' I try to interrupt, but Jane carries on.

'And . . . I think that Will is tired, stressed out with stuff for the project and missing Ellie like crazy. She's the one person he really wants to talk to, and the only one he can't, but even if he could talk to her properly he won't because he feels guilty enough about being away, and

217

he doesn't want to upset her because he knows she's shouldering all the arrangements for the wedding, and that makes him feel guilty too.'

I stare at Jane in amazement. Put like that it seems to make perfect sense. 'Wow! Is that what being a mum means, that you just know all this stuff, as if by magic?'

Jane gives an apologetic smile. 'Partly,' she says. 'It's also because that's exactly how it was with Jack and me when he first started writing. I hated interrupting him when he was holed up for days because I knew how important his writing was to him, and he felt guilty about leaving everything to me when he was holed up for days, so he never discussed anything that was troubling him because he didn't want to add to my burden.' She smiles at the memory. 'We used to leave things brewing gently until – boom! – boiling point was reached. We had some spectacular arguments until we worked out what was going on. Now we know that we have to be open and honest about the realities of life, irrespective of how busy we both are.'

'So Ellie and Will just need to talk to one another, properly like.'

Jane squints up at me through the bright sunlight. 'I guess so. Maybe it is as simple as that. It would certainly put all their fears at rest.'

'She does talk to me about it sometimes, about how she's feeling.'

'But that's great too, Lizzie. Friends are just as important at times like this, but they don't solve the problem. Only the people involved can do that.'

I nod, seeing things more clearly now. 'I'm not sure that Ellie will want to talk to me about it any more, though . . . Some things have happened lately, and I—'

'—mustn't worry about them.' She smiles at me in understanding. 'Ellie mentioned what's been happening recently, and if you don't mind me saying so, I think you're all over-thinking things a bit. To be expected, seeing how busy you all are, but could it be that you're being a tad melodramatic? Don't you think the things that have happened are simply misunderstandings or just plain accidents? Horrible, but accidents nonetheless. I said exactly the same to Ellie on the phone. Try to put things back into perspective and remember that Chinese whispers don't help anyone. Try not to listen to them.'

It's easy to see what she means, sitting here in her peaceful garden, far away from Rowan Hill. I let the wind blow through my hair, and feel Rowan's sleeping body relaxed against mine. I can feel my shoulders start to drop a little. High above my head, birds are circling the sky lazily, their cries for a while the only noise, and I sit for a bit longer, chatting with Jane about anything and everything, munching her biscuits and drinking her tea, until it's time to catch the bus home.

The centre is quiet when I get back, so I don't feel too guilty about my time away, even if it is my day off. Plus, it will mean that my plan could work out rather nicely. It occurred to me as I sat with Jane that what we all needed was a little fun, and a quick stop-off at the local supermarket where I change buses has given me just the thing to provide it – at least that's what I'm hoping.

By four o'clock everyone is getting ready to shut up shop, running through the routine tasks that are required to tidy up and leave things in readiness for the morning. I need to be quick if I want this to work.

I circle around the house and enter the courtyard from the top garden gate rather than the usual entrance; I want my entry to go unnoticed. I peer through the gate, pleased to see, as I hoped, Finn's back retreating down one side of the yard, a coil of hosepipe in his hand, the spray in the other, as he waters each of the troughs and hanging baskets in turn, which are already vibrant with colour.

I cross swiftly to the hay bales in the centre. Arranged in a square to provide seating, they also provide a central hiding place, and I dump my booty quickly, one eye on Finn just in case he spots me before he's supposed to. I could be about to get myself in the most almighty trouble, but I hope I know Finn well enough by now.

He's lost in his own thoughts and the task in hand, and I'm right behind him before he even realises I'm there, my shadow crossing his in the afternoon sun. He turns around, his look of greeting rapidly falling off his face as he sees what's pointing at his chest. I wish I had my phone to film him as his expression changes from surprise to confusion, irritation, a warning and then, finally, I'm pleased to see, amusement.

'Gosh, it's been warm today, Finn,' I say, as I let loose a quick burst of water from the 'gun' in my hand.

It was meant to be a little tease, that's all, but the gun is more powerful than I thought and a huge dark wet patch spreads across his shirt, right in the centre of his chest.

His eyes lock with mine, but there are crinkles at the corner of his mouth, and I sense rather than see his fingers tighten on the spray trigger in his hand.

I know I'm never going to be quick enough, but I leap away just the same, feeling the cold blast from Finn's retaliation shot catching me square in the back. The day might be warm for the time of year, but it's still early, and the water is freezing. Knowing that Finn will need to be careful not to trip over the hose, I dodge sharply to his side, ducking as I do so and quickly fire off another round. I don't mean it to, but it hits him straight between the legs, and I'm so embarrassed I just turn and run. From that moment on it's all-out war.

Our shrieks bring the others running in seconds, by which time I'm desperately trying to reach the other guns I've stashed away, getting wetter and wetter by the minute. It doesn't take them long to realise that there are more guns to be had, and Patience is first into battle, snatching up a water cannon and firing a huge torrent of water at a completely defenceless Patrick, who proceeds to run around the courtyard, with a wildly shouting Patience in tow.

Ellie's too polite to be as ruthless as the rest of us and tries to dodge everyone, but instead runs face first into Fliss's burst of water. She stops, spluttering, gasping for air and desperately trying to stop laughing, but failing miserably, as Finn, creeping up behind her, angles the hosepipe up the hem of her dress. You can probably hear her screaming in the next county.

It's fast, it's furious, it's fun and, almost as soon as it's begun, it's all over. Out of ammo, we fall onto the hay bales, where we collapse in a snorting, coughing, hysterical heap, with Finn waving the hosepipe menacingly, threatening anyone who moves.

It takes a lot longer for the laughter to subside, but when it does it leaves behind a feeling as soft and peaceful as the air itself. It's not until later, as I sit with my book and a cup of tea, smiling at the memory, that I realise who was shooting who.

JUNE

Chapter 25

LIZZIE

The start of the week feels almost normal again, as we all strive to get Patience's order finished. It's busy, frantically so, but there's a routine and a rhythm to the days that isn't disturbed by anything out of the ordinary. Brewing each of Patience's potions seems to take forever, with hours spent stirring slowly, which everyone takes a turn with to share the pain of aching backs and shoulders. It's good thinking time, and although at times my thoughts take me to places I really don't want to go, they are necessary preparation for what I know to be coming soon. Our conversations may be happy as we chat about wedding cake, shoes, flowers and rings, our laughter and excitement mingling with Ellie's, but I can still feel the weight of the coming weeks on my shoulders.

I can only have managed a couple of hours' sleep when my alarm sounds on Friday morning. At least that's what it feels like. I fell asleep soon enough, even though my legs were killing me from standing all day, but

I woke within an hour as my mobile blurted out the arrival of an email. I shouldn't have looked at it. I shouldn't even have left my mobile on – I don't usually – but then I glanced at who it was from, and when I saw Neil's name I had to go and read the whole bloody thing, and that was that, no more sleep for me. I even looked out of my lounge window to check if there were any lights on in the main house, but Ben and Finn's room was in darkness obviously, so I lay there, getting hot and cross. Now I'm standing, swaying gently like I'm drunk or on a ship, and wondering if it's actually possible to sleep in the shower.

Patience is having kittens this morning, even though we've told her time and time again that everything is perfect and she shouldn't worry. I guess I'd feel the same if it were me. I've never known what it feels like to have something in my life that I was so excited about, something that I was totally responsible for. I've never even had a pet. This is like Patience's baby, I think, and as we all gather around Patrick's van, packed and loaded with her first precious order, it's like we're waving it off on the first day of school and hoping it doesn't fall over in the playground.

The faces all around me are tired too, but happy – for Patience, but also for the week that is almost over, and the chance to relax a little. I don't think anyone apart from me even remembers that her order was nearly lost; all they can see is a job well done and a return to what Rowan Hill does best, with everyone working together. Only Ellie still looks like she's constantly trying to catch hold of a thought that won't be caught, but then I guess she has more on her plate than anyone else. Anyhow, she's asked Fliss to wait behind so she can have a word with her about wedding stuff, so perhaps she can get a few things off her chest. I hope so.

The three of us wait at the top of the car park after waving Patrick's van goodbye. The postman's just turned in, and I know he'll stop for a chat, like he always does.

'The kettle's on, Brian,' Ellie calls, as he pulls to a stop, getting out. 'Have you got time for a cuppa today?'

'Nope,' he replies, leaning back in his van to fish out our letters. 'But when has that ever stopped me?' He grins.

'So you haven't got time for a toffee apple muffin then either?'

'Not a chance,' he replies, falling into step beside us as he hands her the post.

She sorts through the thick bundle. 'When are you going to bring us anything exciting?' she comments, eyeing a collection of what look like telephone bills and bank statements.

'I just delivers 'em,' he shrugs. 'Although I did have a big Premium Bond win once upon a time; that was rather nice. You have got a nice one there, though, look.' He takes the pile back from her for a minute, shuffling through them.

'This one, see? Feel the quality.' He rubs the heavy creamy-coloured envelope between his fingers, as we peer at it. 'Oh, it's not for you, sorry,' he adds to Ellie, turning to Fliss instead. 'It's for you, I think; some posh solicitors or other.'

Fliss practically snatches the envelope from him.

'Aye, someone's keen.' He nudges me, handing back the rest of the envelopes to Ellie. 'Perhaps her rich Aunt Mabel's died and left her a shedload of money. Now, wouldn't that be nice!'

But Fliss isn't laughing. 'I don't have an Aunt Mabel,' she replies coldly, as she folds the envelope in half. 'Ellie, can I catch up with you later? I've just remembered I have a phone call to make.'

She doesn't wait for an answer but strides off in the direction of her workshop.

'Brian, for all you know someone has just died,' Ellie scolds. 'That wasn't exactly tactful.'

He has the grace to look a little sheepish as he watches Fliss's retreating back, but then he shrugs again. 'Nah, judging from that reaction, it's more like she's been landed with a huge bill, I'd say.'

She smiles. 'Yes, perhaps.'

'So, not long until the big day then?' he adds.

We're by the tea-room door now, and he holds it open for Ellie and me, bowing like a gentleman to let us pass. I head straight for the tray of muffins.

'Not nearly long enough,' Ellie replies, coming up behind me to sort the tea. 'I'm sure I should be panicking about something.'

'Well, you have a good crowd of people around you,' he smiles. 'I should let them worry about everything if I were you. All you really need to do is turn up, right?'

'Spoken like a true man, Brian, if you don't mind my saying. Would that were true.'

'I'm a bit long in the tooth, I realise that, but it strikes me that you young people like to make things very complicated. Sometimes life's as simple as you care to make it.'

'Well, you may well be right, Brian. Who am I to argue? Now what will it be?' she asks, with a nod at me. 'Lemon meringue muffin or toffee apple?'

I lay Brian's muffin on a napkin for him, knowing that he never eats it there and then, but takes it with him instead. The tea he drinks straight away, pouring it down his throat just as soon as it's in the cup. His mouth must be fireproof. A quick glance at the clock shows me that there's just over ten minutes left until we officially open. I mime a quick 'back in a minute' at Ellie and slip away, leaving them chatting. I have a favour to ask of Ben, and want to catch him before he gets engrossed in his day.

His laptop is right where he said it would be. I hadn't intended to take it straight away, but he assured me that he wouldn't need it for a day or two and I could keep hold of it if I wanted. He didn't even ask me what I wanted it for, but I made up some excuse about wanting to watch a DVD, and he just nodded, smiling. I don't suppose I'll have a chance to look at it during the day – just the thought that it will be there tonight is enough.

My hand is on the back door, ready to pull it closed, when a thought occurs to me and I double back towards the pantry. My fingers linger over the rack of keys hanging there until I find the one I want, unhooking it quickly from its place and spacing out the others so that it won't look so obviously missing. It's in my pocket before you can say "treacherous bitch." Two can play at that game.

Chapter 26

Ellie

I wave a cheery goodbye to Brian and for the next twenty minutes or so concentrate on getting everything set up for the day, but I can't get his words out of my head. They're snagging on something very important, but every time I try to recall what it is that's troubling me, some other thought barges it out of the way and I'm back to square one again.

It's a shame Fliss had to dash off, as I could really do with chatting to her about the wedding arrangements. My brain feels scattered; perhaps it's because I'm not used to feeling so out of control that I feel this odd. It's as though I'm missing something important, and I need to get my arms around it all again, to gather it in, until I feel I own it once more. I'm sure it's simply a question of information, and once I've had a catch-up I'll feel better.

Of course, in typical fashion, the minute the morning rush is over, Helen dashes in wondering if she can borrow Lizzie for a bit while she pops out to see a client who's housebound. I can hardly refuse, and console myself with the thought that the wedding is still three weeks away, and I can meet Fliss later this afternoon. I wave Lizzie away and wander through to the kitchen to collect my mug. Maybe a hot chocolate brimming with cream and marshmallows would help.

The sun is coming around the corner of the house and will soon be flooding the garden with its golden rays. As it hits the window the tea room will light up with its kaleidoscope of colours and patterns, decorating the whitewashed walls. From plain to an array of riches in minutes. Sometimes it quite takes your breath away.

I take a tray to clear some tables while I wait for my drink to cool, pausing at the far end of the room under the window to watch the room's transformation. It still makes the hairs on the back of my neck rise.

'What do you have to do to get a cup of tea around here?'

The voice comes from behind me, startling me out of my reverie, its tone low and grumbling. There are signs on the table menus, but the fact that we don't do table service still catches some people out.

I swing around, my best welcoming smile firmly in place.

'Will!' A flash of heat rises swiftly from my toes as my stomach gives a joyful leap. 'What are you doing here?'

I abandon my tray on the table as I sink into the chair next to him and clasp his outstretched hand. His other caresses my cheek, slipping under my ear and around the back of my neck as he gently pulls me in. His lips are warm, his scent everything that is Will.

'I managed to get another day off, so I thought I'd better put it to good use,' he murmurs around my lips.

I suddenly feel very emotional. The thought of having Will home for the whole weekend – being able to talk, to share, to love – is like a soothing balm, and the realisation of how much I've missed him, the burn.

I pull away, aware of our surroundings, but so far no one seems to have noticed our reunion. I study Will's face for a moment, mentally adding up his features, measuring what I see, but he looks well, relaxed and happy.

His other hand joins mine, his fingers entwining with my own. He dips his head once more until our foreheads touch.

'I've missed you,' he murmurs, 'so much.'

I don't need to speak, my rapid nod and intake of breath belying the level of emotion that threatens to spill down my face.

Neither of us speaks for a moment or two. It's enough just to sit and know that we're home, together. Eventually, the clink of crockery and hum of conversation resume their normal sound levels within my brain and I throw a quick glance around the room. It's nearing lunchtime and the room will be even busier soon.

Reluctantly I let go of Will's hand, feeling the pull of responsibility separate us. He gives a rueful smile and pushes his chair away from the table a little.

'Don't go anywhere,' he smiles. 'I'll be back.'

I break into a broad grin. 'Nope, I'll be right here.'

'Good. Because I'm going to go and catch up with folks, and then when you're finished here, I'm going to catch up with you.'

There's a look in his eye that does unmentionable things to my insides. It's going to be a long afternoon.

Chapter 27

Lizzie

I'm not eavesdropping, not really, and I'm trying really hard not to stare, but for two people just about to start discussing the most important day of their lives, they look really uneasy. In fact, Ellie looks so nervous I'm not sure she's going to keep her cup of tea down. It wasn't exactly an argument, but they were walking across the courtyard quite late last night and my window was open. I couldn't help but overhear their raised voices. I don't blame Will for not wanting to talk about all this today. He's only just come home and would much rather spend the day with Ellie, but my heart goes out to her; she's been so excited about finally being able to tell Will of all the plans for the wedding that this must seem like a real blow.

I dart another glance across at them, as I finish filling a plate with shortbread. Only Fliss looks relaxed, clutching the big flowery notebook that never leaves her side into her chest like an excited child. She must even take it home with her; I couldn't find it anywhere last night. Fliss doesn't seem to have noticed how strained things are between Will and Ellie either, but perhaps that's a good thing – her excited chatter might lift the mood. I reach for the empty cake stand beside me and turn away to fill it.

They've been here for nearly an hour, and although I can only catch odd snippets in between serving customers, so far they've looked at place settings, favours for the guests (whatever those are), table decorations, colours for the napkins as well as the tablecloths, and ribbon colours for the chairs, but then I see Fliss flick over a page in her notebook as Ellie sits up a little straighter.

She picks up another book and pushes it forwards, this time towards Will.

'I wasn't sure about the lilies at first – seeing as this is a country wedding, I thought they might look a bit austere – but I have to admit I'm happy to have been proved wrong. They look spectacular, don't you think?'

Fliss's smile is wide as she shows Will the pictures. I've seen them and they're very striking. There are several different designs, all very simple, and very elegant. In one, a bouquet, a sheaf of blooms is simply draped over a bride's arm, the long green stems vivid against the white dress. In another, a huge pedestal stands against a bright cerise wall, filled with tightly packed flower heads. They're very beautiful, but somehow they're not how I pictured Will and Ellie's wedding would look. They're nowhere near friendly enough, but I know that Ellie is keen to have them for Will's sake. I turn back to my customer, handing over her change together with a couple of napkins.

I don't see the look on Will's face, but I hear him right enough.

'Whose bloody idea was it to have lilies?'

I look at Ellie, a little confused. She looks like she's about to cry, but she pulls together a smile.

'They're your favourite,' she says. 'Aren't they beautiful?'

He ignores her comment.

Fliss looks straight at me for some reason, a frown creasing her brow. 'But they're your favourite flower,' she says, repeating Ellie's words. She turns back through the pages of her notebook, and my heart begins to beat slightly faster; something's not right here.

'I'm sorry, Fliss, but like hell they are. Whatever gave you that idea? Why would I want to have lilies anywhere on our wedding day? Once was enough. They were Caroline's favourite, not mine, and all I remember is that I couldn't get their cloying scent out of my nose for days. It's the last thing I want to be reminded of.'

Ellie shakes her head. 'But it wasn't my idea, Will. I never even knew that.' She looks to Fliss for help, but her head is still stuck in her notebook. 'Wasn't it Patience who told me lilies were Will's favourite, Fliss? When we first got talking about the flowers?'

'Oh dear,' mutters Fliss, tracing a finger down the page in her book. 'Maybe she got it wrong, but I don't think so. Weren't you talking to her about the lilies too, Lizzie? What did you say to her?'

I come over and look to where she's pointing, her finger halfway down a page, hovering over what, I don't know. It's not how I remember the conversation, but the trouble is I can't exactly remember what was said now. I look at Ellie's distraught expression, and back to Will, whose face looks like thunder.

'Well, it doesn't much matter now, does it?' he says. 'I'm sorry, but there's no way I'm having lilies at our wedding, Fliss, whatever you've all decided. We'll have to cancel the order and pick something else.'

Fliss bites her lip. 'Oh, I'm not sure we can cancel really. I mean, they're all paid for. You'll lose your money—'

Will just sits there glaring, saying nothing. He doesn't need to; he's made his point.

'There will be something we can do, Fliss, won't there?' comes Ellie's wobbly voice. 'We'll be able to sort it out, get something different?'

'Maybe . . .' says Fliss quietly, trailing off, her forefinger stroking the page of designs.

'Look, it's not your fault, Fliss,' says Will. 'I can see how much hard work you've put into all of this, but you've obviously been given the wrong information. I've never had a conversation with any of you about flowers, so where this idea came from I don't know.'

He's looking at me now and I can feel my cheeks begin to burn. This isn't my fault, I know it's not, but Will seems to think it is.

He gives Fliss an apologetic smile and stands up. 'I'll see you later,' he says, as he leaves the room.

There's silence for a few moments as our embarrassment swells to fill the room. Eventually Fliss puts her hand on Ellie's arm, nudging her to take the tissue she's holding. 'I'm so sorry, Ellie,' she whispers. 'We'll think of something. Don't worry.'

Ellie takes the tissue from her, her jaw clenched, her eyes filled with tears. She looks up at me sadly; it doesn't matter what I say now, I've blown it.

She puts a hand over Fliss's, which is still resting on her arm in sympathy.

'Thanks, Fliss, I mean, the rest of this is great. You've done so much to help.'

Fliss puts her arm around Ellie's shoulders, giving them a squeeze. 'Hey, what are friends for?'

It's a little awkward after that. Fliss gets up after a few minutes of low muttering and sympathetic noises, leaving Ellie sitting at the table. She doesn't even look at me as she leaves the tea room. I hover around the counter, risking glances at a silent Ellie and wondering how on earth I can make this better.

The door jangles as a couple of walkers enter, and their noise provides the perfect cover for movement. By the time I've exchanged smiles with them and looked back towards Ellie, she's up and by the entrance.

'I might just pop by to see Patience for a few minutes,' she says to the door, and there's nothing I can do to stop her.

Under the circumstances there's only one thing I can do, so I serve and smile, clean and clear, and wonder as each minute ticks past how long Ellie is going to be. She won't be gone all day, and at some point I'll get the chance to explain.

A pinging alert has me rushing to my mobile, and that's when I know it's game over. Instead of the message from Ellie I'd hoped to see, whatever it said, is a message from a number not in my contacts.

You think you're really clever don't you?

But you're not. You're, stupid, stupid, stupid, just like you've always been. Don't think I haven't noticed what you've been up to – such a big mistake. You can't escape your past, Lizzie, and when I'm finished, that's right where you'll be, back in the hell hole where you belong.

Chapter 28

Ellie

I don't go and see Patience straight away. I think about it, but then it occurs to me that I probably don't want to hear what she has to say. I don't need to either. I can work it out by myself, and that's the worst bit, knowing that I've got things so wrong but not having the slightest idea how I'm going to put them right.

There's just a chance that I might be able to find Will and at least try and explain, but he's not anywhere in the house. This isn't necessarily a surprise as I expect he's gone to blow off steam somewhere, but I had thought that perhaps he would have retreated to the sanctity of his studio. He was in here this morning, finishing off some sketches for a new idea he's had, and his workspace is littered with pencils and pages torn from his sketchbook.

A mug sits on top of a pile of catalogues, at a distinct slant, and I automatically cross to move it, lest it topple and do any damage. Just beyond it, propped up against a jar holding more pencils, is the photo I had taken at the wedding fair.

I should be pleased to see it here, propped so obviously where Will can see it every day as he works, but for some reason it makes me feel a little uneasy. I pick it up, bringing it closer to stare at my face in its careful pose. If I didn't know better, I would have wondered who it was. Of course, I've seen the photo in here before, and although I hadn't acknowledged as much, it had prickled at me then too.

It's only now, as I look at the photo again, that I can see I was mistaken. I had thought the picture was making me feel uneasy because I was pretending to be something I'm not. But that's not the reason, not at all, and it hits me then with full force. I had given the photo to Will as a keepsake, something to keep with him during the time he was away, so that he would always have it as a reminder of me while we were apart. And yet here it is, in the one place that he is not.

I've made some very big mistakes over recent months, I can see that now, and I only hope that I've got time enough to put things right – and not only with Will. I replace the photo in its original position, my thoughts no longer on the image it contains, and collect the mug before walking out of the room. Maybe Patience is the best person to chat to, after all.

I'm gone a bit longer than I thought, and after one last check of the house, I circle back to the tea room. I don't really expect to find Will there, but it's getting on for lunchtime and it will be busy soon – and I think I might owe Lizzie an apology as well. To my surprise, it's not Lizzie I find holding the fort, but Finn.

He looks up as the door jangles, a smile on his face as he finishes plating up a scone for the customer he's serving. His eyes flick a warning as I approach the counter, and although I would normally go straight through to the kitchen, something stops me.

It takes a few moments for him to finish serving, and he waits until he can see that his customer is seated and busy with her teapot before speaking to me. He takes my arm and pulls me to one side, away from the counter and to the nearest table, where he makes a show of moving the already perfectly positioned flowers.

'Lizzie's a bit upset,' he says, tilting his head back towards the kitchen. 'I just popped in for elevenses and thought I'd better stay. I don't quite know what's going on. Something to do with Helen, I think.'

'Helen?' I repeat, wondering what on earth Helen could have to do with Lizzie being upset.

'I think that's what she said, but she's not making a lot of sense. I thought I'd better leave her alone for a bit.'

I nod. 'Maybe I should go through and see her. Are you all right out front for a minute?'

'Ben will be wondering where his lemon drizzle is, but apart from that, yeah, it's fine.'

Lizzie is sitting on the floor, her arms wrapped around her long legs, hugging them into her body. She is staring unblinking at the wall in front of her, her face blotchy from dried tears. She looks up as she hears me approach, and then drops her head almost immediately.

'I know you've come to fire me this time,' she mumbles through her hair. 'And it's fine, I'll go, cos I'm so bloody fed up of all of this.'

'Fed up of what, Lizzie?' I ask, moving to sit opposite her and mirroring her position.

Her head raises then, a defiant expression on her face.

'I'm not going to fire you, Lizzie . . . Well, not until I've found out what's going on. Then I might.' I grin at her, hoping to diffuse the tension a little, but if she recognises my attempt at humour, she doesn't respond. Her expression remains the same.

I try again. 'You know, we could sit here all day, Lizzie, but my bones are a lot older than yours, and this floor is bloody cold and uncomfortable. I'm sorry about this morning, but how about you tell me what's happened and we can both give our backsides a break?'

'Go and ask Helen; she'll tell you. I was minding my own business, serving customers and stuff while you weren't here, and then she comes in and accuses me of all sorts. I'm fed up with it. It's always the same; no one ever listens to me, and I get the blame for everything.'

'Lizzie, that's not true. I know things have been a bit difficult lately but I hope that's all in the past now. No one blames you for anything.'

'Try telling Helen that,' she scowls.

I have a feeling this conversation is going to go round and around in circles. 'So what do you think you're being blamed for then?'

Lizzie picks at her fingernail. 'I don't know. Something about the stickers on her wall hangings . . . but I couldn't concentrate on what she was saying properly.'

That's just it, I think. It's what Lizzie always does when she thinks something has gone wrong: she panics and gets confused. I'm sure that's what must have happened.

'I'll tell you what, Lizzie. I think you've misunderstood what Helen was saying to you, that's all. Why don't I pop over and speak to her and then we can sort it all out?'

Both shoulders shrug in unison.

I scrabble to get my feet back underneath me. 'Well, I'm going to see what Helen says anyway. Stay here a minute.'

I turn back to look at her when I get to the door, but all I can see is a curtain of hair hiding her face.

When I reach Helen, she's deep in concentration, poring over a large book at her desk. Her face is flushed red and she looks distinctly agitated. Instead of the usual smile of greeting, I'm alarmed to see a fierce expression on Helen's face as she looks up and sees me, and for the first time ever I feel awkward in her company.

I'm just trying to come up with something to say that won't make the situation any worse when she looks up again and glares at me.

'Whatever you've come to say, Ellie, don't bother – you're wasting your time. I'm sorry, but now it's gone too far. That girl has just lost me a huge amount of money and caused me a great deal of embarrassment at the same time. I don't want to hear it.'

I've never heard Helen speak this way before, but she's obviously very upset. Her usually calm and quiet voice has risen several octaves and has a very noticeable wobble to it. I certainly wasn't expecting this reaction from someone who is usually so rational. Whatever's happened must be very serious, and what's worse is that it doesn't sound like an isolated incident either.

'Hear what, Helen?' I ask gently.

'More bloody excuses, that's what. I've bitten my tongue for long enough because I didn't want to upset you. I know you've been very busy with wedding stuff, but I think I've made enough allowances. It was good of Fliss to try and deal with it, but it's not her problem either. If you won't deal with Lizzie, don't come in here trying to stick up for her either.'

I don't realise my mouth is gaping wide open until I close it with a snap. A little jolt of shock runs through me at Helen's words, not only because I have absolutely no idea what she's talking about, but because the tone of her voice is so harsh and unfriendly. There's a part of me that's panicking too, because all of a sudden everything seems to be unravelling, just like one of Helen's balls of wool, and I don't even know what it is I've done wrong.

Helen's head is bent back to her book and she clearly doesn't want to speak to me, so in the end I just quietly walk away.

I walk blindly back into the tea room and dismiss Finn as quickly as I can in the only way I know how: with a big fake smile on my face that I'm sure fools no one, least of all me. Then I send Lizzie home for the afternoon with a firm reassurance that everything will be okay, and battle my way blindly through a deluge of customers until I can legitimately call it a day. I look up every time the door opens but none of the people that enter is Will.

Chapter 29

Lizzie

It takes me less than twenty minutes to decide. But then again, maybe that's because it's such an easy decision to make. After all, what other choice is there? I've let everyone down so badly, and even though I wanted to put things right, I know that I'm not big enough or strong enough to make that happen.

I look around my tiny flat, more precious to me than anything in my life before, and sieve through the memories that it already contains. I might be going back to my old life, but if I'm going I'm going under my own steam and on my own terms, and that means no mementoes; I don't think I could cope if I took those with me too. Better just to pretend the last few months never happened.

It's not the first time I've been threatened, and it probably won't be the last either, but if you're like me, you get to learn how much of any threat stands a chance of being carried out, and how much is just bollocks. As I was growing up, I learned that it's mostly just a case of acting up to look bigger than you are. Where I come from, that's pretty much all you've got, because the people doing the threatening are in as much shit as you, but here, in this world, things are different. I have no doubt that the person who sent that text has the means to carry out their threat. They're a big person, and I'm small, simply because of who I am.

I leave everything just as I found it. I have all I need, and no more. Ben's laptop has been returned to its rightful place, as has the key. It's finished, but there's one more thing left to do. I reach for the book, still on my shelf, and remove the piece of paper that has acted as a bookmark for so many weeks. I slip it into an envelope and seal my knowledge inside. There's no more I can do here, and to stay will only make things worse. It may seem cowardly to run but at least this way I can only be blamed for the events of the past and not those of the future.

I write the name and address quickly on the outside of the envelope, adding a stamp. Maybe this way someone with a bigger voice than mine can speak and be heard.

My hand is held out to the postbox before I realise that maybe I do have another choice after all. I might be small, but I know now that I'm *not* stupid, and although it's taken me a while to realise this, the thought burns through me like fire. I can only be blamed for events of the past if I leave. But could there be another way? My heart beats a little faster as I look at my watch, knowing I only have moments to make up my mind. Do I stay or do I go?

I drop the letter on its way, giving one last look up the street and ignoring the bus making its way towards me. I'm not going anywhere.

Chapter 30

ELLIE

Ben is stirring something on the Aga by the time I get back to the house and delicious garlicky smells are wafting around the kitchen. His back is towards me as I pass and I'm happy to keep it that way; I have no desire to speak to anyone now, and suspect that if I had to I would be very rude. Ben, of all people, certainly doesn't deserve this. I almost manage to get past him without comment, but then, as I reach the sanctuary of the hallway door, he turns in greeting.

'Tea won't be long, Ellie. I hope you're hungry. I've done my usual trick and catered for about fifteen.'

I daren't turn around. The last thing I want is to have to explain the look on my face. I want nothing more than a shower and the comfort of my room, but even as I acknowledge this I can hear someone jogging down the stairs at the end of the hall, and I know by the sound that it's Finn. I slide a hand through my hair. It's quite dim in the threshold and I pray that this will allow me to escape past him as well.

'It smells gorgeous, Ben, but I'm desperate for a shower. Can you give me ten minutes?'

'No problem,' he calls, already turning back to the stove. 'Give Finn a prod, will you? He had the same idea, but he's been gone so long I think he's probably fallen asleep.'

'I have not,' retorts Finn, sweeping past me with a smile. 'Bloody cheek,' he says, but whereas usually I would have enjoyed their banter, today I'm grateful to have been let go. I practically run up the stairs.

I stand under the water for a long time, turning the shower up gradually until it's as hot as I can possibly stand it and my scalp starts to ache from its force. Finally, when I can bear it no longer, I turn it down and let the soothing warmth calm me.

I feel quite numb. Perhaps the relentless cheerfulness I realise I've been adopting over the last few weeks is finally catching up with me, and now that it's gone I'm left with a space that my mind refuses to fill. If I'm honest with myself, I've seen this coming for a while, but I was just so determined for everyone's sake to pretend that things were fine that I haven't dared to think about it. I haven't been able to make sense of all the things going on around me, so I've been blocking them out. I know I can't run from them any longer, but the trouble is I still have no clue what exactly is going on, or what to do about any of it for that matter. I'm scared things have gone too far between Will and me to ever get back to where we were before.

I step out of the shower and pull my towel around me, grateful for its warmth despite the summer evening. I can't think of a single thing to do beyond getting dry and eating tea, and wonder when I became so useless.

I don't see him at first as I enter our bedroom. The curtains are drawn and the room is cool, dim and silent. It's only when he moves that I notice him, and by the time I do, he has crossed the room to slide the comfort of his arms around me. His hand holds the back of my head as he pulls me into his soft shirt, his own head bending to bury itself in my neck, my wet hair falling against him. His kisses start just behind my ear, dipping to my throat before rising to my cheeks and grazing my lips. A hand comes up then and the other slides from my head until both are holding my face inches from his own. His eyes are closed but he doesn't need to see me to place the gentlest of kisses on each eye, the small sigh of his breath warm against my skin.

When he speaks there's a tight well of emotion in his voice that causes a heat to beat deep inside me.

'I'm so sorry, Ellie,' he murmurs. 'God, I love you.' And my reply is buried in his chest as he holds me to him once more, both of us trembling.

A trickle of water runs down my arm and I give a shiver, moving in tighter under the shelter of Will's arms. I don't want to speak and let words take this moment into something else, but I know that only then will we begin to make any sense of how we're both feeling. The longer I stay like this, the stronger will be the urge to remain silent, and so gradually I pull away until I am holding Will's hands. I pull him towards the bed, where we sit a little shyly, side by side, conscious of the emotional space between us. A tendril of hair slips forwards over my shoulder, where it drips water onto my lap with a soft *plip*. I reach for the bottom of my towel and try to bring it upwards to blot my hair, sensing as I do so the shift of Will's weight from the bed. Moments later the bed dips once more as he returns to kneel behind me, lifting my hair away from my neck and running his fingers through it. A soft towel begins to massage my head gently, and I let my weight sink against Will as I feel the tension in my shoulders start to ease. Ever since I was a child I have loved the feeling of having my hair brushed by someone else, and now as Will slides a comb gently through my tangled curls, a welcome peace begins to push aside all my anxieties. This action conveys far more to me than words ever could, and so for a few moments more neither of us feels the need to say anything at all.

Eventually Will's fingers still and I turn around to face him, his blue eyes almost violet in the dim light.

'I thought you didn't want to speak to me,' I say, not in accusation, but in acknowledgement of my fears. 'I was so scared.'

Will lowers his eyes for a moment. 'I shouldn't have walked out,' he admits. 'I just wanted to spend whatever time I have this weekend with you, not talking about wedding arrangements. I didn't realise quite how many things there were to organise. Bit naive, but there you go. I got impatient listening to all that other stuff, but I can see how hard you and Fliss have worked and I know it's all going to be perfect.'

'But the flowers?'

'Will be beautiful. I'm sorry I got so angry over what was obviously a misunderstanding. Really, it's fine, Ellie.'

I'm not quite sure how to say this. 'Only thing is, I hate the lilies too,' I whisper. 'They're not very friendly, are they?' I pull back slightly, not quite sure what his reaction is going to be. His eyes are fixed on mine. I can see the query in them, and for a moment I'm not quite sure how this is going to go, but then Will exhales a long slow breath, on the back of which is borne a rueful smile that crinkles the corners of his mouth and eyes. He shakes his head gently.

'Well, thank bloody heaven for that,' he grins, and the tension of the moment is released into laughter.

'It's weird, Will. Honest to God the lilies weren't my idea. I'm sure Fliss told me they were your favourite; she certainly gave Patience that idea, and now when I think back I remember having a conversation about them with Alice too, and she seemed rather cool about the idea. I didn't think anything of it at the time, and you know Alice, trying to be diplomatic, but she clearly thought it was an odd choice. Now I know why. I never knew that you had lilies at your wedding with Caroline, but she would have, wouldn't she? And she knew that you didn't like them.'

'Caroline used to fill the house with them, even after the wedding. The smell pervaded everywhere, and when she left Alice threw them all away.'

'So where would Fliss have got that idea from then, if it wasn't you and it wasn't Alice?'

My mind is racing, trying to recall the threads of conversations over the weeks and months. Will shrugs his shoulders just as something registers suddenly, a half-remembered conversation: something that Lizzie had started to say about a mix-up with the flowers, before changing her mind.

I frown gently, biting my lip. 'I've got a horrible feeling I know who it might be,' I say, my mind now firmly back on the events of the afternoon. 'And I'm afraid that's not all she's done either. I can't believe she would have done it deliberately, but there are too many things stacking up now to ignore.'

Will gives me quizzical look.

'Lizzie,' I reply in explanation. 'Let me get dressed. Tea was nearly ready when I came up and I think we need to talk to Finn and Ben about this as well.'

Will eyes my towel with a rueful smile, and for a second I'm torn, but I can't ignore this any longer.

I plant a kiss firmly on Will's lips. 'Later,' I grin, launching myself off the bed and away from his enticing hands.

Finn looks up the minute I walk into the kitchen, his agitated expression fading somewhat as he takes in Will, who's right behind me. I think, not for the first time, how lucky I am to have these wonderful people around me. Finn has always had the ability to sum up a situation in an instant and he has no need to voice his concern. Instead he breaks into a broad grin.

'We left you some tea,' he says, 'so I hope you're hungry; otherwise we'll be eating it for days.' He shoots an affectionate grin at Ben. 'Spaghetti carbonara. Help yourself. There's salad here too.'

My stomach gives a lurch of appreciation at the thought of the garlicky pasta whose comforting smell still lingers in the air. There's a dish of tomatoes drizzled in oil as well, and I spoon copious amounts of both into two bowls.

'Thanks, Ben, this looks fantastic,' says Will, joining me at the table.

Finn rises momentarily, returning to the table with two more bottles of beer, which he places in front of us. 'Apart from anything, it is the weekend, after all,' he says.

Will nods gratefully, acknowledging the reference to the stresses of the day.

I smile around my already full mouth, trying to stop a small explosion of tomato juice from escaping. 'I wonder if I could have a chat with you about something, Finn; well, both of you really . . . about Lizzie?'

The look exchanged between Finn and Ben might as well be emblazoned with flashing lights and heralded by trumpets, it's so obvious. I say nothing but wait for one of them to start speaking. With a sigh and a running of fingers through his hair, it's Finn who starts talking.

'I'm sorry, Ellie, I don't think this is good news,' he says. 'I started thinking about this that night after we went around to Lizzie's, when she found the paper with Patience's order on it.'

I nod for him to continue.

'We said then that maybe it would be wise to check out one or two things about her background, just to be on the safe side . . . and, well, it doesn't make for happy reading, I'm afraid.'

I open my mouth to speak, but Finn carries on.

'I know it doesn't mean anything, and I'm not suggesting for one minute that Lizzie is guilty of anything here. You saw her reaction that night; neither of us could believe her capable of any of the things that have happened recently, but after hearing what I have, I'm beginning to wonder whether she just can't help herself.'

I look over to Will, whose face mirrors my own concern. 'Go on,' I say.

'You might remember one of the lads who came down to do a few sessions with us when Rowan Hill opened. Big lanky lad called Neil, plays the double-bass? Anyhow, he's a community policeman by day and I left a message to ask if he knew much about Lizzie's family. He works the patch where she's from. He's only just got back to me, but he knows the family all right – everybody does apparently; they're not good news. And not only that . . . apparently Lizzie was in touch with him herself about a week ago, saying that she has a "friend" who's in trouble, and asking his advice. I don't think it's any "friend" in trouble, do you?'

'But Lizzie has no family. Her mum died, remember, and she has no idea who her dad is.'

'Whether she does or she doesn't is another matter, but if you had Liam Duncan for a father you'd keep quiet about it too. They're a rough family, Ellie. It's no wonder Lizzie was doing her best to distance herself from them.'

'But Lizzie told me that they only moved to Shrewsbury a few years ago. I don't know where they were living before, but her mum took up with Liam after they moved there.'

'She might have done, but that didn't mean she didn't know him from before. It's very hard to shake off that kind of life. My guess is that wherever they were living Lizzie's mum got herself into some sort of trouble and went back to the only people she thought could help her. I asked Neil to see if he could find out anything more, and the word is very strong that Liam was her mum's pimp, for want of a better word. He's also Lizzie's father.'

I raise a hand to my mouth in shock. 'Oh dear God. She wasn't involved in anything like that, was she?'

Finn is quick to reassure me. 'No, not that he's aware of. In fact, he asked some of his colleagues from the regular force about the incident when Lizzie's mum got into the fight that broke her arm, but not surprisingly the detail is a bit thin. There wasn't exactly a horde of folks queuing up to give evidence, but the general consensus is that she was probably trying to protect Lizzie in her own way, something that didn't go down too well with the punters. Her mum died of an overdose in the end, whether accidently or not it wasn't clear.'

'But Lizzie might still be in danger,' I gulp. 'We might be,' I add, trying not to think of the ordeals that must have faced her on a regular basis.

The three men exchange looks. 'My mate doesn't think so. They won't be bothered about Lizzie, as long as she's out of their hair. Too many other things to worry about.'

'But I still don't really understand what this has to do with the things that have been going on here, things that on the face of it have either been accidents or misunderstandings. Why would Lizzie cause trouble when she doesn't seem to have any reason to do so? It doesn't make sense.'

Finn scratches his head. 'I don't know either, and neither does Neil. In fact, he did say that, on the face of it, Lizzie seemed different from the rest of the family. She had rung him to ask for help, don't forget, and a copper would usually be the last person that anyone from that kind of family would speak to. She doesn't seem to have anything to gain from causing trouble, but I think that maybe when you have the kind of life where you have to lie and cheat just to get through the day, it becomes second nature to you. Like I said, maybe she can't help herself.'

'But Lizzie has always seemed very grateful for everything that she has here. Why would she deliberately jeopardise that? If she were in touch with her family, or they had some hold over her in some way, I could understand her actions, but from what you say she doesn't even seem to be in contact with them.'

'I don't have the answers, Ellie; I'm just repeating what I've heard. I admit it all seems a little strange, especially as from what I can see nobody has stood to gain from what's gone on here.' Finn takes another slurp of beer. 'But I don't think we can ignore it.'

Will rests his fork back in his bowl. 'I have to agree with Finn, I'm afraid. I like Lizzie and I really thought this place would be good for her, but I'm not sure we can carry on as we are. Sooner or later things are going to get out of hand.'

'They may already have,' I say softly, explaining the events of the afternoon. 'I haven't got to the bottom of it yet, but whatever happened with Helen sounded pretty serious, and not like it was an isolated incident either.' I glance at Will. 'It's a small thing, but there's also been a misunderstanding with the wedding flowers, and Lizzie is involved somewhere along the line. Do you remember that comment she made when we went to see her about Ben's keys – something about a mix-up over the flowers? I think Fliss has been trying to cover for her.'

There's silence for a few minutes as we all mull over what has been said. My own head is replaying every one of the odd things that have happened over the last few weeks, and I'm forced to admit that I probably don't know the half of it. I have no idea what upset Helen so much this afternoon, but the clear implication was that I should have known. I may have been a bit preoccupied lately but not to the extent that I would forget something serious like that. It's as if a huge chunk of information is missing.

'So what do we do now?' I say to nobody in particular. 'I can't bear the thought of asking Lizzie to leave.'

'I'm not sure it's come to that yet,' replies Will, 'but we do need to talk to her. Tell her what we know and ask for her explanation.'

'We owe her that at least,' says Ben, 'and for God's sake go easy on her. I can't believe she's behind any of the things that have happened; it just doesn't fit with the Lizzie I know.' He heaves a sigh. 'But I suppose I have to take on board what's been said—'

I don't need to look at any of them to know what's coming my way. I suppose it's only fair really, seeing as I'm the one who spoke up for Lizzie in the first place. I look at my watch and wind some more spaghetti around my fork with a sigh. If I'm to be judge, jury and executioner, I may as well go on a full stomach.

Chapter 31

ELLIE

There's a slight breeze blowing as I cross the courtyard. On any other day I might have stopped to enjoy the perfect evening air, but tonight I'm in no mood to dawdle.

I curl my hand over the key in my pocket, just in case I need it. It's a spare key for Lizzie's flat; I don't suppose she's had the best of afternoons, and there's every possibility she won't want to talk to me at all, but I can't leave without checking that she's all right.

I'm not exactly sure how to make a knock on the door sound friendly but I try all the same. Not a pounding, or a too quiet timid knock, but a sort of breezy 'I was just passing by' *rat-a-tat-tat*. The sort of knock that might sound like a friend popping in for a natter. I don't feel like her friend. I feel like a Judas.

All too predictably there's no reply. Even when I knock again with a bright *Hi, Lizzie, it's only me*, all I can hear is the sound of a distant dog barking and the drone of a nearby lawn mower. There is no sound at all from within.

It's funny how you can tell a place is empty the minute you walk into it. Whether it's the stillness in the air or the lack of energy that used to occupy the space, I don't know, but the minute I open Lizzie's door

I know she's gone. Not popped out to buy a carton of milk gone, but packed up and left gone. There is a flat quality to the place that echoes my own feelings exactly: a sad disappointment at a situation that was looking so good, but that time had turned sour.

It strikes me at first that Lizzie's leaving is tantamount to an admission of guilt, but there is something else here, like a soft whispering at the corners of my mind. There's not a thing out of place here, and I mean not a thing. The flat has been so carefully cleaned and left so ordered it seems at odds with a person who has deliberately set out to cause trouble these past few months. It seems more like the action of someone who wanted others to think well of them, even when they knew this was unlikely: a person who wanted to make as few waves as possible, who wanted to slip by unnoticed, leaving no ripples in her wake, no sign that she was ever here.

The rooms which had held the vibrant and slightly chaotic nature that was Lizzie are now tidy to the point of fastidiousness. Even the bed is stripped, the sheets, pillowcases and duvet cover folded neatly at the end of the bed. Everything she brought with her is gone but, incongruously, everything she added during her time with us remains. Four or five magazines sit in a neat pile at rigid right-angles to the edge of the coffee table. The wool-wrapped jam jar that Helen gave her still sits on the tiny chest of drawers in her bedroom, the fabric flowers they made together carefully arranged within. Even the jar of hand cream that she bought from Patience is left beside the sink in the bathroom.

There is, however, one final detail which makes my heart ache. There in the kitchen, propped against the flowery teapot that Lizzie bought from a market, is a note. I don't have to read it to know what it says, as propped beside it is a pile of ten- and twenty-pound notes. There must be about five hundred pounds altogether, not stolen money or money earned through illicit means, but what is left of the small salary we paid her. Carefully saved for a rainy day, and now that day has come, left behind – for what? Compensation? When I can finally bring myself to read the note there is an apology that it couldn't be more, and a thank you for having had her.

As the tears run silently down my face I feel sure that Lizzie is not guilty of anything here, except being a victim. She has run because it's the only thing she knows how to do. She has slipped by as she must have had to do so many times in her past, taking only what she brought with her, as if she had no claim to anything else.

I feel a well of guilt and shame building up for this young girl who had tried so hard to make a fresh start, but who, in the end, had been let down by the very people who could have made a difference. People who let the weight of her past cling to her like a sour smell she could not evade, and who did so little to help her wash it away.

I hold the note in my hand for a moment, wondering what to do, as my feeling of unease builds. By the time I'm at the door, a real fear has quickened my steps. Lizzie might have run, and I can't do anything about that, but it's where she's run to that scares me.

Shrewsbury is quiet at this time of night. It's too early for the pub- and party-goers, and we are distinctly in the wrong part of town. Every town has streets like these, whether we want to acknowledge it or not, and I'm ashamed that I feel so uncomfortable. I don't even know if this is where Lizzie will have come, but the buses from the village either come north to Shrewsbury or south to Ludlow, a place she doesn't know that well. We've loitered around the bus and train station for an age, the four of us splitting up and searching every corner, checking the places that are still open – the fast-food restaurants and convenience stores – before reluctantly admitting defeat and returning to the car. I have no idea what time Lizzie left Rowan Hill, but I pray that she hasn't journeyed on to Birmingham, or even London. If she has, there's no way we'll find her.

Now we're driving slowly up and down the streets on Neil's patch, near to where Lizzie used to live, something that fills me with unease. The few people who are about stop to watch us, with a look that is not curiosity but a challenge to invade their space. I know I've lived a sheltered and, I can see now, privileged life, but I'm scared for Lizzie. I'm scared of what might happen if she isn't welcomed back into the fold, and I'm equally scared of what might happen if she is.

Two and a half hours later it's fully dark, and we drive silently back home, having seen no sign of Lizzie or anyone who looked even remotely like her. At nearly eleven o'clock there's nothing more we can do for now, and our day of work tomorrow still beckons. My phone has stayed silent the entire time, and although I understand why Lizzie might not want to reply to my messages, I hope that at least they might bring some comfort to her.

As we close up the house for the night, switching off lights and locking doors, there's hardly a word said; it's a sad end to a sorry day as we troop off to bed. I lie curled tightly into the crook of Will's arm, and while this brings some comfort I know that sleep will be hard to find. There will be no respite from my thoughts in the morning, and the dawn, when it comes, will only serve to bring light.

Chapter 32

ELLIE

I have a visitor to the tea room first thing on Monday morning. Someone who, under the circumstances, is the last person I expected to see. She doesn't normally call in this early in the morning, but as I look up at the sound of the door opening, my relief at seeing Helen's smile, albeit rather a cautious one, is heartfelt.

The smile quickly turns to a frown when she sees me.

'Ellie, you look awful,' she exclaims, coming straight over to the counter. 'You look like you haven't slept in a week.'

Now that she's closer I can see black shadows under her eyes too, and the slightly pinched expression left behind by stress.

'Erm, pot, kettle, black?' I venture, not knowing quite how this remark will be taken, something that I wouldn't have thought twice about before.

There's a slight hesitation, and maybe Helen is pondering this too, but very quickly her face opens again and she holds out her arms for a hug.

'I'm so sorry, Ellie,' she says. 'I had a dreadful evening thinking about how vile I was to you . . . and to Lizzie. I've been so on edge lately for some reason, and I was very upset yesterday, but when I sat down and thought about it properly I couldn't think why I behaved the way I did – it wasn't like me at all. I should have come and discussed things with you rationally, so I made up my mind today to do just that . . . and to apologise.' She gives a little glance over my shoulder. 'Is Lizzie here too?' she adds.

I'm not sure what to say. I still have no idea what upset Helen, but it's clear she's still very troubled by what happened, and the last thing I want to do is to give her the impression that Lizzie left because of her. Whichever way I put it will sound wrong.

'She's not here at the minute. I've never seen you so upset, Helen. What on earth happened?'

She studies my face for a moment. 'You don't have any idea, do you?' she asks, looking puzzled.

I shake my head, bemused. 'No, I really don't. It's like I've missed huge chunks of what's been happening, Helen. I could see how upset you were, but that aside, you seem to think I should know about certain other things as well, and that's what I'm finding confusing.' I shake my head. 'I don't know; maybe I'm going doolally.'

It was a light-hearted remark, but to my surprise Helen looks really worried. 'No, I don't think so, but can we sit down for a minute so I can explain?'

'Sure. Pop over there and I'll bring some tea.'

We've only just opened and as yet there's no one else about, but it's probably the only time I've prayed for a lack of customers. I fill a teapot and stack some cups and the milk jug on a tray, adding some shortbread at the last minute.

As I sit down Helen eyes the tray, and reaches out for a piece of the sugary biscuit. 'I remember the first time I came to see you at Rowan Hill. We had shortbread then. It seems like a lifetime ago, and so much has happened since.' She gives me a sad smile. 'Good things, Ellie – I don't want to lose them, or any of you.'

I reach out to touch her arm. 'What's been happening, Helen? Start at the beginning.'

'I thought at first *I* was going doolally. It was just little things: stuff going missing and then turning up in peculiar places, things not being where I know I had left them. Nothing major, but irritating all the same. Then things got a little more serious.'

I pour the tea, nodding at Helen to continue.

'I noticed one day that one of my pictures was looking a bit odd; you know, the woven ones that I keep on display. It looked like it was sagging in the middle, and when I went to have a closer look I realised that a load of the threads had been snipped through at the back. The front thread was still there but was only just hanging on to the canvas as its anchor had gone.'

I halt the flow of tea into the cups, looking up at Helen in shock.

'That's not the only thing, I'm afraid, Ellie. A week or so ago I was finishing off a commission for a wall hanging and had already wrapped the strips of fabric into balls so they were ready to use. They were a particular colour, chosen especially, and all the fabric I had had been cut. As I began to unwind the balls they fell apart. The first few strips around the outside were fine, but then underneath the strips had been recut into pieces only a couple of inches long. Someone had undone the balls and deliberately cut them up. They were completely unusable. The commission was a birthday present and because the fabric was one I ordered specially for it, getting more in time was a real problem. I nearly lost the commission.'

'Why didn't you tell me all this before? This is awful.'

Helen looks down at her cup, swirling the tea around with a spoon. 'I didn't want to worry you, and in any case . . . well, I know now that I should have spoken to you about this myself, but at the time too many other things seemed to be going wrong, and we felt you had enough to deal with. But when the rings went missing as well, we—'

I look up sharply, my cup never making it as far as my lips. 'What rings, Helen?' I say slowly, the shock of her words making my voice sound strident in the empty room.

There is a panicked look on Helen's face as she realises what she's said, possibly a detail that was not hers to share. She doesn't know where to look, and there's an awkward silence for a moment. 'Ellie, I thought you knew, I'm so sorry. Fliss was . . . well, I'm sure she was going to tell you, it's just that—'

'Am I really that bad,' I mutter, 'that no one seems able to share things with me any more? Honestly, what did you all think I would do?'

'It's not like that, Ellie. Please don't get upset. Things have been a bit tough lately, and we all thought it best if we tried to deal with it ourselves. Fliss said that she would talk to you last week. I thought she had. I'm sorry.'

'Is that why you were cross with me yesterday? Because you thought I'd been ignoring what was happening?'

Helen lays her hand over mine. She doesn't need to answer.

'I had no idea, Helen, about any of it.'

'I can see that now,' she replies, her eyes downcast. 'I should have spoken to you myself, like I said, but . . .' she trails off, trying to pick her way through the muddle that we seem to have found ourselves in.

I hardly dare to ask. 'So what happened yesterday? You can tell me now.'

It takes a moment, but Helen finally meets my eyes. There is a soft sigh.

'Well, as you know, I had to go out to meet a client, so Lizzie came over to cover for me. After my meeting I picked up a few supplies and then came back. I'd arranged to meet some more clients back here around lunchtime. They wanted to pick up a picture I had made for them, but when I arrived, thankfully before they did, I discovered it had been sold.'

'But how did that happen?'

'I keep anything that's been sold on display until it's collected, but pieces are marked very clearly with coloured tags so that we can identify what's sold and what isn't. I know this one had the right tag on it, Ellie, because I put it there myself, but when I got back, Lizzie had just accepted a 50 per cent deposit on it. It was marked as if it were available.'

'But that could have been a simple mistake, surely?'

Helen shakes her head violently. 'It wasn't, because when I checked, all the other tags were wrong too. Everything had been swapped around, so that sold pieces were up for sale again and vice versa. It took me all afternoon to sort out the mess, not to mention two very irate customers.'

'I don't know what to say. I'm so sorry.' I expel a slow breath because I know what's coming next. 'And you think Lizzie did all this?' I add quietly.

To my surprise there is a shake of the head, but more in sorrow this time than exasperation. 'I did . . . but now I'm not so sure. The more I think about it, the more it seems so unlikely, but I really can't think who—' Her eyes search mine as she takes in my expression, studying my face for a moment. 'She's not here, is she? She's gone.'

I pinch my lips together.

'Jesus, what a mess. I'm not surprised she's gone, Ellie, to be honest, after what I said to her. I was a right cow to you as well, but I accused Lizzie of all sorts of things, which, let's face it, I have absolutely no proof of, but at the time I was so angry. I shouldn't have taken it out on you either.'

I try a small smile.

'Helen, you were upset about something that's very precious to you.'

'That doesn't excuse my behaviour. Lizzie will probably never speak to me again. Where has she gone?'

I pause for a moment, wondering how I can let Helen down gently, but there's no way I can think of to soften what I'm about to say next.

'I'm sorry, Helen, but no one saw her leave. We don't know where she is.'

Helen stares at me for a moment, her gentle features quite distraught.

'Oh God, what have I done?' she winces, her hand covering her mouth. 'We have to find her, Ellie; she could be in all sorts of trouble. I don't think her family . . . well, you know . . . they're not like yours and mine.'

'I know, but we have to hope that she's okay. She's pretty street-wise. I'm sure she knows how to look after herself.' I'm not really sure I believe that any more, but I need to say it as much to convince myself as Helen. I fill her in on our search over the last couple of days.

'I left countless messages on her phone as well. We just have to hope that she'll find her own way back to us when she's ready. She left behind all the things that matter to her.'

'I hope so, but I can't sit here and do nothing, Ellie. I know you're trying to make me feel better about things, but I still feel responsible for this. Perhaps I should look for her too?'

'I know how you feel, Helen. She's my responsibility as well, but I honestly don't know where to look. She could be anywhere.'

I let my words sit between us for a moment, knowing that Helen feels as guilty as I do right now.

'I'm beginning to get a bit freaked out by all this, to be honest. Everything that has happened recently seems to involve Lizzie in one way or another, and now that she's run off, it looks more than ever like she's to blame. I got the strangest feeling when I was in her flat though, Helen. I can't explain it, and it doesn't make any sense, but the way she'd left it seemed . . . sad, unbearably so. It doesn't fit with someone who's been causing so much trouble.'

'And yet what other explanation is there?'

The door gives its friendly jangling welcome as Fliss comes into the tea room, a beaming smile on her face.

'There you are,' she starts. 'So who's the most amazing wedding organiser ever then? Actually, you don't need to answer that, you're looking at her.' She beams, looking back and forth between the two of us. 'Aren't you going to ask what I've done?' she adds, seeing our blank faces, but then continuing before we have the chance to reply. 'Only gone and sorted out your flowers, once and for all, you'll be pleased to hear. Well, actually, I had a little help . . . It was Lizzie's brilliant idea. I don't know why I didn't think of it before.'

She looks around the room, suddenly realising it's empty save for us. 'Oh, where is she? I thought she'd like to hear how it all turned out.'

Chapter 33

ELLIE

It takes all my powers of persuasion to stop Fliss going out to look for Lizzie too, but eventually she sees my reasoning. I'd lain in bed last night searching my mind for any clues as to where Lizzie might have gone, but despite the fact that she lived in Shrewsbury for some time before she came to us, it's almost as if she blanked out that part of her life, and none of us have ever heard her mention any places other than those we visited together, like Attingham Park or the town-centre shops. I can't believe that she would have returned back to her life before – it doesn't seem like the kind of thing she would do – but however hard we try we cannot think of where else she might have gone.

'But why did she go in the first place, Ellie?' asks Fliss. 'She loves it here, and she's been doing so well.'

Helen makes a small noise at the back of her throat. 'I think that might have been my fault,' she says. 'There was another . . . misunderstanding yesterday and I got a bit worked up about it all. I let Lizzie have it with both barrels, I'm afraid. It's no wonder she's gone.'

'You didn't tell me that,' says Fliss, her face falling in sympathy. 'What happened?'

Helen fidgets with the empty cup in front of her, twisting it around in the saucer. She gives a half-smile. 'I should go,' she starts, looking at her watch. 'I've got a lot to do today. I'll catch up with you later, Fliss, if that's okay – I can tell you then.'

I smile as she stands, rising myself, intent on walking her to the door. She obviously doesn't want to talk any more, and I can't say I blame her. I feel as if I'm going around in circles myself. I'm glad she popped in this morning; it's cleared the air a little, although as we say goodbye I wonder whether it's enough. Perhaps it's my imagination, but her hug feels a little forced.

'I should crack on too,' comes Fliss's voice from behind me. 'It's all go, isn't it? What will you do?' she adds, as I turn around to face her. 'Now that Lizzie has gone, I mean. It leaves you rather in the lurch, doesn't it? You must let me know if you need any help.'

'Thanks, Fliss. I'm more concerned about Lizzie now, rather than what her absence means, but you're right, it will make things a bit harder again. I have Finn popping in later, so I should manage fine.'

She's almost at the door when I remember what it is that I wanted to ask her. 'Fliss, why didn't you tell me you'd had some rings go missing?'

There's a guilty smile of admission. 'I was hoping you wouldn't find out,' she grimaces. 'You've been so stressed lately, Ellie. I didn't want to burden you with that on top of everything else. And it's no biggy really; it won't make any difference. I've still got time to finish them.'

My eyes widen. 'Oh God, it was our rings that went? You should have told me. Apart from anything else, that's theft; they were worth quite a lot of money, never mind all the work you'd already put in.'

'I might have just mislaid them.'

'Really? You honestly expect me to believe that?'

Another sheepish smile. 'No, not really,' she says wearily. 'Just trying to look on the bright side. Anyway, as I said, I've sorted it, so you're not to worry any more.' She takes hold of my hand and gives it a squeeze. 'Try and come over later, if you can. Just for a few minutes. I want to show you what we've done about the flowers. That should cheer you up.'

I collect our cups and plates, trying to think of all the things that have been happening lately and put them in some sort of order. There must be some common denominator, something that might give me a clue, but all I come up with is a list of events, seemingly random and entirely unconnected. The thought that anyone here is responsible is absurd, but in reality it's the only logical conclusion there can be, and this thought above all others haunts me – not only the who, but the why.

I really need to go and speak to Helen again. Something she said a few moments ago is niggling me but I can't remember what it was now; my head is too jumbled. I'm also wondering what changed her mind about Lizzie, but until Finn comes to relieve me later on, I'm on my own. I eye the cakes, freshly made this morning, which are now cool enough to slice, and go and wash my hands. I had better get on, the first of the morning walkers will be through shortly.

I haven't even got as far as drying my hands properly when I hear the doorbell jangle again.

'So where would you like me to start?'

I'd know that voice anywhere.

'Gina!' I exclaim, rushing forwards to throw my arms around the diminutive woman standing there. 'Oh my God, what are you doing here?'

She flashes me a huge grin, the big silver hoops in her ears glinting in the light. 'That's a very long story, which in the end turned out to be a very short story. Which version would you like?'

'Any,' I laugh. 'I don't care, it's so lovely to see you.'

Gina hasn't changed a bit: she still has the same jet-black spiky hair and the same look of a coiled spring about her. She's all of five foot nothing, and doesn't look like she could stand still if she tried.

'I'm so pleased I'm here. Look at this place, Ellie; it looks amazing. And good to see the old tables and chairs are being useful. I thought you might have thrown them all out by now.'

'No way. Everything is still here. Look.' I point to the display cabinet, where a selection of cakes is displayed on huge blue and white floral-print plates. Plates that Gina herself made once upon a time.

She sighs, turning back to me with a wistful expression. 'Christ, it's good to be home, Ellie.'

I narrow my eyes at her. 'That sounds like it could be the long story?' I remark. 'Need a cup of tea? Or a hot chocolate?' I add, remembering Gina's fondness for the stuff.

'Now you're talking,' she says, taking another look at the cabinet. 'And as big a piece of gingerbread as you'll let me have. Then I'll tell you about that arse of a husband of mine, and you can tell me what's going on here. A little bird told me you needed a hand,' she winked.

I can't begin to describe how happy I am to see Gina. It feels like a weight has been lifted off my shoulders. She was one of the first real friends I made when I moved here more than a year and a half ago, before Rowan Hill as it is now existed. I baked cakes for her tea room in the village, and she gave me the first real sense of purpose I'd had since moving here. When she sold up, moving to Northamptonshire with her husband's job, it gave us the perfect opportunity to open up here, and not only that but we bought up her tea-room fittings, lock, stock and barrel. Without Gina, Rowan Hill Tea Room would simply not exist. However, that's not the only reason I'm pleased to see her: Gina is a little powerhouse of energy, and if you ask her to do something, she never asks how but only when by. I suddenly feel like I've gained an important ally, but also, perhaps more importantly right now, a safe pair of hands.

Gina has wandered through to the kitchen while I make her drink, and a loud sigh floats through the door.

'God, I've missed your cakes, Ellie. Look at this lot. Is it wrong that I want a piece of every one of them?'

When I stick my head around the door to reply she already has an apron on. 'Shall I cut them for you?' she asks before I can reply.

As I nod she moves past me to collect the cake stands from the counter. There's not a thing that woman misses.

'So basically,' she says, 'before you ask, my Derek is a complete twazzock. I'm trying to be polite here, you understand?'

I raise an eyebrow at her as I place the hot chocolate down beside her.

'Well, more to the point, he's a lying, cheating bastard, but the strange thing is that after twenty-seven years of marriage, I don't actually mind that much.' She waves the cake slice at me. 'So don't look at me like that.'

I wasn't aware that I was looking at her in any particular way, but given the piece of news I've just heard, I'm not quite sure which face I should be making. Surprise? Disgust? Sympathy? Or, judging by the look of her, encouragement?

'What happened, Gina?'

'Well, we moved, as you know. I hated the place, by the way, folks very unfriendly, and so there I was, busy buying up half the county to try and make our place look habitable, when Derek's boss ups and dies. Two months later and Derek gets made managing director of the firm.'

'Oh God, how awful . . . But quite good for Derek, I suppose.'

'Very good for Derek, seeing as he'd been shagging the MD's wife: the very round Sheila with the fat arse and now, fortuitously, pots of money.'

'Gina!'

'What? I'm only telling the truth. She has got a fat arse.'

'But how long had it been going on?'

'Oh, years . . . The annual conference wasn't an annual conference . . . The area sales meetings he had to stay over for weren't area sales meetings . . . Blah blah blah. You get the idea.' She slides an expertly sliced cake onto a stand. 'So, I thought about what I should do, and the more I thought about it, the more I realised there was only one thing I did want to do. And that was come home, so here I am.'

She flashes me a huge smile, which I can't help but return. 'But what *are* you going to do?'

'I had rather hoped that's where you might come in,' she says, her mood suddenly rather more serious. 'You know how things were with Derek and me. I got bored easily and drove him mad, and so he bought me stuff to keep me happy. Now I know why he did that, of course, but even so I'm not ungrateful. I got to do a few things over the years that I really enjoyed. One of them was running my tea room, and the other was making pots. No offence, Ellie, but there's no point me running a tea room any more, so I thought I might have a go at making my pots again. What do you think?'

I look at the tiny woman standing in front of me waving a cake slice and I feel a little well of excitement building up inside of me. I can't think of anything I'd like more; having Gina here will be the icing on the proverbial cake. There's one small problem, though.

'I think that's an utterly brilliant idea . . . but, Gina, I'm not sure where we'd put you right now.'

'No, I know, but I've got to wait for the sale of our house to go through yet and that could take ages. Derek has moved into Sheila's five-bedroomed colonial, so after some, er, "discussions", we've agreed that what's left from the sale of the house once the mortgage is paid off is mine. It'll be enough to rent somewhere, or build something, or . . . something else that I haven't quite figured out yet.'

I'm suddenly caught by a wave of excitement at her news. 'Oh, I don't care, Gina. We'll make it happen, don't worry; we'll work it out. I'm so glad you're here.'

A thought comes to me then, and I narrow my eyes at her. 'Hang on a minute. Earlier you said a little bird had told you we needed a hand. Which little bird would that be exactly?'

'I spoke to Will yesterday,' she laughs, 'but I made him promise not to tell you. I wanted to keep it as a surprise. He did say that you could put me up here for a little bit, though. Is that okay?'

'Of course it is! The swine, he never mentioned it. I bet they all know, don't they?'

Gina lowers her gaze. 'Well, only Will and Finn to be fair, but Will mentioned things had been a bit iffy here. He thought it would be a nice surprise if I just turned up. I didn't see any point in waiting around, so I jumped in the car and came over. I got here late last night.'

'But where's all your stuff?'

'I stayed at the Morrises' B&B, but I didn't bring much, to be honest, just a couple of cases. I can fetch them later today.' She eyes me suspiciously. 'But first things first. What's been going on?'

I really don't know where to start, and I'm very well aware that when I do begin to tell Gina about it, it's going to sound like I'm being far too dramatic. She never says a word the whole time but stands there looking at me intently. When I've finished she is silent for a few moments more, digesting what I've told her, then she walks out into the main room, surveying the counter with her hands on her hips.

'Right, unless there's anything weird and wonderful that I should know about, I think I'll get the hang of things. Where's your menu?'

I slide one out from its resting place down the side of the till and go to pass it to her, holding it out a little gingerly.

'I won't make any cakes while I'm here, I promise. Now go on, shoo, you have lots to do.'

I still haven't quite relinquished my grip on the menu. I smile at Gina's indignant expression. 'I didn't mean that at all . . . It's just that, well, I can't let you step in here and then leave you all on your own. You've only just got here.'

'And I'll be fine, so yes, you can. Now, menu, please.' She holds out her hand, wiggling her fingers.

'Well, only if you're sure.'

Gina scans the menu quickly. 'Piece of cake.' She grins at me. 'Now go!'

I feel better already.

I'm halfway to the door when it opens and a familiar red uniform comes through.

'Morning, morning,' sings Brian the postie, passing me a handful of letters. He looks past me to the figure behind the counter.

'I heard you were back,' he announces. 'I wondered if this was where you might be hiding out.'

'Well, hello to you too, Brian. That's charming, that is. Anyway, don't just stand there. Come on – I want to know what's been happening in the village; edited highlights only, please.' She throws me a questioning glance. 'Does he still . . . ?'

'Oh yes,' I laugh. 'Toffee apple muffin usually.'

I leave them to catch up, sauntering back to the house, and feeling more relaxed than I have in weeks. As I walk across the yard in the sun I remember a comment Helen made about feeling on edge and I realise that's what I've felt like too. Fliss mentioned that I'd been very stressed recently, and while I hadn't thought this to be the case, it must have seemed that way to other people. It's certainly true that my usual sense of peace has been missing of late. I stop for a moment, raising my head and closing my eyes, trying to feel the air of stillness that always surrounds Rowan Hill. It's particularly strong in the summer, but today, although the birds are singing and the leaves of the trees are rustling, it doesn't seem to go any deeper than that. I look over to the little flat above Patrick's workshop where Lizzie had made her home and think back to the day when we sat together in the gardens at Attingham Park. I know Lizzie could feel it too, and I wonder if she had been able to sense the change at Rowan Hill. I would love to be able to ask her.

A thought comes to me, and I pick up my pace towards the house. I have a million and one things to do, but I know where I'm headed now and who I need to see.

Chapter 34

ELLIE

I had intended to make only a brief stop by the kitchen to put the post on the table, but as I sifted through the pile, one letter stopped me in my tracks.

I'd recognise Lizzie's handwriting anywhere. It's just like she is: tall, loopy and a little bit ditzy. I study the envelope intently, but there are no clues as to where she is. The postmark says Shrewsbury, but that hardly narrows it down. It's the largest sorting office nearby, and letters posted for miles around would still bear the same mark. I perch on the edge of my seat at the table, holding the contents of the letter in a hand which is trembling slightly. It's only Monday today, which means she must have posted this letter on Saturday, the day she left.

I rip the envelope open, hoping to find a note telling me she's fine and that I'm not to worry. Instead I find a small cutting from a newspaper. Nothing else, just a rather worn-looking piece of newspaper print, folded in half, the ink smudged slightly from being handled.

I stare at the words on the clipping, but they mean nothing to me. I read them again in case I've missed something, in case I've skipped over some vital piece of information, but I still draw a blank. One thing is very clear, though: these are life-changing words. For someone, somewhere, these words turned their world upside down. But why did Lizzie choose to send me this? Of all the things she could have sent given the circumstances, she chose an anonymous newspaper clipping, and for some reason it unnerves me a great deal.

I refold the clipping carefully and slide it back into its envelope, heat gathering uncomfortably at the back of my neck. I pull out my phone and stare at the screen, but it's unchanged. There is no message from Lizzie. I look about the kitchen, trying to decide what to do, then realise that my original intention is still a good one and rush from the house.

I turn through the doorway in the right-hand side of the courtyard, an arch that will lead me past the polytunnels and the orchard and on to the back of Alice's house. I follow the red-bricked wall that encloses the garden to the Lodge first of all and then to Alice's garden. Work has halted on the Lodge for the moment as Finn and Ben are spending all their time laying paths through the woodland. It's back-breaking work, but an awful lot easier when it's dry and warm. The Lodge looks very sad with no one to care for it, and from what little I can see, the back garden is in sore need of attention again. I'll be very pleased when it's back in use; I don't like to see it empty and looking so forlorn.

I push open the gate to Alice's garden, smiling as I catch sight of her in the corner, her bright red sun hat bobbing up and down as she dead-heads her roses. I call a greeting and hope I don't startle her, but she lifts a hand and waves me over.

'Make yourself useful, dear,' she says, handing me a spray bottle. 'Give those a good squirt while I finish dead-heading. The greenfly are being such pests this year.'

I take the bottle as directed and start to spray the roses with what looks like soapy water. 'They're still beautiful, Alice. They smell gorgeous.'

'That's because they're proper old-fashioned roses, not those soulless new things that might be all fancy colours and ridiculous names but have no smell at all.'

I smile at Alice's comment. She's certainly not afraid of making her opinion known.

'So, what have you come to tell me then?' she says equally directly. 'Have you had news from Lizzie?'

'No, not exactly,' I start, not quite sure how to finish. After a few beats more, Alice straightens and turns to look at me. She takes another decisive snip at a rose.

'Perhaps it's time I stopped for a cup of tea. Come in, and you can tell me all about it.'

Once settled in the kitchen, Alice wastes no time in her interrogation.

'What does "not exactly" mean then?' she asks. 'Do you mean you have news of her, but not from her? Is that it?'

'Erm . . . that's not exactly right either.' I fish in my pocket. 'This came,' I say, handing her the envelope. 'I know it's from Lizzie, but, well . . . have a look yourself. It's not what I expected at all.'

Alice purses her lips as she slides out the newspaper clipping, her lips moving as she scans the article.

'Oh dear,' she says, 'how horrible. But what has it got to do with Lizzie?'

'I don't know. I'm not really sure it has got anything to do with her. What I can't make out is why she would have sent it to me. Do you think it's some sort of message? Or could it be that she wanted me to have it, to keep it safe perhaps . . . ? I don't know.'

Alice turned the clipping over. 'And this just came, did it, just like that?'

'Yes, in this morning's post. There was no note with it or anything. There's nothing written on it either, I've checked.'

'No. I can see that, dear. But whatever the reason, she sent it to you, no one else. So she must have thought it would have some meaning for you.'

'But it doesn't, Alice. It's from some newspaper in Cumbria. Look, the name is along the bottom of the page, but I don't even know anyone from there.'

'Well, I admit, it's a little strange,' she says, 'but there must be some reason for it. Lizzie might be a bit . . . giddy at times, but she can be very single-minded when she wants to be. That's why I find all this a bit strange. It's not like her at all.'

'What isn't?' I ask, fiddling with the edge of the tea cosy.

'All these things she's supposed to have done. It's completely at odds with everything she thinks about this place.' Alice gives me a very direct look. 'Have you ever asked her how she feels about Rowan Hill? Have any of you?'

I look down at the table, feeling Alice's disapproval. If I had given Lizzie a little more of my time, perhaps I would know where she was now, or at least why she had sent me the newspaper clipping.

'She thinks the world of you, you know. And she would never knowingly do anything to hurt this place, I'm absolutely convinced of that. Whatever has happened here certainly seems to involve Lizzie, I agree, but there has to be more to it than that. I think perhaps you owe it to her to find out, don't you?'

'But I'm not really sure what I can do,' I say. 'She won't answer any of my messages or calls, and if I can't speak to her, how can I find out what's happened?'

Alice looks at me a little sadly. 'But, my dear, she has spoken to you, don't you see?'

She puts the clipping back in the envelope and hands it to me. 'She must have posted this to you on the very day she left. Why would she do that? Why not simply hand it to you or leave it somewhere for you to find? Whatever that article is about must have meant something to

Lizzie, something too important to leave to chance. She wanted to be certain that you received it and, in my opinion, she didn't want anyone else to know about it. Best get on that internet thingy you're all so fond of, and if I were you I'd start by seeing what you can find out from the *Westmorland Gazette*.'

I look up in surprise. 'How did you get to be so wise, Alice?' I smile.

She pats my hand. 'Because I have time to sit back and observe,' she says. 'I'm not busy rushing around all the time like you young things, so my mind can take its time to digest things a little more. Besides which, I couldn't rush round if I wanted to, could I? This old body won't let me.'

Something about her words comes back at me like an echo from a previous conversation. I stare at her for a moment, trying to work out what it is, and then it comes to me. How stupid, when it was the very thing I wanted to talk to Alice about in the first place.

'Alice, this might sound a little odd, but has anything about Rowan Hill changed recently? Does it feel any different to you?'

It's Alice's turn to look surprised. She rests her cup gently back down in her saucer and stares into the dregs of her tea. 'Yes, yes it has,' she says slowly. 'That's very perceptive of you, Ellie . . . although I don't know why I'm surprised really, seeing as it was you who changed it back to how it used to be in the first place.' She catches sight of my stunned expression. 'You remember what I told you, when you first came to me looking for answers about Will's behaviour? I told you about the estate, how it was in his parents' day, the centre of the community.'

I nod. 'Yes, I remember.'

'And I also told you about Caroline, and the change in Will after he met her . . . that was when Rowan Hill changed too. It became cold, just like her, full of quarrels and meanness, hurtful things thought and said amongst us all. Rowan Hill lost her spirit then – and it took a young woman who wouldn't give up on us to change all that and to bring back the sense of community that Rowan Hill thrives on.'

She smiles at me fondly and I can feel my cheeks turning pink, but underneath my embarrassment I know she's right. We're all on edge with one another, just like Helen said too.

'I'm a silly old woman, Ellie, I know that, but I've lived here all my life, and whether you call them memories or vibes I don't know, but Rowan Hill doesn't like it when things are out of balance. Someone here is tipping that balance, and I don't think things will truly come right again until you find out who that person is. I think Lizzie is a very bright, perceptive young woman, and she might just have given you a clue to help you find that out.'

I stare at Alice for a moment, not really seeing her, my mind firmly back on the day I took Lizzie to Attingham Park and the conversation we'd had where I'd asked for her help. I feel a warmth settle around me, and I feel certain now that Lizzie is okay. She has done exactly what I asked her to: she *has* noticed what's been going on around her and, far from running away, she's done the only thing that made any sense to her. Lizzie must have felt that while the blame for what's been happening was being laid at her door, we would never think to look to anyone else for the answers – so she simply removed herself from the equation, forcing us to look elsewhere.

I focus back on Alice's face and see the beginnings of a small smile there, the same smile that is echoed on my own face. We understand each other perfectly.

My mind is a whirl of thoughts as I walk back across the yard. No longer confused thoughts, just rather a lot of them, all jostling for priority. I'll calm them down in a little while, put them all in order, but there's something else I want to do first. It's approaching lunchtime, and I'm going to stop and make something for us all to eat. I've just time to set a certain wheel in motion beforehand. I open up Finn's laptop on the kitchen table and, while I'm waiting for it to boot up, I take the envelope out of my pocket once more, laying the clipping down on the table.

I read the contents again, just to check I've not missed anything, before typing 'The Westmorland Gazette' into the search engine and waiting for the results. It must have been a big story at the time and with any luck the full article will be on the paper's website, rather than just the few lines contained in the clipping, and, if I'm lucky, the name of the reporter who wrote it.

I type in the keywords that I hope will bring up the article, and within seconds five hits are listed. I select the second, my heart beating faster and faster while I wait for it to load. With a flicker it's there before me, the whole story as it appeared in print, ending with the section that appears on the clipping I've placed on the table in front of me:

> . . . *and police are now appealing for any witnesses to the crash to contact them, in order to establish the cause of this horrific accident. The deceased man has yet to be named, and police are keen to make contact with his family as soon as possible. Anyone with any information is urged to make contact with the incident team on the helpline number below, which will operate as normal throughout the Christmas holiday period.*

The article is dated 22 December last year.

Chapter 35

ELLIE

'It's only a few sandwiches and some fruit, I'm afraid, but it should keep the wolf from the door,' I say, as Patience all but snatches the bag out of my hand.

'You are an absolute lifesaver,' she says, beaming, and sinking her teeth straight into her egg and cress. 'I'm so hungry at the minute. I don't know what's wrong with me. I'm ravenous all the time.'

There's a definite twinkle in her eye.

'Keeping your strength up for anyone in particular?' I tease, and Patience's answering blush is all the confirmation I need.

'I'm like a bloody teenager, it's ridiculous,' she mumbles through a mouthful of food. 'But the biggest amount of fun I've ever had. My mother was right, you know, it is the quiet ones you have to watch!' She lowers her voice to a whisper. 'Don't say anything to Patrick, will you? The poor man will die of embarrassment. No one is supposed to know.'

'Well, stop grinning like a Cheshire cat then. That might help. Honestly, Patience, what are you like?' I tut in mock exasperation. 'I am so very pleased for you, though, and for Patrick. It's lovely, and I can see how happy you are.'

'*And* I've had another order from the garden centre. What do you think of that?' She catches sight of my expression. 'Don't worry, I've insisted on a proper amount of time to make things this time around. No need for panic . . . Just as well, given that your wedding is so soon. It's your fault, you know, all this lovey-dovey stuff. It must be catching.'

She takes another bite of her sandwich. 'Not that I'm complaining, mind! Just don't go changing your mind on the flowers again, will you? I don't think I can stand the strain.'

I give her a quizzical look. 'What do you mean, changing my mind again? I haven't changed my mind – the thing with the lilies was just a misunderstanding.'

A flicker of confusion crosses Patience's face but she says nothing.

'I haven't caught up with Fliss yet to find out what we're doing now. She mentioned that Lizzie had had a brilliant idea, and it's all been sorted, but I don't know any more yet.' I wave my bags in the air. 'I thought she might have spoken to you about it . . . I'm on my way there now actually, so I expect it will all become clear.'

Patience smiles. 'I'll wait to hear,' she says. 'Come and have another chat with me as well, once it's sorted, won't you? Just so you can tell me face to face and there's no confusion.'

There's a rather odd expression hovering on her face, like she wants to say something else, but it passes as I watch her, replaced with another beaming smile. 'And bring cake with you next time. I shall need the energy.' She winks.

I'm still smiling as I reach the door to Fliss's studio. Patience needing energy, my eye – poor Patrick is going to need all the help he can get.

At first I think there's no one there, until I hear a muffled expletive from behind the office door. Fliss is on her hands and knees, with her head underneath the desk and her bum rather inelegantly stuck in the air.

'Well, that's a fine greeting,' I say, pulling open the door a little wider. There is a thump as her head connects with the desk's wooden edge.

'Oooh, ouch!' I say on her behalf. 'Sorry. I didn't mean to make you jump.'

I wait while Fliss extracts herself from beneath the desk and slowly gets to her feet. She looks rather agitated.

'Is everything all right? Have you lost something?'

Her face smiles a greeting, but her eyes are still flicking backwards and forwards over the floor.

'No, it's nothing really,' she says, trying to give me her full attention. A horrible thought suddenly flashes through my mind.

'More jewellery hasn't gone missing, has it? What was it? I can help you look.' I take a step further into the room, but instead Fliss takes hold of my arm, pulling me close and guiding me back out into the main room.

'No, no, nothing like that. Just some silly bookmark, that's all; it will be here somewhere. But you haven't come to hear about that, have you? Flowers, that's what – much more exciting! Come on, let's sit over here, and I can show you what we've come up with. I think you're going to love them.'

The sandwiches and fruit salad are a big hit with everyone, not because they're gourmet food, but simply because it's one less thing for everyone to think about in their busy day, and lunch is often the easiest meal to overlook. I've lost count of the amount of times the clock shows half past three and I still haven't eaten. By that time of the day it hardly seems worth bothering, and so it's often tea time before I have anything to eat that isn't cake.

This simple act of community is how it should be, I think, as I'm washing up the few plates and bowls. It's what we wanted from Rowan Hill when the germ of the idea first began to take shape. This shouldn't be just somewhere that people come to work and then go home again; it was supposed to be something for us all to belong to – a family, if you like, living and working together. I've lost sight of that recently and I wonder if it's the same for everyone. Granted, we all pitch in and help one another out, like with Patience and her order, for example, but that was different somehow – that was necessity, and not the same thing as the small spontaneous acts of generosity that used to take place. There is one other reason for my paying everyone a lunchtime visit. It's something that I haven't done in a while, but which I used to do every day, just a few minutes of catching up with folk. Today I wanted everyone to see me and to know that I have my eye very firmly back on the ball.

The dishes done, I return to the laptop to continue with my search. I only have two days to go before the unveiling ceremony for Will's window and, a little over two weeks after that, we get married. So little time to sort all this out really, but I know that I have to, because I'm very clear about one thing: Lizzie *will* be at our wedding, and I'm certain now that until I've discovered what she wanted me to, there's no way she'll come back.

※

I go back to my original search on the website of the *Westmorland Gazette*, calling up the article I had read earlier, but I can't find anything linked to the original story. Instead I type the keywords back into the search function once again and wait for the other four links to appear. I systematically highlight and read through each article, but none of them are related. Snapshots of other people's troubled lives but nothing I can connect back to the snippet Lizzie sent.

I try a different tactic, and type in a general search on Google, but judging by the number of results returned it's going to take some time to look at all of them. I need to relieve Gina for a break, but I've just time to make a quick phone call. Reverting back to the original article, I make a note of the reporter's name and, waving away a persistent fly, pull my mobile towards me.

Ian Edwards is unavailable, but I leave a message with the receptionist stressing how important it is that he rings me back, and then I make my way to the tea room. Gina is most reluctant to have a break of any sort, saying that she's only just got into her stride and it's the first fun she's had in ages. Short of ordering her out of the room there's not a lot I can do about that. Still, the cakes for tomorrow won't make themselves, and as I pull on my apron I'm secretly pleased. It will be nice to have her company while I'm baking, and Gina has always been someone I can confide in.

I broach the subject of Lizzie again once I've weighed out my first set of ingredients. She was suspiciously quiet on the matter when she first got here, but I know that's only because she's thinking and taking everything in before making any comment. It will come in due course, that I'm sure of.

'I had something a bit weird come in the post today,' I start, before filling her in about the contents of Lizzie's letter and my subsequent conversation with Alice. 'But typical, the reporter wasn't available when I rang.'

'Do you think he'll be able to tell you anything?'

'Possibly,' I reply, releasing a burst of fragrance into the room as I start to grate lemons. 'It sounded as if it was a pretty horrific accident, and it was only six months or so ago; I would hope he would remember it. It seems odd that there are no other linked stories on their website. Something like that must have had a follow-up story, surely?'

'Not if whoever died wasn't local.'

I pause, rotating the lemon a little more. 'What do you mean?'

'Well, you said the article was an appeal for witnesses and the person who died wasn't named. The accident happened on a major road: lots of people would have been using it that day, and the chances are that it wasn't even someone from that part of Cumbria. Once the authorities established the person's identity, wouldn't any subsequent story of the death be picked up by the person's local paper instead?'

'Oh God, you're right. I hadn't thought of that. But that makes it worse in a way. This person could be from anywhere, couldn't they?'

'In theory, yes. I guess you'll have to wait and see what your reporter chap says. Perhaps he knows what happened afterwards.'

I tip the pungent zest into the mixing bowl as Gina turns to serve a customer.

'But you trust this Lizzie now?' she asks, returning to the kitchen a few moments later. 'You don't think she had anything to do with the other incidents?'

'I did. I think we all did . . . but no, not any more. She's from a rough background and she's had a tough time of late, but once you get to know Lizzie properly, it's just not something she would do. Not only that, but she'd have nothing to gain by it. She'd lose her home for one thing.'

'Then who does stand to gain by it? Who don't you trust?'

And there it is, in a single sentence. How like Gina to get straight to the heart of the matter.

I stare down at the puddle of juice from the lemon I've just squeezed. 'But that's just it, Gina. I trust everyone here. There isn't anyone who would gain from these things, and we're all friends in any case.'

'You can't be, can you? Someone here is pretending to be something they're not.'

I think about the truth in her words for a moment. I know that she's right. It's the only logical solution, but the thought of it is like an icy blast in the warm kitchen.

'Has anything happened before all this started that someone bears a grudge over?'

'I can't think of anything,' I say, shaking my head. 'I mean, we've all been here right from the start, apart from Lizzie and . . . Fliss, and she's, well, that's plain ridiculous. I mean, she's organising my wedding, for God's sake . . .' I don't mean to let my sentence trail off to quite the extent that it does.

Gina's eyebrows shoot up. 'Oh?' she fires back.

I'm quick to correct her. 'No, no, there's no problem with Fliss. It's nothing like that. It's just that . . . I feel a bit disloyal, actually. I mean, she's done an amazing job for us. I really haven't had the time to sort things properly, and she's organised everything for us beautifully.'

'But?'

'But . . .' I say slowly, 'I think I've got a bit carried away with all the wedding stuff. Originally it was going to be a very quiet affair. We've only got immediate family and very close friends coming, and so it was just a ceremony at a local hotel, with a meal afterwards and a bit of a party back here.' I think back to my recent conversation with Fliss, less than two hours ago. 'It's sort of grown into something a bit more flash and glamorous than I ever intended, and I'm not sure I'm entirely comfortable with it. I don't know how I'm going to tell Fliss, or even whether I should. It's probably too late to do anything about it anyway.'

'But it's your wedding, Ellie.'

'I know. It's awkward, though. Fliss is a friend now, and she's spent hours sorting everything out. It's my fault anyway. I haven't given it enough of my attention, and I was so grateful to her I've sort of gone along with everything she's said.'

Gina snorts, her earrings swinging wildly. 'Even so, surely at the beginning you told her the sort of wedding you wanted? She probably shouldn't have made all those suggestions if they went against what you had planned. It's not her wedding, is it?'

I screw my face up, trying to remember exactly how it had all come about. 'We did talk about it, and Fliss never insisted on anything, but she did point out that perhaps a simple wedding was a bit of a cop-out on my part. I mean, Will made that window out there for me, Gina. You can't get much more of a grand gesture than that, can you? I wanted our wedding to be something that was so perfect it would show Will the strength of my love for him. But I've been seduced by it all, all the beautiful pictures in the magazines and photos that Fliss has shown me, all the "stuff" I've convinced myself we have to have.' I look up at her for a moment. 'It's not what matters, is it? That's not what our wedding should be about. I feel such a fool and, worse, I think I've really let Will down.'

There's no reply, and when I look back to Gina I can see from the expression on her face that she agrees with me. Now that I've said it out loud, I know I wasn't asking Gina for her advice at all. I was only trying to convince myself of something that deep down I know to be right. I can see how ridiculous my ideas were. This is not the way to show Will how much I love him, by turning our wedding day into a stiff, perfectionist stage play. It should be about fun and laughter. We should be relaxed and spontaneous with each other, and I know now that's what's making me nervous about the whole thing. I don't want to spend the day being scared of smudging my make-up or having my hair fall down, because the person in that photograph is not me at all, and it's not the girl that Will fell in love with.

'Do you know how Will feels about all this?'

I give a groan. 'Not exactly. That's the hardest thing. With him away we've had so little opportunity to talk about it all properly. Chatting over the phone is hardly the way to go about it. I was over with Fliss not that long ago, and she says that whenever she's had to check anything with him, he's been really excited about it all. He certainly seems that way to me too, but . . . it still doesn't feel right. Deep down I don't think it's the kind of wedding he wants either. I've let myself be convinced that it was, but now I'm not so sure.'

'Sorry, love, but I think you should speak to her. And you need to speak to Will too, properly this time, and find out what you both really want, before it's too late.'

'I know,' I say, biting my lip. 'I'm scared it's gone too far to put things right now, and what with Lizzie leaving and everything else—'

'One thing at a time, Ellie. You might not be able to do anything about Lizzie immediately, but you can talk to Will. There might be some things – smaller things – that you can change about the wedding, and the very fact of having had a conversation will make you feel better. You've got the dedication ceremony for his window later this week, haven't you? Try to have a chat before then, so that once he's home, you both know how to play things.' She studies my glum face for a moment. 'Listen, I'm sorry. I only got here five minutes ago and I'm bossing you around like a good 'un. I didn't mean to upset you. Look, I'll put the kettle on and we can have a hot chocolate with the works on it. All your problems will dissolve into thin air, and you'll feel so much better.'

'Nice try,' I reply, catching her rueful smile, but I can't help smiling in spite of myself. Gina might be forthright, but sometimes it takes someone who's a little distant from the problem to state the bleeding obvious. As Gina just has, very eloquently.

Five minutes later and I'm sucking a marshmallow from the top of my chocolate, and surprisingly I do feel a little better. Terrified of what I'm going to say to Fliss, and not looking forward one little bit to what I fear might be coming over the next few days, but at least I feel clearer about things and have a course of action in my head. Just knowing I'm doing something feels better than floundering about aimlessly.

Gina blows the froth on her chocolate too. 'So is that what Fliss does for a living then? Is she a wedding planner?'

'God, no, that came about by accident really because of her past experience. She's a jeweller, you see; in fact, she's making our wedding rings. That's how she started, I think; she's an absolute veteran of the wedding fair. She got most of her early business from them, but that was before she moved down here to get a proper workshop.'

'She's not from around here then?'

A sharp flicker of unease pulls at my stomach as I stare at Gina, who's casually slurping her drink, and realise that I have absolutely no idea where Fliss is from.

Chapter 36

Ellie

We're almost finished for the day when my mobile bursts into noisy life. As the afternoon wore on I had resigned myself to not hearing back from the reporter today, but a phone call from a number with a Cumbria area code can only mean one thing. I snatch up my phone, hoping I'm not asking too much from this conversation.

Gina waves me out of the tea room, and I'm grateful for the opportunity for a little privacy. I make my way across the yard as quickly as I can, my opening sentences designed to buy me time until I'm safely in the kitchen.

The reporter sounds bored. It's near the end of his working day and I know I'm an unwelcome intrusion into his workload. I'm sure he's only ringing me back at all because deep down there's still a little spark of the *what if*. What if there's a real story at the end of this conversation, rather than just another bland recounting of facts?

We spend a few moments establishing the reason for my call, and checking the details of what I'm asking. It's clear almost straight away that although he does remember the story, he can't tell me anything that will lead me any further.

'I'm sorry that I can't help. I only remember it because it was a horrible thing to happen so close to Christmas, but we only ever printed the story as you've seen it, and there was no follow up afterwards because it turned out that the man who died wasn't local to us. We only printed the appeal for help at the request of the police, to widen the net as it were.'

'I see. And you can't remember where this man came from?'

'We never knew the details. It's like I told the other lady, we had no reason to follow it up; not our story to tell.'

I feel my spine stiffen.

'Sorry, did you say that you'd spoken to someone about this only recently?'

'Yeah, a couple of weeks ago. She didn't leave her name.'

'It is quite important that I find out the name of the person who died. Is there anything else that you can think of that might help me, anything at all?'

'I'm sorry, love, but there's nothing else I can remember about it. You'll have to trawl the internet and see what you can find. Same advice I gave before.'

I end the call with a sigh of frustration. I hadn't expected anything else really, but to know that I must be following in Lizzie's footsteps is a comfort at least. All I can do now is hope that searching online will turn up some information.

I give my watch a quick glance. I should really go and help Gina finish things up for the day. I'm immensely grateful that she's here, but it would be very unfair to take advantage of her. She'll need to go and get the rest of her things from the B&B, and I did promise I would help her. I look longingly at the laptop, but rise from the table once more, knowing that if I risk even one little look, several hours will pass by almost unnoticed.

It's nearly seven o'clock by the time we get in and, judging by the look of appreciation on the faces of Ben and Finn, the fish and chips that I've brought back are a welcome sight indeed. They are exhausted after a day's hard labour laying paths through the woodland, and I'm not fit for anything much, to be honest. I may not have had the physical toil to tire me out, but I feel emotionally drained from trying to keep up with the thoughts whizzing through my head. I know there will be no respite from them until I find out what I need to know and so, as soon as Gina has gone upstairs to sort out her things, and the boys have flopped in front of the TV, I pull the laptop towards me once more.

It's funny how things can happen when you least expect it. How a day that was sliding into just another evening can be propelled from the mundane to the unforgettable in a single heartbeat. I wasn't sure what I expected to find as I sat calmly at the table, a mug of tea by my side. The news reports that I searched through listed details of other people's lives: places I had never been to, people that I never knew. They told stories of lives that had been delayed, altered or irrevocably changed, but they were always at a distance from me; they never came any closer than the words on the screen in front of me. I never thought for one moment that, when I found the details of the accident I was looking for, they would reveal anything other than an unfamiliar name to be recorded on a notepad. I never thought that the words I saw would live and breathe inside of me, and swallow me whole.

The words spun time away from me, back to a place of pain and betrayal, but also to a period when the first tiny seed of my future was planted, a future that I would now do anything to protect. They took me back to the day almost three years ago when I had a car accident, the day I met Will, the day I discovered that my partner of six years was already married with a child – a lover who, a scant two years later, had ploughed into the back of a jackknifed lorry on an icy road, and who had died in a ball of flame.

I stare at the words on the screen in front of me, my vision already blurred with tears, knowing that I can never undo their power.

The deceased, a thirty-one-year-old IT manager from Edinburgh, has been named as Robbie Fitzpatrick. He is survived by a wife and child.

Survived by a wife and child . . .

And now they scare me, these words, because in an instant everything that has been happening at Rowan Hill has gone from being a random collection of events to something that I now know without a shadow of a doubt is personal. Somehow, everything that has happened here is connected to me. But I have no idea why.

I pick up the piece of newspaper that still lies on the table beside me. A crease cuts the paper in two, and I can imagine it being folded time and time again, being read time and time again, the fingers of the person holding it smudging the ink a little before returning it once more to a place of safety. Except now it's no longer hidden. It has found its way to me through Lizzie; how I don't know, but the last time I saw her, its original owner was searching for it frantically . . .

The tears are running freely down my face, dripping off the end of my chin, shaken loose by the erratic trembling of my body as it propels me across the room to the pantry. I take down a key hanging on the row of hooks, and walk blindly across the yard once more. I need to know if I'm right, and when I find out that I am, I will wish with all my might that I'm wrong.

The room is still light in the evening sunshine, the white walls glowing with soft colour. I know what I'm looking for, but I've no idea where to find it. The cases are bare, emptied of their treasures for the day, and the room looks like the sad and hollow shell it is. Everything here is hollow. It is all just for show. I move into the back room, my heart jittery with the shock of adrenalin that my body is pumping through it.

The desk is neat and ordered. Calculating. And there, among the careful files of invoices and orders, is what I'm looking for. The letter

Brian joked about with us just a few short weeks ago, a letter he guessed might be about an unexpected inheritance, but which was instead an invoice for services in connection with the settlement of the estate of one Robbie Fitzpatrick.

Survived by a wife and child.

I'm not sure how much time passes before Finn finds me, sitting on the floor of Fliss's office, shaking uncontrollably. I hear a voice trying to speak between choking sobs but it cannot be mine; it sounds so far away. Finn pulls me into his arms and I cling to him, feeling his gentle comfort surround me, until eventually I can find the strength to stand.

The whisky burns my throat but I gulp it down, grateful for the opportunity to focus on the heat that follows, for a moment obliterating everything else. I look at the faces of Gina and Ben, across the table from me, taut and worried without even knowing why. Finn is crouched on the floor beside my chair, one hand splayed across my back and the other holding mine in a fierce grip. The kitchen is silent save for the faint whirring noise from the laptop as the fan kicks into life. The screen is as I left it, except that now translucent coloured bubbles bounce over the words as if to make them more palatable.

'What's going on, Ellie?' asks Finn, his thumb stroking the back of my hand. 'We saw the laptop,' he continues, but I know that he's unsure how to frame his next question. 'I'm so sorry. Is that your Robbie?'

My Robbie? I stare at Finn. He hasn't been my Robbie for a long time, but beyond a comprehension of what has happened and the awfulness of it all, I cannot begin to think any further than that. In the days and weeks to come I will torture myself by imagining his final moments of life, and I will grieve for the man I once loved – not because I love him still, but because a life is a life and even though he betrayed me, we shared too many memories for our time together to ever be erased.

I cannot think of any of this now.

'You don't understand.' I begin. 'Fliss is his wife. It's Fliss; it's been her all along.'

There are confused looks over my head.

'What's been Fliss? Ellie, what are you talking about?'

I shake my head at their slowness to understand. 'Everything here that's been going on. It was never Lizzie at all.'

Gina leans forwards then. 'Ellie, has this got to do with the newspaper clipping? Is that how you found out about Robbie?'

When I nod, I see a flicker of recognition in her eyes as she begins to put the few pieces she has of the jigsaw together. She quickly relays what she knows to the others, and I smile gratefully. I'm too tired to put it all into words.

Finn's face is soft as he looks up at me. 'It doesn't make sense, Ellie. Even if Fliss was Robbie's wife, what has that got to do with you? You weren't together at the time of the accident; you hadn't been for a long while. Why would Fliss do all these things?'

'I don't know,' I whisper. 'That's what I'm afraid of.'

Chapter 37

ELLIE

I wake the next morning a little ashamed to find that I'm still curled in the crook of Finn's arm, exactly where I was when I fell asleep. My head feels stiff and tight, as if the information I hold is too big for the space to contain, and although it's warm here, my stomach feels like I'm continually swallowing ice-cold water.

My own room seemed achingly empty without Will, and after a hot bath the night before, Finn's insistence that I was not to be left by myself was one I accepted gladly. Even after the initial shock of my discovery yesterday had subsided, it left in its wake a very real fear that something horrendous was going to happen. I made Finn come back with me to Fliss's workshop to check that everything was exactly how I had found it, but although my fear was probably quite irrational, I couldn't bear to be on my own.

I still can't work out how Lizzie came across the newspaper clipping, or indeed what made her suspicious enough to follow up on the information it contained, but I can only assume that she had known that what she found out was too important to ignore. The sad thing is that even with something as significant as this, she didn't think she'd be believed. Instead she'd had to leave a clue for me so that I could find out for myself what she had. We let her down so badly, when all she ever wanted to do was help.

I ease myself out from under Finn's arm as slowly as I can, and am pleased when he simply rolls over and carries on sleeping. It can only be very early, but I'm in desperate need of a cup of tea.

As soon as I reach the hallway downstairs I can hear muted voices coming from the kitchen, and I'm not surprised to find Ben and Gina already nursing a pot of tea. Ben gets up to fetch another mug as soon as he sees me.

'Did you get any sleep?' he asks, as he passes a steaming cuppa to me.

'Miraculously I think I must have,' I say, 'although I think Finn will have a severely dead arm once he wakes up. Did either of you manage any?'

'On and off,' replies Ben. Gina's response is similar.

'We've been thinking,' he says, getting straight to the point, 'about what we should do now. I wanted to go straight round to Fliss's this morning and demand to know what's been going on, but Gina pointed out that might not be the best thing to do.'

I nod. 'I've been thinking about that too. In fact, I've thought about little else, but at the moment Fliss is completely unaware that anything has changed, and right now it needs to stay that way. Think about what this would mean for Will.'

Gina nods, while Ben just looks puzzled.

I look at Ben's still blank face. 'Tomorrow sees the opening of a project that means more to Will than anything in his life so far. It's all he's focused on for months, and tomorrow sees the end of that, the culmination of all his hard work and the public recognition of it. I don't want to think about what might happen if we confront Fliss today – for Will's sake, I can't risk it. Tomorrow has to happen exactly as planned, and Will mustn't know about any of this yet. I can't do that to him, I just can't.'

Ben nods slowly. 'I take your point. I'm sorry, I hadn't thought of that.'

I take a deep breath. 'I can only think it's safer to carry on as if nothing else has happened and tackle Fliss once Will is home.' My voice starts to crack a little. 'Please . . . I need him here when we do.'

Gina's arm is warm across my back, as she leans up against me. 'Don't forget, all we know for certain is that Fliss was Robbie's wife, and for some reason she's turned up here,' she says. 'I admit this seems to be one hell of an odd coincidence, but beyond that, and apart from my own feelings, and I'm guessing Lizzie's too, we have absolutely no proof that Fliss has done anything wrong. We have nothing that links her with any of the things that have happened here.'

'That's true, I suppose,' I say. 'But do you think Lizzie has proof?'

'She could have. But at the moment we can hardly go around there accusing Fliss without it. Admittedly we could ask her about Robbie, but I would say she's a very accomplished liar. Wouldn't she just give us some soppy cock-and-bull story about sisterhood and wanting to be close to you or something? We'll be no further forward. I agree with you. I think we need to play it cool until we know more for certain.'

I place my mug back on the table, looking at the anxious faces around me. My heartbeat is loud in my ears.

'There's something else too,' I say quietly.

Gina is almost in tears and I know she's figured out what I can hardly bear to say.

'I don't think there's going to be a wedding.'

Finn's voice is suddenly loud in the quiet space. 'What do you mean, there isn't going to be a wedding?'

I look up at his sleep-heavy face as he pads barefoot into the room.

My lips start to tremble. 'I'm so scared of what's going to happen, Finn. I've been trying to think what on earth could cause Fliss to behave the way she has, but I can't come up with anything. I thought she was my friend – we all did – but if we believe that she's somehow caused all the things that have happened here, then she must have a reason for doing so, and a reason that's connected to me. Nothing that's happened so far has directly involved me, just the people I care about, but what if I'm next? What if all this was just leading up to something else, something bigger, and she hasn't finished with me yet? What's the one thing that would hurt me more than anything else?'

'Oh my God,' mutters Ben. 'She's organising your wedding.'

'Or un-organising it,' I add quietly.

The silence in the room grows louder and louder, and I will someone to contradict me, to laugh and call me insane, to reassure me that it couldn't possibly be true, but no one does.

It's Gina who eventually breaks the silence. 'I'm so sorry, Ellie,' she says, the weight of sorrow palpable in her voice. 'What are we going to do?'

Finn comes to sit beside me, wordlessly taking my hand in his.

I raise my chin a little. 'Find out if I'm right, and if I am, we're all going to have to act our socks off tomorrow and pretend to Will that everything is okay. Tomorrow is his day. Fliss may think she's ruined enough in our lives already, but she's not ruining that.'

I try not to notice the tear that Gina flicks from the corner of her eye, or the mute concern on the faces of the men who I have come to love like brothers. For now, I can only concern myself with the need to keep up the pretence for one more day. To act like I have so many times over the last few months, convincing myself and everyone around me that things are okay, when I know now without question that they are not.

Finn's jaw is set in a tight line, but he nods in acquiescence, flicking a glance at his watch. It's time to get ready for the day ahead.

In a way it's remarkably easy to get through the day just as I always have. I'm busy in the tea room for one, and although Gina and I speak in low voices from time to time, I can get by on general chit-chat with everyone else, accepting their good wishes for the coming day with an excitement that I conjure out of thin air.

I can even have a telephone conversation with a very kind lady who tells me that my wedding reception was cancelled over four months ago, and although there's no real need, I make the same call over and over, to the florist, caterers, photographers, and my dress designer, listening to their apologetic tones in numb shock. It's not until very much later, when I'm standing staring out of the window with tears pouring down my face, that I succumb to Finn's silent embrace.

Chapter 38

ELLIE

It's almost unbearable how much I want Will home. His last text to me, received this morning, just said, 3 hours, 19 minutes and 36 seconds. Now I can't get this image of a big digital clock counting down out of my head. It accompanies everything I do, like I'm running two streams of film through my head at the same time, alongside the almost physical ache that catches me every time I think of him.

It's just Alice, Finn and me travelling down to London for the dedication of the window that Will has been working on. It isn't a big do apparently, just Conservation Trust board members and representatives from the local clergy, but I can tell from what Will doesn't say more than from what he does how important it is. It's been six months of his life. Six months that's been borrowed from me, I want to say, but of course I don't.

Things have gone well, Will says. He's pleased with his work and, as his own sternest critic, this is high praise indeed. I know this is probably the most important thing he's ever done, and to leave it all behind will be hard. It will feel like having a part of himself removed and, given what awaits him at home, I'm terrified he'll discover that he misses it more than he's missed me.

Alice is fussing with her handbag, which she has bought especially for the occasion, but now isn't sure goes with her dress. Finn is trying to be reassuring, and I love him for it, but I'm not sure who he's trying to convince, himself or me. I'm a bag of nerves, desperate with longing, and probably withdrawn and monosyllabic to boot. This train journey could well prove to be a very long three hours.

Finn, I know, feels the same way that I do. But under no circumstances must we arrive in London for Will's big day in a bad mood, and with an evil nudge to my ribs he directs my attention to a chap sitting a few seats back, tapping away at his laptop. A copy of the *Financial Times* lies on the table beside him.

'What do you suppose he's writing there?' Finn asks, leaning in, his voice muted.

'I don't know, something for work?'

Finn heaves an exasperated sigh. 'God, you're rubbish at this, aren't you . . . No imagination.' He pauses to check I've caught his meaning. '*I* think he's writing his ad for the lonely hearts column in *Classic Car Monthly*. "City gent seeks mature dominatrix for kinky afternoon sex. No strings".'

'Shhh!' I say in a furious whisper. 'You can't say things like that, Finn.'

'Why not? Just because you can't think of anything better,' he replies, arching his eyebrows in challenge.

'I so can!'

'Go on then.'

'But he'll hear us,' I stall.

Finn's reply is instant. 'No, he won't. Look, he's plugged in,' he argues, directing my attention back to the chap, who has headphone wires trailing across his shirt. I think for a few seconds more.

'You see, that's where you're going wrong,' I start off. 'You'd assumed that he's listening to One Direction on the sly, when actually he's transcribing the notes from his latest surveillance operation. His client, a Mr Roger Smythe, suspects his wife is having an affair . . .' I pretend to type. *'Mrs Annabel Smythe left the house at 9.32 and proceeded down Bishop's Way to the local Tesco store, where she spent a total of £152.17, leaving the store at 10.46. I bought a can of shaving gel and a packet of extra strong mints. (Please see my expenses detail on the last page of my report.) Mrs Smythe returned to the marital home at around 11.15. (Temporary traffic lights on Orbison Drive.)'*

Finn leans in, looking over my shoulder as if to read what I've typed.

'Well, was she?'

'Was she what?'

'Having an affair?'

'I don't know. I haven't got to that bit yet . . . oh, hang on, here's something . . . *At 11.45 I observed a white van arriving at the house purporting to be from an A. P. Turner, domestic appliance repairs. The occupant, a man estimated to be in his late thirties, got out and was greeted by Mrs Smythe, who led him into the house, where I later observed him . . .'*

'Yes . . .'

'. . . *repairing the washing machine.*'

'Oh, shame,' sighs Finn, relaxing back in his seat with a wicked grin. 'You've got the hang of it, though.'

'What on earth are you talking about?' interjects Alice. 'You're behaving like a couple of schoolchildren.'

'I know. Great, isn't it?' grins Finn, totally without shame.

'And totally transparent,' she adds. 'Don't think I don't know what you're up to,' she finishes sternly.

Finn is quiet for a few moments considering this. I sit hunched and nervous. 'Of course you know what I'm up to, Alice,' answers Finn finally. 'You always did know. Even when I was a child I couldn't get anything past you. And, yes, this is a smokescreen, but I'm trying to cheer us all up so that Will won't notice anything wrong. That way, the day will be about him, which is as it should be. Can't you just humour me?'

'You think I disapprove of not telling him?'

'Alice!' says Finn in warning. 'We're having that conversation.'

'No, we're not, dear. I don't disapprove of the decision you've made, and I understand entirely your reasons for not telling him straight away. It's just that, well, you know how he is. He'll be awfully cross that you didn't tell him.'

Finn makes a strangled sound. 'We know exactly how he's going to feel, Alice,' he retorts, his temper flaring. 'But I can't think how telling him sooner would make things any better either. We should tell him the news face to face, while he's at home, not in some anonymous hotel room just before his big moment. That wouldn't be fair, would it?'

'Alice, it's not Finn's fault,' I say quietly. 'It's my fault. For letting things go unnoticed and unchallenged for so long, but I can't tell Will yet; apart from anything, I don't think I could handle that either.'

'I know, Ellie. I understand it's an awful situation,' she sighs. 'Just ignore me, Finn. I'm a doddery old woman, I know, but I can't help thinking that this is prolonging the agony.'

'Prolonging the agony?' says Finn. He glares at Alice, struggling to unfold his long legs from under the table. 'I'm going to get a drink,' he adds, stalking off.

Alice turns to look at me. 'Oh dear,' she murmurs. 'I didn't mean to upset him like that. I just meant—'

'I know. I know,' I croon. 'He'll be all right in a while. He's feeling guilty about Fliss too, thinking that he should have been more aware of what was going on. He has no need to feel guilty at all, of course, but you know Finn. Let him calm down a bit; he'll be fine.'

She watches me for a long moment. 'And you, Ellie. How are you? Honestly now, no pretending.'

I feel my eyes begin to smart again. 'I don't know how I am, Alice, and that's the truth. I feel numb, scared . . . terrified.'

'And you still don't know what all this has been about?'

I shake my head, mutely.

'But what are you going to do? Your beautiful wedding . . .'

'I don't know what we'll do,' I smile half-heartedly, 'but things that have been undone can always be remade, in time . . . I hope. It's not just Will and me, though, is it? Everyone else has suffered too, and I feel so dreadfully responsible for all of it. I've let people down at Rowan Hill by trying to pretend that everything was all right, when it plainly wasn't. I've had my head in the sand for too long, so I only have myself to blame.'

'My dear, you mustn't think like that. People will understand; I'm sure of it.'

'Will they?'

She smiles for a moment, fishing in her handbag. 'You'll find a way through this, dear, like you always do, but you mustn't seek to blame yourself. None of this is anybody's fault. Now, let's have a mint imperial.'

Sensing movement beside me I look up to see Finn sliding back into the seat, carrying a cardboard drinks tray filled with large plastic cups.

'Sorry,' he says immediately, 'for being such a complete arsehole.' His attention is directed just inches off the table.

I nudge his shoulder gently. ''S okay. It's allowed.'

He looks up then, his face sombre, his eyes resting briefly on mine before flicking across to Alice.

'You were quite wrong, Finn,' she says mildly, rushing on before Finn, whose mouth has dropped open, can interrupt. 'That man is neither a lonely heart nor a private investigator. It's Tallulah Lovegood, the well-known writer of bodice-rippers. Chapter sixteen is going extraordinarily well, by the way,' and she flaps at her face as if to cool down her cheeks.

Finn just looks at me, his expression unreadable. 'I love you, Alice,' he says with a perfectly straight face, handing her a cup of coffee.

Chapter 39

Ellie

Peter is charm personified, and looks just how an old professor should: small and wiry with a grey beard and horn-rimmed glasses. His voice as he greets us is soft, with a beautiful Scottish burr.

We're standing in the room that has been home to Will for the past six months, feeling shy and self-conscious with each other as the introductions are performed. I would have preferred to meet up with Will privately, but I understand how Peter, as one of the trustees in charge of the project, feels it's his responsibility to take charge of us all this afternoon. The look in Will's eyes as he sees me will have to sustain me through the proceedings until we're alone later.

'Aye, Finn,' says Peter, clasping his hands warmly. 'I'm pleased to meet with you, son, I've heard a great deal about you.' He continues. 'And Ellie, of course, about whom I've heard a *very* great deal.' He twinkles, planting a kiss on my cheek. 'I'm so glad you could both come.' He turns to Alice then and says simply, 'Enchanted, dear lady,' while holding out his hand. Alice positively simpers. 'Well, folks, the taxi will be here shortly, which will take us to the church for the dedication and reception. Afterwards, we'll go back to the hotel for dinner, just the five of us. I hope that's okay?' He smiles. 'And remember that the purpose of this afternoon as far as I'm concerned is to make as much fuss of Will as possible. He's altogether too modest, and I've told him that, after today, he'd better get used to the compliments.'

Will predictably groans, his hand seeking out mine.

'Don't worry, we won't let you down,' quips Finn.

It's fair to say the church is absolutely nothing like I expected. For one, it's a modern building, and I can't begin to visualise how a traditional stained-glass window could sit inside such a building. It's also something of a work in progress, I realise, as we enter. Long wooden pews are still being moved back into place in one quadrant of the church to our right, behind which a whole section is curtained off, with scaffolding towers still in place. As I look around, trying to make sense of what I can see, Peter, obviously sensing my confusion, starts to explain.

'Of course, it all looks back to front, because we've actually come in through the rear entrance. If you look straight ahead now you'll see the original main entrance, which is the oldest part of the church. This area will be reopened after today to preserve the church's sense of history.'

He's leading us forwards as he speaks, and I can see now that in fact the church is two buildings, the original structure now only a small part of the whole, having had its new counterpart grafted onto it. It's been done well, the renovations not a copycat of the original but a distinct and ultramodern building. In fact, the more I look, the more I realise how clever the design is. Anything less than the very dramatic contrast that is here now would have looked like a rather poor pastiche, a pretend version of the original, which would never have quite become the thing it was trying to be.

'So what's the story here?' asks Finn politely. 'What happened to the original building?'

Peter smiles in a knowing fashion, revelling in his role as storyteller. 'Well, you are in fact standing on a bombsite. St Luke's Church fell victim to the Blitz in 1943 and was more or less abandoned as rebuilding efforts after the war concentrated on the commercial and residential properties in the area. In the 1950s, a replacement building was rebuilt in the grounds. It was rather an unlovely and unloved building, which sort of dwindled away into nothingness. The congregation grew smaller and smaller, and the church couldn't afford to maintain it. It closed for good in 1979, and has been boarded up ever since.'

'But it's still consecrated ground presumably?'

'Oh indeed. You may have seen the massive amount of new development going on in the area on the drive over here. Regeneration is rife in this part of Islington, and fortunately, despite all its problems, there's always been a great community spirit. When the opportunity to receive money from the Millennium Fund came up, St Luke's was given the chance to be reborn. It's taken a good few years, but we're almost there now. Regular services will start again in three weeks' time.'

I'm looking up around me, but still can't see any sign of where Will's work might be. We've come to rest at a point almost in the centre of the space, where a small lectern is standing beside a cloth-covered structure some six feet high. I look at Will, who smiles reassuringly, and Finn, who looks as bemused as I am.

Peter turns at the sound of a door opening. 'Ah, here comes Michael now,' he announces, as a robed man, presumably the vicar, enters the space, followed by two more suited chaps and a lady carrying a small child. We wait patiently until they reach us. Peter holds out his hand and shakes the vicar's warmly, grinning broadly. 'Michael, Will of course you know, and this is Ellie, Finn and Alice,' he says, indicating us in turn. Hands are shaken copiously.

'Guys, this is the Reverend Michael Thomas, his wife Eloise and their daughter Lily. With him are the Trust's chairman, Oliver Scott, and the project manager, James Wilkinson.' Again more hands, and a shy smile from Lily.

The Reverend Michael has a shock of one-inch red hair, more freckles than face, and eyelashes so pale they're almost white. He grasps Will's hand, holding his other hand over it for a minute.

'Big day then, Will?' he affirms. 'I bet you never thought it would come?'

Will nods, finally regaining possession of his hand.

'And a fellow ginger person too, I see,' he adds, looking towards me and showing perfect white teeth. 'God truly does work in mysterious ways, doesn't he?' he beams. 'Welcome to you all.'

I touch a hand to my hair automatically, suddenly doubting my appearance. Will catches my movement and his look is enough to silence any doubts I might have.

Michael gives a quick glance at his watch. 'I'm so pleased you could all come today. I think perhaps, if you're ready, we should crack on. Folks will be arriving soon.'

Folks? What folks? Alice too looks confused.

'Oliver, over to you then.'

Oliver duly walks forwards, nodding, to stand beside us and the covered structure. He raises his hand slightly.

'I would like to start by thanking everyone for coming, and welcoming you to St Luke's Church, which will shortly take its rightful place once more at the heart of this community. On behalf of the Churches Conservation Trust, I am thrilled and honoured to have been part of this historic project, and although our work here is nearly done, its legacy, I hope, will remain part of all our heritage.' He looks around smiling genially.

A photographer comes forwards and fires off a couple of shots. Where the hell did he come from?

'We are, of course, here this afternoon to pay tribute to Will McLennan and his expertise and tenacity in recreating the window that originally stood in this church, and which has been lost for so many years. It will, I know, serve as a constant reminder of the origins of St Luke's and also form the centrepiece of St Luke's new memorial fund.' He pauses here, turning slightly. 'Peter, perhaps we could have the lights on now?'

He waits for a moment as Peter bends down to depress a switch at the base of the shrouded plinth, lifting a corner of the cloth as he does so. There is a momentary pause before the lights come on, one on each corner of the structure, revealing muted colours inside. No detail is evident, but it's clear finally that somehow Will's window is contained within.

Oliver moves to the rear of the structure and reaches to the top, grabbing the cloth, it being almost exactly level with his head. 'Ladies and gentlemen,' he begins, getting ready to pull, 'I give you the St Luke's memorial window!' And with that he removes the cloth with a flourish, whirling it behind him like a matador. He doesn't exactly say *ta-dah*, but I hear a loud one in my head anyway. And there's Will's window. Except it isn't a window. It's a four-foot-high replica hanging inside a glass box, which sits above a plinth containing four halogen bulbs and the inevitable donation box and dedication.

I can't help it. I'm so disappointed I could cry. Oliver's voice continues in ecstatic tones. 'And as you can see, in a wonderful twist of irony, yet so appropriate to the situation, the window depicts Christ coming out of the wilderness.'

A flash of light ricochets off my brain as the photographer moves forwards, preserving the moment for posterity. The next few minutes don't seem real at all. I know that I have a huge smile plastered on my face. I can hear myself saying all the appropriate things and posing for photos and giving hugs and shaking hands. Yet none of it seems to penetrate the cloud that I feel totally overwhelmed by.

I force myself to look at the piece. I know it's beautiful. I can see the skill that has turned two-dimensional pieces of coloured glass into a three-dimensional creation showing movement and depth, the etching and painting perfect in every detail. The joins are seamless, the execution no less than I would have expected from Will, but from what I've seen in his workshop back home, it looks like something he could knock up in a couple of afternoons. It's beautiful, yes, but in the end it's just a well-placed enticement for people to part with their loose change.

I'm aware that the door has been opening and closing repeatedly and that people are starting to mill about. Questioning looks are being exchanged. Will voices a warning to Peter, who apologises, but tells him he'll understand in a minute, and ushers us to sit down on the newly installed pews in front of the section that's still curtained off. There are people filing in behind us, row after row of them.

I sit beside Will, totally bereft of clear or conscious thought. I'm clutching his hand in an effort to remain tethered to reality, when all I want to do is flee. I can't believe my reaction to his work. I should be here showing my love and loyalty, my support and admiration, and I cannot. I'm pretending. Will had not given me an indication at any time that his work was on a grander scale. He had said it was a window and I thought it would be just that, an actual window, the space between two pieces of wall. I have no reason to blame him; no one misled me. It's just that I had built up a picture in my mind of something else, and now I feel let down and cheated – not for me, but for Will. To have only this small piece to show for all his hard work. Someone should have given him more, and I'm ashamed that right now it can't be me.

Peter has come to sit on the other side of Will and Finn, and Alice is to my right; just beyond her, Oliver and James. The Reverend Michael has moved the lectern, and I realise is now standing behind it directly in front of us, the what? Congregation, I assume. My head hurts.

He raises his hands wide in welcome and instantly every voice in the room is still. 'Thank you. Thank you,' he beams. 'I am thrilled that you could all come today, not least because I hope that this will come as the most magnificent surprise for Will, who was expecting a rather more private showing today, but also because it is only fitting for you all to be part of this today, as everyone here has helped in some way to get St Luke's back on its feet.'

There is a rustle of interest and several heads turn to look at Will. He's nervous. I can see his Adam's apple bobbing up and down.

'In three weeks' time this building will become your church, but also, I hope, the centre of the community, and on that day, quite rightly, the focus will be on the church itself and its dedication. However—' He holds up a hand here, to forestall any further discussion. 'I could not let the unveiling of Will's window go unmarked with a clear conscience, and so we all decided to arrange today's little ceremony, for which I know I have both the bishop's and the good Lord's approval.'

There is a ripple of amusement.

'Many of you have had the opportunity to get to know Will over recent weeks and feel, as I do, that he is a spectacularly talented, if far too modest, man. Not only that—' He holds up his hand again as a series of bangs and scrapes comes from the rear. 'Not only that, and incidentally I apologise for the noise – the lads are just removing the last poles from the scaffolding towers – but we have come to appreciate his sense of humour, generosity of spirit and, frustrating though it may have been, his downright inventiveness in keeping us from poking our noses in as we tried in vain to get a sneak preview of his work.' He pauses once more to let the amusement register again, these words obviously ringing true. 'Not even I have seen the finished article.'

There's something not quite right about this last statement, and as I struggle to make out what it is, I almost miss what comes next.

'So without any further ado, let's see what we all think. Lads, if you're ready?' At his signal the curtain behind him is swiftly opened.

What follows is a single moment of utter silence broken only by a collective intake of breath as light flows across us, glowing coloured light that dances at our feet and bounces off the white walls around us.

The piece is abstract, modern and bold, the space somehow divided into sections that stand at juxtapositions to each other, giving the window the look of a faceted diamond. It has none of the embellishment of the memorial window, no paint or etching, but its strength is in its design and use of colour. A myriad colours rise from the ground in a breathtaking riot, deeper at the bottom and then rising, gradually lightening in tone through blue to violet, green, copper and rose, until they reach a crescendo of light and golden hues radiating out from the highest point. If you were to stand at its feet you would feel as if you had disappeared, replaced by colour through and through. It is heart-breakingly beautiful.

Gradually, the noise subsides. I'm shaking, or is it Will? Oliver is there before us then, encouraging Will to his feet, beckoning him for-wards to stand beside Michael, who hugs him unashamedly.

'Ladies and gentlemen,' welcomes Oliver, waiting for quiet. 'For those of you who don't know, our brief for the window was simple: to recreate the original stained-glass window that you can now see under glass to my right. Not an easy task, as none of the original remained. It had to be pieced together from archive descriptions and photographs, not all of them accurate, and sadly most of the photographs in black and white. As you can see, not only has Will recreated that window beautifully, but he had the courage and, may I say, audacity to argue that it simply would not do for the space we had in mind, that it was wrong for the wonderful new building that we see around us today. Instead, with extraordinary breadth of vision, he worked on a new design: his own, very modern interpretation of Christ coming out of the wilderness. The piece is called quite simply *A Change of Light*. Ladies and gentlemen, I give you Will McLennan.'

There is more hearty applause as Oliver moves aside to let Will take possession of the lectern, shaking his hand again for good measure. 'I've been saying it for a while now but, Will, you had better get used to the sound of the telephone ringing.' He laughs.

And then Will is there, and I get to look at him again as if for the first time, his blond hair sticking up a little, tired eyes, but still beauti-ful, smiling shyly, wreaking havoc with my insides. He gives a little cough.

'I'm not sure I can speak actually,' he says. 'I really wasn't expecting this and, well . . . I'm glad you like the window.' He trails off, but then louder. 'Actually, I'd like to thank a few people, if I may? It's not always easy, being an artist. It's a solitary kind of thing but one which you all have made very much easier with your kindness and welcome and . . .' He pauses here to search the crowd. 'Maggie and David, wherever you are, with your endless cups of tea and Hobnobs. In the end it wasn't really such a difficult task. The design is based on one that I had already made at home, and in a way I had the most perfect inspiration. When I thought about what it might feel like to be in the wilderness, to be tested, I realised that it mirrored my own life to some extent, from a very dark time a couple of years ago to the present day, when someone very special brought the light back into my life.' He rubs his chin a little. 'What you've seen here today is simply my own interpretation of what that feels like, and I hope it brings those same sentiments to everyone in this wonderful community that is St Luke's,' he adds, turning to look directly at me. 'In many ways I will be sad to say farewell to you all, but as many of you know, simply because I never shut up about it, I'm marrying my beautiful Ellie in two weeks. I've loved being a part of your lives, but I've been away from her for too long, and it's time to go home.'

There is thunderous applause, as with one single movement the congregation gets to its feet. I'm vaguely aware of heads craning to get a better view of me, but my eyes remain on Will, as do his on mine. There are tears pouring down my face. My heart thumps in my chest at the thought of what is to come, and the moment when I will have to break Will's heart.

It's quite a few hours later by the time we finally sit down for dinner, having done the inevitable refreshments at the church, photo opportunities and 'mingling'. All in all, I think we kept Peter's promise of making as much fuss of Will as possible. Although I feel drained and exhausted, it was the right thing to do; I'm utterly convinced of that.

Only now does Will begin to show what the day has taken out of him. It's a restless sort of tiredness now that everything is over; his body and mind relaxing, though still feeling like they should be rushing around, the disbelief that it has all come to an end and the need to think about what comes next. For now, he's a fish out of water.

The yawns are escalating as we finish dessert, Alice declaring her age to be against her. It has, we all agree, been a day to remember, although Will takes every opportunity to mention his embarrassment at Peter for setting him up.

'You should have seen your face, Ellie, when you thought that little window was all it was. I've never seen such bad acting.'

'Oh?' I say, feigning ignorance. 'I thought I hid it pretty well.'

Will shakes his head. 'I've told you before what an expressive face you have. There's no pulling the wool over my eyes, I'll have you know.' He looks at me, amused, playing with a smile. 'Although the fact that you were so disappointed is actually quite a compliment,' he teases.

Finn gives me a questioning look, and I know he is trying to bring the meal to an end so that we might go back to our rooms. The thought of what might be coming next sits like a fizzing stone in my stomach. I cannot break the news to Will today; I never imagined that things would play out like they have, but to do this to him now would be the cruellest thing. I must give him one last night of peace.

One by one goodbyes are said as we take our leave of one another, Finn very graciously offering to walk Alice to her room. Eventually just Will and I are left, standing a little self-consciously in the hotel corridor, acknowledging that another little chapter in Will's life has come to an end, and that it's time to move on to the next. I wonder if it will always be this way when he finishes future commissions, and I can't help but wonder whether I will be around to see them.

I light the lamp inside our room and slide into Will's welcoming arms. I've waited so long to feel them around me today, but the comfort they provide is a poignant reminder of all I'm about to inflict on the man I love, a man who I know has missed me just as much as I have him, and who, in his exhaustion, just wants to go home, back to the life he left behind, and to the new one he hopes to find as a married man.

Neither of us speaks for some while – it's enough just to be with one another – but eventually a rather pressing need forces me to gently move away. As I cross the room to the bathroom, Will is already moving towards the bed. I take the opportunity to brush my teeth while I'm there, and as I stick my head around the door a few moments later with the offer to run a bath on my lips, I see that he is already stripped and under the sheets, his eyes closed, his breathing soft. I hesitate on the threshold for a moment, my movements undecided, before finally returning to the bathroom to finish getting ready for bed at a more leisurely pace. By the time I slip beneath the sheets, Will's breathing is deep and even. He stirs only slightly to curl an arm around me, and I return his murmured sentence.

'I love you too,' I say, feeling his warm breath against my cheek. Tomorrow is another day.

Chapter 40

ELLIE

Where the evening was quiet and languid, the morning is bright and full of movement. Will's head is no longer bound by the last few months' activity, and in his freedom he just longs to be home. Despite his obvious tiredness he finds an optimistic energy for the day ahead. I wonder if there might be a quiet space of time where I can share the events of the last few days, because I know that once home other things will clamour for his attention, but it's not to be, and as we sit on the train, I feel a deep sense of unease start to grow. I know it's fuelled by the passage of time, but this does little to calm me, and as we approach Shrewsbury I find it harder and harder to respond to Will's cheerful chatter.

The shrill sounding of my mobile jerks me out of a conversation I'm finding it difficult to follow, and I scramble to pull it from my bag. The name lighting up the screen is the very last I expect to see, and I lean forwards in my seat.

'Lizzie,' I exclaim. 'Oh God, please tell me you're all right.'

There is a burst of static before her words reach me: '. . . fine. Where are you?'

'Never mind where I am. Where are you? What on earth happened, Lizzie? Where did you go?'

The conversations around me have stilled. 'Nowhere, I'm here. Ellie, you have to come home. Where are you?'

'Lizzie, we're on our way. What's the matter?' I say, trying to calm the panic in her voice. I can't begin to imagine what put it there. 'Are you okay?'

'I'm fine,' the voice repeats. 'Ellie, I haven't got time to explain properly. I need to find Ben. Please just get here as soon as you can.'

Another crackle of static ends the connection. I redial but it goes straight to answerphone. I stare at Finn, who is looking at me open-mouthed, Lizzie's few words of conversation loud enough for everyone to hear.

'What's going on?' asks Will quietly.

'I don't know. I didn't hear any more than you did.'

'She sounded really upset . . . But then you knew that, didn't you? You knew that she would be.' He studies me for a moment, his blue eyes searching mine. He drops his head, picking at the skin at the side of his fingernail. 'Would someone like to tell me what the bloody hell is going on? You know, I was wondering if it was me that was making you edgy yesterday. At times it felt like you could hardly bear to look at me. And today? Today it's like you're waiting for the executioner's axe to fall. While I'm rather relieved to know that it might not be me that's the problem, I would like to know what's going on.'

I can feel my eyes start to fill with tears. 'Will, I couldn't tell you yesterday, not with everything else happening. I couldn't do that.'

His voice is insistent. 'Tell me what, Ellie? It's not yesterday any more.'

I look at my watch, realising that we must be close to the station. 'Will, I can't tell you here, not like this. Please don't make me.' My throat feels raw with the effort of keeping my emotions locked in.

Even though I'm happy to know that Lizzie is safe and well, something has brought her back, and that makes me even more anxious. I wanted the time to talk to Will, to quietly share the news about our wedding with him, to tell him how little I know of the reasons behind Fliss's actions, and all the while to be safe in the knowledge that whatever happens I will no longer be doing this alone. Will would have been shocked and hugely upset, but I'm sure he would have shown me some perspective, and he would have let me know that everything would be all right. In addition to whatever else Fliss has done, she has robbed me of this too.

Finn is pulling his coat and bag down from the luggage rack. 'Come on, people. We're coming into the station; let's get a ripple on.' He hands Will his jacket.

'Listen, Will, I know this is not ideal, but we had no choice. The short story is that all the things that we thought Lizzie has been involved in turned out to have been Fliss's doing, but we still don't know why as yet. This is the first contact we've had from Lizzie since she took off, and you heard what she said on the phone just now. We need to get home. I know you're not going to like it, but the explanations will have to wait.'

Will stands up, glaring at his brother, before looking back down at me. 'You're really worried about this, aren't you?'

I nod miserably.

He holds out his hand. 'Well, then, come on, let's get home.'

Chapter 41

Lizzie

I hover in the car park, watching as Finn's car pulls onto the private section of the road that leads up to the house. Although it's only late morning, the ropes we use to close off the area when we're shut are already in place, and not a single car is in sight. I don't think I've ever seen Rowan Hill look so sad.

As Finn stops the car, I can see Ellie craning her neck around to catch sight of anything that might give her a clue as to what's going on. I'm not exactly a welcoming committee. Ellie's face is anxious and drawn, but it's Will who is first out of the car.

'What's going on, Lizzie? Are you okay?'

I give a curt nod. 'Come with me, quickly. I've called the police.'

Alice waves Ellie on. 'Go on, you go. I'll follow.' She scrambles out of the car, her legs unwilling to move at speed. Finn and Will are already on the move.

We reach the entrance to the courtyard, where just for a moment all appears as it should. The sun beams down upon the warm stone, which traps the heat within the circle of buildings, where the bright heads of geraniums and begonias stand proudly in their pots. A light breeze brings the scent of lavender from Patience's studio, both familiar and soothing. I can see Ellie's eyes moving over the scene in front of her, and I know the moment a flash of light against glass catches her attention, the sunlight bouncing off the jagged shards that still cling to the frame. She sees the tumble of broken glass in the doorway to Fliss's showroom and would have rushed towards it had I not caught hold of her arm.

'No,' I say. 'This way,' and I lead them onward to the top of the courtyard, to the tea room.

At this time of the day it should be a hubbub of noise: conversation, chinking crockery, laughter ringing out. Even just the hiss of the coffee machine. Today, it is eerily quiet and the doorbell sounds a harsh jangle into the still but not quite empty space.

Sitting at one of the tables are three figures: Fliss, flanked by Ben and Patrick. Their faces are watchful, strained. I want to rush at Fliss, but the air is thick between us and I hold back. Very slowly a chair moves backwards over the tiles with a harsh grating noise, and a figure stands.

'Good to see you home, Ellie,' says Fliss, without a trace of warmth. 'It would seem I'm no longer welcome here, but I couldn't go without saying goodbye, could I? Without having had the opportunity for a little chat.'

'What have you done, Fliss?' Ellie asks carefully.

'What have *I* done? Oh, that's rich, coming from you.' She gives a snort of laughter. 'So have you figured it out yet, what this has all been about? I would have enjoyed watching you work out who was behind it all – the lost order, Ben's poor dresser – but it would seem that dear Lizzie might have found herself a backbone after all, and she rather beat you to it. Of course, she hasn't been able to tell you all about it yet, so I thought I'd save her the bother, although I think you may already have uncovered the biggest surprise of them all, my final parting gift to you.'

I can hear the sound of my heartbeat rushing in my ears, loud against the stillness of the room and the quietness of Fliss's voice, which seeps into my bones with its coldness.

'I think it's only fair to explain, you see – not only to you, Ellie, but to all your lovely friends – exactly why I've done the things I have. And how nice that they're here today to listen to what I've got to say. It makes it all so much more worthwhile, for them to see you squirm like a little worm wriggling on a hook, even now trying to extricate itself from the pain. Do you understand yet just how much I hate you?'

Will gives a gasp of shock beside Ellie. 'What's she talking about?' he hisses.

Fliss's laugh is short and harsh.

'Oh, don't tell me she hasn't told you, Will . . . Oh, that's priceless! How long did you think you could leave it before telling him, Ellie – a day, a week? Or were you going to wait until the big day itself before telling him there is no wedding?'

'What!' Will's eyes are suddenly ablaze.

'Yes, that's right, no wedding. A real shocker, isn't it? Want to know why? Shall I tell him, Ellie?'

'You knew about this,' says Will. It's not a question.

'Of course she knew about it,' spits Fliss, her anger flaring. 'It's her fault. God, you're all so stupid. And you' – she points a finger at Ellie – 'you . . . little Miss Perfect, "I just want everyone to be happy all the time" . . . Well, let me tell you, life's not like that, Ellie. People are not happy all the time. They *were* happy, until you went and ruined things.'

I look from Will to Fliss and back again. I need to defend Ellie but I don't know how. She might not even know about Robbie yet.

Fliss laughs. 'And don't try and protest your innocence, like we're all stupid. I'm sure you do know what this is all about . . . but maybe you're a bit reluctant to own up to your little secret now, aren't you, what with the wedding plans and all that. Tell me something, though, Ellie. Did you even mourn him?'

Ellie's voice is a whisper. 'I didn't even know Robbie was dead, Fliss. I only just found out.'

'Like I believe that. You're more of a bitch than I thought you were. How can you put aside his life like it's an irrelevance? How dare you!'

'But it's true, Fliss,' I protest. 'I told you she had no idea. I sent her the newspaper clipping you kept so that she could work it out. You're bloody barmy, you are. How could Robbie's death possibly have anything to do with Ellie, when she didn't even know he was dead?'

Ben gets to his feet.

'Stay away from me! I'll go when I'm good and ready.'

Will moves his hand to the small of Ellie's back as she sags against him. I can hear her ragged breaths.

'Is this true, Ellie? Is Robbie dead?' he says gently.

She nods, tears threatening to overwhelm her.

'But I did only find out a couple of days ago. I don't know what I'm supposed to have done.'

'Oh, for God's sake, Will, listen to her, you spineless wimp. *I don't know what I'm supposed to have done,*' she mimics. 'It's very simple. Very simple indeed, the oldest explanation in the book, in fact. Your darling Ellie is nothing but an adulterous liar and a cheat.'

'No, she isn't! Don't listen to her, Will,' I shout. 'She's bloody mad.'

'Don't worry, Lizzie,' he reassures. 'I've no intention of believing anything that isn't true.' He turns his attention back to Fliss.

'That's a very serious accusation, Fliss, and I still don't know what gives you the right to make it.'

'Because she stole him from me, that's why. Because she turned my marriage into a sham . . . I had a proper wedding too, far better than your pastiche of an affair. It was so beautiful, a winter wedding, so white and pure . . . But she had to steal him away from me, didn't she? She couldn't just let him go.'

'Fliss, I didn't. I had nothing to do with it. How could I have? I haven't seen Robbie since the day before my accident, nearly three years ago. And you know that. I spoke to you that day, but I swear I've never spoken to Robbie since. Why on earth would I want to?'

Fliss falters for a moment, obviously thinking back to that day, but then shakes her head violently. 'No! You've been having an affair and you know it. Why else would he be coming to see you?'

My stomach flutters in shock.

Ellie shakes her head. 'He wasn't coming to see me, Fliss. I don't know where you got that idea from, but you've got it wrong.'

I see a tiny glimmer of doubt on Fliss's face then, before her features contort once more. She snatches up a piece of paper from the table. 'Then how do you explain this?' she shouts, thrusting the letter at Ellie.

Ben plucks the letter from her hand. 'Don't read it, Ellie. You don't need to.'

'I have to see it, Ben. I need to know.'

Slowly he brings it to her, his gaze not on Ellie, but on Will. His expression is hollow.

'Dear God, no,' is all she can manage before Will has to take her weight.

But Fliss hasn't finished yet.

'So now do you understand? Why I came here? You don't even care that you've taken something precious from me; even now you're denying it. Well, now I've taken something from you, and mixed up your perfect little world, just so you can see how it feels. There will be no wedding, Ellie, not now, not ever, not now people know what you've done.'

She turns and looks behind her, at the window, vibrant in the afternoon light. 'And this, this is the biggest joke of all,' she laughs, a small tinkling sound in the hushed room. 'A showcase of your love for Ellie? I don't think you'll be needing this now, will you?'

I realise what she's about to do the split second she grabs one of the glass vases from the table. I launch myself at her, catching her arm in an attempt to stop her, but she's too fired up and pushes me away roughly like I'm a small child. I can only look on helplessly, panting, as a chorus of shouts rise up around me.

Fliss raises her arm, all her focus directed on the window in front of us.

'Wait!' Will's voice booms loud in my ear, but it's too late.

The vase is curving upwards, the sun catching it as it flashes past. I crash my teeth together as I wait for the deafening noise that must surely come, a high-pitched shriek of falling glass, as it tears itself away from its frame . . .

Except when it does come, it's a small noise, like the tinkling of the doorbell on just another sunny afternoon. I wrench my eyes open, the scream I can feel building within me, dying, stuck in my throat, as the vase passes clean through a rose-coloured pane, two smaller pieces of glass passing with it.

Will is standing motionless, trembling, waiting, breath forgotten, but the frame holds. Apart from one single piece of glass, hardly larger than the vase itself, the window is undamaged.

I hear a new sound then, a fury of noise that should have come moments earlier, as Fliss launches herself at Ellie with a scream of denial, but Will is unmoving in her path and she finds herself held firm. There's a moment when their eyes lock, but she fights against his arms, refusing to hold his gaze as she struggles to free herself.

'Some things endure,' he snarls. 'But relationships built on lies never do. It's time to judge yourself, Fliss, not others.'

Finn and Ben are by her side as she looks up at Will's words. She lets herself be led back to a chair, where she sits, chest heaving, as she struggles for what to say.

'You're a victim of Robbie's too, Fliss, just like Ellie was, allowed to live a lie by a coward who never deserved anyone's love.' Will's face is white with anger. 'I'm sorry for your loss, but it's Robbie you should be angry at. He's the one who betrayed you, not Ellie. Nothing you've done here has made any difference. You haven't won, or triumphed, just poured all your hate into something that was built on a lie. You might have ruined our wedding, but that's all, nothing else. I have all the time in the world to love Ellie.'

Fliss slumps in her chair, her anger all but spent as the door opens once more. I can hear hushed, urgent, but most importantly, familiar voices, as all my friends come into the room, Neil leading the way. Patrick and Finn instantly move to his side as Ben takes up a stance next to Fliss, with a look that tells her in no uncertain terms that this is over.

Ellie is still holding the letter in her hand, and she glances at it one more time. I think of the lines I glimpsed earlier that have caused so much suffering.

I'm sorry, Fliss, I guess I never really stopped loving her . . .

Her tears come as she turns into Will's enfolding embrace, perhaps tears of relief, most certainly tears of love and, if I know Ellie, tears of heart-wrenching sorrow for a life lost – not just Robbie's, but his wife's too.

Chapter 42

ELLIE

The light is golden here in the early evening, but tonight I can't see the window's colours, and I wonder if life will always feel this grey from now on. Fliss has been taken away, of course, to where I'm not entirely sure, but I have no strength for any more questions; it seems as if I've spent the day answering them, and neither the questions nor the answers have brought me any peace. I don't blame Fliss, not really. She's suffered too; she's still suffering, and I fear that the illness that has pursued her since Robbie's death will not be easily beaten. Her sister appeared to claim her, the same sister who has been looking after Fliss's daughter all these months, ever since the post-natal depression that Fliss suffered from returned and developed into something even more serious. I find it hard to believe that Fliss could have woven such a convincing façade around herself, but I've let myself be convinced of so many things over recent months that I'm in no position to judge.

Will is devastated. He's been thrown headlong into a situation that, because of his long absence, must feel like utter madness. The contrast to the celebratory events of yesterday is stark, and although he's holding it together, mostly for me, there is an absence of light in his eyes that couldn't be any clearer. He has been immersed in a world of creativity where his thoughts never ventured much further than the work in hand, and although his heart and soul were in it, as time moved on he longed for a return to normality, and the thought of our wedding gave him the strength to reach the finish line. He doesn't know where he is right now, and to my shame I have nothing to offer him. We've not spoken about the wedding, but there will be a time, soon, when we do, and I can't bear to hear him say he doesn't want to get married any more.

It takes a few minutes before I register that an even darker shadow has fallen over the table. I must have left the door open because I heard no one enter, but with an unusual quietness, Lizzie slips onto the chair beside me. She says nothing, but after a moment her hand finds mine and we sit in silence for a few moments more.

'Have you moved back in now?' I ask eventually. I can't ignore her after she's been brave enough to come and find me. 'I expect you're looking forward to sleeping back in your own bed tonight.'

'Huh, I've slept in a lot worse places than the Lodge, believe me.'

I smile despite myself. 'It's a bit grim at the moment, isn't it? But I'm so glad to know that's where you were. I like the thought that you were here all the time, looking out for us. I just never realised how much.'

'I was only doing what you asked me to. You said I should notice things around here and if I saw anything wrong I should try to fix it, so that's what I've done. Besides, I'd never leave here – well, not unless you really wanted me to – but I knew I had to get away, otherwise you would never have figured it out. I know you all thought it was me doing those things – and I know you didn't mean to; it was only that Fliss was so clever. With me out of the way I hoped you might begin to see things differently.'

'Not all of us thought that way.'

Lizzie cocks her head to one side. 'Maybe not. Not towards the end anyway, but it doesn't matter. It's no more than I'm used to.'

'And even after all that, you still came to our rescue. We owe you a huge apology, Lizzie, and I really don't know how we can make it up to you. We've treated you appallingly, haven't we?'

'Nah, I don't think so. You were only thinking what she wanted you to think, and that's no one's fault, is it? Besides, I wanted to help. After I figured out I wasn't going bonkers after all, I got mad; I mean, really furious. Evil cow. I wasn't going to let her get away with what she was doing. We're family now, aren't we? And that's what families do.'

I squeeze her hand. 'I hope so, I really do. I couldn't ask for a better one.'

'So what will you do now? I could make some cakes if you like?'

There's a part of me that thinks that maybe this is not such a bad idea. That the way through this is to carry on regardless, but I'm just so tired, and right now I need to wallow a little.

'That's really good of you, Lizzie, but honestly I don't think we're going to open tomorrow, maybe not until after the weekend – I don't know. I think we all need a little time; it's been a huge shock, and there's still a huge number of things left to do. The police will want to take further statements, and we need to decide if we want to press charges over the damage done to the studio. Apart from that we have friends and family who still think they're coming to a wedding in two weeks' time. They all need to be contacted.'

Lizzie bites her lip, thoughtful. 'Isn't there any way you can still get married then?'

'I wish that there were, but no, it's just not possible. Even if we still had a venue, there's no flowers or caterers, no photographer, nothing. You couldn't rustle anything up in that space of time. It's peak season; they've all been booked up for months.'

'I should have said something sooner,' replies Lizzie, tears welling in her eyes. 'I knew she'd been causing trouble over the arrangements, deliberately telling one person one thing and another person something else until none of us knew which end was up, but I never thought for one minute she'd cancelled the whole bloody lot. I could have stopped it. Maybe if I'd given you more time . . .'

A little tear trickles down Lizzie's cheek as she falls silent, lost in her own memories of these horrible weeks and months. She sniffs, dragging a hand across her nose.

'I'll tell you something, though. That bitch is not going to win, no way.'

'I don't think she was very well,' I say gently.

'Maybe not. You'd have to be wrong in the head to do stuff like that, wouldn't you? But I meant what I said. When I came here I had nothing, but it's like you said: we're all part of something much bigger here, and for the first time in my life I've felt like I've belonged. I know I got a lot of stuff wrong to start with, but I've become better since I've been here, Ellie, better than I've ever been anywhere in my life before. No one's going to take that away from me. Not ever.'

She smiles at me, more of a grimace really, but even though her words are hard to hear, I draw a small measure of comfort from them.

With another quick squeeze of my hand, and a light kiss to my cheek, Lizzie leaves as silently as she came. There is something different about her tonight. The gangly, rather awkward girl that first came to us all those months before has gone, and in her place is a rather lovely, thoughtful, calmer and altogether more confident person. Even through all that has happened, and the best efforts of one individual to undermine everything we have built up together, maybe Rowan Hill still has the ability to help when we need it to. I can only hope it has a little of its magic left.

Chapter 43

ELLIE

I know I shouldn't be up here, but Lizzie and Gina have all but thrown me out of the tea room. They make quite a pair, Gina taking an immediate liking to her willing protégée, and Lizzie revelling in her newfound confidence. I'm only getting in the way. I'm trying to keep busy but there's really nothing to do. Patience arrived with an update this morning, that she has contacted the last of the wedding guests, and a line is slowly being drawn under the events of the last few days.

It's quiet up here, sitting on the bench looking out over Rowan Hill, and it seems appropriate to be here now, a place where Will and I sat together all that time ago as he first shared his vision for Rowan Hill. The air is soft, this Tuesday morning, settling in gentle currents that drift away from me into the wide open space. I'm hoping my thoughts can find some freedom here, and I send them out, knowing that some of them might return to me, borne on the breeze, while others will stay, adrift from me, released.

I've had so little time to think over the last weekend, or so it would seem. There have been so many decisions to make and practical things to do that the days have emptied themselves into the evening before I've had a chance to stop. It hasn't been obvious, but I've hardly been alone either. It's the same with Will, and although no one has forced their opinions on us, or taken the conversation somewhere we did not wish to follow, the weight of the future hangs over us all. Even Will, having taken a phone call early this morning, has gone back to his studio, glad of the opportunity to lose himself once more, and I can't blame him. I'd do the same if I could.

It's the guilt that has been the hardest to bear. Finn has tried to claim ownership of it too, saying he should have done more to check Fliss out before allowing her to join us at Rowan Hill, and I'm not belittling his emotion – I can see it reflected in everything he says and does – but my own guilt has so many layers to it that just as I seem to pick apart one, another comes to take its place.

Finn was right when he said we had been puppets, dangling on the strings of the puppet master while she played us all for fools. But who is the more foolish: the innocent victim, whose only crime is naivety, or the person who can see that the strings have become tangled and does nothing to set them right? I don't have to answer my own question for I know I've been the biggest fool of them all.

'So, do you like my bench?'

The voice is warm and soft. It carries with it a thread to the past, back to that first day we sat here, when he asked me the very same question. Will had been lost then, damaged by a past that he has since managed to put behind him. It made me smile then, just as it does now.

'Yes, not short of a bit of wood, are you?' I reply, just as I had all that time ago.

Will comes to sit beside me, his hand sliding against mine, his fingers curling around my own.

'How did you know I was up here?' I ask, certain that no one had seen me leave.

'Because it's Rowan Hill, because it's everything we made, the whole of it, the big picture, and because all morning I've been thinking about this place, and now that I'm here, I know why.'

I lean my head against his shoulder. 'I'm sorry, Will,' I say. Again. Will's response is to drop a kiss against my hair. 'You know, it doesn't matter how many times you say that, it's still not necessary.'

I pull away from him. 'How can you say that? After everything I've done. I've let everyone down, I turned our wedding into a ridiculous theatre show . . . Poor Lizzie—'

'—is fine, and quite happy bossing everyone about now that she's suddenly so organised, and as for letting everyone down, what about you? Haven't we all let you down, believing the rubbish that Fliss was bandying about, the lies that she told everyone? We were all taken in by her – even me. She had me believing all sorts about you, things that had I bothered to think about for more than a minute, I would have known weren't true. She played us all off against one another, telling one person one thing, and someone else the opposite, until none of us knew what the truth was.'

'What sort of things? What did she say?'

Will takes hold of my hand. 'Ellie, we don't need to do this—'

'Yes, we do. I want to know.'

Will heaves in a huge breath. 'Well . . . like telling me that you were disappointed in me because we weren't going on a honeymoon, but that she knew exactly where you wanted to go . . .'

'But I didn't want to go away! We agreed that. I couldn't bear to be away from here.'

Will is silent for a minute, his blue eyes soft on mine. 'Neither could I.'

And suddenly I can see the extent of it all, how easy it had been to manipulate us, planting lies and suspicion, until none of us knew what to believe. I look up, holding Will's gaze as his mouth pulls into a slow smile. He leans forwards, catching a hand behind my head and pulling it close. I can still feel a smile on his lips as they touch mine.

'None of this is anyone's fault, Ellie – you have to believe that – least of all yours. We can go on torturing ourselves about this, or we can choose to move on, just like you taught me to do. To put the past behind us and trust in our future. They were wise words. They still are.'

I look out across the wide open space in front of me, watching as a buzzard circles lazily, riding the thermals beneath his wings without a care in the world.

'Was it good news, the phone call that you took this morning?'

'Another commission, if I want it. Smaller this time, and something I can do most of from home, but good, nonetheless – important. I said yes, of course.'

I nod, realising that Will is right. Nothing has really changed, except perhaps our perception. Only now, as the lies fall away, can we see things from an honest and clear point of view. Our future is still as it was, stretching out before us.

However, there is one final thing I have to know, one thing I am still uncertain about. I know in my heart what I believe to be true, but I don't fully trust my feelings, not yet. So I float it out there, to sit between us for a moment.

'We need to talk about children, Will. It's too important a thing to leave unsaid.'

His eyes are clear on mine, as he nods. 'What do you want to know?' he says. 'I agree we need to be honest, and I think things may have become a little . . . unclear.'

My heart begins to beat a little faster. 'If you want children. Only . . . I don't know what to believe. I did . . . I thought, but now . . .'

'What did you think, Ellie? Let's go back to the beginning.'

I screw my eyes up, knowing that I could be about to get this very wrong. 'It's just that I can't imagine you wanting children. I mean, when you're working, you'd live off tea and Hobnobs and pee in a bucket in the corner of the room given half a chance—'

'I would not!' interrupts Will, but there's a huge grin trying to spill out onto his face. 'Oh God, am I really that bad?'

'Yes,' I laugh. 'You really are. But . . . that's one of the things I love about you, Will. I love to see that expression on your face when you're immersed in a piece, when you're totally gripped in the flow of trying to create something so special that you can't rest for a minute until it's the very best that it can be. I can't imagine my ever wanting that to stop.'

Will is quiet for a moment, pondering the words I've just said, considering his response carefully, still not totally sure whether he's letting me down or not.

'I did want children, once. A part of me still does. Having children is one of the most beautiful and responsible things in the world. I look at Jane and Jack sometimes and I love what I see, but I know I can't be like that. It's too important a thing to get wrong and I would get it wrong, very wrong. I'm far too selfish, I think, particularly when I'm working, and, well . . . I'm hoping to do a lot more of that in the future. I can't pretend to be something I'm not, Ellie. I know what I'm like.'

'And you're rather glad that I know what you're like too?'

There's a somewhat sheepish smile. 'But what about you? I—'

'—don't need to worry,' I finish for him, finally sending the last of my fears out into the space before me, where a gentle breeze carries it away.

'And we will get married, Ellie, that I can promise you. It might take a little time to get things sorted, but we have as much time as we need.' He pauses then for a moment, looking up at me through eyes crinkled with amusement. 'But only on one condition.'

'Which is?'

'That I never have to look at another eau de Nil tablecloth as long as I live.'

Chapter 44

ELLIE

The morning is beautiful. Even at this early hour, the sky is a mile high, painted a soft powder blue that will deepen as the day draws on. It's midsummer, the longest day of the year.

I perch on the edge of the bed, scrunching my toes against the soft carpet, and gather my energy to stand once more and face the day. It's been a long week: in many ways a good one, but I'm sure I've counted far more days than the standard week contains. Today, however, is Saturday and I need count no longer. I will be glad when it's over.

A rapid knock at the door heralds the rather energetic figure of Gina, who bustles in with a tray. She doesn't even look at me, but places the tray down on the chest of drawers beside the bed and crosses to the window, flinging back the curtains that I had peeped through only moments earlier.

I stare perplexed at the tray's contents, thankful that I am still in my pyjamas, such is the speed of Gina's movement.

She turns to face me with her hands on her hips, her face split wide into a grin.

'Well, it is absolutely the most perfect day for a wedding out there.'

So this is how we're going to play it today, I think. I thought perhaps there might be a quiet and slightly more solemn atmosphere to the day than usual, or even perhaps a blanket ban on mentioning anything to do with the wedding. I hadn't reckoned on such a blatant *well, the very last thing we're going to do is sweep it under the carpet* attitude. Then again, this is Gina we're talking about; when she's around a spade daren't be anything else.

'I don't wish to sound ungrateful, Gina, but champagne, really? At this time of the morning? I understand the sentiment, but perhaps this is taking things a tad too far, even for you.'

Gina doesn't reply, but crosses to the chest of drawers and hands me the glass. 'Drink this, eat that – all of it, mind – and I'll be back in about half an hour.'

I'm left staring at her retreating back. I look at the tray once more, which holds a glass of orange juice, a croissant and jam – and a full English breakfast. It's bizarrely tempting. I pick up the croissant and pull off the end, chewing it thoughtfully. It certainly won't make the day any worse. I sit back on the bed, swinging my legs back up and propping myself on the pillows, and then I lift the tray onto my lap and munch my way through the whole lot. God, it's good, and I realise that it's probably the first time in a while that I've tucked into a meal with such gusto. Gina might be ever so slightly bonkers, but good bonkers, and I see that her rather forthright approach to today might well be the best way of handling things.

I'm staring out of the window when, true to her word, Gina comes bustling back in. She eyes my empty plate with a smile. 'Thought you might fancy that when you got going. Just the thing to set you up for the day.' She glances at her watch. 'Speaking of which, we'd better get a move on. Time to hit the shower, please.'

I roll my eyes. 'Gina, I think I might just manage to get ready all by myself. You don't need to watch my every move, honestly.'

'Well, that's where you're wrong, clever clogs. Don't argue.' She gives the door a very pointed look. 'Go on, off you go then.'

I stay in the shower for twice as long as I would do normally. I reason that under the circumstances it is allowed, and it's bliss standing there with the steady stream of water calming me from the head down. It would seem as though Gina's tactic for the day is to follow my every move, and these might well be the last few moments I get to myself all day.

I half expect to see her loitering on the landing waiting for me when I emerge from the bathroom, but the house seems quiet. Time to get a move on; it'll be busy in the tea room and I've been pandered to enough for one day. I know that people will understand, but I don't want to be accused of not pulling my weight. It's been tough for everyone since Fliss left, not just me, and no one else has been wallowing in self-pity. It hits me then, in one big rolling wave, just what today actually means, and I have to put out a hand against the wall to steady myself.

Breathing doesn't actually help. It's supposed to, I know; I've heard enough people say it in my life. Big breaths, deep breaths: breathe slowly, in and out. It's supposed to be a cure-all in times of stress, but today it's suddenly hard to breathe at all, never mind the quality or the quantity. I should have been getting married today, and now I'm not, and the grief of that loss hits me like a wall. I don't even know where Will is. He went out ridiculously early. But I feel so utterly foolish, trying to pretend that I could get through the day as if it were the same as any other. I should be with him.

The tears haven't come yet but I can feel them. They're waiting for the safety of our room before they explode from me in huge gulping sobs and there's nothing I can do to stop them.

I almost don't see him; he's standing so still, his back to me, and I'll be honest, he's the very last person I expected to see in my bedroom. The shock of it halts the onslaught of my tears.

'Ben?'

He turns to me then, his face warming to a slow, sweet smile that is full of an unexpected emotion.

'Morning, Ellie,' he replies, a little shyly. 'This day has felt like a long time coming, but I'm very honoured to be standing here right now. It means the world to me to be able to do this for you.'

My mouth must be hanging open; I'm sure of it. What on earth is he talking about? And then he takes a slight step to one side, and I see what I hadn't noticed before: the creamy folds of something hanging on the wardrobe door behind him. My stomach turns over.

'Do you remember all that time ago, when we first saw this? I told you then how beautiful you would look in it.'

I'm not sure I can take in his words. They seem to be suggesting something that shouldn't be possible, and I can't answer. I'm captivated by the dress hanging behind him. It's a stunning piece of design, with a wide and quite low scooped neckline embellished with a large roll collar that would sit beautifully on my shoulders. Close-fitting sleeves that look like they would hang low on the hands. From the neckline the dress just drops away, a single sheath of material, fitted at first then widening through the skirt to pool on the floor, the whole thing the consistency of double cream. Back when Ben was a jobbing carpenter this had hung in a shop in the village that he was helping fit out – now the very same dress seems to be hanging in my bedroom, waiting expectantly for someone to slip it on . . .

'Above anyone else, it was you that taught me that things don't have to turn out the way you think they're going to. You taught me never to give up fighting for my dream, and I know that maybe this isn't the dream you'd planned, but in a way I'm glad that things have happened the way they have; if they hadn't, I would never have been able to give you this.'

Ben moves across the room and takes both my hands, holding them clasped to his chest.

'I'm so proud of you, Ellie, and I wanted to give you this dress to say thank you for all that you've done for me, and for Finn too. For believing that what we had was special and daring us to believe it as well. Wear it knowing how loved you are.' And with that he kisses my cheek. I honestly think he might be about to cry.

I look up into his deep brown eyes. 'It's so beautiful, Ben, I don't know what to say . . . but I will wear it one day, I promise.'

He kisses my hand. 'Not one day . . .' and his eyes give a slight flicker over my shoulder as a gentle breeze from the opening door wafts over me. He pulls away with another smile, still holding my hands so that they stretch out before us. He slips away and Will takes his place, his warm hands sliding over mine.

Within seconds his lips meet mine. 'Hello, you,' he murmurs with a soft sigh. 'It's the perfect day for a wedding out there.'

I pull away to look at him, his blue eyes twinkling above his jeans and a T-shirt. 'Hmm, you're not the first person to tell me that this morning. What's going on, Will?'

'It's really very simple . . . I couldn't bear the thought of us not getting married today, and neither could anybody else. So will you marry me, Elinor Hesketh, today?'

I look back and forth across the room as if that will make any difference. 'But nothing's organised, Will. It was all a sham, how can we—' And then I stop as the words of a very wise postman come back to me: *Sometimes life's as simple as you care to make it . . . All you really need to do is turn up, right?* . . . and I see so clearly the truth in that statement and how I've grieved for a wedding that was a sham in every sense of the word. All I need is to marry Will; that's what's important, not the fancy car or the sequinned shoes or the perfect shade of table napkin. Tears begin to fill my eyes.

As if reading my mind, Will continues, 'Correct me if I'm wrong, but all we need to get married is a marriage licence, somewhere to get married and someone to marry us . . . well, we have the first and the second – and the third . . . ? Well, you'll just have to wait and see.'

I don't think I will ever tire of looking at that face.

'Now I only have a few more minutes before I'm shooed away, but I wanted to show you something.' He fishes in his jeans for his wallet. 'This goes everywhere with me,' he says, handing me a photo.

I look down at the picture. It's of me, taken during the renovations of Rowan Hill, dressed in filthy jeans and a faded baggy T-shirt, with my hair half escaping from a very messy bun. I have my tongue sticking out at a photographer who had dared to take a photo of me when I looked such a mess. The same photographer who's standing before me now.

'Stop frowning,' says Will. 'I knew you'd look like that, but I wanted to show you this today, because I know you've been feeling like everything that's happened is your fault, and that you've let me down, but I wanted to remind you that this is the girl I fell in love with. This is the photo I take out and stare at every time we're apart when I want to be reminded of your smile, your laugh, your mad hair. You don't need to be anybody else, Ellie; you're perfect just as you are, and please don't ever change.'

A single tear escapes to roll down my cheek. A happy tear. I feel a sudden rush of release as the weight of this day is suddenly lifted. Today is no longer a day to feel encumbered by the past or to mourn something that was never really true. Today is a day to welcome as if it were your lover, to clasp it to you and never let it go.

There is an obvious gathering of noise behind the door, of whispers and excited shushing mixed with giggles. Will gives a chuckle.

'See, I told you I was about to be shooed out.' He turns to look at the dress once more. 'Have I told you yet that I love you, Miss Hesketh? See you later.' He winks.

Chapter 45

LIZZIE

'Surprise!' shouts a noisy chorus as the door bursts open and me, Gina, Helen, Jane and Patience all fall into the room. There's a rattling clink of glasses.

'Come on, you, out,' I grin, poking Will in the arm. 'No men allowed. It's time to make Ellie even more beautiful.'

Once Will is firmly out of the way, Ellie is quickly enveloped in a jumble of arms as all five of us try to hug her at the same time.

'You should have seen your face this morning, Ellie. It was an absolute picture,' laughs Gina. 'You really had no idea, did you?'

'You've been planning this the last couple of weeks, haven't you?' she replies, as the penny finally drops. 'You rotten lot. You might have given me some idea.'

'What and spoil the fun?' replies Helen. 'No way. Today is all about you and Will, and thanks to Lizzie, I think you might be rather surprised as the day goes by. Isn't that right, Lizzie?'

I give an enthusiastic nod. 'Yes, and it might be more of a surprise than any of us bargained for. Some of it is a little, er, uncertain. If it happens, it happens. Much more fun this way.'

Ellie's eyes are shining as she looks straight at me. 'You've done of all this?'

'No . . . I had help from all of your friends, Ellie. Isn't that what we're all about here?'

'Still, I can't believe this is happening. It shouldn't be possible at all, but somehow here you all are, here I am, and . . . Oh my God, by the end of the day I'm going to be Mrs McLennan!' she squeals.

There is a massive bubble of excitement building up inside me, which I just might have to let out in one very big girly scream. Either that or turn cartwheels down the hallway. 'So what do you want to do first?'

Patience gives a snort of laughter. 'You have to ask?' she drawls, bringing forth a bottle of champagne and a glass. 'First, we're all going to sink a glass of the good stuff.'

She hands Ellie a glass and proceeds to undo the foil wrapping around the champagne cork. She eases open the wires. 'What do we think, ladies? Polite and dignified or wild and exuberant?'

There is a chorus of 'Wild!', just as I knew there would be, and Patience sends the cork shooting off into the ceiling with a loud pop.

For a few minutes no one can say anything amid the gales of laughter, but eventually it subsides and we're left, first grinning at each other like lunatics, and then a little calmer as the mood suddenly becomes very poignant.

'I want to explain how I feel,' begins Ellie, 'what the last few months have been about, and to apologise for being so caught up in my own delusions that I've neglected you all. I don't deserve today, not really. I don't deserve your generosity or your unfailing loyalty—'

I reach out my hand to Ellie's, clutching her warm fingers. 'No need to say any more, Ellie. Isn't that right, girls? No bones to pick, no explanations required. We all know the real you, don't forget, not the version that Fliss was parading around. Today is a celebration for you and Will, but also for the true meaning of friendship, and don't you ever forget that.'

My eyes are clear and bright, and not a trace of my earlier anxieties remains. I've grown immeasurably over the last few months, without even noticing, and now I can stand before them all, calmer and more confident than I've ever been before. No longer a small person, but their equal. It's time to move forwards now, and to stop looking over my shoulder.

'I'm going to do your make-up, Ellie,' I say, winking at her, 'and then Jane and Helen are going to do your hair.' I roll up my sleeves. 'So we'd best get a move on.'

Gina picks up her cue, checking her watch. 'Yes, come on, girls, it's time we weren't here; things to do and all that.'

'Now, don't worry, Ellie; we've got plenty of time. The wedding's not until twelve and it's not going to take us that long to make you look gorgeous!'

'It might,' she says, wiping underneath her eyes again. 'If I can't stop crying.'

'Ahh,' adds Helen, 'but we came prepared . . . waterproof mascara.'

In a few moments only Ellie and I remain. She takes a seat at the dressing table, inhales a deep breath and relaxes. She's in safe hands.

It's a strange reversal, this, with me in charge for a change, and I realise that I no longer need to feel like she's my teacher, or my protector. It's a subtle shift in our relationship, but a good one. Ellie smiles, almost as if she can sense what I'm thinking.

'Bit weird this, isn't it?' I say, as I squeeze a small amount of foundation onto the back of my hand. 'I bet you never thought you'd be sitting there with me doing this, did you?'

'I didn't,' she whispers back, her face strangely taut, as if she's not entirely sure how much she should be moving her face. 'It feels nice, though.'

'I've been practising too, just so you know. I'm not about to turn you into a Barbie doll.'

She groans slightly. 'Do you remember that photo of me? The one I had done at the wedding fair. Wasn't it awful?'

I chew at my lip. 'Not awful. It looked beautiful actually . . . It's just a shame that it wasn't you who looked beautiful.'

Her expression tells me she knows exactly what I mean.

'So I thought we'd go for a rather more natural look today.'

She laughs then. 'Always good for the groom to recognise the bride on their wedding day.'

'That's what I'm hoping . . .' I answer, picking up a brush.

There is silence for a few minutes, before Ellie's eyes flicker open again.

'Will and I were chatting the other day about the Lodge. The trail is almost laid now, and Finn reckons they've only got another week's work or so before they're done. They should have time then to concentrate on the Lodge again, and we, well . . . we wondered if you would like it, Lizzie? To have as your home?'

I still the brush for a moment, slowly lowering it, and moving back slightly so that I can focus on the whole of Ellie and not just her face.

'It was weird staying there,' I say. 'And not just because of what was going on and the fact that I was sort of camping, but all it did was make me miss my little flat even more.' I bite my lip again, struggling to find the right words. 'It also felt a little bit . . . removed. Does that make sense?'

Ellie takes hold of my hand. 'Yeah, I get that and, Lizzie, it's your choice, there's no right or wrong answer.'

I look at her steadily for a moment. 'In that case, it's really generous of you and Will, but I think I'd like to stay where I am. I like it, being in the middle of everything . . . where I can keep an eye on you all.' I blush. 'God, listen to me.'

She smiles back. 'Well, then, that's settled, I think. And for what it's worth, Lizzie, I think it's an excellent choice. We'll all sleep a little more soundly in our beds, knowing you have our backs.'

'Maybe one day, I dunno . . . but for now, you know you could always let Gina have it.'

'We could.' She nods, probably thinking how perfectly this might work. 'Especially now that she's going to be taking on Fliss's empty unit as well. That sounds like a fine idea.'

<hr />

There are no crowds of people when Ellie is finally ready. No photographer waiting to snap her *ta-dah* moment, only three of her best friends, and I can't help but think that's exactly how it should be. There were laughs during the process, a few more tears, but no trace of anxiety or nerves, and as I swing Ellie's chair back around so that she can look in the mirror, her reflection shows her everything that is right about today.

The room is full of sunshine, but even so she looks as if light has been poured onto her face. There is no plastic mask, no pretence of any kind. That's what happiness does for you. She sits there, freckles and all, but with a complexion more creamy than I've ever seen it, the lightest of blushes on her cheeks, and her lips a gentle inviting rose. Tendrils of hair curl around her face and shoulders, weaving their way around the tiny sprigs of heather and pale tuberoses whose glorious scent wafts through the air. She looks just as I'd always imagined she would. My heart is beating fast in the still, quiet air. Gina was right. It is the most beautiful day for a wedding.

Chapter 46

Ellie

The kitchen is quiet as I make my careful way downstairs. There will be riotous activity somewhere, but here for a few moments more all is calm. The others have left to get ready themselves and attend to more preparations, I'm told. I'm allowed downstairs but am under orders not to leave the kitchen, or open any doors. The room is as I left it last night, except for the addition of one single thing.

On the table, laid with the utmost care, is a card, which simply reads *For Ellie*. I'd know that exuberant handwriting anywhere, and my throat tightens as my eyes linger on the gathering of flowers beside it that Patience has left for me.

There are roses of the softest pink, with pale sweet peas and love-in-a-mist, phlox and white dahlias between heathers and more tuberoses, tiny feathered astilbes, and curling stems of gentians. As I gather the bouquet into my arms, I couldn't have wished for anything more perfect. It is the garden here at Rowan Hill, and what could be more special on a day like today?

The time is a quarter to twelve, and I stand breathing deeply like countless brides before me, willing myself not to forget every moment of this day and every subsequent day after, as I step into the world a married woman. A world made stronger and richer for the vows that have preceded it.

A tiny click behind me alerts me to the fact that I am no longer on my own. I don't even have to turn around to know who it is; after all, there is only one man who could possibly escort me to wherever it is we're going.

'Hello, Finn,' I say, as he comes to stand beside me.

He looks impossibly handsome in his dark suit, a sprig of heather and a rosebud tucked into his buttonhole.

'Morning,' he says with a lopsided grin. 'Don't you scrub up well?'

I reach up to straighten his tie. 'You're going to break a few hearts today, Finn, that's for sure,' I say, kissing his cheek.

He looks down at me, his eyes bright and shining. 'Well, if you're ready, Miss Hesketh . . . shall we?' And he takes my arm, leading me out into the blue of the day.

Parked outside is his pick-up truck, clean and shiny, and adorned with ribbon.

I burst out laughing. 'Oh God, I love it, Finn! But where on earth am I going to sit? You'll never get my dress in there.'

'Fear not,' he says, with a slight bow. 'For today, madam will be riding in the rear of the carriage.'

He sees my confusion and leads me to one side, where I can see that the back of the truck now looks like something from a carnival parade. Ribbons are hung all along the sides and a piece of red carpet fills the truck bed. Goodness knows where that came from. The floor is strewn with petals and in its centre sits a hay bale, draped in a cream fabric. There's even a small pair of steps at the rear.

'I can't believe this; it's amazing,' I exclaim, taking his hand and gingerly climbing the steps. 'Please tell me we haven't got far to go,' I add, wondering where on earth he's taking me.

Finn chuckles as he climbs into the cab. 'Wait and see,' he says, and that's all.

We pull out through the gates of Rowan Hill and into the village, where a crowd of people sends us on our way with a cheer and much arm waving. I feel a bit like the queen. After about a minute at a slow crawl, Finn stops again, and I hear the cab door open.

'Sorry it took so long,' he laughs, offering me his hand once again.

'Finn McLennan, you're bloody mad, you are. Come on, tell me. Where are we going?'

He looks up and down the street. 'Well, where do people usually go to get married?' he says, amused.

I register then where we're standing, as my eye follows the trail of people across the road, the lychgate closing behind them with a creak as they make their way through the churchyard. I look at him in confusion.

'But we can't be getting married here. The vicar is busy. There's another wedding in the neighbouring parish. It was one of the first things we checked at the beginning of the year.'

'What, and he's the only vicar in the whole wide world?' Finn gives his watch a pointed look. 'Please don't make my brother wait any longer than he has to. I don't think I can stand the pressure.'

My heart begins to beat even faster as we walk up the path to the church. I've just caught sign of Jane and Lizzie by the door, and judging by the matching blush-pink dresses they're wearing, and smiles as wide as heaven, I think I have two bridesmaids. I take the deepest of breaths, adjust my hold on Finn's arm and turn to follow them both inside the church.

It's quiet inside, there's no organ music, but the peaceful air is perfect as I walk between the sea of faces, drinking in everything I see. It's as if time has slowed down to such a point that I can even see the dusk motes sparking in the sunlight, like tiny diamonds drifting into an already golden day. I know all the faces here: my friends, my family, everyone from Rowan Hill and, right at the top, my parents, my mother already dabbing at her eyes. And finally, as I look from one smiling face to another, I get to see Will for the first time, and then everything stops as I take in every inch of his face, and his beautiful blue eyes.

I take his hand as everyone else melts away and a new figure steps forwards. A figure with a shock of red hair that I last saw just over two weeks ago.

He smiles warmly at the congregation, and then bends to me. 'Did I not tell you that God works in mysterious ways, Ellie? Truly glorious and mysterious ways,' he whispers, before turning back to the congregation and raising his hands.

And then the Reverend Michael delivers the line I've been longing to hear all morning.

'Dearly beloved, we are gathered here today . . .'

Chapter 47

LIZZIE

'Whatever happened to "life's as simple as you care to make it", Brian?'
I tease, nudging his arm. 'You said, "All you really have to do is turn
up, right?" What about this lot then?' I grin at him, waving my arm in
front of me.

The old postman blushes deeply. 'Well, that's still true, right
enough, but actually it's even better when you turn up and there's a bit
of food,' he laughs.

'A bit of food! There's enough here to feed the whole village . . .
although it looks as if the whole village may well have turned up.' I take
hold of his arm then, and kiss his cheek, which is already turning pink. 'I
know I have you to thank for a lot of this, Brian, and I can't begin to tell
you how much your help will mean to Ellie. What did you do?'

'Well, you know me, I like to have a bit of a chat with folks as I go
about my round, and Gina might have a voice like a foghorn, but you
can't beat the personal touch, can you? Folks were only too happy to
help once they heard of the pickle you were in, and once I explained
what we needed, well, they came up trumps, didn't they?'

'They certainly did,' I say, looking at the collection of tables in the
courtyard, all groaning with food. 'I can't believe it.'

'This place has been good for the village. It's brought more folks into the shops, and people like it. It has a good feeling about it.'

It certainly does today. The courtyard is pretty much standing room only, and I'm thrilled that Ellie and Will got to share their wedding day with the village. After all, none of this would have been possible without them. They turned out in force to take photos of the wedding as we couldn't get a photographer, and donated flowers from their own gardens to decorate the church and Rowan Hill itself, which also hangs with rows and rows of bunting. There's no way Helen could have made all this by herself and, try as I might, I'm completely useless with a sewing machine. It must have taken an army of people to hang it all this morning, let alone all the other things that have been done.

Rowan Hill has found its magic again, through the people that truly love it, just as I do now. This is my home, and we may have had a rough few months, but we feel stronger now than we've ever been – just like a marriage, really. As I catch sight of Patience and Patrick slow-dancing, I smile, and know that things can only get better.

I think of Fliss as well, of course, now that we know the whole story, and of Robbie, who wanted to have his cake and eat it too. He'd ruined two lives: not just Ellie's but Fliss's, leaving her so full of anger and bitterness that she had taken it out on the only person she could. Ellie certainly didn't deserve it, but I can see now that neither did Fliss. She'd had her dream wedding, she'd felt just as Ellie does now, but then she had it all snatched away from her by a weak and selfish man. Robbie had paid the ultimate price for his behaviour, but who was the real victim, I wonder.

As I watch the happy faces around me, I hear a shout rise up across the crowd – *one, two, three, four* – and the band strikes up in unison, a joyful surge of folk music this time, played loud and fast. Ben and Finn will be at the helm, of course. Oh, how I love those boys. I look across to them now, catching sight of Neil, whose eyes seem to find mine again, and I feel a little flutter inside of me. He has such a kind face.

I wander down the length of the courtyard once more, stopping to chat to my friends, and to nibble on the sausage rolls along the way. I can see Will and Ellie doing the same thing, thanking people for coming, and every once in a while stopping the world for a moment to steal a kiss. It's like he said: they have all the time in the world to love each other, and today is the start of a long but happy journey for them.

My journey has ended right here. I've found a place to call home, where I can stand each day; no longer in the shadows, but instead with my face turned towards the sun. I know that I will never want to be anywhere else.

As the day moves into night, there comes a quieter time, a peaceful release from the energy of earlier, as Rowan Hill takes her place among the stars and is lit with a thousand twinkling fairy lights. Soon the bells of the church ring out the chimes of midnight and, as the people drift away, a figure comes to stand at my side, holding a champagne glass shyly. We stand to welcome the coming dawn. No more the longest day but, instead, in its place, a new day.

AUTHOR'S NOTE

I hope you've enjoyed your visit to Rowan Hill. The setting and cast of characters are ones I first brought to life in my debut novel, *Letting in Light*, and I really couldn't resist visiting them once more, just to keep an eye on them, you understand, and see how they're all doing. They're so much a part of my life that I feel rather protective of them, but you know, I think they're going to be okay . . .

Writing a book is not a quick process. A lot can happen during the time from when the first word goes on the page to the sign-off of the last edits, which is why I'm so grateful (and lucky) to have the support of some truly wonderful people around me. My agent, Peta Nightingale, is everything an agent should be: eternally wise, incredibly supportive, funny, warm, astute, and very talented. Just knowing that she's there at the end of the phone is enough to bring my blood pressure back down! My wonderful editors Sammia Hamer at Amazon and Sophie Missing are just a joy to work with, and their tactful, skilful advice is worth its weight in gold. *Turn Towards the Sun* is a very different book because of them, and I am so very grateful to have the opportunity to work with them.

On the first of March this year (2016) I learned of the very sad death of someone who at one time in my life was very special to me. As was only right and natural as our lives moved on, we lost touch over the years, but I'm so very grateful to his lovely sister for finding me to let me know. She had found me through social media, and as we chatted she mentioned that she never knew I was now a writer, and that her brother would have been proud of me. In a way it's sad that he never got to read *Letting in Light*; I think for many reasons he would have enjoyed it. It also reminded me that his hugely selfless act all those years ago was the one that ultimately brought me my wonderful husband, with whom I'm soon to celebrate twenty years of marriage, and our three amazing children. I'm sorry that I never got the chance to thank him properly, but I'm sure that one way or another he knows. I hope so. I'm so lucky to have such a wonderful family, and there aren't enough thanks in the world for all that they do.

I'd also like to thank Bekah Graham at Amazon, who suggested the brilliant title for this book. Not only is it wonderfully appropriate for the book, and echoes all the sentiments within it, but inadvertently she also provided me with a timely reminder. 2016 has been a particularly turbulent and challenging year, both for the world, but also for our family, as we changed jobs, went through GCSEs and A-levels, suffered an extremely stressful house move, and coped with the sad decline of my mother-in-law into dementia. There have, of course, also been many things to celebrate and rejoice in, and I guess that's why Bekah's title suggestion struck such a huge chord with me – that throughout our lives, whatever challenges and sadnesses we face, we should never give up, or give in to negativity, but instead remain always with our faces turned towards the sun.

ABOUT THE AUTHOR

 Emma Davies once worked for a design studio, where she was asked to write an autobiographical note. 'I am a bestselling novelist,' she began, 'currently masquerading as a thirty-something mother of three.' That job didn't work out, but she's now a forty-something mother of three, and she's working on the rest. For years Emma was a finance manager who spent her days looking at numbers, so at night she would throw them away and play with words, practising putting them together into sentences. She now writes in all the gaps between real life. Visit her website, www.emmadaviesauthor.com, where, amongst other things, you can read about her passion for Pringles and singing loudly in the car. You can also find Emma at www.facebook.com/emmadaviesauthor and www.twitter.com/emdavies68.